D0786729

and its best music and understands in her very soul how to (stealthily, quietly) keep her reader spellbound. She is the rarest sort of disciplined writer, possessed of an intuition for the art of sorting out the telling incident, the perfect line of dialogue, the signal impulse in a character's life, or in her own, and excluding the dross. With Wendell Berry and Robert Penn Warren she is one of Kentucky's greatest literary artists, meaning she is one of the world's greatest, nothing less."
—James Robison, author of *The Illustrator*

"With *Patchwork,* fans including me have a rare opportunity in the literary world: to savor a body of work as a whole in one volume and to learn from the author herself about the wellspring of her writing life. Here we find an overview, an essence, of Mason's pithy, sparkling, often funny stories, her lovely reminiscences of life in rural western Kentucky, her literary essays and interviews, and her hilarious *New Yorker* riffs on subjects as different as sheep in New Zealand, a Picasso exhibition at New York's Museum of Modern Art, and President Clinton's phrase 'Adam's off ox.' If you're wondering about this writer's range, consider her pivot from Vladimir Nabokov to Mark Twain to Elvis Presley. As a kind of provisional summing up, *Patchwork* is an indispensable addition to any shelf of her novels and stories. Enjoy the delicious feast."—James Reston, author of *A Rift in the Earth: Art, Memory, and the Fight for a Vietnam War Memorial* patchwork

# patchwork

A
## Bobbie Ann Mason
Reader

Introduction by
## George Saunders

UNIVERSITY PRESS OF KENTUCKY

Copyright © 2018 by The University Press of Kentucky

Scholarly publisher for the Commonwealth,
serving Bellarmine University, Berea College, Centre College of Kentucky, Eastern Kentucky University, The Filson Historical Society, Georgetown College, Kentucky Historical Society, Kentucky State University, Morehead State University, Murray State University, Northern Kentucky University, Transylvania University, University of Kentucky, University of Louisville, and Western Kentucky University.
All rights reserved.

*Editorial and Sales Offices:* The University Press of Kentucky
663 South Limestone Street, Lexington, Kentucky 40508-4008
www.kentuckypress.com

Cataloging-in-Publication data available from the Library of Congress

ISBN 978-0-8131-7545-4 (hardcover : alk. paper)
ISBN 978-0-8131-7550-8 (epub)
ISBN 978-0-8131-7549-2 (pdf)

This book is printed on acid-free paper meeting
the requirements of the American National Standard
for Permanence in Paper for Printed Library Materials.

Manufactured in the United States of America.

Member of the Association of University Presses

# Contents

# Preface

Jonathan Allison

The University Press of Kentucky is proud to publish *Patchwork: A Bobbie Ann Mason Reader,* which brings together many of the author's most beloved short stories and excerpts from her novels and memoirs, as well as essays, interviews, and recent work. In its variety and brilliance, it is certainly a "patchwork," as the title suggests, but the contents have been carefully selected by the author to highlight themes such as war, love, marriage, and family history.

As a writer, Mason rose swiftly to the national stage. Publication of her first story, "Offerings," in the *New Yorker* marked the beginning of a long relationship with that magazine, where she has published many stories and pieces of reporting, some of which appear in the present volume. Her work, although often regional in setting, has national and international significance and appeal. If Mason is a great southern writer, she is also a great American writer and, as one critic noted, one of those writers who, "by concentrating their attention on a few square miles of native turf, are able to open up new and surprisingly wide worlds for the delighted reader" (*New York Review of Books*).

"Shiloh" portrays the relationship between Leroy, a truck driver, and his wife, Norma Jean, who are haunted by the memory of their child, who died in infancy. Complex, compassionate, and poignant, the story became a contemporary classic and is one of the most widely anthologized stories in high school and college textbooks. The book that soon followed, *Shiloh and Other Stories,* won the PEN/Hemingway Award for Debut Fiction and was a finalist for the PEN/Faulkner Award for Fiction, the American Book Award, and the National Book Critics Circle Award. Reviewing the collection in the *New Republic,* Anne Tyler described Mason as "a full-fledged master of the short story." Critics began associating her with a new wave of short fiction emerging in the 1980s, including Raymond Carver, Ann Beattie, and Richard Ford. Reflecting on this period, Mason recalled, "My work was about working-class characters whose inner lives were not often portrayed in the pages of the *New Yorker* magazine, so this created a stir," and she began to feel "freer to write about so-called ordinary people, with the conviction that no one, after all, is ordinary."

She says her style "comes out of a way of hearing people talk." She has a good ear for ordinary speech, and few authors depict the understated but subtly revealing dialogue of friends, mothers, daughters, and married couples better than she does. She identified with Elvis Presley because he "was so familiar—and he was ours! I don't remember the controversy he stirred up because everything he did seemed so natural and real, and he was one of us, a country person who spoke our language." This says something about her impulses as a writer: staying true to a voice, a tonality, and a form of language. "I write in plain straightforward English," she says, "often in the language and cadences of rural and small-town Kentuckians. I hear the music of their speech, and I feel it conveys their attitudes toward the world. It is in that language that I tell their stories."

Much of her work deals with war and the grief and trauma that it leaves behind. Michiko Kakutani in the *New York Times* described her first novel, *In Country,* as "a novel that, like a flashbulb, burns an afterimage in our minds." It concerns a seventeen-year-old girl, Sam Hughes, whose father died in combat before she was born, and through memories gathered from her taciturn uncle and others she tries to imagine what the experience of Vietnam was really like, as opposed to the fantasies conveyed by TV and movies. When she finally reads her late father's overwhelmingly blunt, factual war diary, she realizes how many illusions she has nursed for years. The novel begins and closes with a journey to the Vietnam War Memorial, where the splintered, multigenerational family is finally united in grief as they stand before the etching of Sam's father's name. As in much of Mason's work, sprawling suburban and country landscapes are described in pithy detail, including the Howard Johnsons, Country Kitchens, and Exxon gas stations along the interstate. Popular music is everywhere on radios and stereos, from the Doors to Bruce Springsteen, sifted through the sensibility of the narrator, creating a vivid soundscape.

Mason's world is a place you can see clearly, but it is also a world of feeling. She has an extraordinary eye for detail, as when Leroy in "Shiloh" notices for the first time "the peculiar way goldfinches fly past the window. They close their wings, then fall, then spread their wings to catch themselves." Her characters appear with clarity preceding a particularly dramatic revelation, as when Norma Jean is depicted "picking cake crumbs from the cellophane wrapper, like a fussy bird," just before she declares, unexpectedly, "I want to leave you." In *Nancy Culpepper,* Nancy watches her boyfriend during a tense moment at her parents' dinner table: she "watched him trim the fat from his ham as precisely as if he were using an X-Acto knife on mat board." Below the surface of the details, there are currents of feeling. When he tries to understand his relationship with the past, at the Shiloh historic battleground, Leroy realizes the limits of his capacity to understand even his own past: "Leroy knows he is leaving out a lot. He is leaving out the insides of history." It is precisely "the insides of history" and of lived experience that Bobbie Ann Mason recovers in her fiction, portraying with consummate artistry the relationship between the world she observes and her characters' inner lives, with all their hopes and dreams.

# Introduction

George Saunders

## 1.

When I was a grad student back in the 1980s, Bobbie Ann Mason was considered one of the Southern reps of the so-called "dirty realists" or "Kmart realists." Her work was praised for its frank, unabashed inclusion of elements then supposedly unusual in American literary fiction—television, brand names, pop culture, apartment complexes, malls, etc. Although she was rightly considered a master of the short story in this mode, reading her work again, I see what a short-sell this view was. Bobbie Ann Mason is a strange and beautiful writer indeed, and if she is a realist, she is that best kind of realist: an emotional realist. Her stories exist to gently touch on, and praise, even mourn, what it feels like to be alive in this moment, or in any moment, and her representations of American life are beautifully compressed and distorted, as all great art must be—to purpose—and that purpose is to embody an organic beauty that melds sound, sense, and substance.

The first book she ever wrote was an unpublished riff on Donald Barthelme's *Snow White*, on the subject of the Beatles. To my ear, even her more realist stories—the ones that began appearing to great acclaim in the *New Yorker* in the early 1980s—retain that essential postmodern energy. Though they concern ostensibly real people, often working-class, from Kentucky, and don't include any overtly po-mo elements, their shapes are new and odd and truthful. (Also ornery and funny.) Like the Russian absurdist Daniil Kharms, Mason seems to reflexively reject the compunctions of Freytag's Triangle, that creative writing chestnut that would divide stories into Exposition, Rising Action, and Climax. Especially her stories seem averse, in their endings, to the too-easy solution of the existential problems they have worked so hard (in their beginnings and middles) to construct. A Mason story quietly builds to a point of tension (a tension often sorrowful), and then, in a move that feels courageous and culminant, the story refuses to explode falsely. The characters are often left right there on the hook, or on a nearby, similar hook. ("The goal," she has said, "is to leave the story at the most appropriate point, with the fullest sense of what it comes to, with a passage that has resonance and brings into focus the whole story. It has to sound right and seem right, even if its meaning isn't obvious.") Even when a character takes action, the reader may not be convinced that this new direction will lead to real freedom or happiness. Mason's is an approach devoid of falsification. She is OK, it seems, with the notion that American lives (and life in general) may be fundamentally sad, at least upon first examination.

## 2.

An early influence was Nabokov, and Mason's stories contain some of the most precise and therefore poetic descriptions of nature in contemporary American literature. There are beautifully real gardens in her work, the kinds of gardens people actually have, and descriptions of fruits and vegetables and fields and flowers and weeds that will make you want to go sit in your own neglected yard and try, for once, to *observe* the way Mason does, which is to say, with all the senses engaged and the language center set on wide-open. These descriptions are the result of awareness-of-world, and that awareness extends even to the non-agrarian, reminding us of how pleasurable it is to read depictions of actual human *noticing*. (In her first *New Yorker* story, "Offerings," for example, there appears this zinger: "Later, with a perverse delight, she sees a fly go by, actually trailing a wisp of cat hair and dust.")

These reminders of the freshness and immanence of the natural world are all the more moving because we feel that the more complete and organic relation to the land that, say, the grandparents of these characters might have had is coming to an end, and that the knowledge these descendants retain of nature is vestigial and fading.

## 3.

In Mason's work people are often struggling under that particular form of contemporary distress brought about by paucity of resources, both material and spiritual. Distant forces seem to be conspiring to make these people peripheral, inconsequential. The stories are full of divorces, separations, marriages barely holding together; and the characters take up hobbies to fill the void, including minor fascinations with pop-cultural figures, those tentative mini-Gods. True religion has moved away from these people, or they from it, and where religion exists, it seems to share some taint of the material: it serves as a cudgel, or a social marker, a way for one person to assert superiority over another. (When someone, in a Mason story, invites someone to church, it is often a way of saying, "I feel there is something wrong with you" or "I know something you don't.")

So you could say, as critics have, that Mason is writing about a particular form of late-twentieth-century American sadness, a moment during which something has fundamentally shifted in the American ethos. The way I would say it is that she is bearing witness to our descent into a new era of pure materialism. This, for me, is the essential energy of Mason's work: the sense of loving, vibrant human beings stymied by the systemic rebuttal of their vitality.

But ultimately she is writing about something bigger and more universal, which is that, here on earth, in these human bodies, it is hard to be happy. We suffer from that eternal sorrow that Buddhists call samsara: the cycle of futility that comes from believing that happiness will be found in the satisfaction of our desire.

These stories are full of sorrow and loneliness and the human heart pushing back against these.

## 4.

Although I don't know if Mason would agree with this assessment, I feel, reading her work, that her prose is guided by a sense of musicality—sound in cahoots with meaning. Her stories are language-forms, and proceed that way—a fact that was, I think, missing in the early rush to understand her stories as simple representations of some exotic (Southern, working-class) Other. Of course, no good story is ever strictly realistic—the stories of Raymond Carver are full of distortions and compressions, as are those of Flaubert, Munro, et al.

Stories are scale-models for the world that benefit by willful exaggeration. They are like model railroad towns whose construction is guided by delight—the things the author likes to do and is good at doing, which, in turn, produce a distorted-but-fun little place. The doorways of this writer's town are full of quarreling couples; this writer's town is perpetually snowbound; this one's has more flowers than any real town could possibly sustain (growing on the roofs of cars and up the side of the bell tower); in the streets of this writer's town, everyone walks happily arm-in-arm, but there are plastic mini-dragons situated in the alleys. And yet, somehow, actions occurring within these distorted towns produce heightened, meaningful representations of the real world. The distortions help us see, in extremis, parts of our everyday lives that normally remain submerged. (Everyone behaves fairly normally in "The Metamorphosis," but that big bug in Gregor's room causes us to reexamine the notion of "normal behavior.")

These offsets can be slight but are always present, even in the most ostensibly "realistic" work. There are the first-order offsets caused by the necessary compression and omission. (Think of all the things omitted by the simple utterance "Jim sat down with his cup of coffee." The clouds overhead! The thousand bugs in the bushes just outside! The scandalous thing just uttered by a drunk in the church next door!) But the most important offsets are the ones the author applies via her sentence-to-sentence habits of thought and preference, actualized through the process of revision. The best writers—writers like Mason—steer not by convention, or a desire to teach us something or export some worldview, but by this inner sense of preference, in a spirit of exploration, asking, through the enactment of a highly personal artistic method: *What is it, after all, that I believe?*

## 5.

So: what does the universe look like, refracted through the distortive preferential principles of Bobbie Ann Mason?

First, I note that the calm richness of the language produces a difficult-to-achieve fictional effect: that of nonjudgment. It is easy enough for a writer to be harsh. It is equally easy to be reflexively anti-harsh—to be sentimentally oversupportive of one's characters. But to make a character about whom we feel an *ongoing engaged ambiguity,* or an *expanding hopeful curiosity,* is the hardest thing. The preferred relation of reader to invented world should mimic the relation between reader and actual world, in those moments when the reader is most fully alive to that actual world: befuddled, confused, engaged, brought to the edge of her seat, so to speak, by the vagaries and infinite variety of reality. When a writer puts us in *that* relation to her subject, that is real writing.

This quality of nonjudgment is one that Mason shares with the Chekhov of the two masterpieces "In the Cart" and "In the Ravine." Mason, like the Russian master, is comfortable standing in the face of sorrow and loneliness. She does not have the reflexive aversion to these sentiments that might cause a writer to mock her characters or provide too-easy solutions, but, rather, through the calmness with which she abides there, collecting and sharing their (perhaps sad) data, she communicates a sense of compassion. Sorrow and loneliness are real, she seems to say, and much more common than we like to admit, but maybe not so terrible or unusual after all; haven't we all felt these? Don't we, in fact, feel them nearly every day? Mason refuses—structurally, I would say—to participate in our familiar American business of cloaking ourselves in denial. Is there unhappiness? Let it be so, she seems to say. This is the comfort Mason offers: the comfort that comes when we see someone not in denial of an evident darkness. This quality comes to feel, a few stories in, like a form of kindness: courageous and hopeful. There is, in my reading, a sort of motherliness about this: we come home hurt, terrified of what we might have done to ourselves; and what a comfort it is to have someone quietly look at the wound, no flinching, no gasping—just calm regard, a regard that offers its own form of healing.

6.

Another redemptive feature in a Mason story is the kindness and neighborly tolerance these characters show one another. Emmett in "In Country," to cite just one example, is a particularly believable uncle figure, whose relation to his niece feels just right: he is fond of her. He is protective of her, a friend to her, to the extent that he can be, given the damage done him by the war in Vietnam. A reader habituated by an overhelping of mediocre contemporary fiction might find himself waiting for these characters to suddenly erupt in abusiveness, or at least to snarkify a bit—to take jabs at one another in their frustration—but Mason's characters are stronger than that. They tend to be courteous, to decline to say the most hurtful thing. A reader also notes that Mason is this way herself—she resists the gratuitous comic dig that might serve to put author and reader firmly above the character, looking smugly down. And in this, she allies herself with her characters, and allies us with them too, and so we form a tight little empathetic bundle—a pleasant place to be, and one that improves us. It mimics the effect of standing beside a friend while a third person (a stranger, maybe) tells a somewhat odd story, and noting that the friend (unlike ourselves) is not rushing to a too-hasty or too-dismissive judgment of the stranger but, instead, is really *listening*. This is instructive; it teaches us that we, too, might be capable of such patient abiding.

But Mason is no sentimentalist. Tricky systems of psychological warfare are enacted beneath these calm surfaces; witness the way, in "Shiloh," Norma Jean's mother passive-aggressively brings up the notion of "neglect" after she has caught Norma Jean smoking, and Norma Jean (and the reader) understands this as an underhanded reference to a grandchild lost to SIDS: a deep and terrible insight into the way cruelty actually proceeds.

So, her characters are mostly gentle, but also vulnerable to sudden lurches to the dark side, which even they may not be fully aware they are making. In a more recent story called "The Horsehair Ball Gown," Mason masterfully summarizes the life of a family and its hidden tragedy and, in the process, creates an unforgettable pair of siblings who, though they are old within the story, appear to the reader to be many ages at once, each of these selves simultaneously guilty and innocent—a beautiful story, full of tragedy and fun. The feeling you get reading this later work is that this is a writer who has spent a lifetime carefully watching people. She knows some things about us, and these are generous things, mostly; but a few of the things she knows have made her a touch skeptical about human beings, wise to the ways they can go off-track.

7.

Fiction, at its best, is not mere depiction, but effects a change upon the reader so as to prepare her for more enlightened living in the world—as Kafka famously says, it "prepares us for tenderness." This is not to say that fiction should preach, or offer some canned, simple solution. On the contrary: fiction often simply lays out the difficulties we face; underscores the challenges presented to human happiness. The work of Bobbie Ann Mason, it seems to me, does this in a particularly loving fashion, full of truth, characterized by a refusal of the sentimental and an embracing of a muscular form of hope.

These are, to my ear, radical stories. That which we so ardently seek, these stories say, may not save us. Of her youth in Kentucky, Mason has said, "Primarily I rebelled against apathy and limited education. I was rejecting a whole way of life that I thought trapped everyone." This strikes me as a pretty good starting place for understanding the body of her work, which includes five short story collections, five novels, a memoir, and a rich bounty of personal and critical essays, a good sampling of which you are about to have the pleasure of reading. Here, if I may briefly project my politics onto Mason's work, I find myself thinking of her fictive world as a scale model in which good people—the longing-filled descendants of settlers and dreamers—wander through a still-beautiful, yet somehow hostile American dreamscape: a system of aggressive banality, constructed to serve distant capital, that thereby short-changes the individual and denies her celebration and sensuality and true liberty.

What is the antidote? Well, for starters, a lively and fearless awareness of the affliction, as evidenced in the pages you are about to read. Art, Chekhov claimed, does not need to solve problems, only to formulate them correctly. The stories of Bobbie Ann Mason formulate the problem of living this way: people, even good, kind people, will sometimes find themselves suffering, lonely, and frustrated, especially, perhaps, in an age like ours, where we have misplaced certain key values, become obsessed with things, and grown selfish. But then again, these stories say (and demonstrate, through their perceptivity and humor and what I believe used to be called "sass") that there are ways back, and we are always trying to find them—ways back to happiness, to more authentic selves, to happier times, to love. Within that dreamscape, there is beauty. The beauty of friendship, and wit; the beauty of continuing to try. And stepping back, then, to include the creator of that work, we find more grounds for hope: we see an artist, equipped with her lovely heart, prodigious powers of observation, and a lean-but-lush American poetic tendency, gazing down at these imaginary people as she creates them, her eyes full of tenderness and genuine concern.

# A Note to the Reader
# about This Reader

Bobbie Ann Mason

A collection like this is a patchwork autobiography of sorts. I see in it my lifelong tendency to look for patterns, and I see my rebellion against them too.

I grew up with scraps and scissors and paper dolls and colors and jigsaw puzzles. I helped my grandmother piece quilts—geometric designs of stars and flowers. And I learned sewing from my mother, a seamstress with a flair. After opening the compact package of a Butterick or Simplicity dress pattern, you had to cut out the pattern pieces, scissoring along the dark lines of the thin tissue paper. Cutting out material, piecing, sewing straight seams, working jigsaw puzzles, solving mysteries—all these simple but absorbing endeavors of my childhood became more intricate over time, yet design itself became more and more elusive. The simple quilt pieces of my childhood led me to the subtle shades of exquisite patterns in literature.

Writing fiction is a way of making patterns, discovering them hiding in the words and sensations of the story. It is a way of exploring what you know but didn't know that you knew. And it is a way of finding out what you never knew but should have known long before. Fiction gives you an illusion of coherence, the possibility that things actually make sense. Images and words relate to each other in satisfyingly coherent ways, but they keep you on edge, wondering. Why doesn't everything fit together the way it is supposed to?

Fiction takes you on an adventure into a world you thought you knew but that you find out is both familiar and unfamiliar. It twists your mind and makes you jump. As a reader I want to be shaken and disturbed, nudged and whirled. I want to be amazed and gobsmacked. I want to write fiction that does that to you when you read it and to me as I write it. I don't want fiction to pacify or congratulate. It shouldn't confirm your prejudices or simply mirror your own life. Fiction, I learned, should offer more than the gratification of connecting the dots, or the comfort of a warm quilt. The joy is finding the downy little feather that pokes through the fabric. "The detail is all," wrote Vladimir Nabokov in his novel *Ada, or Ardor.*

Cutting out a Simplicity dress pattern along the dark lines is not much of a challenge, but ending up with a dress is. My mother could create a dress without a pattern to follow, but the pattern was there, and she knew she would find it. And she knew the design is never complete. Something is always mysterious and unfinished. Likewise, a story with an ambiguous ending is a reminder of the uncertainty and mystery—and hope—we live with, an ending that isn't there yet. A definite ending would be final, with nothing left to treasure.

# I

# First Stories

*My first published story appeared in* Stylus, *the University of Kentucky's literary magazine. It was the era before the MFA, so instead of pursuing creative writing in graduate school, I studied literature. Suddenly Donald Barthelme's novella* Snow White *(1967) turned my head around. Sneaking off from graduate studies that summer, I tried writing a novel about the Beatles from a Barthelme slant.*

*Eventually, in the 1980s, when I began to write fiction in earnest, which I had wanted to do all along, I found myself in the middle of a hopping renaissance of the short story. All around me superb fiction writers were producing extraordinary fiction. Raymond Carver, Tobias Wolff, Ann Beattie, Mary Robison, and Alice Munro were all the rage. Critics searched for labels for the new direction.*

*The surge of good fiction was stimulating and encouraging. The MFA programs had not yet reached their heyday, and everything seemed new.*

*My own stories, coming out of a rural western Kentucky world of unsettling change, seemed unfamiliar to many readers, but others were relieved to see fiction about people like those they knew—a truck driver, a drugstore clerk, a bus driver, a preacher, a retired couple headed for Florida. The reviewer Anatole Broyard wrote that my characters were "more foreign and incomprehensible" than European peasants, a line I treasure for its comic absurdity.*

—BAM

# Offerings

FROM *Shiloh and Other Stories* (1982)

Sandra's maternal grandmother died of childbed fever at the age of twenty-six. Mama was four. After Sandra was born, Mama developed an infection but was afraid to see the doctor. It would go away, she insisted. The infection disappeared, but a few years later inexplicable pains pierced her like needles. Blushing with shame, and regretting her choice of polka-dotted panties, she learned the worst. It was lucky they caught it in time, the doctor said. During the operation, Mama was semiconscious, with a spinal anesthetic, and she could hear the surgeons discussing a basketball game. Through blurred eyes, she could see a red expanse below her waist. It resembled the Red Sea parting, she said.

Sandra grows vegetables and counts her cats. It is late summer and her woodpile is low. She should find time to insulate the attic and to fix the leak in the basement. Her husband is gone. Jerry is in Louisville, working at a K Mart. Sandra has stayed behind, reluctant to spend her weekends with him watching go-go dancers in smoky bars. In the garden, Sandra loads a bucket with tomatoes and picks some dill, a cucumber, a handful of beans. The dead bird is on a stump, untouched since yesterday. When she rescued the bird from the cat, it seemed only stunned, and she put it on a table out on the porch, to let it recover. The bird had a spotted breast, a pink throat, and black-and-gray wings—a flicker, she thought. Its curved beak reminded her of Heckle and Jeckle. A while later, it tried to flap its wings, while gasping and contorting its body, and she decided to put it outside. As she opened the door, the dog rushed out eagerly ahead of her, and the bird died in her hand. Its head went limp.

Sandra never dusts. Only now, with her mother and grandmother coming to visit, does she notice that cobwebs are strung across corners of the

3

ceiling in the living room. Later, with a perverse delight, she sees a fly go by, actually trailing a wisp of cat hair and dust. Her grandmother always told her to dust under her bed, so the dust bunnies would not multiply and take over, as she would say, like Wandering Jew among the flowers.

Grandmother Stamper is her father's mother. Mama is bringing her all the way from Paducah to see where Sandra is living now. They aren't going to tell Grandmother about the separation. Mama insisted about that. Mama has never told Grandmother about her own hysterectomy. She will not even smoke in front of Grandmother Stamper. For twenty-five years, Mama has sneaked smokes whenever her mother-in-law is around.

Stamper is not Grandmother's most familiar name. After Sandra's grandfather, Bob Turnbow, died, Grandmother moved to Paducah, and later she married Joe Stamper, who owned a shoe store there. Now she lives in a small apartment on a city street, and—as she likes to say, laughing—has more shoes than she has places to go. Sandra's grandfather had a slow, wasting illness—Parkinson's disease. For five years, Grandmother waited on him, feeding him with a spoon, changing the bed, and trying her best to look after their dying farm. Sandra remembers a thin, twisted man, his face shaking, saying, "She's a good woman. She lights up the fires in the sky."

"I declare, Sandy Lee, you have moved plumb out into the wilderness," says Grandmother.

In her white pants suit, Sandra's grandmother looks like a waitress. The dog pokes at her crotch as she picks her way down the stone path to the porch. Sandra has not mowed in three weeks. The mower is broken, and there are little bushes of ragweed all over the yard.

"See how beautiful it is," says Mama. "It's just as pretty as a picture." She waves at a hillside of wild apple trees and weeds, with a patch of woods at the top. A long-haired calico cat sits under an overgrown lilac bush, also admiring the view.

"You need you some goats on that hill," says Grandmother. Sandra tells them about the raccoon she saw as she came home one night. At first, she thought it was a porcupine. It was very large, with slow, methodical movements. She followed it as far as she could with her headlights. It climbed a bank with grasping little hands. It occurs to Sandra that porcupines have quills like those thin pencils *Time* magazine sends with its subscription offers.

"Did you ever find out what went with your little white cat?" Mama asks as they go inside.

"No. I think maybe he got shot," Sandra says. "There's been somebody shooting people's cats around here ever since spring." The screen door bangs behind her.

The oven is not dependable, and supper is delayed. Grandmother is restless, walking around the kitchen, pretending not to see the dirty linoleum, the rusty, splotched sink, the peeling wallpaper. She puzzles over the bunches of dill and parsley hanging in the window. Mama has explained about the night shift and overtime, but when Sandra sees Grandmother examining the row of outdoor shoes on the porch and, later, the hunting rifle on the wall, she realizes that Grandmother is looking for Jerry. Jerry took his hunting boots with him, and Sandra has a feeling he may come back for the rifle soon.

It's the cats' suppertime, and they sing a chorus at Sandra's feet. She talks to them and gives them chicken broth and Cat Chow. She goes outside to shoo in the ducks for the night, but tonight they will not leave the pond. She will have to return later. If the ducks are not shut in their pen, the fox may kill them, one by one, in a fit—amazed at how easy it is. A bat circles above the barn. The ducks are splashing. A bird Sandra can't identify calls a mournful good night.

"Those silly ducks wouldn't come in," she says, setting the table. Her mother and grandmother stand around and watch her with starved looks.

"I'm collecting duck expressions," she goes on. "'Lucky duck,' 'duck your head,' 'set your ducks in a row,' 'a sitting duck.' I see where they all come from now."

"Have a rubber duck," says Mama. "Or a duck fit."

"Duck soup," says Grandmother.

"Duck soup?" Sandra says. "What does that mean?"

"It means something is real easy," says Grandmother. "Easy as pie."

"It was an old picture show too," Mama says. "The name of the show was *Duck Soup*."

They eat on the porch, and the moths come visiting, flapping against the screen. A few mosquitoes squeeze through and whine about their heads. Grandmother's fork jerks; the corn slips from her hand. Sandra notices that her dishes don't match. Mama and Grandmother exclaim over the meal, praising the tomatoes, the fresh corn. Grandmother takes another piece of chicken. "It has such a crispy crust!" she says.

Sandra will not admit the chicken is crisp. It is not even brown, she says to herself.

"How did you do that?" Grandmother wants to know.

"I boiled it first. It's faster."

"I never heard of doing it that way," Grandmother says.

"You'll have to try that, Ethel," says Mama.

Sandra flips a bug off her plate.

Her grandmother sneezes. "It's the ragweed," she says apologetically. "It's the time of the year for it. Doesn't it make you sneeze?"

"No," says Sandra.

"It never used to do you that way," Mama says.

"I know," says Grandmother. "I helped hay many a time when I was young. I can't remember it bothering me none."

The dog is barking. Sandra calls him into the house. He wants to greet the visitors, but she tells him to go to his bed, under the divan, and he obeys.

Sandra sits down at the table again and presses Grandmother to talk about the past, to tell about the farm Sandra can barely remember. She recalls the dizzying porch swing, a dog with a bushy tail, the daisy-edged field of corn, and a litter of squirming kittens like a deep pile of mated socks in a drawer. She wants to know about the trees. She remembers the fruit trees and the gigantic walnuts, with their sweeping arms and their hard, green balls that sometimes hit her on the head. She also remembers the day the trees came down.

"The peaches made such a mess on the grass you couldn't walk," her grandmother explains. "And there were so many cherries I couldn't pick them all. I had three peach trees taken down and one cherry tree."

"That was when your granddaddy was so bad," Mama says to Sandra. "She had to watch him night and day and turn him ever' so often. He didn't even know who she was."

"I just couldn't have all those in the yard anymore," says Grandmother. "I couldn't keep up with them. But the walnut trees were the worst. Those squirrels would get the nuts and roll them all over the porch and sometimes I'd step on one and fall down. Them old squirrels would snarl at me and chatter. Law me."

"Bessie Grissom had a tree taken down last week," says Mama. "She thought it would fall on the house, it was so old. A tornado might set down."

"How much did she have to pay?" asks Grandmother.

"A hundred dollars."

"When I had all them walnut trees taken down back then, it cost me sixty dollars. That just goes to show you."

Sandra serves instant butterscotch pudding for dessert. Grandmother eats greedily, telling Sandra that butterscotch is her favorite. She clashes her spoon as she cleans the dish. Sandra does not eat any dessert. She is thinking how she would like to have a bourbon-and-Coke. She might conceal it in a coffee cup. But she would not be able to explain why she was drinking coffee at night.

After supper, when Grandmother is in the bathroom, Mama says she will wash the dishes, but Sandra refuses.

"Do you hear anything from Jerry?" Mama asks.

Sandra shrugs. "No. He'd better not waltz back in here. I'm through waiting on him." In a sharp whisper, she says, "I don't know how long I can keep up that night-shift lie."

"But she's been through so much," Mama says. "She thinks the world of you, Sandra."

"I know."

"She thinks Jerry hung the moon."

"I tell you, if he so much as walks through that door—"

"I love those cosmos you planted," Mama says. "They're the prettiest I've ever seen. I'd give anything if I could get mine to do like that."

"They're volunteers. I didn't do a thing."

"You didn't?"

"I didn't thin them either. I just hated to thin them."

"I know what you mean," says Mama. "It always broke my heart to thin corn. But you learn."

A movie, *That's Entertainment!*, is on TV. Sandra stands in the doorway to watch Fred Astaire dancing with Eleanor Powell, who is as loose as a rag doll. She is wearing a little-girl dress with squared shoulders.

"Fred Astaire is the limberest thing I ever saw," says Mama.

"I remember his sister Adele," says Grandmother. "She could really dance."

"Her name was Estelle," says Mama.

"Estelle Astaire?" says Sandra. For some reason, she remembers a girl she knew in grade school named Sandy Beach.

Sandra makes tomato sauce, and they offer to help, but she tells them to relax and watch the movie. As she scalds tomatoes and presses hot pulp through a food mill, she listens to the singing and tap-dancing from the next room. She comes to the doorway to watch Gene Kelly do his famous "Singin' in the Rain" number. His suit is soaked, and he jumps into puddles with both feet, like a child. A policeman scowls at his antics. Grandmother laughs. When the sauce boils down, Sandra pours it into bowls to cool. She sees bowls of blood lined up on the counter. Sandra watches Esther Williams dive through a ring of fire and splash in the center of a star formed by women, with spread legs, lying on their backs in the water.

During a commercial, Sandra asks her mother if she wants to come to the barn with her, to help with the ducks. The dog bounds out the door with them, happy at this unexpected excursion. Out in the yard, Mama lights a cigarette.

"Finally!" Mama says with a sigh. "That feels good."

Two cats, Blackie and Bubbles, join them. Sandra wonders if Bubbles remembers the mole she caught yesterday. The mole had a star-shaped nose, which Bubbles ate first, like a delicacy.

The ducks are not in the barn, and Sandra and her mother walk down a narrow path through the weeds to the pond. The pond is quiet as they approach. Then they can make out patches of white on the dark water. The ducks hear them and begin diving, fleeing to the far shore in panic.

"There's no way to drive ducks in from a pond," Mama says.

"Sometimes they just take a notion to stay out here all night," says Sandra.

They stand side by side at the edge of the pond while Mama smokes. The sounds of evening are at their fullest now, and lightning bugs wink frantically. Sometimes Sandra has heard foxes at night, their menacing yaps echoing on the hillside. Once, she saw three fox pups playing in the full moon, like dancers in a spotlight. And just last week she heard a baby screaming in terror. It was the sound of a wildcat—a thrill she listens for every night now. It occurs to her that she would not mind if the wildcat took her ducks. They are her offering.

Mama throws her cigarette in the pond, and a duck splashes. The night is peaceful, and Sandra thinks of the thousands of large golden garden spiders hidden in the field. In the early morning the dew shines on their trampolines, and she can imagine bouncing with an excited spring from web to web, all the way up the hill to the woods.

# Shiloh

FROM *Shiloh and Other Stories* (1982)

Leroy Moffitt's wife, Norma Jean, is working on her pectorals. She lifts three-pound dumbbells to warm up, then progresses to a twenty-pound barbell. Standing with her legs apart, she reminds Leroy of Wonder Woman.

"I'd give anything if I could just get these muscles to where they're real hard," says Norma Jean. "Feel this arm. It's not as hard as the other one."

"That's 'cause you're right-handed," says Leroy, dodging as she swings the barbell in an arc.

"Do you think so?"

"Sure."

Leroy is a truckdriver. He injured his leg in a highway accident four months ago, and his physical therapy, which involves weights and a pulley, prompted Norma Jean to try building herself up. Now she is attending a body-building class. Leroy has been collecting temporary disability since his tractor-trailer jackknifed in Missouri, badly twisting his left leg in its socket. He has a steel pin in his hip. He will probably not be able to drive his rig again. It sits in the backyard, like a gigantic bird that has flown home to roost. Leroy has been home in Kentucky for three months, and his leg is almost healed, but the accident frightened him and he does not want to drive any more long hauls. He is not sure what to do next. In the meantime, he makes things from craft kits. He started by building a miniature log cabin from notched Popsicle sticks. He varnished it and placed it on the TV set, where it remains. It reminds him of a rustic Nativity scene. Then he tried string art (sailing ships on black velvet), a macramé owl kit, a snap-together B-17 Flying Fortress, and a lamp made out of a model truck, with a light fixture screwed in the top of the cab. At first the kits were diversions, something to kill time, but now he is thinking about building a full-scale

log house from a kit. It would be considerably cheaper than building a regular house, and besides, Leroy has grown to appreciate how things are put
together. He has begun to realize that in all the years he was on the road he
never took time to examine anything. He was always flying past scenery.

"They won't let you build a log cabin in any of the new subdivisions,"
Norma Jean tells him.

"They will if I tell them it's for you," he says, teasing her. Ever since
they were married, he has promised Norma Jean he would build her a new
home one day. They have always rented, and the house they live in is small
and nondescript. It does not even feel like a home, Leroy realizes now.

Norma Jean works at the Rexall drugstore, and she has acquired an
amazing amount of information about cosmetics. When she explains to Leroy the three stages of complexion care, involving creams, toners, and mois-
turizers, he thinks happily of other petroleum products—axle grease, diesel
fuel. This is a connection between him and Norma Jean. Since he has been
home, he has felt unusually tender about his wife and guilty over his long
absences. But he can't tell what she feels about him. Norma Jean has never
complained about his traveling; she has never made hurt remarks, like calling his truck a "widow-maker." He is reasonably certain she has been faith-
ful to him, but he wishes she would celebrate his permanent homecoming
more happily. Norma Jean is often startled to find Leroy at home, and he
thinks she seems a little disappointed about it. Perhaps he reminds her too
much of the early days of their marriage, before he went on the road. They
had a child who died as an infant, years ago. They never speak about their
memories of Randy, which have almost faded, but now that Leroy is home
all the time, they sometimes feel awkward around each other, and Leroy
wonders if one of them should mention the child. He has the feeling that they
are waking up out of a dream together—that they must create a new marriage, start afresh. They are lucky they are still married. Leroy has read that
for most people losing a child destroys the marriage—or else he heard this
on *Donahue*. He can't always remember where he learns things anymore.

At Christmas, Leroy bought an electric organ for Norma Jean. She used
to play the piano when she was in high school. "It don't leave you," she told
him once. "It's like riding a bicycle."

The new instrument had so many keys and buttons that she was bewildered by it at first. She touched the keys tentatively, pushed some buttons,

then pecked out "Chopsticks." It came out in an amplified fox-trot rhythm, with marimba sounds.

"It's an orchestra!" she cried.

The organ had a pecan-look finish and eighteen preset chords, with optional flute, violin, trumpet, clarinet, and banjo accompaniments. Norma Jean mastered the organ almost immediately. At first she played Christmas songs. Then she bought *The Sixties Songbook* and learned every tune in it, adding variations to each with the rows of brightly colored buttons.

"I didn't like these old songs back then," she said. "But I have this crazy feeling I missed something."

"You didn't miss a thing," said Leroy.

Leroy likes to lie on the couch and smoke a joint and listen to Norma Jean play "Can't Take My Eyes Off You" and "I'll Be Back." He is back again. After fifteen years on the road, he is finally settling down with the woman he loves. She is still pretty. Her skin is flawless. Her frosted curls resemble pencil trimmings.

Now that Leroy has come home to stay, he notices how much the town has changed. Subdivisions are spreading across western Kentucky like an oil slick. The sign at the edge of town says "Pop: 11,500"—only seven hundred more than it said twenty years before. Leroy can't figure out who is living in all the new houses. The farmers who used to gather around the courthouse square on Saturday afternoons to play checkers and spit tobacco juice have gone. It has been years since Leroy has thought about the farmers, and they have disappeared without his noticing.

Leroy meets a kid named Stevie Hamilton in the parking lot at the new shopping center. While they pretend to be strangers meeting over a stalled car, Stevie tosses an ounce of marijuana under the front seat of Leroy's car. Stevie is wearing orange jogging shoes and a T-shirt that says CHAT-TAHOOCHEE SUPER-RAT. His father is a prominent doctor who lives in one of the expensive subdivisions in a new white-columned brick house that looks like a funeral parlor. In the phone book under his name there is a separate number, with the listing "Teenagers."

"Where do you get this stuff?" asks Leroy. "From your pappy?"

"That's for me to know and you to find out," Stevie says. He is slit-eyed and skinny.

"What else you got?"

"What you interested in?"

"Nothing special. Just wondered."

Leroy used to take speed on the road. Now he has to go slowly. He needs to be mellow. He leans back against the car and says, "I'm aiming to build me a log house, soon as I get time. My wife, though, I don't think she likes the idea."

"Well, let me know when you want me again," Stevie says. He has a cigarette in his cupped palm, as though sheltering it from the wind. He takes a long drag, then stomps it on the asphalt and slouches away.

Stevie's father was two years ahead of Leroy in high school. Leroy is thirty-four. He married Norma Jean when they were both eighteen, and their child Randy was born a few months later, but he died at the age of four months and three days. He would be about Stevie's age now. Norma Jean and Leroy were at the drive-in, watching a double feature (*Dr. Strangelove* and *Lover Come Back*), and the baby was sleeping in the back seat. When the first movie ended, the baby was dead. It was the sudden infant death syndrome. Leroy remembers handing Randy to a nurse at the emergency room, as though he were offering her a large doll as a present. A dead baby feels like a sack of flour. "It just happens sometimes," said the doctor, in what Leroy always recalls as a nonchalant tone. Leroy can hardly remember the child anymore, but he still sees vividly a scene from *Dr. Strangelove* in which the President of the United States was talking in a folksy voice on the hot line to the Soviet premier about the bomber accidentally headed toward Russia. He was in the War Room, and the world map was lit up. Leroy remembers Norma Jean standing catatonically beside him in the hospital and himself thinking: Who is this strange girl? He had forgotten who she was. Now scientists are saying that crib death is caused by a virus. Nobody knows anything, Leroy thinks. The answers are always changing.

When Leroy gets home from the shopping center, Norma Jean's mother, Mabel Beasley, is there. Until this year, Leroy has not realized how much time she spends with Norma Jean. When she visits, she inspects the closets and then the plants, informing Norma Jean when a plant is droopy or yellow. Mabel calls the plants "flowers," although there are never any blooms. She always notices if Norma Jean's laundry is piling up. Mabel is a short, overweight woman whose tight, brown-dyed curls look more like a wig than the actual wig she sometimes wears. Today she has brought Norma Jean an off-white dust ruffle she made for the bed; Mabel works in a custom-upholstery shop.

"This is the tenth one I made this year," Mabel says. "I got started and couldn't stop."

"It's real pretty," says Norma Jean.

"Now we can hide things under the bed," says Leroy, who gets along with his mother-in-law primarily by joking with her. Mabel has never really forgiven him for disgracing her by getting Norma Jean pregnant. When the baby died, she said that fate was mocking her.

"What's that thing?" Mabel says to Leroy in a loud voice, pointing to a tangle of yarn on a piece of canvas.

Leroy holds it up for Mabel to see. "It's my needlepoint," he explains. "This is a *Star Trek* pillow cover."

"That's what a woman would do," says Mabel. "Great day in the morning!"

"All the big football players on TV do it," he says.

"Why, Leroy, you're always trying to fool me. I don't believe you for one minute. You don't know what to do with yourself—that's the whole trouble. Sewing!"

"I'm aiming to build us a log house," says Leroy. "Soon as my plans come."

"Like heck you are," says Norma Jean. She takes Leroy's needlepoint and shoves it into a drawer. "You have to find a job first. Nobody can afford to build now anyway."

Mabel straightens her girdle and says, "I still think before you get tied down y'all ought to take a little run to Shiloh."

"One of these days, Mama," Norma Jean says impatiently.

Mabel is talking about Shiloh, Tennessee. For the past few years, she has been urging Leroy and Norma Jean to visit the Civil War battleground there. Mabel went there on her honeymoon—the only real trip she ever took. Her husband died of a perforated ulcer when Norma Jean was ten, but Mabel, who was accepted into the United Daughters of the Confederacy in 1975, is still preoccupied with going back to Shiloh.

"I've been to kingdom come and back in that truck out yonder," Leroy says to Mabel, "but we never yet set foot in that battleground. Ain't that something? How did I miss it?"

"It's not even that far," Mabel says.

After Mabel leaves, Norma Jean reads to Leroy from a list she has made. "Things you could do," she announces. "You could get a job as a guard at Union Carbide, where they'd let you set on a stool. You could get on at the lumberyard. You could do a little carpenter work, if you want to build so bad. You could—"

"I can't do something where I'd have to stand up all day."

"You ought to try standing up all day behind a cosmetics counter. It's amazing that I have strong feet, coming from two parents that never had strong feet at all." At the moment Norma Jean is holding on to the kitchen counter, raising her knees one at a time as she talks. She is wearing two-pound ankle weights.

"Don't worry," says Leroy. "I'll do something."

"You could truck calves to slaughter for somebody. You wouldn't have to drive any big old truck for that."

"I'm going to build you this house," says Leroy. "I want to make you a real home."

"I don't want to live in any log cabin."

"It's not a cabin. It's a house."

"I don't care. It looks like a cabin."

"You and me together could lift those logs. It's just like lifting weights."

Norma Jean doesn't answer. Under her breath, she is counting. Now she is marching through the kitchen. She is doing goose steps.

Before his accident, when Leroy came home he used to stay in the house with Norma Jean, watching TV in bed and playing cards. She would cook fried chicken, picnic ham, chocolate pie—all his favorites. Now he is home alone much of the time. In the mornings, Norma Jean disappears, leaving a cooling place in the bed. She eats a cereal called Body Buddies, and she leaves the bowl on the table, with the soggy tan balls floating in a milk puddle. He sees things about Norma Jean that he never realized before. When she chops onions, she stares off into a corner, as if she can't bear to look. She puts on her house slippers almost precisely at nine o'clock every evening and nudges her jogging shoes under the couch. She saves bread heels for the birds. Leroy watches the birds at the feeder. He notices the peculiar way goldfinches fly past the window. They close their wings, then fall, then spread their wings to catch and lift themselves. He wonders if they close their eyes when they fall. Norma Jean closes her eyes when they are in bed. She wants the lights turned out. Even then, he is sure she closes her eyes.

He goes for long drives around town. He tends to drive a car rather carelessly. Power steering and an automatic shift make a car feel so small and inconsequential that his body is hardly involved in the driving process. His injured leg stretches out comfortably. Once or twice he has almost hit something, but even the prospect of an accident seems minor in a car. He cruises the new subdivisions, feeling like a criminal rehearsing for a robbery. Norma Jean is probably right about a log house being inappropriate here in the new subdivisions. All the houses look grand and complicated. They depress him.

One day when Leroy comes home from a drive he finds Norma Jean in tears. She is in the kitchen making a potato and mushroom-soup casserole, with grated-cheese topping. She is crying because her mother caught her smoking.

"I didn't hear her coming. I was standing here puffing away pretty as you please," Norma Jean says, wiping her eyes.

"I knew it would happen sooner or later," says Leroy, putting his arm around her.

"She don't know the meaning of the word 'knock,'" says Norma Jean. "It's a wonder she hadn't caught me years ago."

"Think of it this way," Leroy says. "What if she caught me with a joint?"

"You better not let her!" Norma Jean shrieks. "I'm warning you, Leroy Moffitt!"

"I'm just kidding. Here, play me a tune. That'll help you relax."

Norma Jean puts the casserole in the oven and sets the timer. Then she plays a ragtime tune, with horns and banjo, as Leroy lights up a joint and lies on the couch, laughing to himself about Mabel's catching him at it. He thinks of Stevie Hamilton—a doctor's son pushing grass. Everything is funny. The whole town seems crazy and small. He is reminded of Virgil Mathis, a boastful policeman Leroy used to shoot pool with. Virgil recently led a drug bust in a back room at a bowling alley, where he seized ten thousand dollars' worth of marijuana. The newspaper had a picture of him holding up the bags of grass and grinning widely. Right now, Leroy can imagine Virgil breaking down the door and arresting him with a lung-ful of smoke. Virgil would probably have been alerted to the scene because of all the racket Norma Jean is making. Now she sounds like a hard-rock band. Norma Jean is terrific. When she switches to a Latin-rhythm version of "Sunshine Superman," Leroy hums along. Norma Jean's foot goes up and down, up and down.

"Well, what do you think?" Leroy says, when Norma Jean pauses to search through her music.

"What do I think about what?"

His mind has gone blank. Then he says, "I'll sell my rig and build us a house." That wasn't what he wanted to say. He wanted to know what she thought—what she *really* thought—about them.

"Don't start in on that again," says Norma Jean. She begins playing "Who'll Be the Next in Line?"

Leroy used to tell hitchhikers his whole life story—about his travels, his hometown, the baby. He would end with a question: "Well, what do you think?" It was just a rhetorical question. In time, he had the feeling that he'd been telling the same story over and over to the same hitchhikers. He quit talking to hitchhikers when he realized how his voice sounded—whin-ing and self-pitying, like some teenage-tragedy song. Now Leroy has the sudden impulse to tell Norma Jean about himself, as if he had just met her. They have known each other so long they have forgotten a lot about each other. They could become reacquainted. But when the oven timer goes off and she runs to the kitchen, he forgets why he wants to do this.

The next day, Mabel drops by. It is Saturday and Norma Jean is cleaning. Leroy is studying the plans of his log house, which have finally come in the mail. He has them spread out on the table—big sheets of stiff blue paper, with diagrams and numbers printed in white. While Norma Jean runs the vacuum, Mabel drinks coffee. She sets her coffee cup on a blueprint.

"I'm just waiting for time to pass," she says to Leroy, drumming her fingers on the table.

As soon as Norma Jean switches off the vacuum, Mabel says in a loud voice, "Did you hear about the datsun dog that killed the baby?"

Norma Jean says, "The word is 'dachshund.'"

"They put the dog on trial. It chewed the baby's legs off. The mother was in the next room all the time." She raises her voice. "They thought it was neglect."

Norma Jean is holding her ears. Leroy manages to open the refrigerator and get some Diet Pepsi to offer Mabel. Mabel still has some coffee and she waves away the Pepsi.

"Datsuns are like that," Mabel says. "They're jealous dogs. They'll tear a place to pieces if you don't keep an eye on them."

"You better watch out what you're saying, Mabel," says Leroy.

"Well, facts is facts."

Leroy looks out the window at his rig. It is like a huge piece of furniture gathering dust in the backyard. Pretty soon it will be an antique. He hears the vacuum cleaner. Norma Jean seems to be cleaning the living room rug again.

Later, she says to Leroy, "She just said that about the baby because she caught me smoking. She's trying to pay me back."

"What are you talking about?" Leroy says, nervously shuffling blueprints.

"You know good and well," Norma Jean says. She is sitting in a kitchen chair with her feet up and her arms wrapped around her knees. She looks small and helpless. She says, "The very idea, her bringing up a subject like that! Saying it was neglect."

"She didn't mean that," Leroy says.

"She might not have *thought* she meant it. She always says things like that. You don't know how she goes on."

"But she didn't really mean it. She was just talking."

Leroy opens a king-sized bottle of beer and pours it into two glasses, dividing it carefully. He hands a glass to Norma Jean and she takes it from him mechanically. For a long time, they sit by the kitchen window watching the birds at the feeder.

Something is happening. Norma Jean is going to night school. She has graduated from her six-week body-building course and now she is taking an adult-education course in composition at Paducah Community College. She spends her evenings outlining paragraphs.

"First you have a topic sentence," she explains to Leroy. "Then you divide it up. Your secondary topic has to be connected to your primary topic."

To Leroy, this sounds intimidating. "I never was any good in English," he says.

"It makes a lot of sense."

"What are you doing this for, anyhow?"

She shrugs. "It's something to do." She stands up and lifts her dumbbells a few times.

"Driving a rig, nobody cared about my English."

"I'm not criticizing your English."

Norma Jean used to say, "If I lose ten minutes' sleep, I just drag all day." Now she stays up late, writing compositions. She got a B on her first paper—a how-to theme on soup-based casseroles. Recently Norma Jean has been cooking unusual food—tacos, lasagna, Bombay chicken. She doesn't play the organ anymore, though her second paper was called "Why Music Is Important to Me." She sits at the kitchen table, concentrating on her outlines, while Leroy plays with his log house plans, practicing with a set of Lincoln Logs. The thought of getting a truckload of notched, numbered logs scares him, and he wants to be prepared. As he and Norma Jean work together at the kitchen table, Leroy has the hopeful thought that they are sharing something, but he knows he is a fool to think this. Norma Jean is miles away. He knows he is going to lose her. Like Mabel, he is just waiting for time to pass.

One day, Mabel is there before Norma Jean gets home from work, and Leroy finds himself confiding in her. Mabel, he realizes, must know Norma Jean better than he does.

"I don't know what's got into that girl," Mabel says. "She used to go to bed with the chickens. Now you say she's up all hours. Plus her a-smoking. I like to died."

"I want to make her this beautiful home," Leroy says, indicating the Lincoln Logs. "I don't think she even wants it. Maybe she was happier with me gone."

"She don't know what to make of you, coming home like this."

"Is that it?"

Mabel takes the roof off his Lincoln Log cabin. "You couldn't get *me* in a log cabin," she says. "I was raised in one. It's no picnic, let me tell you."

"They're different now," says Leroy.

"I tell you what," Mabel says, smiling oddly at Leroy.

"What?"

"Take her on down to Shiloh. Y'all need to get out together, stir a little. Her brain's all balled up over them books."

Leroy can see traces of Norma Jean's features in her mother's face. Mabel's worn face has the texture of crinkled cotton, but suddenly she looks pretty. It occurs to Leroy that Mabel has been hinting all along that she wants them to take her with them to Shiloh.

"Let's all go to Shiloh," he says. "You and me and her. Come Sunday."

Mabel throws up her hands in protest. "Oh, no, not me. Young folks want to be by theirselves."

When Norma Jean comes in with groceries, Leroy says excitedly, "Your mama here's been dying to go to Shiloh for thirty-five years. It's about time we went, don't you think?"

"I'm not going to butt in on anybody's second honeymoon," Mabel says.

"Who's going on a honeymoon, for Christ's sake?" Norma Jean says loudly.

"I never raised no daughter of mine to talk that-a-way," Mabel says.

"You ain't seen nothing yet," says Norma Jean. She starts putting away boxes and cans, slamming cabinet doors.

"There's a log cabin at Shiloh," Mabel says. "It was there during the battle. There's bullet holes in it."

"When are you going to *shut up* about Shiloh, Mama?" asks Norma Jean.

"I always thought Shiloh was the prettiest place, so full of history," Mabel goes on. "I just hoped y'all could see it once before I die, so you could tell me about it." Later, she whispers to Leroy, "You do what I said. A little change is what she needs."

"Your name means 'the king,'" Norma Jean says to Leroy that evening. He is trying to get her to go to Shiloh, and she is reading a book about another century.

"Well, I reckon I ought to be right proud."

"I guess so."

"Am I still king around here?"

Norma Jean flexes her biceps and feels them for hardness. "I'm not fooling around with anybody, if that's what you mean," she says.

"Would you tell me if you were?"

"I don't know."

"What does *your* name mean?"

"It was Marilyn Monroe's real name."

"No kidding!"

"Norma comes from the Normans. They were invaders," she says. She closes her book and looks hard at Leroy. "I'll go to Shiloh with you if you'll stop staring at me."

On Sunday, Norma Jean packs a picnic and they go to Shiloh. To Leroy's relief, Mabel says she does not want to come with them. Norma Jean drives, and Leroy, sitting beside her, feels like some boring hitchhiker she has picked up. He tries some conversation, but she answers him in monosyllables. At Shiloh, she drives aimlessly through the park, past bluffs and trails and steep ravines. Shiloh is an immense place, and Leroy cannot see it as a battleground. It is not what he expected. He thought it would look like a golf course. Monuments are everywhere, showing through the thick clusters of trees. Norma Jean passes the log cabin Mabel mentioned. It is surrounded by tourists looking for bullet holes.

"That's not the kind of log house I've got in mind," says Leroy apologetically.

"I know *that*."

"This is a pretty place. Your mama was right."

"It's O.K.," says Norma Jean. "Well, we've seen it. I hope she's satisfied." They burst out laughing together.

At the park museum, a movie on Shiloh is shown every half hour, but they decide that they don't want to see it. They buy a souvenir Confederate flag for Mabel, and then they find a picnic spot near the cemetery. Norma Jean has brought a picnic cooler, with pimiento sandwiches, soft drinks, and Yodels. Leroy eats a sandwich and then smokes a joint, hiding it behind the picnic cooler. Norma Jean has quit smoking altogether. She is picking cake crumbs from the cellophane wrapper, like a fussy bird.

Leroy says, "So the boys in gray ended up in Corinth. The Union soldiers zapped 'em finally. April 7, 1862."

They both know that he doesn't know any history. He is just talking about some of the historical plaques they have read. He feels awkward, like a boy on a date with an older girl. They are still just making conversation.

"Corinth is where Mama eloped to," says Norma Jean. They sit in silence and stare at the cemetery for the Union dead and, beyond, at a tall cluster of trees. Campers are parked nearby, bumper to bumper, and small children in bright clothing are cavorting and squealing. Norma Jean wads up the cake wrapper and squeezes it tightly in her hand. Without looking at Leroy, she says, "I want to leave you."

Leroy takes a bottle of Coke out of the cooler and flips off the cap. He holds the bottle poised near his mouth but cannot remember to take a drink. Finally he says, "No, you don't."

"Yes, I do."

"I won't let you."

"You can't stop me."

"Don't do me that way."

Leroy knows Norma Jean will have her own way. "Didn't I promise to be home from now on?" he says.

"In some ways, a woman prefers a man who wanders," says Norma Jean. "That sounds crazy, I know."

"You're not crazy."

Leroy remembers to drink from his Coke. Then he says, "Yes, you *are* crazy. You and me could start all over again. Right back at the beginning."

"We *have* started all over again," says Norma Jean. "And this is how it turned out."

"What did I do wrong?"

"Nothing."

"Is this one of those women's lib things?" Leroy asks.

"Don't be funny."

The cemetery, a green slope dotted with white markers, looks like a subdivision site. Leroy is trying to comprehend that his marriage is breaking up, but for some reason he is wondering about white slabs in a graveyard.

"Everything was fine till Mama caught me smoking," says Norma Jean, standing up. "That set something off."

"What are you talking about?"

"She won't leave me alone—*you* won't leave me alone." Norma Jean seems to be crying, but she is looking away from him. "I feel eighteen again.

I can't face that all over again." She starts walking away. "No, it *wasn't* fine. I don't know what I'm saying. Forget it."

Leroy takes a lungful of smoke and closes his eyes as Norma Jean's words sink in. He tries to focus on the fact that thirty-five hundred soldiers died on the grounds around him. He can only think of that war as a board game with plastic soldiers. Leroy almost smiles, as he compares the Confederates' daring attack on the Union camps and Virgil Mathis's raid on the bowling alley. General Grant, drunk and furious, shoved the Southerners back to Corinth, where Mabel and Jet Beasley were married years later, when Mabel was still thin and good-looking. The next day, Mabel and Jet visited the battleground, and then Norma Jean was born, and then she married Leroy and they had a baby, which they lost, and now Leroy and Norma Jean are here at the same battleground. Leroy knows he is leaving out a lot. He is leaving out the insides of history. History was always just names and dates to him. It occurs to him that building a house out of logs is similarly empty—too simple. And the real inner workings of a marriage, like most of history, have escaped him. Now he sees that building a log house is the dumbest idea he could have had. It was clumsy of him to think Norma Jean would want a log house. It was a crazy idea. He'll have to think of something else, quickly. He will wad the blueprints into tight balls and fling them into the lake. Then he'll get moving again. He opens his eyes. Norma Jean has moved away and is walking through the cemetery, following a serpentine brick path.

Leroy gets up to follow his wife, but his good leg is asleep and his bad leg still hurts him. Norma Jean is far away, walking rapidly toward the bluff by the river, and he tries to hobble toward her. Some children run past him, screaming noisily. Norma Jean has reached the bluff, and she is looking out over the Tennessee River. Now she turns toward Leroy and waves her arms. Is she beckoning to him? She seems to be doing an exercise for her chest muscles. The sky is unusually pale—the color of the dust ruffle Mabel made for their bed.

# Third Monday

FROM *Shiloh and Other Stories* (1982)

Ruby watches Linda exclaiming over a bib, then a terry cloth sleeper. It is an amazing baby shower because Linda is thirty-seven and unmarried. Ruby admires that. Linda even refused to marry the baby's father, a man from out of town who had promised to get Linda a laundromat franchise. It turned out that he didn't own any laundromats; he was only trying to impress her. Linda doesn't know where he is now. Maybe Nashville.

Linda smiles at a large bakery cake with pink decorations and the message, WELCOME, HOLLY. "I'm glad I know it's going to be a girl," she says. "But in a way it's like knowing ahead of time what you're going to get for Christmas."

"The twentieth century's taking all the mysteries out of life," says Ruby breezily.

Ruby is as much a guest of honor here as Linda is. Betty Lewis brings Ruby's cake and ice cream to her and makes sure she has a comfortable chair. Ever since Ruby had a radical mastectomy, Betty and Linda and the other women on her bowling team have been awed by her. They praise her bravery and her sense of humor. Just before she had the operation, they suddenly brimmed over with inspiring tales about women who had had successful mastectomies. They reminded her about Betty Ford and Happy Rockefeller. Happy . . . Everyone is happy now. Linda looks happy because Nancy Featherstone has taken all the ribbons from the presents and threaded them through holes in a paper plate to fashion a funny bridal bouquet. Nancy, who is artistic, explains that this is a tradition at showers. Linda is pleased. She twirls the bouquet, and the ends of the ribbons dangle like tentacles on a jellyfish.

After Ruby found the lump in her breast, the doctor recommended a mammogram. In an X-ray room, she hugged a Styrofoam basketball hanging from a metal cone and stared at the two lights overhead. The technician, a frail man in plaid pants and a smock, flipped a switch and left the room. The machine hummed. He took several X-rays, like a photographer shooting various poses of a model, and used his hands to measure distances, as one would to determine the height of a horse. "My guidelight is out," he explained. Ruby lay on her back with her breasts flattened out, and the technician slid an X-ray plate into the drawer beneath the table. He tilted her hip and propped it against a cushion. "I have to repeat that last one," he said. "The angle was wrong." He told her not to breathe. The machine buzzed and shook. After she was dressed, he showed her the X-rays, which were printed on Xerox paper. Ruby looked for the lump in the squiggly lines, which resembled a rainfall map in a geography book. The outline of her breast was lovely—a lilting, soft curve. The technician would not comment on what he saw in the pictures. "Let the radiologist interpret them," he said with a peculiar smile. "He's our chief tea-leaf reader." Ruby told the women in her bowling club that she had had her breasts Xeroxed.

The man she cares about does not know. She has been out of the hospital for a week, and in ten days he will be in town again. She wonders whether he will be disgusted and treat her as though she has been raped, his property violated. According to an article she read, this is what to expect. But Buddy is not that kind of man, and she is not his property. She sees him only once a month. He could have a wife somewhere, or other girlfriends, but she doesn't believe that. He promised to take her home with him the next time he comes to western Kentucky. He lives far away, in East Tennessee, and he travels the flea-market circuit, trading hunting dogs and pocket knives. She met him at the fairgrounds at Third Monday—the flea market held the third Monday of each month. Ruby had first gone there on a day off from work with Janice Leggett to look for some Depression glass to match Janice's sugar bowl. Ruby lingered in the fringe of trees near the highway, the oak grove where hundreds of dogs were whining and barking, while Janice wandered ahead to the tables of figurines and old dishes. Ruby intended to catch up with Janice shortly, but she became absorbed in the dogs. Their mournful eyes and pitiful yelps made her sad. When she was a child, her dog had been accidentally locked in the corncrib and died of heat exhaustion. She was aware of a man watching her watching the dogs. He wore a billed cap that shaded his sharp eyes like an awning. His blue jacket said HEART VALLEY COON CLUB on the back in gold-embroidered stitching. His red shirt had pearl snaps, and his jeans were creased, as though a woman had ironed them. He grabbed Ruby's arm suddenly and said, "What are you staring at, little lady! Have you got something treed?"

He was Buddy Landon, and he tried to sell her a hunting dog. He seemed perfectly serious. Did she want a Coonhound or a bird dog? The thing wrong with bird dogs was that they liked to run so much they often strayed, he said. He recommended the Georgia redbone hound for intelligence and patience. "The redbone can jump and tree, but he doesn't bark too much," he said. "He don't cry wolf on you, and he's a good lighter."

"What do I need a coon dog for?" said Ruby, wishing he had a good answer.

"You must be after a bird dog then," he said. "Do you prefer hunting ducks or wild geese? I had some hounds that led me on a wild-goose chase one time after an old wildcat. That thing led us over half of Kentucky. That sucker never would climb a tree! He wore my dogs out." He whooped and clapped his hands.

There were eight empty dog crates in the back of his pickup, and he had chained the dogs to a line between two trees. Ruby approached them cautiously, and they all leaped into the air before their chains jerked them back.

"That little beagle there's the best in the field," Buddy said to a man in a blue cap who had sidled up beside them.

"What kind of voice has he got?" the man said.

"It's music to your ears!"

"I don't need a rabbit dog," the man said. "I don't even have any rabbits left in my fields. I need me a good coon dog."

"This black-and-tan's ambitious," said Buddy, patting a black spot on a dog's head. The spot was like a little beanie. "His mama and daddy were both ambitious, and *he's* ambitious. This dog won't run trash."

"What's trash?" Ruby asked.

"Skunk. Possum," Buddy explained.

"I've only knowed two women in my life that I could get out coon hunting," the man in the blue cap said.

"This lady claims she wants a bird dog, but I think I can make a coon hunter out of her," said Buddy, grinning at Ruby.

The man walked away, hunched over a cigarette he was lighting, and Buddy Landon started to sing "You Ain't Nothin' But A Hound Dog." He said to Ruby, "I could have been Elvis Presley. But thank God I wasn't. Look what happened to him. Got fat and died." He sang, "'Crying all the time. You ain't never caught a rabbit . . . ' I love dogs. But I tell you one thing. I'd never let a dog in the house. You know why? It would get too tame and forget its job. Don't forget, a dog is a dog."

Buddy took Ruby by the elbow and steered her through the fairgrounds, guiding her past tables of old plastic toys and kitchen utensils. "Junk," he said. He bought Ruby a Coke in a can, and then he bought some sweet corn from a farmer. "I'm going to have me some roastin' ears tonight," he said.

"I hear your dogs calling for you," said Ruby, listening to the distant bugle voices of the beagles.

"They love me. Stick around and you'll love me too."

"What makes you think you're so cute?" said Ruby. "What makes you think I need a dog?"

He answered her questions with a flirtatious grin. His belt had a large silver buckle, with a floppy-eared dog's head engraved on it. His hands were thick and strong, with margins of dirt under his large, flat nails. Ruby liked his mustache and the way his chin and the bill of his cap seemed to yearn toward each other.

"How much do you want for that speckled hound dog?" she asked him.

He brought the sweet corn and some steaks to her house that evening. By then, the shucks on the corn were wilting. Ruby grilled the steaks and boiled the ears of corn while Buddy unloaded the dogs from his pickup. He tied them to her clothesline and fed and watered them. The pickup truck in Ruby's driveway seemed as startling as the sight of the "Action News" TV van would have been. She hoped her neighbors would notice. She could have a man there if she wanted to.

After supper, Buddy gave the dogs the leftover bones and steak fat. Leaping and snapping, they snatched at the scraps, but Buddy snarled back at them and made them cringe. "You have to let them know who's boss," he called to Ruby, who was looking on admiringly from the back porch. It was like watching a group of people playing "May I?"

Later, Buddy brought his sleeping roll in from the truck and settled in the living room, and Ruby did not resist when he came into her bedroom and said he couldn't sleep. She thought her timing was appropriate; she had recently bought a double bed. They talked until late in the night, and he told her hunting stories, still pretending that she was interested in acquiring a hunting dog. She pretended she was, too, and asked him dozens of questions. He said he traded things—anything he could make a nickel from: retreaded tires, cars, old milk cans and cream separators. He was fond of the dogs he raised and trained, but it did not hurt him to sell them. There were always more dogs.

"Loving a dog is like trying to love the Mississippi River," he said. "It's constantly shifting and changing color and sound and course, but it's just the same old river."

Suddenly he asked Ruby, "Didn't you ever get married?"

"No."

"Don't it bother you?"

"No. What of it?" She wondered if he thought she was a lesbian.

He said, "You're too pretty and nice. I can't believe you never married."

"All the men around here are ignorant," she said. "I never wanted to marry any of them. Were you ever married?"

"Yeah. Once or twice is all. I didn't take to it."

Later, in the hospital, on Sodium Pentothal, Ruby realized that she had about a hundred pictures of Clint Eastwood, her favorite actor, and none of Buddy. His indistinct face wavered in her memory as she rolled down a corridor on a narrow bed. He didn't have a picture of her, either. In a drawer somewhere she had a handful of prints of her high school graduation picture, taken years ago. Ruby Jane MacPherson in a beehive and a Peter Pan collar. She should remember to give him one for his billfold someday. She felt cautious around Buddy, she realized, the way she did in high school, when it had seemed so important to keep so many things hidden from boys. "Don't let your brother find your sanitary things," she could hear her mother saying.

In the recovery room, she slowly awoke at the end of a long dream, to blurred sounds and bright lights—gold and silver flashes moving past like fish—and a pain in her chest that she at first thought was a large bird with a hooked beak suckling her breast. The problem, she kept thinking, was that she was lying down, when in order to nurse the creature properly, she ought to sit up. The mound of bandages mystified her.

"We didn't have to take very much," a nurse said. "The doctor didn't have to go way up under your arm."

Someone was squeezing her hand. She heard her mother telling someone, "They think they got it all."

A strange fat woman with orange hair was holding her hand. "You're just fine, sugar," she said.

When Ruby began meeting Buddy at the fairgrounds on Third Mondays, he always seemed to have a new set of dogs. One morning he traded two pocket knives for a black-and-tan coonhound with limp ears and starstruck eyes. By afternoon, he had made a profit of ten dollars, and the dog had shifted owners again without even getting a meal from Buddy. After a few months, Ruby lost track of all the different dogs. In a way, she realized, their identities did flow together like a river. She thought often of Buddy's remark about the Mississippi River. He was like the river. She didn't even have an address for him, but he always showed up on Third Mondays and spent the night at her house. If he'd had a profitable day, he would take her to the Burger Chef or McDonald's. He never did the usual things, such as carry out her trash or open the truck door for her. If she were a smoker, he probably wouldn't light her cigarette.

Ruby liked his distance. He didn't act possessive. He called her up from Tennessee once to tell her he had bought a dog and named it Ruby. Then he sold the dog before he got back to town. When it was Ruby's birthday, he made nothing of that, but on another day at the fairgrounds he bought her a bracelet of Mexican silver from a wrinkled old black woman in a baseball cap who called everybody "darling." Her name was Gladys. Ruby loved the way Buddy got along with Gladys, teasing her about being his girlfriend.

"Me and Gladys go 'way back," he said, embracing the old woman flamboyantly.

"Don't believe anything this old boy tells you," said Gladys with a grin.

"Don't say I never gave you nothing," Buddy said to Ruby as he paid for the bracelet. He didn't fasten the bracelet on her wrist for her, just as he never opened the truck door for her.

The bracelet cost only three dollars, and Ruby wondered if it was authentic. "What's *Mexican* silver anyway?" she asked.

"It's good," he said. "Gladys wouldn't cheat me."

Later, Ruby kept thinking of the old woman. Her merchandise was set out on the tailgate of her station wagon—odds and ends of carnival glass, some costume jewelry, and six Barbie dolls. On the ground she had several crates of banties and guineas and pigeons. Their intermingled coos and chirps made Ruby wonder if Gladys slept in her station wagon listening to the music of her birds, the way Buddy slept in his truck with his dogs.

The last time he'd come to town—the week before her operation— Ruby traveled with him to a place over in the Ozarks to buy some pit bull terriers. They drove several hours on interstates, and Buddy rambled on excitedly about the new dogs, as though there were something he could discover about the nature of dogs by owning a pit bull terrier. Ruby, who had traveled little, was intensely interested in the scenery, but she said, "If these are mountains, then I'm disappointed."

"You ought to see the Rockies," said Buddy knowingly. "Talk about mountains."

At a little grocery store, they asked for directions, and Buddy swigged on a Dr Pepper. Ruby had a Coke and a bag of pork rinds. Buddy paced around nervously outside, then unexpectedly slammed his drink bottle in the tilted crate of empties with such force that several bottles fell out and broke. At that moment, Ruby knew she probably was irrevocably in love with him, but she was afraid it was only because she needed someone. She wanted to love him for better reasons. She knew about the knot in her breast and had already scheduled the mammogram, but she didn't want to tell him. Her body made her angry, interfering that way, like a nosy neighbor.

They drove up a winding mountain road that changed to gravel, then to dirt. A bearded man without a shirt emerged from a house trailer and showed them a dozen dogs pacing in makeshift kennel runs. Ruby talked to the dogs while Buddy and the man hunkered down together under a persimmon tree. The dogs were squat and broad-shouldered, with squinty eyes. They were the same kind of dog the Little Rascals had had in the movies. They hurled themselves against the shaky wire, and Ruby told them to hush. They looked at her with cocked heads. When Buddy finally crated up four dogs, the owner looked as though he would cry.

At a motel that night—the first time Ruby had ever stayed in a motel with a man—she felt that the knot in her breast had a presence of its own. Her awareness of it made it seem like a little energy source, like the radium dial of a watch glowing in the dark. Lying close to Buddy, she had the crazy feeling that it would burn a hole through him.

During *The Tonight Show,* she massaged his back with baby oil, rubbing it in thoroughly, as if she were polishing a piece of fine furniture.

"Beat on me," he said. "Just like you were tenderizing steak."

"Like this?" She pounded his hard muscles with the edge of her hand.

"That feels wonderful."

"Why are you so tensed up?"

"Just so I can get you to do this. Don't stop."

Ruby pummeled his shoulder with her fist. Outside, a dog barked. "That man you bought the dogs from looked so funny," she said. "I thought he was going to cry. He must have loved those dogs."

"He was just scared."

"How come?"

"He didn't want to get in trouble." Buddy raised up on an elbow and looked at her. "He was afraid I was going to use those dogs in a dogfight, and he didn't want to be traced."

"I thought they were hunting dogs."

"No. He trained them to fight." He grasped her hand and guided it to a spot on his back. "Right there. Work that place out for me." As Ruby rubbed in a hard circle with her knuckles, he said, "They're good friendly dogs if they're treated right."

Buddy punched off the TV button and smoked a cigarette in the dark, lying with one arm under her shoulders. "You know what I'd like?" he said suddenly. "I'd like to build me a log cabin somewhere—off in the mountains maybe. Just a place for me and some dogs."

"Just you? I'd come with you if you went to the Rocky Mountains."

"How good are you at survival techniques?" he said. "Can you fish? Can you chop wood? Could you live without a purse?"

"I might could." Ruby smiled to herself at the thought.

"Women always have to have a lot of baggage along—placemats and teapots and stuff."

"I wouldn't."

"You're funny."

"Not as funny as you." Ruby shifted her position. His hand under her was hurting her ribs.

"I'll tell you a story. Listen." He sounded suddenly confessional. He sat up and flicked sparks at the ashtray. He said, "My daddy died last year, and this old lady he married was just out to get what he had. He heired her two thousand dollars, and my sister and me were to get the homeplace— the house, the barn, and thirty acres of bottomland. But before he was cold in the ground, she had stripped the place and sold every stick of furniture. Everything that was loose, she took."

"That's terrible."

"My sister sells Tupperware, and she was in somebody's house, and she recognized the bedroom suit. She said, 'Don't I know that?' and this person said, 'Why, yes, I believe that was your daddy's. I bought it at such-and-such auction.'"

"What an awful thing to do to your daddy!" Ruby said.

"He taught me everything I know about training dogs. I learned it from him and he picked it up from his daddy." Buddy jabbed his cigarette in the ashtray. "He knew everything there was to know about field dogs."

"I bet you don't have much to do with your stepmother now."

"She really showed her butt," he said with a bitter laugh. "But really it's my sister who's hurt. She wanted all those keepsakes. There was a lot of Mama's stuff. Listen, I see that kind of sorrow every day in my line of work—all those stupid, homeless dishes people trade. People buy all that stuff and decorate with it and think it means something."

"I don't do that," Ruby said.

"I don't keep anything. I don't want anything to remind me of *anything*."

Ruby sat up and tried to see him in the dark, but he was a shadowy form, like the strange little mountains she had seen outside at twilight. The new dogs were noisy—bawling and groaning fitfully. Ruby said, "Hey, you're not going to get them dogs to fight, are you?"

"Nope. But I'm not responsible for what anybody else wants to do. I'm just the middleman."

Buddy turned on the light to find his cigarettes. With relief, Ruby saw how familiar he was—his tanned, chunky arms, and the mustache under his nose like the brush on her vacuum cleaner. He was tame and gentle, like his best dogs. "They make good watchdogs," he said. "Listen at 'em!" He laughed like a man watching a funny movie.

"They must see the moon," Ruby said. She turned out the light and tiptoed across the scratchy carpet. Through a crack in the curtains she could see the dark humps of the hills against the pale sky, but it was cloudy and she could not see the moon.

Everything is round and full now, like the moon. Linda's belly. Bowling balls. On TV, Steve Martin does a comedy routine, a parody of the song, "I Believe." He stands before a gigantic American flag and recites his beliefs. He says he doesn't believe a woman's breasts should be referred to derogatorily as jugs, or boobs, or Winnebagos. "I believe they should be referred to as hooters," he says solemnly. Winnebagos? Ruby wonders.

After the operation, she does everything left-handed. She has learned to extend her right arm and raise it slightly. Next, the doctors have told her, she will gradually reach higher and higher—an idea that thrills her, as though there were something tangible above her to reach for. It surprises her, too, to learn what her left hand has been missing. She feels like a newly blind person discovering the subtleties of sound.

Trying to sympathize with her, the women on her bowling team offer their confessions. Nancy has such severe monthly cramps that even the new miracle pills on the market don't work. Linda had a miscarriage when she was in high school. Betty admits her secret, something Ruby suspected anyway: Betty shaves her face every morning with a Lady Sunbeam. Her birth-control pills had stimulated facial hair. She stopped taking the pills years ago but still has the beard.

Ruby's mother calls these problems "female trouble." It is Mom's theory that Ruby injured her breasts by lifting too many heavy boxes in her job with a wholesale grocer. Several of her friends have tipped or fallen wombs caused by lifting heavy objects, Mom says.

"I don't see the connection," says Ruby. It hurts her chest when she laughs, and her mother looks offended. Mom, who has been keeping Ruby company in the afternoons since she came home from the hospital, today is making Ruby some curtains to match the new bedspread on her double bed.

"When you have a weakness, disease can take hold," Mom explains. "When you abuse the body, it shows up in all kinds of ways. And women just weren't built to do man's work. You were always so independent you ended up doing man's work and woman's work both."

"Let's not get into why I never married," says Ruby.

Mom's sewing is meticulous and definite, work that would burn about two calories an hour. She creases a hem with her thumb and folds the curtain neatly. Then she stands up and embraces Ruby carefully, favoring her daughter's right side. She says, "Honey, if there was such of a thing as a transplant, I'd give you one of mine."

"That's O.K., Mom. Your big hooters wouldn't fit me."

At the bowling alley, Ruby watches while her team, Garrison Life Insurance, bowls against Thomas & Sons Plumbing. Her team is getting smacked.

"We're pitiful without you and Linda," Betty tells her.

"Linda's got too big to bowl. I told her to come anyway and watch, but she wouldn't listen. I think maybe she is embarrassed to be seen in public, despite what she said."

"She doesn't give a damn what people think," says Ruby, as eight pins crash for Thomas & Sons. "Me neither," she adds, tilting her can of Coke.

"Did you hear she's getting a heavy-duty washer? She says a heavy-duty holds forty-five diapers."

Ruby lets a giggle escape. "She's not going to any more laundromats and get knocked up again."

"Are you still going with that guy you met at Third Monday?"

"I'll see him Monday. He's supposed to take me home with him to Tennessee, but the doctor said I can't go yet."

"I heard he didn't know about your operation," says Betty, giving her bowling ball a little hug.

Ruby takes a drink of Coke and belches. "He'll find out soon enough."

"Well, you stand your ground, Ruby Jane. If he can't love you for yourself, then to heck with him."

"But people always love each other for the wrong reasons!" Ruby says. "Don't you know that?"

Betty stands up, ignoring Ruby. It's her turn to bowl. She says, "Just be thankful, Ruby. I like the way you get out and go. Later on, bowling will be just the right thing to build back your strength."

"I can already reach to here," says Ruby, lifting her right hand to touch Betty's arm. Ruby smiles. Betty has five-o'clock shadow.

The familiar crying of the dogs at Third Monday makes Ruby anxious and jumpy. They howl and yelp and jerk their chains—sound effects in a horror movie. As Ruby walks through the oak grove, the dogs lunge toward her, begging recognition. A black Lab in a tiny cage glares at her savagely. She notices dozens of blueticks and beagles, but she doesn't see Buddy's truck. As she hurries past some crates of ducks and rabbits and pullets, a man in overalls stops her. He is holding a pocket knife and, in one hand, an apple cut so precisely that the core is a perfect rectangle.

"I can't 'call your name," he says to her. "But I know I know you."

"I don't know *you*," says Ruby. Embarrassed, the man backs away.

The day is already growing hot. Ruby buys a Coke from a man with a washtub of ice and holds it with her right hand, testing the tension on her right side. The Coke seems extremely heavy. She lifts it to her lips with her left hand. Buddy's truck is not there.

Out in the sun, she browses through a box of *National Enquirers* and paperback romances, then wanders past tables of picture frames, clocks, quilts, dishes. The dishes are dirty and mismatched—odd plates and cups and gravy boats. There is nothing she would want. She skirts a truckload of shock absorbers. The heat is making her dizzy. She is still weak from her operation. "I wouldn't pay fifteen dollars for a corn sheller," someone says. The remark seems funny to Ruby, like something she might have heard on Sodium Pentothal. Then a man bumps into her with a wire basket containing two young gray cats. A short, dumpy woman shouts to her, "Don't listen to him. He's trying to sell you them cats. Who ever heard of buying cats?"

Gladys has rigged up a canvas canopy extending out from the back of her station wagon. She is sitting in an aluminum folding chair, with her hands crossed in her lap, looking cool. Ruby longs to confide in her. She seems to be a trusty fixture, something stable in the current, like a cypress stump.

"Buy some mushmelons, darling," says Gladys. Gladys is selling banties, Fiestaware, and mushmelons today.

"Mushmelons give me gas."

Gladys picks up a newspaper and fans her face. "Them seeds been in my family over a hundred years. We always saved the seed."

"Is that all the way back to slave times?"

Gladys laughs as though Ruby has told a hilarious joke. "These here's my roots!" she says. "Honey, we's *in* slave times, if you ask me. Slave times ain't never gone out of style, if you know what I mean."

Ruby leans forward to catch the breeze from the woman's newspaper. She says, "Have you seen Buddy, the guy I run around with? He's usually here in a truck with a bunch of dogs?"

"That pretty boy that bought you that bracelet?"

"I was looking for him."

"Well, you better look hard, darling, if you want to find him. He got picked up over in Missouri for peddling a hot TV. They caught him on the spot. They'd been watching him. You don't believe me, but it's true. Oh, honey, I'm sorry, but he'll be back! He'll be back!"

In the waiting room at the clinic, the buzz of a tall floor fan sounds like a June bug on a screen door. The fan waves its head wildly from side to side. Ruby has an appointment for her checkup at three o'clock. She is afraid they will give her radiation treatments, or maybe even chemotherapy. No one is saying exactly what will happen next. But she expects to be baptized in a vat of chemicals, burning her skin and sizzling her hair. Ruby recalls an old comedy sketch, in which one of the Smothers Brothers fell into a vat of chocolate. Buddy Landon used to dunk his dogs in a tub of flea dip. She never saw him do it, but she pictures it in her mind—the stifling smell of Happy Jack mange medicine, the surprised dogs shaking themselves afterward, the rippling black water. It's not hard to imagine Buddy in a jail cell either—thrashing around sleeplessly in a hard bunk, reaching over to squash a cigarette butt on the concrete floor—but the image is so inappropriate it is like something from a bad dream. Ruby keeps imagining different scenes in which he comes back to town and they take off for the Rocky Mountains together. Everyone has always said she had imagination—imagination and a sense of humor.

A pudgy man with fat fists and thick lips sits next to her on the bench at the clinic, humming. With him is a woman in a peach-colored pants suit and with tight white curls. The man grins and points to a child across the room. "That's my baby," he says to Ruby. The little girl, squealing with joy, is riding up and down on her mother's knee. The pudgy man says something unintelligible.

"He loves children," says the white-haired woman.

"My baby," he says, making a cradle with his arms and rocking them.

"He has to have those brain tests once a year," says the woman to Ruby in a confidential whisper.

The man picks up a magazine and says, "This is my baby." He hugs the magazine and rocks it in his arms. His broad smile curves like the crescent phase of the moon.

# II

# War

*I did not expect to write a novel about the Vietnam War. During the war, I did not know anyone who went to Vietnam. No personal loss or connection motivated the writing of* In Country. *The story grew out of a group of characters who came into my mind and danced around aimlessly for well over a year before I got a sense of their direction. Then I realized that Sam, a young girl of seventeen, is coming of age, and she would naturally ask questions about her missing father. As soon as it occurred to me that her father must have died in Vietnam, I knew I had a novel and that it had a universal theme. Although I was reluctant at first to write about war, I soon realized that war wasn't only battle. It was also the shattering effects on the people at home.*

—BAM

# FROM *In Country* (1985)

PART 1, CHAPTER 1

"I have to stop again, hon," Sam's grandmother says, tapping her on the shoulder. Sam Hughes is driving, with her uncle, Emmett Smith, half asleep beside her.

"Where are we?" grunts Emmett.

"Still on I-64. Mamaw has to go to the restroom."

"I forgot to take my pill when we stopped last," Mamaw says.

"Do you want me to drive now?" Emmett asks, whipping out a cigarette. He smokes Kents, and he has smoked seven in the two hours they have been on the road today.

"If Emmett drives, I could set up front," says Mamaw, leaning forward between the front seats. "I'm crammed in the back here like a sack of sausage."

"Are you sure you feel like driving, Emmett?"

"It don't make no difference."

"I was just getting into it," says Sam, irritated.

It is *her* new car. Emmett drove through the heavy traffic around Lexington, because Sam wasn't experienced at city driving, but the interstate is easy. She could glide like this all the way across America.

At the next exit, Exxon, Chevron, and Sunoco loom up, big faces on stilts. There's a Country Kitchen, a McDonald's, and a Stuckey's. Sam has heard that Stuckey's is terrible and the Country Kitchen is good. She notices a hillside with some white box shapes—either beehives or a small family cemetery—under some trees. She shoots onto the exit ramp a little too fast, and the tires squeal. Mamaw gasps and clutches the back of Sam's seat, but Emmett just fiddles with the buttons on the old Army jacket in his lap. Emmett dragged it out of his closet before they left. He said it might be cold in Washington. It is summer, and Sam doesn't believe him.

Sam pulls in at the Sunoco and springs out of the car to let Mamaw out. Mamaw has barrel hips and rolls of fat around her waist. She is so fat she has to sleep in a special brassiere. She shakes out her legs and stretches her arms. She is wearing peach-colored knit pants and a flowered blouse, with white socks and blue tennis shoes. Sam does not know Mamaw Hughes as well as she does her other grandmother, Emmett's mother, whom she calls Grandma, but Mamaw acts like she knows everything about Sam. It's spooky. Mamaw is always saying, "Why, that's just like you, Sam," or "That's your daddy in you, for the world." She makes Sam feel as though she has been spied on for years. Bringing Mamaw along was Emmett's idea. He is staring off at a bird flying over the Sunoco sign.

"Regular?" a blond boy in a Sunoco shirt asks.

"Yeah. Fill 'er up." Sam likes saying "Fill 'er up." Buying gas is one of the pleasures of owning a car at last. "Come on, Mamaw," she says, touching her grandmother's arm. "Take care of the car, would you, Emmett?"

He nods, still looking in the direction of the bird.

The restroom is locked, and Sam has to go back and ask the boy for the key. The key is on a ring with a clumsy plastic Sunoco sign. The restroom is pink and filthy, with sticky floors. In her stall, Sam reads several phone numbers written in lipstick. A message says, "The mass of the ass plus the angle of the dangle equals the scream of the cream." She wishes she had known that one when she took algebra. She would have written it on an assignment.

Mamaw lets loose a stream as loud as a cow's. This trip is crazy. It reminds Sam of that Chevy Chase movie about a family on vacation, with an old woman tagging along. She died on the trip and they had to roll her inside a blanket on the roof of the station wagon because the children refused to sit beside a dead body. This trip is just as weird. A month ago, Emmett wouldn't have gone to Washington for a million dollars, but after everything that happened this summer, he changed his mind and now is hell-bent on going and dragging Mamaw along with them.

"I was about to pop," Mamaw says.

That was a lie about her pill. Mamaw just didn't want Emmett to know she had to pee.

When they return the key, Mamaw buys some potato chips at a vending machine. "Irene didn't feed us enough for breakfast this morning," she says. "Do you want anything?"

"No. I'm not hungry."

"You're too skinny, Sam. You look holler-eyed."

Irene is Sam's mother, Emmett's sister. They spent the night in Lexington with her in her new house—a brick ranch house with a patio and wall-to-wall carpeting. Irene has a new baby at the age of thirty-seven. The baby is cute, but Irene's new husband has no personality. His name is Larry Joiner, but Sam calls him Lorenzo Jones. In social studies class, Sam's teacher used to play tapes of old radio shows. *Lorenzo Jones* was an old soap opera. Sam's mother's life is a soap opera. The trip would be so different if her mother could have come. But Sam has her mother's credit card, and it is burning a hole in her pocket. She hasn't used it yet. It is for emergencies.

Emmett is in the driver's seat, with the engine running. He is drinking a can of Pepsi. "Are y'all ready?" he asks, flicking cigarette ash on the asphalt. He has moved the car, but it's still close to the gas pumps. A scene of a sky-high explosion, like an ammunitions dump blowing up, rushes through Sam's mind.

"Give me a swig of that," says Sam. "Did you pay?" She takes a drink of Emmett's Pepsi and hands it back.

"Yeah. It was six dollars and thirty cents. I wrote down the mileage. We averaged thirty-one to the gallon."

"That's good!"

The gas gauge is broken, and Sam has to estimate when to get gas. To be safe, she gets gas every two hundred miles. The VW is a seventy-three, with a rebuilt engine. Tom Hudson sold it to her less than two weeks ago. His fingerprints are still on it, no doubt—on the engine and the hubcaps and the gas cap. His presence is everywhere in the car.

"I love this car," Sam says, giving the VW an affectionate slap. "She's a good little bird." She suddenly feels strange saying that. Emmett is always watching birds and writing them down on his life list. There is a certain kind of exotic bird he has been looking for. He claimed such birds sometimes stopped off in Kentucky on their way to Florida, and he keeps looking for one, but he has never seen one in Kentucky. When Sam suggested that they could see one in the Washington zoo, he said it wouldn't be the same as seeing it in the wild.

Sam climbs in the back, and Mamaw starts to get in, but then Mamaw says, "I better check on my flowers. I should have watered them this morning."

She walks behind the car and peers through the back window.

"They don't look droopy," Sam says, glancing at the pot of geraniums wedged behind the seat.

"I reckon they're O.K.," says Mamaw doubtfully. "I'm just afraid the blooms will fall off before we get there." She gets in the front seat. "I'm still so embarrassed, spilling dirt on Irene's nice floor. I guess she thought I was just a country hick, dragging in dirt."

Emmett stubs out his cigarette and takes off, sailing into fourth gear by the time they hit the highway.

"Reckon we'll ever get there?" Mamaw asks. "We'll probably get lost."

"Don't worry, Mrs. Hughes. We've got a map."

"You can't get lost in the United States," Sam says. "I wish I could, though. I wish I'd wake up and not know where I was."

"Lands, child, where do you get your ideas?" Mamaw says.

Emmett drives in silence, intent on his job, like a bus driver. Emmett is a large man of thirty-five with pimples on his face. He has been very quiet since they left Hopewell yesterday, probably because Mamaw is getting on his nerves. He has bad nerves.

"This transmission's getting worse," he says after a while. He glances back at Sam. "It just popped out of fourth gear again."

"Tom said he worked on that transmission. It's supposed to be O.K."

"Well, it's popping out. Just thought I'd tell you."

"Well, I'm not sorry I bought the car, so don't throw it in my face!"

She leans her head against the pillow they borrowed from her mother and watches the cars fire past. On the shoulder are blown-out truck tires, scraps of rubber flung out like abandoned toys. The scenery is funny little hills shaped like scoops of ice cream. Where she lives is flat. She has never been this far away from home before. She is nearly eighteen years old and out to see the world. She would like to move somewhere far away—Miami or San Francisco maybe. She wants to live anywhere but Hopewell. On the road, everything seems more real than it has ever been. It's as though nothing has really registered on her until just recently—since the night last week when she ran off to the swamp. The feeling reminds her of her aerobics instructor, Ms. Hotpants—she had some hard-to-pronounce foreign name—when they did the pelvic tilt in gym last year. A row of girls with their asses reaching for heaven. "Squeeze your butt-ox. Squeeze tight, girls," she would say, and they would grit their teeth and flex their butts, and hold for a count of five, and then she would say, "Now squeeze one layer deeper." That is what the new feeling is like: you know something as well as you can and then you squeeze one layer deeper and something more is there.

Emmett's cigarette smoke floats back and strangles her. She is glad when a while later he lets her have the wheel again. She's proud of the car. It is off-white, with bright orange patches where Tom fixed the spots of rust. The rebuilt engine sounds good.

"This car will look better when I get a paint job," she says.

"What color do you aim to paint it, hon?" Mamaw asks.

"Black." Sam has been thinking that when winter comes she will get a black motorcycle jacket and dye her old tan cowhide boots black. They lace up, and they will look sinister if she dyes them black. A truck that she passed two minutes ago passes her now, with a wheeze and a honk. She slams the horn at him. Trucker-fucker, she mutters to herself.

"Why, look at that, would you!" cries Emmett, pointing to a station wagon pulling a small flat-bed trailer loaded with a dish antenna. "The license plate says Arizona. They've hauled that all the way from Arizona. Imagine having one of those. You could watch everything on earth with that."

"It probably belongs to Big Brother," says Sam.

"Yeah. He's probably got one of those, and his own satellite too," Emmett says thoughtfully.

"Whose brother are y'all talking about?" Mamaw wants to know.

"Big Brother in *Nineteen Eighty-four*. It's a book I had to read in English."

"There goes that transmission again," Emmett says.

"Oh, shit," groans Sam, not loud enough for her grandmother to hear. Cussing shocks Mamaw.

Actually, Sam never really cussed much before this summer. But now she feels like letting loose. She has so much evil and bad stuff in her now. It feels good to say shit, even if it's only under her breath.

PART 2, CHAPTER 1

It was the summer of the Michael Jackson *Victory* tour and the Bruce Springsteen *Born in the U.S.A.* tour, neither of which Sam got to go to. At her graduation, the commencement speaker, a Methodist minister, had preached about keeping the country strong, stressing sacrifice. He made Sam nervous. She started thinking about war, and it stayed on her mind all summer.

Emmett came back from Vietnam, but Sam's father did not. After his discharge, Emmett stayed with his parents two weeks, then left. He couldn't adjust. Several months later, he returned, and Sam's mother let him live with them, in the house she had bought with her husband's life insurance policy. Emmett stayed, helping out around the house. People said Irene babied him. She treated him like someone disabled, and she never expected him to get a job. She always said the war "messed him up." She had worked as a receptionist for a dentist, and she received compensation payments from the government. In retrospect, Sam realized how strange those early years were. When Emmett moved in, he brought some friends with him—hippies. Hopewell didn't have any hippies, or war protesters, and when Emmett showed up with three scruffy guys in ponytails and beads, they created a sensation. The friends came from places out west—Albuquerque, Eugene, Santa Cruz. Boys in Hopewell didn't even wear long hair until the seventies, when it finally became fashionable. Sam had a strong memory of Emmett in his Army jacket and black boots, with a purple headband running through his wild hair. She remembered his friends piling out of a psychedelic van, but she remembered little else about them. People in town still talked about the time Emmett and the hippies flew a Vietcong flag from the courthouse tower. One bleak day in early winter, they entered the courthouse through separate doors and converged at the base of the clock tower. The county circuit court clerk saw them head up the stairs and said later she knew something was about to happen. They fastened the flag to the side of the tower with masking tape, covering part of the clock face. Merchants around the square got nervous and had them arrested for disturbing the peace. The funny part, Emmett always said, was that nobody had even recognized that it was a Vietcong flag. He had had it made by a tailor in Pleiku, the way one might order a wedding suit. Soon after the flag incident, when burglars broke into a building supply company on Main Street, using a concrete block to smash a window, people were suspicious of Emmett's crowd, but no one ever proved anything.

The friends went away eventually, and Emmett calmed down. For a couple of years, he attended Murray State, but then he dropped out. He did odd jobs—mowing yards, repairing small appliances—and got by. Now and then a rumor would surface. At one time, neighbors had the idea that Patty Hearst was hiding out with Emmett and Irene. For a week, Sam had been too embarrassed to go to school, but later she was proud of Emmett. He was like a brother. She and Emmett were still pals, and he didn't try to boss her around. They liked the same music—mostly golden oldies. Emmett's favorite current groups were the Cars and the Talking Heads.

Irene's new husband got a good job in Lexington, but Sam refused to move there with them. Somebody had to watch out for Emmett, Sam insisted, and she didn't want to change schools her senior year. The house was paid for, and Sam still got government benefits. After her mother went away last year, Sam and Emmett got into the habit of watching *M*A*S*H* every evening. Usually, they grilled something and then watched the news, two reruns of *M*A*S*H,* and a movie on Home Box Office or Cinemax. Sam's boyfriend, Lonnie Malone, used to join them before he started working late at Kroger's. Sam's favorite *M*A*S*H* was the one in which Hot Lips Houlihan kicked a door down when she learned that her husband, Donald Penobscott, had requested a transfer to San Francisco without telling her. Emmett preferred the early episodes, with Colonel Henry Blake and Frank Burns. Burns reminded him, he said, of his C.O. in Vietnam, a real idiot. That was about all Emmett would say about Vietnam these days. Emmett had a hearty, good-natured laugh like Hawkeye's. Hawkeye's laughter was so infectious that sometimes when Hawkeye and Trapper John let loose, Sam and Emmett couldn't stop laughing, just laughing for pure joy.

Years ago, when Colonel Blake was killed, Sam was so shocked she went around stunned for days. She was only a child then, and his death on the program was more real to her than the death of her own father. Even on the repeats, it was unsettling. Each time she saw that episode, it grew clearer that her father had been killed in a war. She had always taken his death for granted, but the reality of it took hold gradually. Now, when the episode was repeated, and she saw Radar report to the surgeons in the O.R. that Colonel Blake's plane had gone down over the Sea of Japan, she felt it was poignant because Radar had looked up to the Colonel like a father. The Colonel's last words to Radar had been, "You'd better behave or I'm going to come back and kick your butt."

The summer had been wet. Early in June, a tornado touched down on the main highway south of Hopewell and knocked a few trailers together, but no one was hurt. One night a week later, another tornado watch was in effect. Emmett had been nervous all evening as he listened to the weather channel on the radio. It was ten twenty-four by the kitchen clock that sticky night before the storm. The air conditioning was grinding and thumping, and the TV was on, but above the noise Sam heard Lonnie's van turn into the driveway. The van had a faulty post-ignition shut-off jet, which meant that the engine bucked along for a few moments after Lonnie turned it off, like a stubborn child making an annoying sound.

"Did you get off from work early?" Sam yelled under the porch light. A moth flew in and whizzed around the bulb on the hallway ceiling.

Lonnie Malone was a bag boy at Kroger's. He had a six-pack of Falls City with him and an open can in one hand. He was five-eleven and muscular, and he had brown hair with a kink in it. Sam thought he had a sexy build. On his chest he had a beautiful birthmark, a splotch the shape of an Izod alligator. Lonnie had been a guard for the Hopewell Indians. When he reached the porch, Sam pushed his hair back over his ear and smacked him on the lips. He smelled like beer. Beer smelled something like a run-over skunk.

"I saw a cop on I-24, and I was going sixty," he said with a grin.

"You're lucky he didn't catch you with this beer," Sam said. The screen door slammed behind them, and like an echo, thunder scattered across the sky. "Where'd you get it anyway?"

"Down at the Bottom. I got a guy to go in for me. Crazy old coot. He was just setting out on the county line, straddling it in his pickup. He was swigging from a bottle of Jim Beam in a sack and just daring somebody to look at him wrong."

"Is it storming down that way yet?"

"No. There's a tornado watch, but I don't think it'll hit here." Emmett appeared in the kitchen doorway, filling it up so completely that he shut out the light from the kitchen. "Hey, I'm making muffelatas, y'all," he said. "Do you want one, Lonnie?"

"Yeah, I'm starving. All I had for supper was a hamburger." Lonnie jerked one of the cans from its plastic noose and handed it to Emmett. "Have a beer, Emmett, good buddy."

Emmett opened the can and took a drink. Then with his oven mitt he swatted at the moth and missed.

Lonnie had done a double take when he saw Emmett in his wraparound skirt. He was wearing a long, thin Indian-print skirt with elephants and peacocks on it. Now Lonnie burst out laughing.

"Where'd you get that skirt, Emmett?" he asked.

"It's a joke because Klinger wears dresses on *M\*A\*S\*H*," Sam said.

Emmett struck an exaggerated fashion-model pose against the kitchen door facing, with his cigarette dangling from the corner of his mouth. "I got it at the mall in Paducah," he said.

"Are you bucking for a Section 8, like Klinger?" Lonnie asked.

"Wouldn't hurt," Emmett said with a grin.

Sam suspected Emmett was using the skirt to draw attention away from the pimples on his face. They had been getting worse. She was dying to squeeze them, but he wouldn't let her.

Emmett shoved the muffelatas in the oven and then turned around and pranced like Boy George, modeling his skirt. Emmett had a gleeful expression that said he had gotten away with murder.

"Far out!" Lonnie said, grinning at Emmett. Lonnie emulated Emmett, and they often shot baskets together at the high school. Lonnie even had an Army jacket that he had found at the surplus store, but Sam knew he would never wear a skirt just because Emmett wore one. He wouldn't go that far. Lonnie didn't even like Boy George.

"How come you're here at this hour of the night?" Sam said, sitting down on the lumpy couch in the living room. The couch tilted at an angle.

"I quit," said Lonnie. He wasn't looking at her. He was looking across the room to a rock group riding on a roller coaster on the television screen. He took such a huge slug of beer that his cheeks bulged out.

"Oh, shit," Sam groaned.

"What happened this time, Lonnie?" Emmett asked sympathetically.

"It wasn't for me. I want to have my own business someday, and I wasn't getting anywhere there." Lonnie paused and lit a cigarette. "I'd like to do something outdoors, where I'm my own boss. I've got to be independent."

"Good for you," Emmett said.

Lonnie laughed and took a shot of beer. "At least now I can catch up on my video games with the guys, if I can scrape up enough quarters."

"You can play with Emmett's Atari," said Sam.

"Emmett ain't got *Donkey Kong.* Or *Hard Hat Mack.*"

"Hey, Lonnie, I scored over fifty thousand today on *Pac-Man,*" said Emmett.

"Gah!" Lonnie blew smoke out slowly. "I'll never catch you, Emmett. You're too good."

"I've figured out the secret of *Pac-Man.* The trick is you ignore all them little vitamin pills. They're just there to distract you and make you think you can get something for nothing. But if you keep your mind on your business, you can just keep going forever." Emmett drank some beer and added, "That's the Zen of *Pac-Man.*"

"I'll have to try that," Lonnie said.

"It's too bad you quit your job, Lonnie. I need to borrow some money to pay back a debt I owe the government."

"How much do you owe?"

"Over five hundred dollars." Emmett lifted his skirt and fanned his legs. "They hit me over the head with it. I'd forgot all about it."

"It was that semester he dropped out of Murray," Sam explained. Emmett had dropped his courses but kept collecting monthly checks from the V.A. all semester.

"They won't take me to court, though," Emmett said. "It's not enough money for them to fool with. And I don't have no salary to garnishee." He laughed.

"You can take my education benefits and pay for those classes," Sam said. "I don't want to go to college that bad."

"That reminds me, Sam. Your mama called this evening when you were out running. She wants to know if you're going to U.K. this fall."

"I don't want to go to the same school as my mother. That would be too weird for words. Did she want me to call back?"

"No. She just said to tell you she still wanted you to come up there."

"Don't go," Lonnie said, reaching for her hand. "I need you here to help me get started."

"I'm not going to Lexington. The track team's better at Murray than U.K. anyway. It's more personal." Sam had been accepted at both the University of Kentucky and Murray State University, and Murray was nearby. She hoped to commute.

Emmett gave Sam a can of beer. "Go ahead and drink it. I won't tell on you. It'll give you carbohydrates so you can run tomorrow."

Sam sipped the beer. It didn't taste as bad as it smelled. She and Lonnie were sitting close to each other on the couch. Sam's bare legs brushed against Lonnie's jeans and made her feel a stir of desire. The couch was fuzzy and scratched her legs. Emmett had bought the couch at a yard sale. Emmett did most of his shopping at yard sales. All their stuff was junk. She felt empty and disappointed. Lonnie didn't have a job, and he wasn't going to college. Sam had worked at the Burger Boy after school for two years, but in March she had quit so she could have more time to study. She had been promised her old job back in the fall.

Emmett took the muffelatas from the oven and transferred them to melamine plates that Sam's mother had left behind. She had taken her good dishes. He brought the muffelatas in to Sam and Lonnie.

"Thanks, Emmett," said Lonnie. "This is what I call service." He stubbed out his cigarette in Emmett's Kentucky Lake ashtray.

"Don't mean nothing," said Emmett.

Sam didn't really like the taste of beer, but the muffelata was delicious. Emmett knew how to make muffelatas just right, with lots of olives and onions. Irene never made muffelatas.

"I don't think that storm's coming," Emmett said when he brought in his own plate.

"What's on HBO tonight?" asked Lonnie. "This MTV crap is too weird."

Billy Joel was singing "Uptown Girl." He was in a garage mechanic's coveralls, lusting after Christie Brinkley. Sam said, "HBO is pukey tonight—*Humanoids from the Deep*. But there's an R-rated movie on Cinemax at midnight."

"Oh, good!" Lonnie's parents wouldn't get cable because of all the R-rated movies. Two weeks ago, someone had blown up the cable man's mailbox with a cherry bomb.

Emmett punched the buttons on the selector box. Surfers rode by, then policemen. He settled on Johnny Carson and sat down with his plate, scooting the cat to one side. His skirt fell on the cat, but Moon Pie didn't budge. He was black with white armpits and a big saucer face. Emmett was so crazy about the cat he even slept with him. Moon Pie always woke him up at 4 A.M., and Emmett would get up and feed him, but lately Emmett had been keeping a packet of Tender Vittles under his pillow and a bowl beside the bed so he could feed Moon Pie practically in his sleep.

"How do you know *Humanoids from the Deep* is no good?" said Lonnie.

"*Hemorrhoids* from the Deep," said Sam. "I've seen it and it stinks. Oh, look at Johnny's suit!" she cried, pointing. Johnny Carson's suit made rainbows under the TV lights—soft, glistening colors like those in a puddle of oil. The colors reminded Sam of the Jupiterscope her mother had sent her for her birthday last year. She had bought it in a museum in Cincinnati. The Jupiterscope was a circle of plastic, like a large soft contact lens, that turned scenery into shimmering colors when you looked through it. It was a silly present.

Lonnie laughed. "Hey, can you imagine Johnny Carson wearing a skirt?" he said. "I dare you to wear that skirt out in public, Emmett."

"It's healthier for a man to wear a skirt," Emmett said solemnly. "He's not all cramped up and stuff."

Sam said to Lonnie, "It makes me so mad about that rash on his face. He won't see about it."

"What's wrong with your face, Emmett? I wasn't going to mention it."

"It's just adolescence. Haven't you noticed how my voice is changing?" Emmett spoke deliberately in an unnaturally squeaky voice.

"Be serious," said Sam. "You've got Agent Orange. Those pimples are exactly how they described them on the news." Agent Orange terrified her. It had been in the news so much lately.

"I wasn't exposed to Agent Orange," Emmett said.

"You might have been around it and not known it."

"Maybe you could get some money out of the government, Emmett," Lonnie said. "Then you could pay them back what you owe."

"What would be the point of that? A lot of rigamarole and we'd end up where we started. So let 'em keep the money to begin with." Emmett touched his face. "This ain't nothing," he said. He shrugged, then cocked his head. Thunder. "Socrates wore a toga," he said, petting Moon Pie. "All them Greeks and Romans wore dresses."

Sam laughed. "Are you going to wear it to McDonald's in the morning, Emmett?" Emmett always had breakfast at McDonald's with his friends.

"I don't want anybody to get any wrong ideas."

Sam and Lonnie laughed. "What would they think, Emmett?" said Lonnie.

They knew what people thought. There were a lot of stories floating around about Emmett. Emmett was the leading dope dealer in town. Emmett slept with his niece. Emmett lived off his sister. Emmett seduced high school girls. He had killed babies in Vietnam. But he was popular, and Emmett didn't care what some people said.

Ed McMahon blasted out one of his phony belly laughs, and then a loud thunderclap made the light flicker. Emmett suddenly bent over and clutched his chest.

"What's wrong, Emmett?" Lonnie asked.

Emmett was grimacing with pain.

"You've got heartburns again," Sam said. "It's those tacos you ate at supper." Sam explained to Lonnie, "He's been getting gas. I told him not to eat tacos with hot-stuff. It always makes him belch."

"I guess so," Emmett said, straightening up and shaking his shoulders. Thunder crashed again, and Emmett cringed. Sam was scared. She had never had heartburns herself, and she didn't know if heart attacks were related.

"Are you all right, Emmett?" asked Lonnie. "Don't you go kicking the bucket without making out your will first."

"It's all right," Emmett said. "It went away."

Emmett looked stately in his skirt—tall and broad, like a middle-aged woman who had had several children. Sam and Lonnie sat on the couch with their hands on each other's thighs while Emmett cautiously sat down in the vinyl chair, fluffing up his skirt to let air flood his legs.

"We'll be right back," said Johnny.

PART 2, CHAPTER 2

The storm broke soon after that and they raced around, unplugging appliances. During the storm, Emmett huddled on the stairs with Moon Pie. The rain was so hard the water rushed across the yard from the downspouts. The basement was probably flooding again.

In the hallway, in the dark, Lonnie grabbed Sam and held her close to him. "Are you disappointed in me?" he asked, after they kissed.

"I thought you liked Kroger's. You liked that job better than you liked working at Shumley's." Shumley's was the large farm-equipment plant where Lonnie had been a trainee after school during the winter. Lonnie had to buy expensive safety shoes for the job, but then he had been laid off. Now he had no use for the safety shoes, which had hard, bulbous toes.

"Kroger's was a dead end," Lonnie said. "It was boring, and I goofed off. I'd put all the cans in one sack just for meanness."

"I'm not disappointed in you. But I'm disappointed."

"Maybe I could apply at Ingersoll-Rand."

"They're not hiring."

"Mama and Daddy will have a fit, though." They had wanted Lonnie to go to vocational school to learn a trade, but Lonnie didn't know what he wanted to do, now that he couldn't play basketball. He was famous for sinking ten out of twelve jump shots in a winning game against Hopewell's biggest rivals, the Bingley Bulldogs. People in Hopewell still talked fondly about how Lonnie had done that.

The lightning and the thunder coincided then. The storm was right there, over the house. Sam stood in the hall, clutching Lonnie. In the flash of lightning, she saw Emmett on the stairway, smoking a cigarette. They stayed there in the dark for a long time, and then abruptly the wash of rain let up and the lightning was just a flicker.

After the storm died down, Lonnie kissed Sam and said, "I know what I'm going to do now."

"What?"

"Get drunk."

In the dark, he took a beer from the refrigerator and opened it. "Hey, Emmett," Lonnie said. "The storm's let up. Let's go somewhere."

"It's almost time for the eleven-thirty *M\*A\*S\*H*," Emmett said. He was smoking another cigarette. He and Moon Pie were on the couch now.

"Couldn't you skip one?" said Lonnie.

"But this is my special outfit for watching *M\*A\*S\*H* in," Emmett said, flipping the hem of his skirt. "I miss *M\*A\*S\*H*. I've been homesick for it since the series ended. *AfterMash* just ain't the same."

"They couldn't fight the Korean War forever, Emmett," said Lonnie.

Emmett grabbed his cigarettes from the end table and stuck them in his skirt pocket. "Let's go, then. Where to? The Bottom?"

"I've already been there once tonight," said Lonnie. "We could drive around and see if the storm wrecked anything."

"I know where let's go," Emmett said, taking the last beer from the re-frigerator. "Let's go to Cawood's Pond."

"Are you serious, Emmett?" cried Lonnie. "I thought that place spooked you."

Cawood's Pond was Sam and Lonnie's favorite place to go parking. It wasn't really a pond but a snake-infested swamp with sinkholes. Sam had even heard there were alligators there. Emmett used to go there when he was a boy, but he stopped going. Sam was surprised that he suggested it.

"I ain't scared," said Emmett. "Let's go. I might even have some sweet stuff around here somewhere." He took a cocoa-mix can from a kitchen cabinet. "Ah-ha!" he said, looking inside.

Emmett found a sweatshirt and sniffed the armpits before pulling it over his head. He touched his face. He had one pimple about to pop.

"Let's go to the pond!" he cried. "Don't let Moon Pie out," he said as they left the house. "At night is when cats get run over. Headlights confuse them." Emmett was still wearing the skirt. He was so large he looked ri-diculous in it. Sam had to laugh.

The street lights were shining in new puddles. Sam soaked both run-ning shoes. She felt drunk on that beer. She lay down on the mattress in the back of Lonnie's van, and Lonnie and Emmett sat up front. She bounced along on the mattress, feeling like a soldier in an armored personnel carrier because she couldn't see where they were going. Emmett had once told her how claustrophobic those vehicles were, with a dozen guys packed together on benches, their rifles poking each other, and one guy in a tiny cubbyhole driving, with only a periscope to see his way. It was like being in a submarine, Emmett had said.

"There's a bulldozer over yonder," Emmett said when they reached the gravel road that led to the pond. "They're draining the swamp and rerouting the creek. The biologists are going crazy. They say it'll starve out the snakes, and birds won't land."

"I can do without the snakes," said Sam.

Cawood's Pond was named for a notorious outlaw, Andrew Cawood, who had once hidden out here and was believed to have fallen into a sinkhole. The university biologists had cleared a place for cars to park and built a boardwalk that looped out over the swamp. Sam and Lonnie had spent the night out here in the van a couple of times.

"The insects are having a conversation," said Emmett. "They're talking about me. I know 'cause my ears are burning."

"They're saying, 'Who's that weirdo in the skirt?'" Lonnie teased.

When Lonnie turned the lights off, and they sat there in the silence, they saw how the swampy woods made a black rim around the graveled clearing.

Emmett and Lonnie climbed over the seat of the van and sat down in back with Sam. Emmett pulled his sweet stuff from his cigarette pack. He lit a joint and passed it to Lonnie. The night was pleasant after the rain, and now and then a little breeze stirred and they could hear drops of water shaking from the leaves of the trees.

"Where are all the birds, Emmett?" Sam asked.

"They sleep at night. Except owls."

"Where do birds sleep, Emmett?" asked Lonnie, with a giggle.

"In bird beds."

"Hey, tell about that bird you're always looking for," Sam said. "Maybe there's one here right now."

"You couldn't see it at night."

"If it's white, wouldn't it look like a ghost?"

"What kind of bird is it?" Lonnie asked.

Emmett hesitated before answering. "An egret."

"What are egrets like?" Sam asked. "Are you sure they're around here?"

Emmett drank some beer. "I believe egrets are the state bird of Florida." He took the joint Lonnie passed him and puffed it.

Sam said to Lonnie, "This was a bird he used to see in Vietnam."

"Really?"

Emmett exhaled slowly. "Yeah. You'd see it in the rice paddies, dipping its head down in the water, feeling around for things to eat. It's a wader."

"They might be here, then," Lonnie said. "In a swamp like this."

"Why do you want to see that bird so bad?" Sam asked cautiously.

"It was so pretty. It was the prettiest bird I ever saw, all white and long-legged." Emmett worked at the tab on the beer can. "They're like cowbirds, but cowbirds aren't pretty. Sometimes you'd see these water buffalo and every one of them would have one of these birds sitting beside it, like a little pet."

"Why did they do that?" Lonnie asked.

"The bird would eat things the buffalo turned up, and it would pick ticks off the buffalo's head. Sometimes you'd see the bird setting on the buffalo's back. He didn't care."

"Won't it bring back bad memories if you see a bird like that again?" Sam asked.

"No. That was a good memory. The only fucking one. That beautiful bird just going about its business with all that crazy stuff going on around it. Whole flocks of them would fly over. They fold their long necks up when they fly." Emmett rolled the beer can in his palms, and the aluminum crinkled. He said, "Once a grenade hit close to some trees and there were these birds taking off like quail, ever' which way. We thought it was snowing up instead of down."

"Did you see a lot of action like that over there?" Lonnie asked.

"Some. I nearly got my ass killed once or twice."

"How?"

"Oh, you don't want to know."

Sam passed Lonnie the joint. She exhaled and coughed. She could almost see that bird. She felt peaceful, but her head was spinning with thoughts about Emmett. He hadn't said this much about Vietnam in years. Watching *M\*A\*S\*H* so much must be bringing it out, she thought. Emmett used to have a girlfriend, Anita Stevens, but he had broken up with her at Christmas. He never said why. He took her out for Shrimp Night at the Holiday Inn and gave her a fancy cheese basket from the Party Mart in Paducah. Anita playfully called it her Easter basket and asked Emmett where the sweet stuff was. The basket had so much cheese and salami in it she probably still had some in her refrigerator.

"Hey, Emmett," Sam blurted out. "I wish we had Anita with us. Why don't you call her up?"

"Sure. Hand me the phone."

"I'm serious. Why don't you call her up tomorrow?"

"Anita doesn't want a bird-watcher in a skirt," Emmett said flatly.

"Well, don't wear a skirt then," Sam said.

Emmett mumbled something. He sat propped against the spare tire in the back of the van. The glow from his cigarette reminded Sam of Mars, the way it popped out in the summer sky, burning bright orange, seeming to move toward the earth.

Lonnie turned on the radio, and Bruce Springsteen yelled out, "I'm a cool rocking Daddy in the U.S.A.!" It was from his new album. For a while, they sang along with the songs on the university FM station, Rock-95. Sam watched the moon inch from behind the broken clouds. The night was clearing, and the radio was playing "Ain't Gonna Bump No More with No Big Fat Woman," a song Emmett loved. Anita wasn't a big fat woman. She was pretty, and Sam was sure Anita still cared about Emmett. Sam felt Lonnie pulling at her, wanting to smooch with her, but her mind was whirling around in the darkness and she couldn't catch it.

Emmett and Lonnie went outside, and Sam lost track of time. Maybe she dozed off. She felt afraid. With the moon out, this was a perfect setting for a horror movie. Gradually, she became aware of a familiar yet strange sound on the radio. It was a song by the Beatles, but it was not a song she knew. Sam thought she knew every one of their songs, because her mother owned all their records. She had left them with Sam when she moved to Lexington. "You better leave my kitten all alone," they were singing. How could the Beatles have a new record, she wondered groggily.

"We've got to be quiet," Emmett muttered when he and Lonnie returned to the van. "Lonnie, keep your cigarette inside your hand. Don't show it."

"Take it easy, Emmett. It's all right." Lonnie climbed in the driver's seat and turned the key.

"Jesus fucking Christ, Lonnie!" said Emmett in a loud, hot whisper.

"Be quiet! And don't turn your lights on. Cut that engine! Let's coast down to Highway 1."

"No sweat, Emmett. Just hold tight."

"What did you see, Emmett?" asked Sam, reaching to touch his shoulder.

"Don't do that!" Emmett cried, jerking away from her.

"He just got spooked," Lonnie said, backing out of the clearing. "It wasn't anything."

"Oh, shit," Sam said. "Are you O.K., Emmett?"

Emmett mumbled. "Hurry," he said. "I can't stand this."

"We're going home, Emmett," said Lonnie as they bumped across the gravel in the moonlight. "Keep your skirt on."

# An Appreciation of Tim O'Brien's
*The Things They Carried*

Of all the stories I've read in the last decade, Tim O'Brien's *The Things They Carried* hit me hardest. It knocked me down, just as if a hundred-pound rucksack had been thrown right at me. The weight of the things the American soldiers carried on their interminable journey through the jungle in Vietnam sets the tone for this story. But the power of it is not just the poundage they were humping on their backs. The story's list of "things they carried" extends to the burden of memory and desire and confusion and grief. It's the weight of America's involvement in the war. You can hardly bear to contemplate all that this story evokes with its matter-of-fact yet electrifying details.

The way this story works makes me think of the Vietnam Veterans Memorial in Washington. The memorial is just a list of names, in a simple, dark—yet soaring—design. Its power is in the simplicity of presentation and in what lies behind each of those names.

In the story, there is a central incident, the company's first casualty on its march through the jungle. But the immediate drama is the effort—by the main character, by the narrator, by the writer himself—to contain the emotion, to carry it. When faced with a subject almost too great to manage or confront, the mind wants to organize, to categorize, to simplify. Restraint and matter-of-factness are appropriate deflective techniques for dealing with pain, and they work on several levels in the story. Sometimes it is more affecting to see someone dealing with pain than it is to know about the pain itself. That's what's happening here.

By using the simplicity of a list and trying to categorize the simple items the soldiers carried, O'Brien reveals the real terror of the war itself. And the categories go from the tangible—foot powder, photographs, chewing gum—to the intangible. They carried disease; memory. When it rained, they carried the sky. The weight of what they carried moves expansively, opens out, grows from the stuff in the rucksack to the whole weight of the American war chest, with its litter of ammo and packaging through the landscape of Vietnam. And then it moves back, away from the huge outer world, back into the interior of the self. The story details the way they carried themselves (dignity, laughter, words) as well as what they carried inside (fear, "emotional baggage").

And within the solemn effort to list and categorize, a story unfolds. PFO Ted Lavender, a grunt who carries tranquilizers, is on his way back from relieving himself in the jungle when he is shot by a sniper. The irony and horror of it are unbearable. Almost instantaneously, it seems, the central character, Lieutenant Cross, changes from a romantic youth to a man of action and duty. With his new, hard clarity, he is carried forward by his determination not to be caught unprepared again. And the way he prepares to lead his group is to list his resolves. He has to assert power over the event by detaching himself. It is a life-and-death matter.

So this effort to detach and control becomes both the drama and the technique of the story. For it is our impulse to deal with the unspeakable horror and sadness by fashioning some kind of order, story, to clarify and contain our emotions. As the writer, Tim O'Brien stands back far enough not to be seen but not so far that he isn't in charge.

"They carried all they could bear, and then some, including a silent awe for the terrible power of the things they carried."

# Big Bertha Stories

FROM *Love Life* (1989)

Donald is home again, laughing and singing. He comes home from Central City, near the strip mines, only when he feels like it, like an absentee landlord checking on his property. He is always in such a good humor when he returns that Jeannette forgives him. She cooks for him—ugly, pasty things she gets with food stamps. Sometimes he brings steaks and ice cream, occasionally money. Rodney, their child, hides in the closet when he arrives, and Donald goes around the house talking loudly about the little boy named Rodney who used to live there—the one who fell into a septic tank, or the one stolen by gypsies. The stories change. Rodney usually stays in the closet until he has to pee, and then he hugs his father's knees, forgiving him, just as Jeannette does. The way Donald saunters through the door, swinging a six-pack of beer, with a big grin on his face, takes her breath away. He leans against the door facing, looking sexy in his baseball cap and his shaggy red beard and his sunglasses. He wears sunglasses to be like the Blues Brothers, but he in no way resembles either of the Blues Brothers. I should have my head examined, Jeannette thinks.

The last time Donald was home, they went to the shopping center to buy Rodney some shoes advertised on sale. They stayed at the shopping center half the afternoon, just looking around. Donald and Rodney played video games. Jeannette felt they were a normal family. Then, in the parking lot, they stopped to watch a man on a platform demonstrating snakes. Children were petting a twelve-foot python coiled around the man's shoulders. Jeannette felt faint.

"Snakes won't hurt you unless you hurt them," said Donald as Rodney stroked the snake.

"It feels like chocolate," he said.

The snake man took a tarantula from a plastic box and held it lovingly in his palm. He said, "If you drop a tarantula, it will shatter like a Christmas ornament."

"I hate this," said Jeannette.

"Let's get out of here," said Donald.

Jeannette felt her family disintegrating like a spider shattering as Donald hurried them away from the shopping center. Rodney squalled and Donald dragged him along. Jeannette wanted to stop for ice cream. She wanted them all to sit quietly together in a booth, but Donald rushed them to the car, and he drove them home in silence, his face growing grim.

"Did you have bad dreams about the snakes?" Jeannette asked Rodney the next morning at breakfast. They were eating pancakes made with generic pancake mix. Rodney slapped his fork in the pond of syrup on his pancakes. "The black racer is the farmer's friend," he said soberly, repeating a fact learned from the snake man.

"Big Bertha kept black racers," said Donald. "She trained them for the 500." Donald doesn't tell Rodney ordinary children's stories. He tells him a series of strange stories he makes up about Big Bertha. Big Bertha is what he calls the huge strip-mining machine in Muhlenberg County, but he has Rodney believing that Big Bertha is a female version of Paul Bunyan.

"Snakes don't run in the 500," said Rodney.

"This wasn't the Indy 500 or the Daytona 500—none of your well-known 500s," said Donald. "This was the Possum Trot 500, and it was a long time ago. Big Bertha started the original 500, with snakes. Black racers and blue racers mainly. Also some red-and-white-striped racers, but those are rare."

"We always ran for the hoe if we saw a black racer," Jeannette said, remembering her childhood in the country.

In a way, Donald's absences are a fine arrangement, even considerate. He is sparing them his darkest moods, when he can't cope with his memories of Vietnam. Vietnam had never seemed such a meaningful fact until a couple of years ago, when he grew depressed and moody, and then he started going away to Central City. He frightened Jeannette, and she always said the wrong thing in her efforts to soothe him. If the welfare people find out he is spending occasional weekends at home, and even bringing some money, they will cut off her assistance. She applied for welfare because she can't depend on him to send money, but she knows he blames her for losing faith in him. He isn't really working regularly at the strip mines. He is mostly just hanging around there, watching the land being scraped away, trees coming down, bushes flung in the air. Sometimes he operates a steam shovel, and when he comes home his clothes are filled with the clay and it is caked on his shoes. The clay is the color of butterscotch pudding.

At first, he tried to explain to Jeannette. He said, "If we could have had tanks over there as big as Big Bertha, we wouldn't have lost the war. Strip mining is just like what we were doing over there. We were stripping off the top. The topsoil is like the culture and the people, the best part of the land and the country. America was just stripping off the top, the best. We ruined it. Here, at least the coal companies have to plant vetch and loblolly pines and all kinds of trees and bushes. If we'd done that in Vietnam, maybe we'd have left that country in better shape."

"Wasn't Vietnam a long time ago?" Jeanette asked.

She didn't want to hear about Vietnam. She thought it was unhealthy to dwell on it so much. He should live in the present. Her mother is afraid Donald will do something violent, because she once read in the newspaper that a veteran in Louisville held his little girl hostage in their apartment until he had a shootout with the police and was killed. But Jeannette can't imagine Donald doing anything so extreme. When she first met him, several years ago, at her parents' pit-barbecue luncheonette, where she was working then, he had a good job at a lumberyard and he dressed nicely. He took her out to eat at a fancy restaurant. They got plastered and ended up in a motel in Tupelo, Mississippi, on Elvis Presley Boulevard. Back then, he talked nostalgically about his year in Vietnam, about how beautiful it was, how different the people were. He could never seem to explain what he meant. "They're just different," he said.

They went riding around in a yellow 1957 Chevy convertible. He drives too fast now, but he didn't then, maybe because he was so protective of the car. It was a classic. He sold it three years ago and made a good profit. About the time he sold the Chevy, his moods began changing, his even-tempered nature shifting, like driving on a smooth interstate and then switching to a secondary road. He had headaches and bad dreams. But his nightmares seemed trivial. He dreamed of riding a train through the Rocky Mountains, of hijacking a plane to Cuba, of stringing up barbed wire around the house. He dreamed he lost a doll. He got drunk and rammed the car, the Chevy's successor, into a Civil War statue in front of the courthouse. When he got depressed over the meaninglessness of his job, Jeannette felt guilty about spending money on something nice for the house, and she tried to make him feel his job had meaning by reminding him that, after all, they had a child to think of. "I don't like his name," Donald said once. "What a stupid name. Rodney. I never did like it."

Rodney has dreams about Big Bertha, echoes of his father's nightmare, like TV cartoon versions of Donald's memories of the war. But Rodney loves the stories, even though they are confusing, with lots of loose ends. The latest in the Big Bertha series is "Big Bertha and the Neutron Bomb." Last week it was "Big Bertha and the MX Missile." In the new story, Big Bertha takes a trip to California to go surfing with Big Mo, her male counterpart. On the beach, corn dogs and snow cones are free and the surfboards turn into dolphins. Everyone is having fun until the neutron bomb comes. Rodney loves the part where everyone keels over dead. Donald acts it out, collapsing on the rug. All the dolphins and the surfers keel over, everyone except Big Bertha. Big Bertha is so big she is immune to the neutron bomb.

"Those stories aren't true," Jeannette tells Rodney.

Rodney staggers and falls down on the rug, his arms and legs akimbo. He gets the giggles and can't stop. When his spasms finally subside, he says, "I told Scottie Bidwell about Big Bertha and he didn't believe me."

Donald picks Rodney up under the armpits and sets him upright. "You tell Scottie Bidwell if he saw Big Bertha he would pee in his pants on the spot, he would be so impressed."

"Are you scared of Big Bertha?"

"No, I'm not. Big Bertha is just like a wonderful woman, a big fat woman who can sing the blues. Have you ever heard Big Mama Thornton?"

"No."

"Well, Big Bertha's like her, only she's the size of a tall building. She's slow as a turtle and when she crosses the road they have to reroute traffic. She's big enough to straddle a four-lane highway. She's so tall she can see all the way to Tennessee, and when she belches, there's a tornado. She's really something. She can even fly."

"She's too big to fly," Rodney says doubtfully. He makes a face like a wadded-up washrag and Donald wrestles him to the floor again.

Donald has been drinking all evening, but he isn't drunk. The ice cubes melt and he pours the drink out and refills it. He keeps on talking. Jeannette cannot remember him talking so much about the war. He is telling her about an ammunitions dump. Jeannette had the vague idea that an ammo dump is a mound of shotgun shells, heaps of cartridge casings and bomb shells, or whatever is left over, a vast waste pile from the war, but Donald says that is wrong. He has spent an hour describing it in detail, so that she will understand.

He refills the glass with ice, some 7-Up, and a shot of Jim Beam. He slams doors and drawers, looking for a compass. Jeannette can't keep track of the conversation. It doesn't matter that her hair is uncombed and her lipstick eaten away. He isn't seeing her.

"I want to draw the compound for you," he says, sitting down at the table with a sheet of Rodney's tablet paper.

Donald draws the map in red and blue ballpoint, with asterisks and technical labels that mean nothing to her. He draws some circles with the compass and measures some angles. He makes a red dot on an oblique line, a path that leads to the ammo dump.

"That's where I was. Right there," he says. "There was a water buffalo that tripped a land mine and its horn just flew off and stuck in the wall of the barracks like a machete thrown backhanded." He puts a dot where the land mine was, and he doodles awhile with the red ballpoint pen, scribbling something on the edge of the map that looks like feathers. "The dump was here and I was there and over there was where we piled the sandbags. And here were the tanks." He draws tanks, a row of squares with handles— guns sticking out.

"Why are you going to so much trouble to tell me about a buffalo horn that got stuck in a wall?" she wants to know.

But Donald just looks at her as though she has asked something obvious.

"Maybe I *could* understand if you'd let me," she says cautiously.

"You could never understand." He draws another tank.

In bed, it is the same as it has been since he started going away to Central City—the way he claims his side of the bed, turning away from her.

Tonight, she reaches for him and he lets her be close to him. She cries for a while and he lies there, waiting for her to finish, as though she were merely putting on makeup.

"Do you want me to tell you a Big Bertha story?" he asks playfully.

"You act like you're in love with Big Bertha."

He laughs, breathing on her. But he won't come closer.

"You don't care what I look like anymore," she says. "What am I supposed to think?"

"There's nobody else. There's not anybody but you."

Loving a giant machine is incomprehensible to Jeannette. There must be another woman, someone that large in his mind. Jeannette has seen the strip-mining machine. The top of the crane is visible beyond a rise along the parkway. The strip mining is kept just out of sight of travelers because it would give them a poor image of Kentucky.

For three weeks, Jeannette has been seeing a psychologist at the free mental health clinic. He's a small man from out of state. His name is Dr. Robinson, but she calls him The Rapist, because the word *therapist* can be divided into two words, *the rapist*. He doesn't think her joke is clever, and he acts as though he has heard it a thousand times before. He has a habit of saying, "Go with that feeling," the same way Bob Newhart did on his old TV show. It's probably the first lesson in the textbook, Jeannette thinks.

She told him about Donald's last days on his job at the lumberyard—how he let the stack of lumber fall deliberately and didn't know why, and about how he went away soon after that, and how the Big Bertha stories started. Dr. Robinson seems to be waiting for her to make something out of it all, but it's maddening that he won't tell her what to do. After three visits, Jeannette has grown angry with him, and now she's holding back things. She won't tell him whether Donald slept with her or not when he came home last. Let him guess, she thinks.

"Talk about yourself," he says.

"What about me?"

"You speak so vaguely about Donald that I get the feeling that you see him as somebody larger than life. I can't quite picture him. That makes me wonder what that says about you." He touches the end of his tie to his nose and sniffs it.

When Jeannette suggests that she bring Donald in, the therapist looks bored and says nothing.

"He had another nightmare when he was home last," Jeannette says. "He dreamed he was crawling through tall grass and people were after him."

"How do *you* feel about that?" The Rapist asks eagerly.

"I didn't have the nightmare," she says coldly. "Donald did. I came to you to get advice about Donald, and you're acting like I'm the one who's crazy. I'm not crazy. But I'm lonely."

Jeannette's mother, behind the counter of the luncheonette, looks lovingly at Rodney pushing buttons on the jukebox in the corner. "It's a shame about that youngun," she says tearfully. "That boy needs a daddy."

"What are you trying to tell me? That I should file for divorce and get Rodney a new daddy?"

Her mother looks hurt. "No, honey," she says. "You need to get Donald to seek the Lord. And you need to pray more. You haven't been going to church lately."

"Have some barbecue," Jeannette's father booms, as he comes in from the back kitchen. "And I want you to take a pound home with you. You've got a growing boy to feed."

"I want to take Rodney to church," Mama says. "I want to show him off, and it might do some good."

"People will think he's an orphan," Dad says.

"I don't care," Mama says. "I just love him to pieces and I want to take him to church. Do you care if I take him to church, Jeannette?"

"No. I don't care if you take him to church." She takes the pound of barbecue from her father. Grease splotches the brown wrapping paper. Dad has given them so much barbecue that Rodney is burned out on it and won't eat it anymore.

Jeannette wonders if she would file for divorce if she could get a job. It is a thought—for the child's sake, she thinks. But there aren't many jobs around. With the cost of a baby-sitter, it doesn't pay her to work. When Donald first went away, her mother kept Rodney and she had a good job, waitressing at a steak house, but the steak house burned down one night—

a grease fire in the kitchen. After that, she couldn't find a steady job, and she was reluctant to ask her mother to keep Rodney again because of her bad hip. At the steak house, men gave her tips and left their telephone numbers on the bill when they paid. They tucked dollar bills and notes in the pockets of her apron. One note said, "I want to hold your muffins." They were real-estate developers and businessmen on important missions for the Tennessee Valley Authority. They were boisterous and they drank too much. They said they'd take her for a cruise on the *Delta Queen,* but she didn't believe them. She knew how expensive that was. They talked about their speedboats and invited her for rides on Lake Barkley, or for spins in their private planes. They always used the word *spin.* The idea made her dizzy. Once, Jeannette let an electronics salesman take her for a ride in his Cadillac, and they breezed down the wilderness road through the Land Between the Lakes. His car had automatic windows and a stereo system and lighted computer-screen numbers on the dash that told him how many miles to the gallon he was getting and other statistics. He said the numbers distracted him and he had almost had several wrecks. At the restaurant, he had been flamboyant, admired by his companions. Alone with Jeannette in the Cadillac, on The Trace, he was shy and awkward, and really not very interesting. The most interesting thing about him, Jeannette thought, was all the lighted numbers on his dashboard. The Cadillac had everything but video games. But she'd rather be riding around with Donald, no matter where they ended up.

While the social worker is there, filling out her report, Jeannette listens for Donald's car. When the social worker drove up, the flutter and wheeze of her car sounded like Donald's old Chevy, and for a moment Jeannette's mind lapsed back in time. Now she listens, hoping he won't drive up. The social worker is younger than Jeannette and has been to college. Her name is Miss Bailey, and she's excessively cheerful, as though in her line of work she has seen hardships that make Jeannette's troubles seem like a trip to Hawaii.

"Is your little boy still having those bad dreams?" Miss Bailey asks, looking up from her clipboard.

Jeannette nods and looks at Rodney, who has his finger in his mouth and won't speak.

"Has the cat got your tongue?" Miss Bailey asks.

"Show her your pictures, Rodney." Jeannette explains, "He won't talk about the dreams, but he draws pictures of them."

Rodney brings his tablet of pictures and flips through them silently. Miss Bailey says, "Hmm." They are stark line drawings, remarkably steady lines for his age. "What is this one?" she asks. "Let me guess. Two scoops of ice cream?"

The picture is two huge circles, filling the page, with three tiny stick people in the corner.

"These are Big Bertha's titties," says Rodney.

Miss Bailey chuckles and winks at Jeannette. "What do you like to read, hon?" she asks Rodney.

"Nothing."

"He can read," says Jeannette. "He's smart."

"Do you like to read?" Miss Bailey asks Jeannette. She glances at the pile of paperbacks on the coffee table. She is probably going to ask where Jeannette got the money for them.

"I don't read," says Jeannette. "If I read, I just go crazy."

When she told The Rapist she couldn't concentrate on anything serious, he said she read romance novels in order to escape from reality. "Reality, hell!" she had said. "Reality's my whole problem."

"It's too bad Rodney's not here," Donald is saying. Rodney is in the closet again. "Santa Claus has to take back all these toys. Rodney would love this bicycle! And this Pac-Man game. Santa has to take back so many things he'll have to have a pickup truck!"

"You didn't bring him anything. You never bring him anything," says Jeannette.

He has brought doughnuts and dirty laundry. The clothes he is wearing are caked with clay. His beard is lighter from working out in the sun, and he looks his usual joyful self, the way he always is before his moods take over, like migraine headaches, which some people describe as storms.

Donald coaxes Rodney out of the closet with the doughnuts.

"Were you a good boy this week?"

"I don't know."

"I hear you went to the shopping center and showed out." It is not true that Rodney made a big scene. Jeannette has already explained that Rodney was upset because she wouldn't buy him an Atari. But she didn't blame him for crying. She was tired of being unable to buy him anything.

Rodney eats two doughnuts and Donald tells him a long, confusing story about Big Bertha and a rock-and-roll band. Rodney interrupts him with dozens of questions. In the story, the rock-and-roll band gives a concert in a place that turns out to be a toxic-waste dump and the contamination is spread all over the country. Big Bertha's solution to this problem is not at all clear. Jeannette stays in the kitchen, trying to think of something original to do with instant potatoes and leftover barbecue.

"We can't go on like this," she says that evening in bed. "We're just hurting each other. Something has to change."

He grins like a kid. "Coming home from Muhlenberg County is like R and R—rest and recreation. I explain that in case you think R and R means rock and roll. Or maybe rumps and rears. Or rust and rot." He laughs and draws a circle in the air with his cigarette.

"I'm not that dumb."

"When I leave, I go back to the mines." He sighs, as though the mines were some eternal burden.

Her mind skips ahead to the future: Donald locked away somewhere, coloring in a coloring book and making clay pots, her and Rodney in some other town, with another man—someone dull and not at all sexy. Summoning up her courage, she says, "I haven't been through what you've been through and maybe I don't have a right to say this, but sometimes I think you act superior because you went to Vietnam, like nobody can ever know what you know. Well, maybe not. But you've still got your legs, even if you don't know what to do with what's between them anymore." Bursting into tears of apology, she can't help adding, "You can't go on telling Rodney those awful stories. He has nightmares when you're gone."

Donald rises from bed and grabs Rodney's picture from the dresser, holding it as he might have held a hand grenade. "Kids betray you," he says, turning the picture in his hand.

"If you cared about him, you'd stay here." As he sets the picture down, she asks, "What can I do? How can I understand what's going on in your mind? Why do you go there? Strip mining's bad for the ecology and you don't have any business strip mining."

"My job is serious, Jeannette. I run that steam shovel and put the top-soil back on. I'm reclaiming the land." He keeps talking, in a gentler voice, about strip mining, the same old things she has heard before, comparing Big Bertha to a supertank. If only they had had Big Bertha in Vietnam. He says, "When they strip off the top, I keep looking for those tunnels where the Viet Cong hid. They had so many tunnels it was unbelievable. Imagine Mammoth Cave going all the way across Kentucky."

"Mammoth Cave's one of the natural wonders of the world," says Jeannette brightly. She is saying the wrong thing again.

At the kitchen table at 2 A.M., he's telling about C-5A's. A C-5A is so big it can carry troops and tanks and helicopters, but it's not big enough to hold Big Bertha. Nothing could hold Big Bertha. He rambles on, and when Jeannette shows him Rodney's drawing of the circles, Donald smiles. Dreamily, he begins talking about women's breasts and thighs—the large, round thighs and big round breasts of American women, contrasted with the frail, delicate beauty of the Orientals. It is like comparing oven broilers and banties, he says. Jeannette relaxes. A confession about another lover from long ago is not so hard to take. He seems stuck on the breasts and thighs of American women—insisting that she understand how small and delicate the Orientals are, but then he abruptly returns to tanks and helicopters.

"A Bell Huey Cobra—my God, what a beautiful machine. So efficient!" Donald takes the food processor blade from the drawer where Jeannette keeps it. He says, "A rotor blade from a chopper could just slice anything to bits."

"Don't do that," Jeannette says.

He is trying to spin the blade on the counter, like a top. "Here's what would happen when a chopper blade hits a power line—not many of those over there!—or a tree. Not many trees, either, come to think of it, after all the Agent Orange." He drops the blade and it glances off the open drawer and falls to the floor, spiking the vinyl.

At first, Jeannette thinks the screams are hers, but they are his. She watches him cry. She has never seen anyone cry so hard, like an intense summer thundershower. All she knows to do is shove Kleenex at him. Finally, he is able to say, "You thought I was going to hurt you. That's why I'm crying."

"Go ahead and cry," Jeannette says, holding him close.

"Don't go away."

"I'm right here. I'm not going anywhere."

In the night, she still listens, knowing his monologue is being burned like a tattoo into her brain. She will never forget it. His voice grows soft and he plays with a ballpoint pen, jabbing holes in a paper towel. Bullet holes, she thinks. His beard is like a bird's nest, woven with dark corn silks.

"This is just a story," he says. "Don't mean nothing. Just relax." She is sitting on the hard edge of the kitchen chair, her toes cold on the floor, waiting. His tears have dried up and left a slight catch in his voice.

"We were in a big camp near a village. It was pretty routine and kind of soft there for a while. Now and then we'd go into Da Nang and whoop it up. We had been in the jungle for several months, so the two months at this village was a sort of rest—an R and R almost. Don't shiver. This is just a little story. Don't mean nothing! This is nothing, compared to what I could tell you. Just listen. We lost our fear. At night there would be some incoming and we'd see these tracers in the sky, like shooting stars up close, but it was all pretty minor and we didn't take it seriously, after what we'd been through. In the village I knew this Vietnamese family—a woman and her two daughters. They sold Cokes and beer to GIs. The oldest daughter was named Phan. She could speak a little English. She was really smart. I used to go see them in their hooch in the afternoons—in the siesta time of day. It was so hot there. Phan was beautiful, like the country. The village was ratty, but the country was pretty. And she was beautiful, just like she had grown up out of the jungle, like one of those flowers that bloomed high up in the trees and freaked us out sometimes, thinking it was a sniper. She was so gentle, with these eyes shaped like peach pits, and she was no bigger than a child of maybe thirteen or fourteen. I felt funny about her size at first, but later it didn't matter. It was just some wonderful feature about her, like a woman's hair, or her breasts."

He stops and listens, the way they used to listen for crying sounds when Rodney was a baby. He says, "She'd take those big banana leaves and fan me while I lay there in the heat."

"I didn't know they had bananas over there."

"There's a lot you don't know! Listen! Phan was twenty-three, and her brothers were off fighting. I never even asked which side they were fighting on." He laughs. "She got a kick out of the word *fan*. I told her that *fan* was the same word as her name. She thought I meant her name was banana. In Vietnamese the same word can have a dozen different meanings, depending on your tone of voice. I bet you didn't know that, did you?"

"No. What happened to her?"

"I don't know."

"Is that the end of the story?"

"I don't know." Donald pauses, then goes on talking about the village, the girl, the banana leaves, talking in a monotone that is making Jeannette's flesh crawl. He could be the news radio from the next room.

"You must have really liked that place. Do you wish you could go back there to find out what happened to her?"

"It's not there anymore," he says. "It blew up."

Donald abruptly goes to the bathroom. She hears the water running, the pipes in the basement shaking.

"It was so pretty," he says when he returns. He rubs his elbow absent-mindedly. "That jungle was the most beautiful place in the world. You'd have thought you were in paradise. But we blew it sky-high."

In her arms, he is shaking, like the pipes in the basement, which are still vibrating. Then the pipes let go, after a long shudder, but he continues to tremble.

They are driving to the Veterans Hospital. It was Donald's idea. She didn't have to persuade him. When she made up the bed that morning—with a finality that shocked her, as though she knew they wouldn't be in it again together—he told her it would be like R and R. Rest was what he needed. Neither of them had slept at all during the night. Jeannette felt she had to stay awake, to listen for more.

"Talk about strip mining," she says now. "That's what they'll do to your head. They'll dig out all those ugly memories, I hope. We don't need them around here." She pats his knee.

It is a cloudless day, not the setting for this sober journey. She drives and Donald goes along obediently, with the resignation of an old man being taken to a rest home. They are driving through southern Illinois, known as Little Egypt, for some obscure reason Jeannette has never understood.

Donald still talks, but very quietly, without urgency. When he points out the scenery, Jeannette thinks of the early days of their marriage, when they would take a drive like this and laugh hysterically. Now Jeannette points out funny things they see. The Little Egypt Hot Dog World, Pharaoh Cleaners, Pyramid Body Shop. She is scarcely aware that she is driving, and when she sees a sign, LITTLE EGYPT STARLITE CLUB, she is confused for a moment, wondering where she has been transported.

As they part, he asks, "What will you tell Rodney if I don't come back? What if they keep me here indefinitely?"

"You're coming back. I'm telling him you're coming back soon."

"Tell him I went off with Big Bertha. Tell him she's taking me on a sea cruise, to the South Seas."

"No. You can tell him that yourself."

He starts singing "Sea Cruise." He grins at her and pokes her in the ribs.

"You're coming back," she says.

Donald writes from the VA Hospital, saying that he is making progress. They are running tests, and he meets in a therapy group in which all the veterans trade memories. Jeannette is no longer on welfare because she now has a job waitressing at Fred's Family Restaurant. She waits on families, waits for Donald to come home so they can come here and eat together like a family. The fathers look at her with downcast eyes, and the children throw food. While Donald is gone, she rearranges the furniture. She reads some books from the library. She does a lot of thinking. It occurs to her that even though she loved him, she has thought of Donald primarily as a husband, a provider, someone whose name she shared, the father of her child, someone like the fathers who come to the Wednesday night all-you-can-eat fish fry. She hasn't thought of him as himself. She wasn't brought up that way, to examine someone's soul. When it comes to something deep inside, nobody will take it out and examine it, the way they will look at clothing in a store for flaws in the manufacturing. She tries to explain all this to The Rapist, and he says she's looking better, got sparkle in her eyes. "Big deal," says Jeannette. "Is that all you can say?"

She takes Rodney to the shopping center, their favorite thing to do together, even though Rodney always begs to buy something. They go to

Penney's perfume counter. There, she usually hits a sample bottle of co-
logne—Chantilly or Charlie or something strong. Today she hits two or
three and comes out of Penney's smelling like a flower garden.

"You stink!" Rodney cries, wrinkling his nose like a rabbit.

"Big Bertha smells like this, only a thousand times worse, she's so big,"
says Jeannette impulsively. "Didn't Daddy tell you that?"

"Daddy's a messenger from the devil."

This is an idea he must have gotten from church. Her parents have been
taking him every Sunday. When Jeannette tries to reassure him about his
father, Rodney is skeptical. "He gets that funny look on his face like he can
see through me," the child says.

"Something's missing," Jeannette says, with a rush of optimism, a feeling of recognition. "Something happened to him once and took out the part
that shows how much he cares about us."

"The way we had the cat fixed?"

"I guess. Something like that." The appropriateness of his remark stuns
her, as though, in a way, her child has understood Donald all along. Rodney's pictures have been more peaceful lately, pictures of skinny trees and
airplanes flying low. This morning he drew pictures of tall grass, with creatures hiding in it. The grass is tilted at an angle, as though a light breeze is
blowing through it.

With her paycheck, Jeannette buys Rodney a present, a miniature trampoline they have seen advertised on television. It is called Mr. Bouncer.
Rodney is thrilled about the trampoline, and he jumps on it until his face is
red. Jeannette discovers that she enjoys it, too. She puts it out on the grass,
and they take turns jumping. She has an image of herself on the trampoline,
her sailor collar flapping, at the moment when Donald returns and sees her
flying. One day a neighbor driving by slows down and calls out to Jeannette as she is bouncing on the trampoline, "You'll tear your insides loose!"
Jeannette starts thinking about that, and the idea is so horrifying she stops
jumping so much. That night, she has a nightmare about the trampoline.
In her dream, she is jumping on soft moss, and then it turns into a springy
pile of dead bodies.

III

# Love Lives

*There's always sadness lurking in our love lives—missed opportunities, missed connections, a string of losses. But both memory and anticipation propel us along, sometimes on an exhilarating ride. Tone is my guide to the inner lives of the characters. Tone is the sound of their inner voices, how they express themselves to themselves. Finding the right tone for the story means the characters can come alive. And then, whether they're sad or happy, we are there with them, and we are more alive ourselves.*

—BAM

# Love Life

FROM *Love Life* (1989)

Opal lolls in her recliner, wearing the Coors cap her niece Jenny brought her from Colorado. She fumbles for the remote-control paddle and fires a button. Her swollen knuckles hurt. On TV, a boy is dancing in the street. Some other boys dressed in black are banging guitars and drums. This is her favorite program. It is always on, night or day. The show is songs, with accompanying stories. It's the music channel. Opal never cared for stories—she detests those soap operas her friends watch—but these fascinate her. The colors and the costumes change and flow with the music, erratically, the way her mind does these days. Now the TV is playing a song in which all the boys are long-haired cops chasing a dangerous woman in a tweed cap and a checked shirt. The woman's picture is in all their billfolds. They chase her through a cold-storage room filled with sides of beef. She hops on a motorcycle, and they set up a roadblock, but she jumps it with her motorcycle. Finally, she slips onto a train and glides away from them, waving a smiling goodbye.

On the table beside Opal is a Kleenex box, her glasses case, a glass of Coke with ice, and a cut-glass decanter of clear liquid that could be just water for the plants. Opal pours some of the liquid into the Coke and sips slowly. It tastes like peppermint candy, and it feels soothing. Her fingers tingle. She feels happy. Now that she is retired, she doesn't have to sneak into the teachers' lounge for a little swig from the jar in her pocketbook. She still dreams algebra problems, complicated quadratic equations with shifting values and no solutions. Now kids are using algebra to program computers. The kids in the TV stories remind her of her students at Hopewell High. Old age could have a grandeur about it, she thinks now as the music surges through her, if only it weren't so scary.

But she doesn't feel lonely, especially now that her sister Alice's girl, Jenny, has moved back here, to Kentucky. Jenny seems so confident, the way she sprawls on the couch, with that backpack she carries everywhere. Alice was always so delicate and feminine, but Jenny is enough like Opal to be her own daughter. She has Opal's light, thin hair, her large shoulders and big bones and long legs. Jenny even has a way of laughing that reminds Opal of her own laughter, the boisterous scoff she always saved for certain company but never allowed herself in school. Now and then Jenny lets loose one of those laughs and Opal is pleased. It occurs to her that Jenny, who is already past thirty, has left behind a trail of men, like that girl in the song. Jenny has lived with a couple of men, here and there. Opal can't keep track of all of the men Jenny has mentioned. They have names like John and Skip and Michael. She's not in a hurry to get married, she says. She says she is going to buy a house trailer and live in the woods like a hermit. She's full of ideas, and she exaggerates. She uses the words "gorgeous," "adorable," and "wonderful" interchangeably and persistently.

Last night, Jenny was here, with her latest boyfriend, Randy Newcomb. Opal remembers when he sat in the back row in her geometry class. He was an ordinary kid, not especially smart, and often late with his lessons. Now he has a real-estate agency and drives a Cadillac. Jenny kissed him in front of Opal and told him he was gorgeous. She said the placemats were gorgeous, too.

Jenny was asking to see those old quilts again. "Why do you hide away your nice things, Aunt Opal?" she said. Opal doesn't think they're that nice, and she doesn't want to have to look at them all the time. Opal showed Jenny and Randy Newcomb the double-wedding-ring quilt, the star quilt, and some of the crazy quilts, but she wouldn't show them the craziest one—the burial quilt, the one Jenny kept asking about. Did Jenny come back home just to hunt up that old rag? The thought makes Opal shudder.

The doorbell rings. Opal has to rearrange her comforter and magazines in order to get up. Her joints are stiff. She leaves the TV blaring a song she knows, with balloons and bombs in it.

At the door is Velma Shaw, who lives in the duplex next to Opal. She has just come home from her job at Shop World. "Have you gone out of your mind, Opal?" cries Velma. She has on a plum-colored print blouse and a plum skirt and a little green scarf with a gold pin holding it down. Velma shouts, "You can hear that racket clear across the street!"

"Rock and roll is never too loud," says Opal. This is a line from a song she has heard.

Opal releases one of her saved-up laughs, and Velma backs away. Velma is still trying to be sexy, in those little color-coordinated outfits she wears, but it is hopeless, Opal thinks with a smile. She closes the door and scoots back to her recliner.

Opal is Jenny's favorite aunt. Jenny likes the way Opal ties her hair in a ponytail with a ribbon. She wears muumuus and socks. She is tall and only a little thick in the middle. She told Jenny that middle-age spread was caused by the ribs expanding and that it doesn't matter what you eat. Opal kids around about "old Arthur"—her arthritis, visiting her on damp days.

Jenny has been in town six months. She works at the courthouse, typing records—marriages, divorces, deaths, drunk-driving convictions. Frequently, the same names are on more than one list. Before she returned to Kentucky, Jenny was waitressing in Denver, but she was growing restless again, and the idea of going home seized her. Her old rebellion against small-town conventions gave way to curiosity.

In the South, the shimmer of the heat seems to distort everything, like old glass with impurities in it. During her first two days there, she saw two people with artificial legs, a blind man, a man with hooks for hands, and a man without an arm. It seemed unreal. In a parking lot, a pit bull terrier in a Camaro attacked her from behind the closed window. He barked viciously, his nose stabbing the window. She stood in the parking lot, letting the pit bull attack, imagining herself in an arena, with a crowd watching. The South makes her nervous. Randy Newcomb told her she had just been away too long. "We're not as countrified down here now as people think," he said.

Jenny has been going with Randy for three months. The first night she went out with him, he took her to a fancy place that served shrimp flown in from New Orleans, and then to a little bar over in Hopkinsville. They went with Kathy Steers, a friend from work, and Kathy's husband, Bob. Kathy and Bob weren't getting along and they carped at each other all evening. In the bar, an attractive, cheerful woman sang requests for tips, and her companion, a blind man, played the guitar. When she sang, she looked straight at him, singing to him, smiling at him reassuringly. In the background, men played pool with their girlfriends, and Jenny noticed the sharp creases in the men's jeans and imagined the women ironing them. When she mentioned it, Kathy said she took Bob's jeans to the laundromat to use the machine there that puts knifelike creases in them. The men in the bar had two kinds of women with them: innocent-looking women with pastel skirts and careful hairdos, and hard-looking women without makeup, in T-shirts and jeans. Jenny imagined that each type could be either a girlfriend or a wife. She felt odd. She was neither type. The singer sang "Happy Birthday" to a popular regular named Will Ed, and after the set she danced with him, while the jukebox took over. She had a limp, as though one leg were shorter than the other. The leg was stiff under her jeans, and when the woman danced Jenny could see that the leg was not real.

"There, but for the grace of God, go I," Randy whispered to Jenny. He squeezed her hand, and his heavy turquoise ring dug into her knuckle.

"Those quilts would bring a good price at an estate auction," Randy says to Jenny as they leave her aunt's one evening and head for his real-estate office. They are in his burgundy Cadillac. "One of those star quilts used to bring twenty-five dollars. Now it might run three hundred."

"My aunt doesn't think they're worth anything. She hides all her nice stuff, like she's ashamed of it. She's got beautiful dresser scarves and starched doilies she made years ago. But she's getting a little weird. All she does is watch MTV."

"I think she misses the kids," Randy says. Then he bursts out laughing. "She used to put the fear of God in all her students! I never will forget the time she told me to stop watching so much television and read some books. It was like an order from God Almighty. I didn't dare not do what she said. I read *Crime and Punishment*. I never would have read it if she hadn't shamed me into it. But I appreciated that. I don't even remember what *Crime and Punishment* was about, except there was an ax murderer in it."

"That was basically it," Jenny says. "He got caught. Crime and punishment—just like any old TV show."

Randy touches some controls on the dashboard and Waylon Jennings starts singing. The sound system is remarkable. Everything Randy owns is quality. He has been looking for some land for Jenny to buy—a couple of acres of woods—but so far nothing on his listings has met with his approval. He is concerned about zoning and power lines and frontage. All Jenny wants is a remote place where she can have a dog and grow some tomatoes. She knows that what she really needs is a better car, but she doesn't want to go anywhere.

Later, at Randy's office, Jenny studies the photos of houses on display, while he talks on the telephone to someone about dividing up a sixty-acre farm into farmettes. His photograph is on several certificates on the wall. He has a full, well-fed face in the pictures, but he is thinner now and looks better. He has a boyish, endearing smile, like Dennis Quaid, Jenny's favorite actor. She likes Randy's smile. It seems so innocent, as though he would do anything in the world for someone he cared about. He doesn't really want to sell her any land. He says he is afraid she will get raped if she lives alone in the woods.

"I'm impressed," she says when he slams down the telephone. She points to his new regional award for the fastest-growing agency of the year.

"Isn't that something? Three branch offices in a territory this size—I can't complain. There's a lot of turnover in real estate now. People are never satisfied. You know that? That's the truth about human nature." He laughs. "That's the secret of my success."

"It's been two years since Barbara divorced me," he says later, on the way to Jenny's apartment. "I can't say it hasn't been fun being free, but my kids are in college, and it's like starting over. I'm ready for a new life. The business has been so great, I couldn't really ask for more, but I've been thinking—Don't laugh, please, but what I was thinking was if you want to share it with me, I'll treat you good. I swear."

At a stoplight, he paws at her hand. On one corner is the Pepsi bottling plant, and across from it is the Broad Street House, a restaurant with an old-fashioned statue of a jockey out front. People are painting the black faces on those little statues white now, but this one has been painted bright green all over. Jenny can't keep from laughing at it.

"I wasn't laughing at you—honest!" she says apologetically. "That statue always cracks me up."

"You don't have to give me an answer now."

"I don't know what to say."

"I can get us a real good deal on a house," he says. "I can get any house I've got listed. I can even get us a farmette, if you want trees so bad. You won't have to spend your money on a piece of land."

"I'll have to think about it." Randy scares her. She likes him, but there is something strange about his energy and optimism. Everyone around her seems to be bursting at the seams, like that pit bull terrier.

"I'll let you think on it," he says, pulling up to her apartment. "Life has been good to me. Business is good, and my kids didn't turn out to be dope fiends. That's about all you can hope for in this day and time."

Jenny is having lunch with Kathy Steers at the Broad Street House. The iced tea is mixed with white grape juice. It took Jenny a long time to identify the flavor, and the Broad Street House won't admit it's grape juice. Their iced tea is supposed to have a mystique about it, probably because they can't sell drinks in this dry county. In the daylight, the statue out front is the color of the Jolly Green Giant.

People confide in Jenny, but Jenny doesn't always tell things back. It's an unfair exchange, though it often goes unnoticed. She is curious, eager to hear other people's stories, and she asks more questions than is appropriate. Kathy's life is a tangle of deceptions. Kathy stayed with her husband, Bob, because he had opened his own body shop and she didn't want him to start out a new business with a rocky marriage, but she acknowledges now it was a mistake.

"What about Jimmy and Willette?" Jenny asks. Jimmy and Willette are the other characters in Kathy's story.

"That mess went on for months. When you started work at the office, remember how nervous I was? I thought I was getting an ulcer." Kathy lights a cigarette and blows at the wall. "You see, I didn't know what Bob and Willette were up to, and they didn't know about me and Jimmy. That went on for two years before you came. And when it started to come apart—I mean, we had *hell!* I'd say things to Jimmy and then it would get back to Bob because Jimmy would tell Willette. It was an unreal circle. I was pregnant with Jason and you get real sensitive then. I thought Bob was screwing around on me, but it never dawned on me it was with Willette."

The fat waitress says, "Is everything all right?"

Kathy says, "No, but it's not your fault. Do you know what I'm going to do?" she asks Jenny.

"No, what?"

"I'm taking Jason and moving in with my sister. She has a sort of apartment upstairs. Bob can do what he wants to with the house. I've waited too long to do this, but it's time. My sister keeps the baby anyway, so why shouldn't I just live there?"

She puffs the cigarette again and levels her eyes at Jenny. "You know what I admire about you? You're so independent. You say what you think. When you started work at the office, I said to myself, 'I wish I could be like that.' I could tell you had been around. You've inspired me. That's how come I decided to move out."

Jenny plays with the lemon slice in the saucer holding her iced-tea glass. She picks a seed out of it. She can't bring herself to confide in Kathy about Randy Newcomb's offer. For some reason, she is embarrassed by it.

"I haven't spoken to Willette since September third," says Kathy.

Kathy keeps talking, and Jenny listens, suspicious of her interest in Kathy's problems. She notices how Kathy is enjoying herself. Kathy is looking forward to leaving her husband the same way she must have enjoyed her fling with Jimmy, the way she is enjoying not speaking to Willette.

"Let's go out and get drunk tonight," Kathy says cheerfully. "Let's celebrate my decision."

"I can't. I'm going to see my aunt this evening. I have to take her some booze. She gives me money to buy her vodka and peppermint schnapps, and she tells me not to stop at the same liquor store too often. She says she doesn't want me to get a reputation for drinking! I have to go all the way to Hopkinsville to get it."

"Your aunt tickles me. She's a pistol."

The waitress clears away the dishes and slaps down dessert menus. They order chocolate pecan pie, the day's special.

"You know the worst part of this whole deal?" Kathy says. "It's the years it takes to get smart. But I'm going to make up for lost time. You can bet on that. And there's not a thing Bob can do about it."

Opal's house has a veranda. Jenny thinks that verandas seem to imply a history of some sort—people in rocking chairs telling stories. But Opal doesn't tell any stories. It is exasperating, because Jenny wants to know about her aunt's past love life, but Opal won't reveal her secrets. They sit on the veranda and observe each other. They smile, and now and then roar with laughter over something ridiculous. In the bedroom, where she snoops after using the bathroom, Jenny notices the layers of old wallpaper in the closet, peeling back and spilling crumbs of gaudy ancient flower prints onto Opal's muumuus.

Downstairs, Opal asks, "Do you want some cake, Jenny?"

"Of course. I'm crazy about your cake, Aunt Opal."

"I didn't beat the egg whites long enough. Old Arthur's visiting again." Opal flexes her fingers and smiles. "That sounds like the curse. Girls used to say they had the curse. Or they had a visitor." She looks down at her knuckles shyly. "Nowadays, of course, they just say what they mean."

The cake is delicious—an old-fashioned lemon chiffon made from scratch. Jenny's cooking ranges from English-muffin mini-pizzas to brownie mixes. After gorging on the cake, Jenny blurts out, "Aunt Opal, aren't you sorry you never got married? Tell the truth, now."

Opal laughs. "I was talking to Ella Mae Smith the other day—she's a retired geography teacher?—and she said, 'I've got twelve great-great-grandchildren, and when we get together I say, "Law me, look what I started!"'" Opal mimics Ella Mae Smith, giving her a mindless, chirpy tone of voice. "Why, I'd have to use quadratic equations to count up all the people that woman has caused," she goes on. "All with a streak of her petty narrow-mindedness in them. I don't call that a contribution to the world." Opal laughs and sips from her glass of schnapps. "What about you, Jenny? Are you ever going to get married?"

"Marriage is outdated. I don't know anybody who's married and happy."

Opal names three schoolteachers she has known who have been married for decades.

"But are they really happy?"

"Oh, foot, Jenny! What you're saying is why are *you* not married and why are *you* not happy. What's wrong with little Randy Newcomb? Isn't that funny? I always think of him as little Randy."

"Show me those quilts again, Aunt Opal."

"I'll show you the crazies but not the one you keep after me about."

"O.K., show me the crazies."

Upstairs, her aunt lays crazy quilts on the bed. They are bright-colored patches of soft velvet and plaids and prints stitched together with silky embroidery. Several pieces have initials embroidered on them. The haphazard shapes make Jenny imagine odd, twisted lives represented in these quilts.

She says, "Mom gave me a quilt once, but I didn't appreciate the value of it and I washed it until it fell apart."

"I'll give you one of these crazies when you stop moving around," Opal says. "You couldn't fit it in that backpack of yours." She polishes her glasses thoughtfully. "Do you know what those quilts mean to me?"

"No, what?"

"A lot of desperate old women ruining their eyes. Do you know what I think I'll do?"

"No, what?"

"I think I'll take up aerobic dancing. Or maybe I'll learn to ride a motorcycle. I try to be modern."

"You're funny, Aunt Opal. You're hilarious."

"Am I gorgeous, too?"

"Adorable," says Jenny.

After her niece leaves, Opal hums a tune and dances a stiff little jig. She nestles among her books and punches her remote-control paddle. Years ago, she was allowed to paddle students who misbehaved. She used a wooden paddle from a butter churn, with holes drilled in it. The holes made a satisfying sting. On TV, a 1950s convertible is out of gas. This is one of her favorites. It has an adorable couple in it. The girl is wearing bobby socks and saddle oxfords, and the boy has on a basketball jacket. They look the way children looked before the hippie element took over. But the boy begins growing cat whiskers and big cat ears, and then his face gets furry and leathery, while the girl screams bloody murder. Opal sips some peppermint and watches his face change. The red and gold of his basketball jacket are the Hopewell school colors. He chases the girl. Now he has grown long claws.

The boy is dancing energetically with a bunch of ghouls who have escaped from their coffins. Then Vincent Price starts talking in the background. The girl is very frightened. The ghouls are so old and ugly. That's

how kids see us, Opal thinks. She loves this story. She even loves the cred-
its—scary music by Elmer Bernstein. This is a story with a meaning. It suggests all the feelings of terror and horror that must be hidden inside young
people. And inside, deep down, there really are monsters. An old person
waits, a nearly dead body that can still dance.

Opal pours another drink. She feels relaxed, her joints loose like a
dancer's now.

Jenny is so nosy. Her questions are so blunt. Did Opal ever have a crush
on a student? Only once or twice. She was in her twenties then, and it
seemed scandalous. Nothing happened—just daydreams. When she was
thirty, she had another attachment to a boy, and it seemed all right then,
but it was worse again at thirty-five, when another pretty boy stayed after
class to talk. After that, she kept her distance.

But Opal is not wholly without experience. There have been men, over
the years, though nothing like the casual affairs Jenny has had. Opal remembers a certain motel room in Nashville. She was only forty. The man
drove a gray Chrysler Imperial. When she was telling about him to a friend,
who was sworn to secrecy, she called him "Imperial," in a joking way. She
went with him because she knew he would take her somewhere, in such a
fine car, and they would sleep together. She always remembered how clean
and empty the room was, how devoid of history and association. In the
mirror, she saw a scared woman with a pasty face and a shrimpy little man
who needed a shave. In the morning he went out somewhere and brought
back coffee and orange juice. They had bought some doughnuts at the new
doughnut shop in town before they left. While he was out, she made up
the bed and put her things in her bag, to make it as neat as if she had never
been there. She was fully dressed when he returned, with her garter belt
and stockings on, and when they finished the doughnuts she cleaned up all
the paper and the cups and wiped the crumbs from the table by the bed.
He said, "Come with me and I'll take you to Idaho." "Why Idaho?" she
wanted to know, but his answer was vague. Idaho sounded cold, and she
didn't want to tell him how she disliked his scratchy whiskers and the hard,
powdery doughnuts. It seemed unkind of her, but if he had been nicer-look-
ing, without such a demanding dark beard, she might have gone with him
to Idaho in that shining Imperial. She hadn't even given him a chance, she
thought later. She had been so scared. If anyone from school had seen her

at that motel, she could have lost her job. "I need a woman," he had said. "A woman like you."

On a hot Saturday afternoon, with rain threatening, Jenny sits under a tent on a folding chair while Randy auctions off four hundred acres of woods on Lake Barkley. He had a road bulldozed into the property, and he divided it up into lots. The lakefront lots are going for as much as two thousand an acre, and the others are bringing up to a thousand. Randy has several assistants with him, and there is even a concession stand, offering hot dogs and cold drinks.

In the middle of the auction, they wait for a thundershower to pass. Sitting in her folding chair under a canopy reminds Jenny of graveside services. As soon as the rain slacks up, the auction continues. In his cowboy hat and blue blazer, Randy struts around with a microphone as proudly as a banty rooster. With his folksy chatter, he knows exactly how to work the crowd. "Y'all get yourselves a cold drink and relax now and just imagine the fishing you'll do in this dreamland. This land is good for vacation, second home, investment—heck, you can just park here in your camper and live. It's going to be paradise when that marina gets built on the lake there and we get some lots cleared."

The four-hundred-acre tract looks like a wilderness. Jenny loves the way the sun splashes on the water after the rain, and the way it comes through the trees, hitting the flickering leaves like lights on a disco ball. A marina here seems farfetched. She could pitch a tent here until she could afford to buy a used trailer. She could swim at dawn, the way she did on a camping trip out West, long ago. All of a sudden, she finds herself bidding on a lot.

The bidding passes four hundred, and she sails on, bidding against a man from Missouri who tells the people around him that he's looking for a place to retire.

"Sold to the young lady with the backpack," Randy says when she bids six hundred. He gives her a crestfallen look, and she feels embarrassed.

As she waits for Randy to wind up his business after the auction, Jenny locates her acre from the map of the plots of land. It is along a gravel road and marked off with stakes tied with hot-pink survey tape. It is a small section of the woods—her block on the quilt, she thinks. These are her trees. The vines and underbrush are thick and spotted with raindrops. She notices a windfall leaning on a maple, like a lover dying in its arms. Maples are strong, she thinks, but she feels like getting an ax and chopping that windfall down, to save the maple. In the distance, the whining of a speedboat cuts into the day.

They meet afterward at Randy's van, his mobile real-estate office, with a little shingled roof raised in the center to look rustic. It looks like an outhouse on wheels. A painted message on the side says, "REALITY IS REAL ESTATE." As Randy plows through the mud on the new road, Jenny apologizes. Buying the lot was like laughing at the statue at the wrong moment—something he would take the wrong way, an insult to his attentions.

"I can't reach you," he says. "You say you want to live out in the wilderness and grow your own vegetables, but you act like you're somewhere in outer space. You can't grow vegetables in outer space. You can't even grow them in the woods unless you clear some ground."

"I'm looking for a place to land."

"What do I have to do to get through to you?"

"I don't know. I need more time."

He turns onto the highway, patterned with muddy tire tracks from the cars at the auction. "I said I'd wait, so I guess I'll have to," he says, flashing his Dennis Quaid smile. "You take as long as you want to, then. I learned my lesson with Barbara. You've got to be understanding with the women. That's the key to a successful relationship." Frowning, he slams his hand on the steering wheel. "That's what they tell me, anyhow."

Jenny is having coffee with Opal. She arrived unexpectedly. It's very early. She looks as though she has been up all night.

"Please show me your quilts," Jenny says. "I don't mean your crazy quilts. I want to see that special quilt. Mom said it had the family tree."

Opal spills coffee in her saucer. "What is wrong with young people today?" she asks.

"I want to know why it's called a burial quilt," Jenny says. "Are you planning to be buried in it?"

Opal wishes she had a shot of peppermint in her coffee. It sounds like a delicious idea. She starts toward the den with the coffee cup rattling in its saucer, and she splatters drops on the rug. Never mind it now, she thinks, turning back.

"It's just a family history," she says.

"Why's it called a burial quilt?" Jenny asks.

Jenny's face is pale. She has blue pouches under her eyes and blue eye shadow on her eyelids.

"See that closet in the hall?" Opal says. "Get a chair and we'll get the quilt down."

Jenny stands on a kitchen chair and removes the quilt from beneath several others. It's wrapped in blue plastic and Jenny hugs it closely as she steps down with it.

They spread it out on the couch, and the blue plastic floats off somewhere. Jenny looks like someone in love as she gazes at the quilt. "It's gorgeous," she murmurs. "How beautiful."

"Shoot!" says Opal. "It's ugly as homemade sin."

Jenny runs her fingers over the rough textures of the quilt. The quilt is dark and somber. The backing is a heavy gray gabardine, and the nine-inch-square blocks are pieced of smaller blocks of varying shades of gray and brown and black. They are wools, apparently made from men's winter suits. On each block is an appliquéd off-white tombstone—a comical shape, like Casper the ghost. Each tombstone has a name and date on it.

Jenny recognizes some of the names. Myrtle Williams. Voris Williams. Thelma Lee Freeman. The oldest gravestone is "Eulalee Freeman 1857–1900." The shape of the quilt is irregular, a rectangle with a clumsy foot sticking out from one corner. The quilt is knotted with yarn, and the edging is open, for more blocks to be added.

"Eulalee's daughter started it," says Opal. "But that thing has been carried through this family like a plague. Did you ever see such horrible old dark colors? I pieced on it some when I was younger, but it was too depressing. I think some of the kinfolks must have died without a square, so there may be several to catch up on."

"I'll do it," says Jenny. "I could learn to quilt."

"Traditionally, the quilt stops when the family name stops," Opal says. "And since my parents didn't have a boy, that was the end of the Freeman line on this particular branch of the tree. So the last old maids finish the quilt." She lets out a wild cackle. "Theoretically, a quilt like this could keep going till doomsday."

"Do you care if I have this quilt?" asks Jenny.

"What would you do with it? It's too ugly to put on a bed and too morbid to work on."

"I think it's kind of neat," says Jenny. She strokes the rough tweed. Already it is starting to decay, and it has moth holes. Jenny feels tears start to drip down her face.

"Don't you go putting my name on that thing," her aunt says.

Jenny has taken the quilt to her apartment. She explained that she is going to study the family tree, or that she is going to finish the quilt. If she's smart, Opal thinks, she will let Randy Newcomb auction it off. The way Jenny took it, cramming it into the blue plastic, was like snatching something that was free. Opal feels relieved, as though she has pushed the burden of that ratty old quilt onto her niece. All those miserable, cranky women, straining their eyes, stitching on those dark scraps of material.

For a long time, Jenny wouldn't tell why she was crying, and when she started to tell, Opal was uncomfortable, afraid she'd be required to tell something comparable of her own, but as she listened she found herself caught up in Jenny's story. Jenny said it was a man. That was always the case, Opal thought. It was five years earlier. A man Jenny knew in a place by the sea. Opal imagined seagulls, pretty sand. There were no palm trees. It was up North. The young man worked with Jenny in a restaurant with glass walls facing the ocean. They waited on tables and collected enough tips to take a trip together near the end of the summer. Jenny made it sound like an idyllic time, waiting on tables by the sea. She started crying again when she told about the trip, but the trip sounded nice. Opal listened hungrily, imagining the young man, thinking that he would have had handsome, smooth cheeks, and hair that fell attractively over his forehead. He would have had good manners, being a waiter. Jenny and the man, whose name was Jim, flew to Denver, Colorado, and they rented a car and drove around out West. They visited the Grand Canyon and Yellowstone and other places Opal had heard about. They grilled salmon on the beach, on another ocean. They camped out in the redwoods, trees so big they hid the sky. Jenny described all these scenes, and the man sounded like a good man. His brother had died in Vietnam and he felt guilty that he had been the one spared, because his brother was a swimmer and could have gone to the Olympics. Jim wasn't athletic. He had a bad knee and hammertoes.

He slept fitfully in the tent, and Jenny said soothing things to him, and she cared about him, but by the time they had curved northward and over to Yellowstone the trip was becoming unpleasant. The romance wore off. She loved him, but she couldn't deal with his needs. One of the last nights they spent together, it rained all night long. He told her not to touch the tent material, because somehow the pressure of a finger on the nylon would make it start to leak at that spot. Lying there in the rain, Jenny couldn't resist touching a spot where water was collecting in a little sag in the top of the tent. The drip started then, and it grew worse, until they got so wet they had to get in the car. Not long afterward, when they ran short of money, they parted. Jenny got a job in Denver. She never saw him again.

Opal listened eagerly to the details about grilling the fish together, about the zip-together sleeping bags and setting up the tent and washing themselves in the cold stream. But when Jenny brought the story up to the present, Opal was not prepared. She felt she had been dunked in the cold water and left gasping. Jenny said she had heard a couple of times through a mutual friend that Jim had spent some time in Mexico. And then, she said, this week she had begun thinking about him, because of all the trees at the lake, and she had an overwhelming desire to see him again. She had been unfair, she knew now. She telephoned the friend, who had worked with them in the restaurant by the sea. He hadn't known where to locate her, he said, and so he couldn't tell her that Jim had been killed in Colorado over a year ago. His four-wheel-drive had plunged off a mountain curve.

"I feel some trick has been played on me. It seems so unreal." Jenny tugged at the old quilt, and her eyes darkened. "I was in Colorado, and I didn't even know he was there. If I still knew him, I would know how to mourn, but now I don't know how. And it was over a year ago. So I don't know what to feel."

"Don't look back, hon," Opal said, hugging her niece closely. But she was shaking, and Jenny shook with her.

Opal makes herself a snack, thinking it will pick up her strength. She is very tired. On the tray, she places an apple and a paring knife and some milk and cookies. She touches the remote-control button, and the picture blossoms. She was wise to buy a large TV, the one listed as the best in the consumer magazine. The color needs a little adjustment, though. She eases up the volume and starts peeling the apple. She has a little bump on one knuckle. In the old days, people would take the family Bible and bust a cyst like that with it. Just slam it hard.

On the screen, a Scoutmaster is telling a story to some Boy Scouts around a campfire. The campfire is only a fireplace, with electric logs. Opal loses track of time, and the songs flow together. A woman is lying on her stomach on a car hood in a desert full of gas pumps. TV sets crash. Smoke emerges from an eyeball. A page of sky turns like a page in a book. Then, at a desk in a classroom, a cocky blond kid with a pack of cigarettes rolled in the sleeve of his T-shirt is singing about a sexy girl with a tattoo on her back who is sitting on a commode and smoking a cigarette. In the classroom, all the kids are gyrating and snapping their fingers to wild music. The teacher at the blackboard with her white hair in a bun looks disapproving, but the kids in the class don't know what's on her mind. The teacher is thinking about how, when the bell rings, she will hit the road to Nashville.

# Coyotes

FROM *Love Life* (1989)

Cobb's fiancée, Lynnette Johnson, wasn't interested in bridal magazines or china patterns or any of that girl stuff. Even when he brought up the subject of honeymoons she would joke about some impossible place—Bulgaria, Hong Kong, Lapland, Peru.

"I just want to go no-frills," she said. "What kind of wedding do *you* want?" She was sitting astride his lap in a kitchen chair.

"I want the kinky-sex, thank-God-it's-Friday, double-Dutch-chocolate special," he said, playing with her hair. It smelled like peppermint.

She was warm and heavy in his lap, and she had her arms around him like a sleepy child. It bothered him that she hadn't even told her folks yet about him, but he had put off taking her to meet his mother, so he thought he understood.

It was the weekend, and they were trying to decide whether to go out for dinner. They were at his apartment at Orchard Acres—two-fifty a month, twice as much as he had paid for his previous apartment. His new place was nice, with a garbage disposal and a patio. He had moved out of his rat-hole when he began working with the soil-conservation service, but now he wished he had saved to buy a house instead of splurging on an expensive apartment with a two-year lease. She kept clothes in his closet and in the chest of drawers, and the bathroom was littered with her things, but she was adamant about holding on to her own place for the time being. Lynnette had such definite ways. She always got up early and ran six or eight miles, even in the winter. She ate peanut butter for breakfast—for protein, she told him. She claimed weeds were beautiful. She had arranged some dried brown weeds in a jug on the dining table. She had picked the weeds from a field when they went pecan-hunting back in the fall. Wild pecans were small, and the nuts were hard to pick out. Cobb still had most of them in a cracker box.

"You wouldn't believe the pictures I saw today," she said a bit later when they were lolling in bed, still undecided about going out to eat. Cobb was trying to lose weight.

Lynnette worked in a film-developing place that rushed out photos in twenty-four hours. The pictures rolled off the chain-drive assembly and through the cutter, and she examined and counted them before slipping them into envelopes.

"There was a man and a woman and a dog," she said. "A baby was asleep in a bassinet at the foot of the bed. Some of the pictures were of the man in bed with the dog—posed together like they were having breakfast in bed. The dog was sitting up on its haunches against the pillow. And in some of the pictures the woman was in bed with the dog. You couldn't really tell, but I don't think either of these people had a stitch of clothes on. They were laughing. The dog, I swear, was laughing, too."

"What kind of dog?"

"A big one. Blond, with his tongue hanging out."

"Sounds like a happy family scene," said Cobb, noticing that he and Lynnette were sitting up against their pillows the way she said the people in the photos were. "It was probably Sunday morning," he said. "And they were fooling around before the baby woke up."

"No, I think it was something really weird." She held her wrist up near the lamp and studied her watch. Getting out of bed, she said, "I saw the woman come in and pick up the pictures. A really nice woman—middle-aged, but still pretty. You'd never suspect anything. But she was too old to have a baby."

Some of the pictures Lynnette told him about frightened her. She saw people posing with guns and knives, grinning and pointing their weapons at each other. But the nudes were more disturbing. The lab wasn't supposed to print them, but when she examined negatives for printing she saw plenty of nude shots, mostly close-ups of private parts or couples photographing themselves in the mirror in much the same pose they would have struck beside some monument on their vacation. Once, Lynnette saw a set of negatives that must have been from an orgy—a dozen or more naked people. One was a group shot, like a class picture, taken beside a barbecue grill.

Cobb suggested that they might have been a nudist society, but Lynnette said nudists were too casual to take photographs of this kind. Those people weren't casual, she said.

Cobb was his real name, but people assumed it was a nickname—implying "rough as a cob." Rough in that sense, he thought, meant prickly, touchy, capable of great ups and downs. But Cobb knew he wasn't really like that. He guessed he hadn't lived up to his name, or grown into it, as people were said to do, and this left him feeling a little vague about himself. Cobb was twenty-eight, and he had had a number of girlfriends, but none like Lynnette. Ironically, he first met her when he took in a roll of film to be developed—his trip to Florida with Laura Morgan. He had dated Laura for about a year. They had driven down in her Thunderbird, spending a week at Daytona and then a couple of days at Disney World. They took pictures of the motels, the palm trees, the usual stuff. When he went to get the pictures, he struck up a conversation with Lynnette. From something she said, he realized she had seen his photos. He suddenly realized how trite they were. She saw pictures like that come through her machine every day. He felt his life take a turn, a hard jolt. They started going out—at first secretly, because it took Cobb a few weeks to work matters out with Laura. Laura wouldn't speak to him now when he ran into her in the hall at work. She was the type who would have wanted a wedding reception at the Holiday Inn, a ranch house in a cozy subdivision, church on Sunday. But Lynnette made him feel there were different ways to look at the world. She brought out something fresh and unexpected in him. She made him see that anything conventional—Friday-night strolls at the mall or an assortment of baked-potato toppings at a restaurant—was funny and absurd. They went around town together trading on that feeling, finding the unusual in the everyday, laughing at things most people didn't see the humor in. "You're just in love," his older brother, George, said when Cobb tried to explain his excitement.

Cobb went to his mother's for supper on Tuesdays, when his stepfather, Jim Dance, an accountant, was out at his Optimist Club meetings. Their house made Cobb uncomfortable. The furnishings defied classification. He hadn't grown up with any of it; it was all acquired after his mother, Gloria, married Jim. The walls were covered with needlepoint scenes of castles and reproductions of paintings of Amish families in buggies. The dining room had three curio cabinets, as well as Gloria's collection of souvenir coasters, representing all fifty states. In the living room, Early American clashed with low modern chairs upholstered with fat pillows. The room was filled with glass paperweights and glass globes and ashtrays, all swirling with colors like the planet Jupiter.

Cobb had come over to tell her he was going to marry Lynnette. His mother was overjoyed and gave him a hug. He could feel the flour on her hands making prints on his sweater.

"Is she a good cook?" she wanted to know.

"I don't know. We always eat out. I don't want any ham," he said, indicating the platter of ham on the table. "Do you want me to marry a good cook who will fatten me up or a lousy cook who'll keep me trim? What's your standard, Mom?"

Gloria forked a piece of ham onto his plate. "What are her people like?" She tore into the ham on her own plate.

"They're not in jail. They're not on welfare. They don't walk around with knives. They're not cross-eyed or anything."

"Why am I surprised?" she said.

"I don't even know them," Cobb said. "They're not from around here. She moved down here from Wisconsin when she was in high school. Her daddy worked at Ingersoll, but now he's been transferred to Texas."

Gloria smiled. "It'll be awful hot in Texas by June. Are they going to have a big shindig?"

"I don't think we'll get married there." Hesitantly, he said, "Lynnette's different, Mom. She's real serious and she doesn't like anything fancy."

"You ought to learn something about her people," Gloria said anxiously. "You never know."

"She's real nice. You'll like her."

Gloria poured more iced tea into her tall blue glass. "Well, it's about time you married," she said. "You know, when you were a baby you walked and talked earlier than any of the others. I had faith that you'd turn out fine, no matter what I did. But when you were about thirteen you went through a stage. You got real moody, and you slept all the time. After that, you never were the same lively boy again." Gloria bowed her head. "I never did understand that."

"That was probably when I found out about nuclear war. That's a real downer when it dawns on you."

"I never worry about nuclear war and such as that! The evil of the day is enough to keep me busy." Sullenly, she chomped on a biscuit.

"The evil of the day is where it's at, Mom," said Cobb.

After supper, when he returned from the bathroom, she was standing by a lamp, consulting the *TV Guide,* with the magazine's cover curled back. "On 'Moonlighting' they just talk-talk-talk," she said. "It drives you up the wall."

He flipped through her coffee-table books: *The Book of Barbecue, The Art of Breathing, The Perils of Retirement.* Everything was either an art or a peril these days. When he was growing up, his mother didn't read much. She was always too tired. She worked at a clothing store, and his dad drove a bread truck. There were four children. Nobody ever did anything especially outrageous or strange. Once, they went to the Memphis zoo, their only overnight family trip. In a petting-zoo area, a llama tried to hump his sister. Now his sister was living in Indiana, and his daddy was in Chicago with some woman.

Cobb noticed how people always seemed to be explaining themselves. If his stepfather was eating a hamburger, he'd immediately get defensive about cholesterol, even though no one had commented on it. Cobb never felt he had to explain himself. He was always just himself. But he was beginning to think there was a screwy little note, like a wormhole, in that attitude of his. He had a sweatshirt that said "PADUCAH, THE FLAT SQUIRREL CAPITAL OF THE WORLD." Lynnette was giving him a terrible time about it. The sweatshirt showed a flattened squirrel. It wasn't realistic, with fur and eyes and a fluffy tail or anything; it was just a black abstract shape.

"It's in extremely bad taste," Lynnette said. "I can't even stand to mash a bug. So I can't begin to laugh at a steamrollered creature."

It was the first thing that had really come between them, so he apologized and stopped wearing the sweatshirt. The shirt was just stating a fact, though. Driving down Broadway one day in the fall, Cobb counted three dead squirrels in three blocks. It was all those enormous oak trees.

"You're sweet," Lynnette said, forgiving him. "But sometimes, Cobb, you just don't think."

The incident made him wonder. It startled him that he had done something others would instantly consider so thoughtless. He wondered how much of his behavior was like that, how much Lynnette would discover about him that was questionable. He felt defenseless, in the dark. He didn't know how serious she was about getting married. She told him she couldn't ask her folks to throw a big wedding. It would make them nervous, she said. He figured they couldn't afford it, so he didn't press her. She never asked for much from him, but her reaction to the sweatshirt seemed blown out of proportion. He did not tell her he'd been out rabbit hunting a few times with his brother George.

Cobb saw a strange scene in the Wal-Mart. He had gone in to buy rubber boots to wear hunting on George's property, which was certain to be muddy after the recent thaw. Cobb was trying to find a pair of size-9 boots when he noticed one of the clerks, a teenager, calling to a couple over in the housewares aisle. "I've got something to tell y'all," she said. The boy and girl came over. They were about the same age as the clerk and were dressed alike in flannel shirts and new jeans. The clerk had on a pale-blue sweater and jeans and pink basketball shoes. She wore a work smock, unbuttoned, over her sweater.

"Well, we got married," she said in a flat tone, holding her hand up to show them her ring.

"I thought y'all were going to wait," said the girl, fiddling with a package of cassette tapes she was holding.

"Yeah, we got tired of waiting and we were setting around and Kevin said why not, this weekend's as good as any, so we just went ahead and did it."

"Kevin never could stand to wait around," said the boy, smiling faintly.

His girlfriend asked, "Did y'all go anywhere?"

"Just to the lake. We stayed all night in one of those motels." She pushed and pulled at her ring awkwardly, as if she was trying to think of something interesting to say about the trip. The boy and girl said they were going to Soul Night at Skate City, even though it was always so crowded. Another explanation, Cobb realized. They drifted off, the girl tugging at the boy's belt loop.

Cobb momentarily forgot what he had come for. His eyes roamed the store. A bargain table of snow boots, a table of tube socks. His mother and the CPA had been to Gatlinburg, where they saw tube socks spun in a sock store. She said it was fascinating. At a museum there, she saw a violin made from a ham can. Cobb was confused. Why weren't these three young people excited and happy? Why would anybody go all the way to Gatlinburg to see how tube socks were made?

George's place used to be in the country, but now a subdivision was working its way out in his direction and a nearby radio transmitter loomed skyward. When Cobb arrived, the dog, Ruffy, greeted him lazily from a sunny spot on the deck George had built onto the back of his house. Above a patch of grass beside a stump, a wind sock shaped like a goose was bobbing realistically, puffed with wind.

"Hey, Cobb," said George, opening the back door. "That thing fooled you, didn't it?" He laughed uproariously.

George worked a swing shift and didn't have to go in till four. His wife, Ceci, was at work, waitressing at the Cracker Barrel. Toys and clothes and dirty dishes were strewn about. Cobb stepped around a large aluminum turkey-roasting pan caked with grease.

After George put on his boots and jacket and located a box of shotgun shells, they headed through the fields back to a pond where George had set some muskrat traps. It was a biting, damp day. Cobb's new boots were too roomy inside, and the chill penetrated the rubber. Tube socks, he thought.

"I hate winter," George said. "I sure will be glad when it warms up."

Cobb said, "I like it O.K. I like all weather."

"You would."

"I like not knowing what it's going to be. Even when they say what it's going to be, you're still not sure."

"You ain't changed a bit, Cobb. I thought you were getting serious about that Johnson girl. I thought you were ready to settle down."

"What does that mean? Settle down?"

George just laughed at Cobb. George was nine years older, and he had always treated him like a child.

"If you're going to get married, my advice is not to expect too much," George said. "It's give-and-take. As long as you understand that, maybe you won't screw it up."

"What makes you think I might screw it up?"

George whooped loudly. "My God, Cobb, you could fuck up an *anvil*."

"Thanks for the vote of confidence."

A car horn sounded in the direction of George's house. "Hell. There she is, home early, wanting me to go after that shoulder we had barbecued at It's the Pits. Well, she can wait till we check these traps."

There was nothing in the traps. One of them had been sprung, apparently by a falling twig. Cobb felt glad. He thought he would tell Lynnette how he felt. Then he wondered if he was trying too hard to please her.

George said, "I was half expecting to catch a coyote."

"I thought coyotes lived out West." George pronounced "coyote" like "high oat," but Cobb pronounced the *e*. He didn't know which was right.

"They're moving this way," George said. "A fellow down the street shot one, and there was one killed up on the highway. I haven't seen any, but when an ambulance goes on, they howl. I've heard 'em." George formed his lips in a circle and howled a high "woo-woo" sound that gave Cobb chill bumps.

Cobb couldn't stop thinking about the teenage bride at the Wal-Mart. He invented some explanations for the behavior of those three teenagers: Maybe the girl wasn't great friends with the couple and so she was shy about telling them her news. Or maybe the guy was her former boyfriend and so she felt awkward telling about her marriage. Cobb remembered the smock she was wearing and the gray-green color of the cheap boots lined up on the wall behind her. When he told Lynnette about the girl and how empty she had seemed, Lynnette said, "She probably doesn't get enough exercise. Teenagers are in notoriously bad shape. All that junk food."

Lynnette was never still. She did warm-up and cool-down stretches. Even talking, she used her whole body. She was always ready to make love, even after the late movie on TV. At his apartment that weekend, they watched *The Tomb of Ligeia*. She wanted to make love during the scary parts.

It was almost one in the morning when the movie ended. She got up and brought yogurt back from the refrigerator—blueberry for him, strawberry for her. He liked to watch her eat yogurt. He shook his carton up until the yogurt was mixed and liquefied enough to drink, but she ate hers carefully—plunging her spoon into the cup vertically, all the way to the bottom, then bringing it up coated with plain yogurt and a bit of the fruit at the tip. He liked to watch her lick the spoon. George would probably say that this was a pleasure that wouldn't last, but Cobb felt he could watch Lynnette eat yogurt every day of their lives. There would be infinite variety in her actions.

Each of them seemed to have an off-limits area, a place they were afraid to reveal. He couldn't explain to her what it felt like to get up before dawn to go deer hunting—to feel for his clothes in the dark, to fortify himself with hot oats and black coffee, and then to plunge out in the cold, quiet morning, crunching frost with his hard boots. Hardly daring to breathe, he crouched in the blind, listening for a telltale snort and quiver, leaves rustling, a blur of white in the growing dawn, then a sudden clatter of hooves and a flash of joy.

There were some new pictures from work that Lynnette was telling him about now. "It was a Florida vacation," she said. "Old couple. Palm trees, blue water. But no typical shots—no Disney World, no leaping dolphins. Instead, there are these pictures of mud, pictures of tree roots and bark. Trees up close. And all these views of a small stucco house. Pictures of cars at motels, cars on the beach, cars in a parking lot at a supermarket. A sort of boardwalk trail in the woods. Then a guy holding up something small. You can't tell what it is."

"How small?" Cobb was trying to follow her description with his eyes closed.

"Like a quarter he's about to flip."

"Tell me one of your stories about the pictures."

"Let's see, they used to live there long ago. They raised their kids there, then moved far away. Now . . . they're retired now and so they go back, but everything's changed. The trees are bigger. There are more cars. The old motels look—well, old. Someone else owns their house, and the crepe myrtle and the azaleas she planted have grown into monsters. But she recognizes them—the same shade of purple, the same place she planted them by the driveway. They go and spy on the house and get chased away. Then they go to one of the parks where there's a boardwalk through the woods. A man raped her there once, when she was young and pretty, but after all these years going back there doesn't mean much. Then she loses her wedding ring and they retrace their steps, looking for it. They look through cracks in the boardwalk. They take all these pictures, in case the ring shows up in the pictures and they'll be able to tell later. Like in that old movie we saw, *Blow-Up?* Then they find the ring, and she photographs him holding it up. But it doesn't show up in the picture."

"That didn't happen to you, did it?"

"What?"

"Getting raped."

"No. I just made it up."

Turning over and opening his eyes, he said, "The way you do that, make up stories—you wouldn't change that, would you? When we're old, you should still do that."

"I hope I have a better job by then."

"No, I mean the way you can look at something and have a take on it. Not just take it for granted."

"It's no big deal," she said, squirming.

"It is to me."

She set her yogurt on the lamp table and suddenly pounded her pillow. "You know what I hate the most?" she said. "Those spread shots guys take of their wives or girlfriends. I think about those whenever I do my stretches for running." She shuddered. "It's disgusting—like something a gynecologist would see. It's not even sexy."

"Maybe you shouldn't look at them."

She ate some yogurt, and a strange look came on her face, as though she had just tasted a spot of mold. "You don't expect a nurse or a doctor to go to pieces when they see blood, so I should at least be able to look at those negatives. It's not personal. It's not my life—right?"

"Right. It's like TV or movies. It's not real." Cobb tried to comfort her, but she wriggled out of his grasp.

"It *is* real," she said.

Cobb kicked at the bedspread, rearranging it. "I don't always understand you," he said, reaching for her again. "I'm afraid I'll screw things up between us. I'm afraid I'll make some mistake and not know it till it's too late."

"What are you talking about?"

"I don't know, something my brother said."

"It's a mistake to listen to your relatives," she said, spooning the last of her yogurt. "They always believe the worst."

That weekend, he took Lynnette to his mother's for Sunday dinner. His mother would have liked it better if he had taken Lynnette to Sunday-morning church services first, but he couldn't do that to her. And he didn't want to start something false he'd have to keep up indefinitely.

"You're not going to believe her house," said Cobb on the way. Lynnette was wearing a black miniskirt, yellow tights, short black boots, a long yellow sweater. She looked great in yellow, like a yellow-legged shorebird with black feet he'd sometimes seen at the lake.

"Why are you so nervous about her house?" she asked. "All women have a unique way of relating to their house. I think it's interesting."

"This is more than interesting. It's a case study."

His mother was in the kitchen frying chicken. She wore an apron over her church clothes, a gray ensemble with flecks of pink scattered all over it. She said, "I would have stayed here this morning and had dinner ready for you, but we had this new young man at church giving a talk before the service. He came to work with the youth. He was so nice! The nicest young man you'd ever want to meet. He's called a Christian communicator." She laughed and rolled her hands in her apron.

Cobb tried to see his mother's house through Lynnette's eyes. All the glass objects made him suddenly see his mother's fragility. She was almost sixty years old, but she had no gray hair. It dawned on him that she must have been dyeing it for years. His mother didn't look at Lynnette or talk to her directly. She spoke to Lynnette through Cobb—a strange way to carry on a conversation, but something he had often noticed that people did.

Jim, the CPA, shooed them into the living room while Gloria cooked. Smoking a pipe, he fired questions at Lynnette as though he were interviewing her for the position of Cobb's wife: "Are you related to the Johnsons out on Jubilee Road? What does your daddy do? Who does your taxes?"

"I always do my own taxes," Lynnette said. "It's pretty simple."

"She's not but twenty-three," Cobb said to his stepfather. "You think she's into capital gains and tax shelters?"

At the table, Cobb remarked, "George called this morning and said he saw one of those coyotes out at his place. We're going out this afternoon."

"We're going to look for coyotes," Lynnette said enthusiastically. She pronounced "coyotes" with an *e* at the end, the way he did, so Cobb figured that was the correct way.

"Lynnette likes to go walking out in the fields," Cobb said. "She's a real nature girl."

Gloria said, "George is after me every summer to go back on that creek and look for blackberries, but now I wouldn't go for love nor money—not if there's wild coyotes."

"George says they're moving in because of all the garbage around," Cobb explained. "They catch rabbits out in the fields and then at night scoot into town and raid the garbage cans. They've got it made in the shade."

"Y'all better be careful," Gloria said.

"They don't attack people," Lynnette said. During the meal, she talked about her job. She said, "Sometimes I'll read about a wreck in the paper and then the pictures show up and I recognize the victim. The sheriff brings a roll in now and then when their equipment isn't working."

"I sure would hate that," said Gloria.

Lynnette, spearing a carrot slice, said, "We get amazing pictures—gunshot wounds and drownings, all mixed in with vacations and children. And the thing is, they're not unusual at all. They're everywhere, all the time. It's life."

Jim and Gloria nodded doubtfully, and Lynnette went on, "I couldn't sleep last night, thinking about some pictures that came in Friday—a whole roll of film of a murder victim on a metal table. The sheriff brought the roll in Friday morning and picked them up after lunch. I recognized the body from the guy's picture in the newspaper. I couldn't keep from looking."

"I saw that in the paper!" said Cobb's stepfather. "He owed money and the other guy got tired of waiting for it. So he got drunk and blasted him out. That's the way it is with some of these people—scum."

Lynnette dabbed her mouth with a mustard-yellow napkin and said, "It was weird to see somebody's picture in the newspaper and then see the person all strung out on a table with bullet holes in his head, and still be able to recognize the person. The picture they ran in the paper was a school picture. That was really sad. School pictures are always so embarrassing."

"Would you like some more chicken?" Gloria asked her. "Cobb, do you mean you're eating squash? I thought I'd never see the day."

That afternoon was pleasant and sunny, still nippy but with a springlike feel to the air. Cobb and Lynnette drove out to George's, stopping at Lynnette's apartment first so that she could change clothes. Cobb was glad to get out of his mother's house. He thought with a sinking feeling what it might be like in the coming years to go there regularly for Sunday dinner. He had never seen Lynnette seem so morbid, as though her whole personality had congealed and couldn't be released in its usual vivacious way.

George popped out on the deck as soon as they pulled up. The dog barked, then sniffed Lynnette.

"Ruffy was barking last night about eleven," George told them, before Cobb could introduce Lynnette. "I turned on the outside light, and Ruffy come running up to the deck, scared to death. There was this damned coyote out in the yard stalking that goose! It was fluttering in the wind and the coyote had his eye on it. Ruffy didn't know what to think." George pointed at the wind sock and made hulking, stalking motions with his body. He laughed.

"The goose looks absolutely real," Lynnette said, stooping to pet the dog. "I can see why a coyote would make a mistake."

"I tell you, it was the funniest thing," George said, overcome with his news. He stood up straight, containing his laughter, and then said, "Damn, Cobb, where'd you get such a good-looking girl?"

"At the gittin' place," Cobb said with a grin.

Ceci was there, along with the three kids. "Don't look at this mess," Ceci said when they went inside. "I gave up a long time ago trying to keep house." Ceci shoved at her two-year-old, Candy, who was tugging at her elbow. The little girl had about ten rubber bands wound tightly around her arm. As Ceci methodically worked them off, she said, "We're still eating on that shoulder, Cobb. I'll fix y'all a sandwich to take back to the creek if you want me to."

Cobb shook his head no. "Mom just loaded us up with fried chicken and I can't hardly walk."

Lynnette, who must have spotted the gun rack in the den, asked George, "Are you going to shoot the coyote?"

George shook his head. "Not on Sunday. I can't shoot him with a shotgun anyway. I'd need a high-powered rifle."

"I'd love to see a coyote," Lynnette said.

"Well, you can have him," said Ceci. "I don't want to see no coyotes."

"Maybe we'll run into one back at the creek," Cobb said to Lynnette in an assuring voice. He caressed her back protectively.

"They're probably all laying up asleep at this time of day," said George. "If I could get out there about six in the morning, then I might see one. But I can't get out of bed that early anymore."

"Lynnette gets up and runs six miles at daylight," Cobb said.

"That must be why she's so skinny," said George to Cobb, grinning to include Lynnette but not looking at her.

Ceci said, "I couldn't run that far if my life depended on it."

"You have to work up to it," said Lynnette.

Ceci finished removing the rubber bands from Candy's arm and said to the child, "We don't want to see no old coyote, do we, sugar?"

Ceci's tone with Lynnette bothered Cobb. It implied that Ceci felt superior for *not* being able to run six miles. Cobb hated the way people twisted around their own lack of confidence to claim it as a point of pride. Agitated, he hurried Lynnette on out to the fields for their walk.

George yelled after them, "Be sure to keep count of how many coyotes y'all see."

Lynnette hooked her hand onto Cobb's elbow, and they started out through a bare cornfield spotted with stubble. "I wish we'd see one," she said. "I'd talk to it. I bet you could tame it if you were patient enough. I could see myself doing that."

"I wouldn't be surprised if you could." He laughed and draped his arm around her shoulders.

Lynnette said, "I used to know a family that had a tame deer that came to a salt lick they put out. The deer got so tame it would come in the house and watch TV with them."

"I don't believe you!" Cobb said. "You're joking."

"No, I'm not! During hunting season they'd tie a big red ribbon around her neck."

The mud from earlier in the week had dried, but Cobb was wearing his new rubber boots. Lynnette had changed into black high-top shoes and jeans. She wasn't wearing a cap. He loved her for the way she could take the cold.

"Are you O.K.?" he said. "Is it too windy?"

"It's fine. It's just—" She gave a sigh of exasperation. "I shouldn't have talked about those pictures at your mother's."

"Yes, you should. It was exactly what she needed to hear."

"No, I should've kept my mouth shut. But her house brought out something in me. I wanted to shock her."

"I know what you mean. I always want to break all that glass." He booted a clod of dirt. "Families," he said disgustedly.

"It's all right," she said. "It's just one of those things." She bent to pick up a blue-jay feather. She twirled it in her fingers.

George had bush-hogged a path along the creek, and they followed it. When they started down into the creek, Cobb held on to Lynnette, drawing aside branches so they wouldn't slap her face. The water had subsided, and there were a few places of exposed gravel where they could walk. They made their way along the edge of the water for a while, then came to a part of the creek where the water was a few inches deep. Cobb carried Lynnette across, piggyback. She squealed and started to laugh. He sloshed through the puddle and carefully let her loose on the other side. She took a few steps, then squatted to examine some footprints.

"A coyote has been here!" she said excitedly. "Or maybe a fox."

The prints, like dog-paw rosettes, were indistinct. Cobb remembered seeing a red fox running through a field of winter wheat one spring when he was a child. The wheat was several inches high, and the fox made a path through it, leaving a wake like a boat. All Cobb could see was the path through the wheat and the tail surfacing occasionally. He had never seen a small animal travel so fast. It was like watching time, the fastest thing there was.

They sat down on a fallen log next to an animal den in the bank, beneath the exposed roots of a sycamore tree. Dried, tangled vines hung down near the opening, and a dirt path led down the bank to the creek bed.

"What did you really think of my mom?" Cobb asked, taking Lynnette's hand.

"The knickknacks made me sad." Lynnette pulled at some tough vines on the ground. Cobb made sure the vine wasn't poison ivy; he watched her slender fingers worry and work with the flexible stems as she spoke. She said, "I don't want my mom to have to deal with a wedding."

"Why not?"

"She couldn't handle it."

"We don't have to have anything big."

Lynnette pulled away from him. "She's one of these people who have to make lists and check and recheck things," she said. "You know—the type of person who has to go back and make sure they turned off the oven when they left the house? She's that way, only real bad. It prevents her from functioning. She can't make a phone call without checking the number ten times."

Lynnette's mother sounded nuts, Cobb decided. He had seen her picture. She was pretty, with a generous smile. Cobb had imagined her, somehow, as a delicate woman who nevertheless had strong ideas. Her smile reminded him of Dolly Parton before she lost all that weight.

Lynnette said, "When I was a senior in high school, my mom tried to kill herself. She took a lot of Valium. I was at band practice and I got a call at the principal's office to go to the hospital. It was a total surprise. I never would have imagined she'd do that." Lynnette was still twiddling the feather as she talked, even though Cobb had her hand, squeezing it.

"Why did she do it?" he asked.

"For a long time I blamed myself. I thought I hadn't shown her enough love. I was always so busy with band practice and all that teenage shit. And I remembered that I had upset her once when I said something mean about Dad. But then only a couple of years ago I found out my dad was shacking up back then with some woman from the country club. And looking back, I realized that all Mom had was that house. She used to work before we moved here, but then she couldn't get a job, and she didn't have many friends, and her house was all she had. I remember coming home and she'd be dusting all her knickknacks or pasting up wallpaper or arranging artificial flowers. I used to make fun of it, and I'd never help out. That's when it started, the way she'd pick over things and count them and try to keep track of them. I didn't think it was strange then." Lynnette shuddered in disgust. "I remember when the Welcome Wagon came—these two grinning fat women. They brought us some junk from the stores, coupons and little things. There was a tiny cedar chest from a furniture store. Your mother has one something like it, on that whatnot in the hall."

"One of her Gatlinburg souvenirs," Cobb said.

"I hated the Welcome Wagon. I thought they just came to check us over, to see if we were the country-club type. And we weren't. And then to think my dad would fool around with one of those country-club women—a golfer. I could have died of shame."

Cobb held Lynnette closely. "Every day I get to know you better," he said. "This is just the beginning." He flailed around for some comparison. "This is just the yogurt on top, and there's the fruit to come."

She giggled. "That's the silliest thing I ever heard! That's why I care about you. You're not afraid to say something that ridiculous. And you really mean it, too." She dropped the blue-jay feather, and it swirled in the water for a moment, then caught on a leaf. "But I'm afraid, Cobb. I'm afraid I might do something like she did—for different reasons."

"What reasons?"

"I don't know."

"But you're not like that."

"But I might get like that."

"No, you won't. That's crazy." Cobb caught himself saying the wrong word. "No, that's ridiculous," he said. "You won't get like that."

"When I started seeing those pictures at work I'd imagine pictures of my—if my mother had succeeded that day."

Cobb watched the feather loosen from the leaf and begin to float away in the little trickle of water in the creek bed. He tried to comprehend all that might happen to that feather as it wore away to bits—a strange thought. In a dozen years, he thought, he might look back on this moment and know that it was precisely when he should have stopped and made a rational decision to go no further, but he couldn't know that now.

She said, "Do you have any idea how complicated it's going to be?"

Cobb nodded. "That's what I like," he said confidently. "Down here, we just call that taking care of business."

Tufts of her hair fluttered slightly in the breeze, but she didn't notice. She couldn't see the way the light came through her hair like the light in spring through a leaving tree.

# Bumblebees

FROM *Love Life* (1989)

From the porch, Barbara watches her daughter, Allison, photographing Ruth Jones out in the orchard. Allison is home from college for the summer. Barbara cannot hear what they are saying. Ruth is swinging her hands enthusiastically, pointing first to the apricot tree and then to the peach tree, twenty feet away. No doubt Ruth is explaining to Allison her notion that the apricot and the peach cross-pollinate. Barbara doesn't know where Ruth got such an idea. The apricot tree, filled with green fruit, has heart-shaped leaves that twirl in clusters on delicate red stems. Earlier in the year, the tree in bloom resembled pink lace.

Allison focuses the camera on Ruth. Ruth's hand is curled in her apron. Her other hand brushes her face shyly, straightening her glasses. Then she lifts her head and smiles. She looks very young out there among the dwarf trees.

Barbara wonders if Ruth is still disappointed that one of the peach trees, the Belle of Georgia, which Barbara chose, is a freestone. "Cling-stones are the best peaches," Ruth said when they planted the trees. It is odd that Ruth had such a definite opinion about old-fashioned clingstones. Barbara agrees that clingstones are better; it was just an accident that she picked Belle of Georgia.

They were impatient about the trees. Goebel Petty, the old man Barbara and Ruth bought the small farm from two years before, let them come and plant the trees before the sale was final. It was already late spring. Barbara chose two varieties of peach trees, the apricot, two McIntoshes, and a damson plum, and Ruth selected a Sweet Melody nectarine, two Redheart plums, and a Priscilla apple. Ruth said she liked the names.

The day they planted the trees was breezy, with a hint of rain—a raw spring day. Mr. Petty watched them from the porch as they prepared the holes with peat moss. When they finished setting the balled-and-burlapped roots into the hard clay, he called out, "Y'all picked a bad place—right in the middle of that field. I had fescue planted there." Later, he said to them, "The wind will come rip-roaring down that hill and blow them trees over."

Barbara could have cried. It had been so long since she had planted things. She had forgotten that Georgia Belles were freestones. She didn't notice the fescue. And she didn't know about the wind then. After they moved in, she heard it rumble over the top of the hill, sounding like a freight train. There were few real hills in this part of Kentucky, but the house was halfway up a small one, at the end of a private road. The wind whipped across the hickory ridge. Barbara later discovered that particular kind of wind in a Wordsworth poem: "subterraneous music, like the noise of bagpipers on distant Highland hills."

Now, as Ruth and Allison reach the porch, Ruth is laughing and Allison is saying, "But they never teach you that in school. They keep it a secret and expect you to find it out for yourself." Allison tosses her hair and Barbara sees that several strands stick to the Vaseline she always has on her lips to keep them from chapping. Allison brushes the hair away.

"Ruth, do you remember what you said that day we planted those trees?" asks Barbara.

"No. What?" Ruth has a lazy, broad smile, like someone who will never lose her good humor—like Amelia Earhart, in one of those photographs of her smiling beside her airplane.

Barbara says, "You said you wondered if we'd last out here together long enough to see those trees bear."

"I reckon we're going to make it, then," Ruth says, her smile fading.

"Y'all are crazy," says Allison, picking a blade of grass from her bare knee. "You could go out and meet some men, but here you are hanging around a remote old farm."

Barbara and Ruth both laugh at the absurdity of the idea. Barbara is still bitter about her divorce, and Ruth is still recovering from the shock of the car accident three years before, when her husband and daughter were killed. Barbara and Ruth, both teachers at the new consolidated county high school, have been rebuilding their lives. Barbara took the initiative, saying Ruth needed the challenge of fixing up an old farmhouse. Together, they were able to afford the place.

"We're not ready for men yet," Ruth says to Allison.

"Maybe in the fall," Barbara says idly.

"Maybe a guy will come waltzing up this road someday and you can fight over him," Allison says.

"I could go for that Tom Selleck on 'Magnum, P.I.,'" Ruth says.

"Maybe he'll come up our road," Barbara says, laughing. She feels good about the summer. Even Allison seems cheerful now. Allison had a fight with her boyfriend at the end of the school year, and she has been moody. Barbara has been worried that having Allison around will be too painful for Ruth, whose daughter, Kimberly, had been Allison's age. Barbara knows that Ruth can't sleep until Allison arrives home safely at night. Allison works evenings at McDonald's, coming home after midnight. The light under Ruth's door vanishes then.

"I never heard of two women buying a farm together," Mr. Petty said when they bought the farm. They ignored him. Their venture was reckless—exactly what they wanted at that time. Barbara was in love with the fields and the hillside of wild apples, and she couldn't wait to have a garden. All her married life she had lived in town, in a space too small for a garden. Once she got the farm, she envisioned perennials, a berry patch, a tall row of nodding, top-heavy sunflowers. She didn't mind the dilapidated condition of the old house. Ruth was so excited about remodeling it that when they first went indoors she didn't really mind the cracked linoleum floors littered with newspapers and Mr. Petty's dirty clothes. She was attracted by the Larkin desk and the upright piano. The barn was filled with Depression-style furniture, which Ruth later refinished, painstakingly brushing the spindles of the chairs to remove the accumulated grime. The house was filthy, and the floor of an upstairs room was covered with dead bumblebees. Later, in the unfinished attic they found broken appliances and some unidentifiable automobile parts. Dirt-dauber nests, like little castles, clung to the rafters.

On the day they planted the fruit trees, they explored the house a second time, reevaluating the work necessary to make the place livable. The old man said apologetically, "Reckon I better get things cleaned up before you move in." As they watched, he opened a closet in the upstairs room with the bumblebees and yanked out a dozen hangers holding forties-style dresses—his mother's dresses. He flung them out the open window. When Barbara and Ruth took possession of the property two weeks later, they discovered that he had apparently burned the dresses in a trash barrel, but almost everything else was just as it had been—even the dead bumblebees littering the floor. Their crisp, dried husks were like a carpet of autumn leaves.

Ruth would not move in until carpenters had installed new plasterboard upstairs to keep bees from entering through the cracks in the walls. In the fall, Barbara and Ruth had storm windows put up, and Barbara caulked the cracks. One day the following spring, Ruth suddenly shrieked and dropped a skillet of grease. Barbara ran to the kitchen. On the windowpane was a black-and-yellow creature with spraddled legs, something like a spider. It was a huge bumblebee, waking up from the winter and sluggishly creeping up the pane. It was trapped between the window and the storm pane. When it started buzzing, Barbara decided to open the window. With a broom, she guided the bee out the door, while Ruth hid upstairs. After that, bees popped up in various windows, and Barbara rescued them. Ruth wouldn't go outdoors bareheaded. She had heard that a sting on the temple could be fatal. Later, when the carpenters came to hang Masonite siding on the exterior of the house, the bees stung them. "Those fellows turned the air blue with their cussing!" Ruth told friends. In the evenings, Barbara and Ruth could hear the wall buzzing, but the sounds gradually died away. One day after the carpenters left, Barbara heard a trapped bird fluttering behind the north wall of the living room, but she did not mention it to Ruth. This summer, Barbara has noticed that the bees have found a nook under the eaves next to the attic. Sometimes they zoom through the garden, like truck drivers on an interstate, on their way to some more exotic blossoms than her functional marigolds, planted to repel insects from the tomatoes.

Barbara's daughter has changed so much at college that having her here this summer is strange—with her cigarettes, her thick novels, her box of dog biscuits that she uses to train the dog. The dog, a skinny stray who appeared at the farm in the spring, prowls through the fields with her. Allison calls him Red, although he is white with brown spots. He scratches his fleas constantly and has licked a place raw on his foreleg. Allison has bandaged the spot with a sanitary napkin and some wide adhesive tape. Allison used to be impatient, but now she will often go out at midday with the dog and sit in the sun and stare for hours at a patch of weeds. Barbara once asked Allison what she was staring at. "I'm just trying to get centered," Allison said with a shrug.

"Don't you think Ruth looks good?" Barbara asks Allison as they are hoeing the garden one morning. Allison has already chopped down two lima bean plants by mistake. "I like to see her spending more time out-of-doors."

"She still seems jittery to me."

"But her color looks good, and her eyes sparkle now."

"I saw her poking in my things."

"Really? I'm surprised." Barbara straightens up and arches her back. She is stiff from stooping. "What on earth did she think she was doing?"

"It made me feel crummy," Allison says.

"But at least she's coming out of her shell. I wish you'd try to be nice to her. Just think how I'd feel if you'd been killed in a wreck."

"If you caught me snooping, you'd knock me in the head."

"Oh, Allison—"

Allison lights a cigarette in the shade of the sumac, at the edge of the runoff stream that feeds into the creek below. She touches a thistle blossom.

"Come and feel how soft this flower is, Mom," she says. "It's not what you'd expect."

Barbara steps into the shade and caresses the thistle flower with her rough hands. It is a purple powder puff, the texture of duck down. Honeybees are crawling on some of the flowers on the stalk.

Allison picks a stalk of dried grass with a crisp beige glob stuck on it. "Here's another one of those funny egg cases," she says. "It's all hatched out. I think it's from a praying mantis. I saw it in my biology book." She laughs. "It looks like a hot dog on a stick."

Every day Allison brings in some treasure: the cracked shell of a freckled sparrow egg, a butterfly wing with yellow dust on it, a cocoon on a twig. She keeps her findings in a cigar box that has odd items glued on the lid: screws, thimbles, washers, pencils, bobbins. The box is spray-painted gold. Allison found it in the attic. Barbara has the feeling that her daughter, deprived of so much of the natural world during her childhood in town, is going through a delayed phase of discovery now, at the same time she is learning about cigarettes and sex.

Now Allison crushes her cigarette into the ground and resumes her hoeing, scooping young growth from the dry dirt. Barbara yanks pigweed from the carrot row. It hasn't rained in two weeks, and the garden is drying up. The lettuce has shot up in gangly stalks, and the radishes went to seed long ago.

Barbara lays down her hoe and begins fastening up one long arm of a tomato plant that has fallen from its stake. "Let me show you how to pinch suckers off a tomato vine," she says to Allison.

"How do you know these things, Mom? Did you take biology?"

"No. I was raised in the country—don't you remember? Here, watch. Just pinch this little pair of leaves that's peeping up from where it forks. If you pinch that out, then there will be more tomatoes. Don't ask me why."

"Why?" says Allison.

In her garden diary, Barbara writes, "Thistles in bloom. Allison finds praying mantis egg carton." It is midmorning, and the three of them are having Cokes on the porch. Ruth is working on quilt pieces, sewing diamonds together to make stars. Her hands are prematurely wrinkled. "I have old-people hands and feet," she once told Barbara merrily. Ruth's face doesn't match. Even at forty, she has a young woman's face.

A moment ago, Allison said something to Ruth about her daughter and husband, and Ruth, after pausing to knot a thread and break it with her teeth, says now, "The reason I don't have their pictures scattered around the house is I overdid it at first. I couldn't read a book without using an old school picture of Kimberly for a bookmark. I had her pictures everywhere. I didn't have many pictures of him, but I had lots of her. Then one day I realized that I knew the faces in the pictures better than I knew my memories of their faces. It was like the pictures had replaced them. And pictures lie. So I put away the pictures, hoping my memories would come back to me."

"Has it worked?"

"A little bit, yes. Sometimes I'll wake up in the morning and her face will come to me for a second, and it's so vivid and true. A moment like that is better than seeing the pictures all the time. I'm thinking the memory will get clearer and clearer if I just let it come." Ruth threads her needle in one purposeful jab and draws the ends of the thread together, twisting them into a knot. "I was at my sister's in Nashville that night and we stayed out late and they couldn't get in touch with us. I can't forgive myself for that."

"You couldn't help it, Ruth," Barbara says impatiently. Ruth has told the story so many times Barbara knows it by heart. Allison has heard it, too.

As Ruth tells about the accident, Allison keeps her book open, her hand on the dog. She is reading *Zen and the Art of Motorcycle Maintenance*. It isn't just about motorcycles, she has told them.

Her needle working swiftly, Ruth says, "It was still daylight, and they had pulled up to the stop sign and then started to cross the intersection when a pickup truck carrying a load of turnips rammed into them. He didn't stop and he just ran into them. There were turnips everywhere. Richard was taking Kimberly to baton practice—she was a third-place twirler at the state championships the year before." Ruth smooths out the star she has completed and creases open the seams carefully with her thumbnail. "He died instantly, but she just lingered on for a week, in a coma. I talked to that child till I was blue in the face. I read stories to her. They kept saying she never heard a word, but I had to do it anyway. She might have heard. They said there wasn't any hope." Ruth's voice rises. "When Princess Grace died and they turned off her machines? They never should have done that, because there might have been a miracle. You can't dismiss the possibility of miracles. And medical science doesn't know everything. For months I had dreams about those turnips, and I never even saw them! I wasn't there. But those turnips are clearer in my mind than my own child's face."

The mail carrier chugs up the hill in his jeep. Allison stays on the porch, shaded by the volunteer peach tree that sprang up at the corner of the porch—probably grown from a seed somebody spit out once—until the jeep is gone. Then she dashes down to the mailbox.

"Didn't you hear from your boyfriend, hon?" Ruth asks when Allison returns.

"No." She has a circular and a sporting-goods catalogue, with guns and dogs on the front. She drops the mail on the table and plops down in the porch swing.

"Why don't you write him a letter?" Ruth asks.

"I wrote him once and he didn't answer. He told me he'd write me."

"Maybe he's busy working," Ruth says kindly. "If he's working construction, then he's out in the hot sun all day and he probably doesn't feel like writing a letter. Time flies in the summer." Ruth fans herself with the circular. "He's not the only fish in the sea, though, Allison. Plenty of boys out there can see what a pretty girl you are. The sweetest girl!" She pats Allison's knee.

Barbara sees the three of them, on the porch on that hillside, as though they are in a painting: Allison in shorts, her shins scratched by stubble in the field, smoking defiantly with a vacant gaze on her face and one hand on the head of the dog (the dog, panting and grinning, its spots the color of ruined meat); Ruth in the center of the arrangement, her hair falling from its bobby pins, saying something absurdly cheerful about something she thinks is beautiful, such as a family picture in a magazine; and Barbara a little off to the side, her rough hands showing dirt under the fingernails, and her coarse hair creeping out from under the feed cap she wears. (Her hair won't hold curl, because she perspires so much out in the sun.) Barbara sees herself in her garden, standing against her hoe handle like a scarecrow at the mercy of the breezes that barrel over the ridge.

In the afternoon, Barbara and Ruth are working a side dressing of compost into the soil around the fruit trees. The ground is so hard that Barbara has to chop at the dirt. The apricot is the only tree in the orchard with fruit, and some of the apricots are beginning to blush with yellow. But the apple leaves are turning brown. Caterpillars have shrouded themselves in the outermost leaves and metamorphosed already into moths.

Ruth says, "Imagine a truckload of apricots. It almost seems funny that it would be turnips. You might think of apples or watermelons. You see trucks of watermelons all the time, and sometimes you hear about them rolling all over the highway when there's a wreck. But turnips!" She picks up her shovel and plunges it into the ground. "God was being original," she says.

"The nectarine tree looks puny," Barbara says abruptly. "I had my doubts about growing nectarines."

"That man that ran into them in his turnip truck? They said he didn't look. He just plowed right into them. The police swore he hadn't been drinking, but I believe he was on dope. I bet you anything—"

Suddenly screams waft up from the house. It is Allison shrieking. Barbara rushes down the path and sees her daughter in front of the house shaking her head wildly. Then Allison starts running, circling the house, pulling at her hair, following her own voice around the house. Her hair was in ponytail holders, but when she reappears it is falling down and she is snatching the bands out of her hair. As she disappears around a corner again, Barbara yells, "Mash it, Allison! Mash that bee against your head!"

Allison slams to a stop in front of the porch as Barbara catches her. In a second Barbara smacks the bumblebee against the back of her daughter's head.

"He was mad at me," sobs Allison. "He was chasing me."

"It's that perfume you've got on," says Barbara, searching through Allison's hair.

"It's just bath oil. Oh, my head's stung all over!"

"Be still."

Barbara grabs one of Allison's cigarettes from the package in her shirt pocket. She pushes Allison up onto the porch, where she sits down, trembling, in the wicker rocker. Barbara tears the paper of the cigarette and makes a paste out of tobacco shreds and spit in the palm of her hand. She rubs the paste carefully into the red spots on Allison's scalp.

"That will take the sting out," she says. "Now just relax."

"Oh, it hurts," says Allison, cradling her head in her hands.

"It won't last," Barbara says soothingly, pulling her daughter close, stroking her hair. "There, now."

"What's wrong with Allison?" asks Ruth, appearing from behind the lilac bush as though she has been hiding there, observing the scene. Barbara keeps holding Allison, kissing Allison's hair, watching the pain on Ruth's face.

After that, Ruth refuses to wear her glasses outdoors, because the tiny gold *R* decorating the outer corner of the left lens makes her think a bee is trying to get at her eye. But now the bees are hiding from the rain. For two days, it has been raining steadily, without storming. It rarely rains like this, and Barbara's garden is drowning. In the drizzle, she straightens the Kentucky Wonder vines, training them up their poles. The peppers and peas are turning yellow, and the leaves of the lima beans are bug-eaten. The weeds are shooting up, impossible to hoe out in the mud. The sunflowers bend and break.

With the three of them cooped up, trying to stay out of each other's way, Barbara feels that the strings holding them together are both taut and fragile, like the tiny tendrils on English-pea vines, which grasp at the first thing handy. She's restless, and for the first time in a long while she longs for the company of a man, a stranger with sexy eyes and good-smelling aftershave. The rain brings out nasty smells in the old house. Despite their work on the place, years of filth are ingrained in it. Dust still settles on everything. Ruth discovers a white mold that has crept over the encyclopedia. "An outer-space invasion," Allison says gleefully. "It's going to eat us all up." Ruth bakes cookies for her, and on Friday evening, when Allison has to work, Ruth videotapes "Miami Vice" for her. Allison's tan is fading slightly in the gloomy weather, and her freckles remind Barbara of the breast of a thrush.

The creek is rising, and the dog whines under the front porch. Allison brings him onto the enclosed back porch. His bandage is muddy and shredded. She has the mail with her, including a letter from her father, who lives in Mobile. "Daddy wants me to come down this fall and live," she tells Barbara.

"Are you going?"

"No. I've made a decision," Allison says in the tone of an announcement.

"What, honey?" Ruth asks. She is mixing applesauce cake, from a recipe of her grandmother's she promised to make for Allison.

"I'm going to quit school for a year and get a job and an apartment in Lexington."

"Lexington?" Barbara and Ruth say simultaneously. Lexington is more than two hundred miles away.

Allison explains that her friend Cindy and she are going to share an apartment. "It'll be good for us to get out in the real world," she says. "School's a drag right now."

"You'll be sorry if you don't finish school, honey," Ruth says.

"It doesn't fit my needs right now." Allison picks up her music and heads for the piano. "Look, think of this as junior year abroad, O.K.? Except I won't be speaking French."

Barbara jerks on her rain slicker and galoshes. In the light drizzle, she starts digging a trench along the upper side of the garden, to divert the water away from it. The peppers are dying. The cabbages are packed with fat slugs. She works quickly, fighting the rivulets of water that seep through the garden. The task seems useless, but belligerently she goes on, doing what she can.

Ruth comes slogging up the muddy path in her galoshes, blinking at the rain. She's not wearing her glasses. "Are you going to let her go to Lexington?" Ruth asks.

"She's grown," Barbara says.

"How can you let her go?"

"What can I do about it?"

Ruth wipes the raindrops from her face. "Don't you think she's making a mistake?"

"Of course, God damn it! But that's what children are—people with a special mission in life to hurt their parents."

"You don't have to tell me about hurt, Barbara. Do you think *you* know anything about that?"

Furiously, Barbara slaps the mud with her hoe. Next year she will relocate the garden above the house, where the drainage will be better.

The next day, the rain lets up, but it is still humid and dark, and a breeze is stirring over the ridge, as though a storm is on its way. Allison is off from work, and she has been playing the piano, picking out nonsense compositions of her own. Barbara is reading. Suddenly, through the picture window, Barbara sees Ruth in the orchard, pumping spray onto a peach tree. Barbara rushes outside, crying, "Ruth, are you crazy!"

The cloud of spray envelops Ruth. Barbara yells, "No, Ruth! Not on a windy evening! Don't spray against the wind!"

"The borers were going to eat up the peach tree!" Ruth cries, letting the sprayer dangle from her hand. She grabs a blob of peach-tree gum from the bark and shows it to Barbara. "Look!"

"The wind's blowing the spray all over you, not the tree," Barbara says sharply.

"Did I do wrong?"

"Let's go inside. The storm's coming."

"I wanted to help," Ruth says, in tears. "I wanted to save the tree."

Later, when Barbara and Allison are preparing supper and Ruth is in the shower washing off the insecticide, Allison says, "Mom, when did you realize you weren't in love with Daddy anymore?"

"The exact moment?"

"Yeah. Was there one?"

"I guess so. It might have been when I asked him to go have a picnic with us over at the lake one day. It was the summer you were a lifeguard there, and I thought we could go over there and be together—go on one of those outdoor trails—and he made some excuse. I realized I'd been married to the wrong man all those years."

"I think I know what you mean. I don't think I'm in love with Gerald anymore." Studiously, Allison chops peppers with the paring knife.

Barbara smiles. "You don't have to be in a hurry. That was my trouble. I was in a hurry. I married too young." Hastily, she adds, "But that's O.K. I got you in the bargain."

Allison nods thoughtfully. "What if you wanted to get married again? What would you do about Ruth?"

"I don't know."

"You'd have to get a divorce from *her* this time," Allison says teasingly.

"It would be hard to sell this place and divide it up." Barbara is not sure she could give it up.

"What's going on with Ruth, anyway?" Allison is asking. "She's so weird."

"She used to be worse," Barbara says reassuringly. "You remember how she was at first—she couldn't even finish the school year."

"I didn't want to tell you this, but I think Ruth's been pilfering," Allison says. "I can't find my purple barrette and that scarf Grandma gave me. I bet Ruth took them." Allison looks straight out the window at the water washing down the runoff stream, and a slight curl of satisfaction is on her lips. Barbara stares at the dish of bread-and-butter pickles she is holding and for a moment cannot identify them. Images rush through her mind—chocolate chips, leftover squash, persimmons.

That night, Allison has gone out to a movie, and Barbara cannot sleep. The rain is still falling lightly, with brief spurts of heavy rain. It is past midnight when Allison's car drives up. The dog barks, and Ruth's light switches off, as if this were all some musical sequence. Earlier in the evening, Barbara glimpsed Ruth in her room, shuffling and spreading her pictures on the bed like cards in a game of solitaire. She keeps them in a box, with other mementos of Kimberly and Richard. Barbara wanted to go to her with some consolation, but she resisted, as she resisted mothering Allison too closely. She had the feeling that she was tending too many gardens; everything around her was growing in some sick or stunted way, and it made her feel cramped. As she hears Allison tiptoeing down the hall, Barbara closes her eyes and sees contorted black motorcycles, shiny in the rain.

Early the next morning, Allison calls them outdoors. "Look how the creek's up," she cries in a shrill voice.

The creek has flooded its banks, and the bridge is underwater, its iron railing still visible.

"Oh, wow," Allison says. "Look at all that water. I wish I was a duck."

"It's a flood," Barbara says matter-of-factly. Her garden is already ruined, and she has decided not to care what happens next.

At breakfast, a thunderous crack and a roar send them out to the porch. As they watch, the bridge over the creek tears loose and tumbles over, the railing black against the brown, muddy stream. The violence of it is shocking, like something one sees in the movies.

"Oh, my God," Ruth says quietly, her fingers working at her shirt.

"We're stranded!" says Allison. "Oh, wow."

"Oh, Lord, what will we do?" Ruth cries.

"We'll just have to wait till the water goes down," Barbara says, but they don't hear her.

"I won't have to work," Allison says. "I'll tell McDonald's I can't get there, unless they want to send a rescue helicopter for me. Or they could send the McDonald's blimp. That would be neat."

"Isn't this sort of thrilling?" Barbara says. "I've got goose bumps." She turns, but Ruth has gone indoors, and then Allison wanders off with the dog.

Barbara heads out through the field. From the edge of the woods, she looks out over the valley at the mist rising. In the two years Barbara and Ruth have lived here, it has become so familiar that Barbara can close her eyes and see clearly any place on the farm—the paths, the stand of willows by the runoff stream that courses down the hill to feed the creek. But sometimes it suddenly all seems strange, like something she has never seen before. Today she has one of those sensations, as she watches Allison down by the house playing with the dog, teaching him to fetch a stick. It is the kind of thing Allison has always done. She is always toying with something, prodding and experimenting. Yet in this light, with this particular dog, with his frayed bandage, and that particular stick and the wet grass that needs mowing—it is something Barbara has never seen before in her life.

She continues up the hill, past the woods. On the path, the mushrooms are a fantastic array, like a display of hats in a store—shiny red Chinese parasols, heavy globular things like brains, prim flat white toadstools. The mushrooms are so unexpected, it is as though they had grown up in a magical but clumsy compensation for the ruined garden. Barbara sidesteps a patch of dangerous-looking round black mushrooms. And ahead on the path lies a carpet of bright-orange fungi, curled like blossoms. She reaches in the pocket of her smock for her garden diary.

On Tuesday the sun emerges. The yard is littered with rocks washed out of the stream, and the long grass is flattened. The bumblebees, solar-activated, buzz through the orchard.

From the orchard, Barbara and Ruth gaze down the hill. The run-off stream still rushes downhill, brown and muddy, and Barbara's trench above the garden has widened.

"The apricots are falling off," Ruth says, picking up a sodden, bug-pocked fruit.

"It's O.K.," Barbara says, toeing the humps of a mole tunnel.

"I thought I'd fix up a room for Allison so she won't have to sleep in the living room," Ruth says. "I could clean out the attic and fix up a nice little window seat."

"You don't need to do that, Ruth. Don't you have something of your own to do?"

"I thought it would be nice."

"Allison won't be around that long. Where is she, anyway? I thought she was going to try to wade the creek and meet her ride to work."

"She was exploring the attic," Ruth says, looking suddenly alarmed. "Maybe she's getting into something she shouldn't."

"What do you mean, Ruth? Are you afraid she'll get in your box?"

Ruth doesn't answer. She is striding toward the house, calling for Allison.

Allison appears on the porch with a dusty cloth bundle she says she has found under a loose floorboard in the attic.

"Burn it!" Ruth cries. "No telling what germs are in it."

"I want to look inside it," Allison says. "It might be a hidden treasure."

"You've been reading too many stories, Allison," says Barbara.

"Take it out in the driveway where you can burn it, child," Ruth says anxiously. "It looks filthy."

Allison fumbles with the knot, and Ruth stands back, as though watching someone light a firecracker.

"It's just a bunch of rags," says Barbara skeptically. "What we used to call a granny bag."

"I bet there's a dead baby in here," says Allison.

"Allison!" Ruth cries, covering her face with her hands. "Stop it!"

"No, let her do it, Ruth," says Barbara. "And you watch."

The rags come apart. They are just stockings wound tightly around each other—old stockings with runs. They are disintegrating.

"My old granny used to wear her stockings till they hung in shreds," Barbara says breezily, staring at Ruth. Ruth stares back with frightened eyes. "Then she'd roll them up in a bundle of rags, just like this. That's all it is."

"Oh, crap," says Allison, disappointed. "There's nothing in here."

She drops the stockings on the damp gravel and reaches in her pocket for a cigarette. She strikes a match, holds it to her cigarette and inhales, then touches the match to the rags. In the damp air, the flame burns slowly, and then the rags suddenly catch. The smell of burning dust is very precise. It is like the essence of the old house. It is concentrated filth, and Allison is burning it up for them.

# IV

# Beginnings

*The radio, girl detective books, and Louisa May Alcott were my early escapes from the isolation of country life. I wanted to go to radioland. I wanted to drive a roadster and solve mysteries. I couldn't sing or play a guitar, but Alcott showed me the true direction. She and her energetic character Jo March wrote books.*

—BAM

# FROM *The Girl Sleuth* (1975)

Writing is the closest you can come to being a girl detective in real life at that age. I wrote the Carson Girls series, and I still have *The Carson Girls Go Abroad*. A glance at my little mystery story reveals no child prodigy, no creative imagination blossoming, only a frustrated but nevertheless determined child who was busily resisting the Honey Bunch/Junior Miss model. My little story reveals a desperate dependence on escapist fantasies. It was an amalgamation of Nancy Drew, the Danas, the Bobbseys, Vicki Barr, and Cherry Ames. I couldn't even think of an original name for my girls. I took it simply from Nancy Drew's father, Carson Drew.

*The Carson Girls Go Abroad* was about twins, Sue and Jean, whose father was a famous detective and whose mother was significantly nonexistent. The girls had a modest flair for solving mysteries. Jean was the serious, practical twin—grimly mature and already latched to a boyfriend. Sue, the more adventurous, tomboyish twin (a thin projection of myself), was resentful of her sister's boyfriend and had no plans to marry. She wanted to be an airline hostess and she bought a book, *How to Become a Stewardess in Five Easy Lessons*. Jean planned to be a nurse: she was more feminine, good at making beds and fixing food. As the book opened they were choosing their careers and celebrating their eighteenth birthdays with a surprise party (with ice cream, dainty sandwiches, pickles, candies, puddings, cakes, and pies) and a trip to the State Fair in Louisville (with cotton candy and candied apples and lemonade) where Sue had a narrow escape from the Snake Woman. Nothing happened to Jean, who was protected by her boyfriend.

The mystery was about a stolen stamp collection (the fictional version of my own dime-store album). A prominent citizen had his valuable collection stolen but it was mysteriously returned the next day. Then the Carson Girls heard a burglar in their own house and soon afterward discovered that one of their stamps, an odd Romanian portrait of a bespectacled man whose hairline was askew, had faded. The Carson Girls, according to the newspaper, theorized that a ring of counterfeiters was operating in the vicinity, "borrowing" stamp collections and making copies of valuable stamps.

In the meantime, the Carson Twins went on a trip to France with their father and their French maid, Mlle. Bleax (my conception of a French name). Jean's boyfriend piloted his own private plane across the ocean and Sue played air hostess. Jean wore a helmet and goggles and sat in the cockpit with her boyfriend and also played ship's nurse. When they got to France, they toured the provinces and saw the famous Percheron horses Sue had read about in geography. While they were in France, they became curious about a stamp shop and soon became involved in a fascinating set of adventures. As it turned out, the counterfeiting ring was operating right there in provincial France, and the Carson Girls solved the mystery, mainly because of Sue's daring and logical mind. Jean was too busy with her boyfriend to contribute much. The twins won a fabulous reward for catching the crooks, and with the reward they would be able to go to airline hostess and nursing school.

# Reaching the Stars: My Life as a Fifties Groupie

Featured in the *New Yorker,* May 26, 1986

In the late nineteen-fifties, when I was a teenager, I held a national office, published a journal, was interviewed on television and radio, and travelled widely to places like Cincinnati and Detroit and Blytheville, Arkansas. I was a shy, backward, anti-social country kid living on a farm near Mayfield, Kentucky, a hundred and fifty miles from the nearest city, Nashville, but I was ambitious and determined to hit the big time—or at least meet somebody famous. The first star I met was Gene Autry's dumpy sidekick in the floppy hat, Smiley Burnette. I was about thirteen when he came to town for a show at the Princess Theatre. You could buy a picture of him for a dollar or pay a dollar to have your picture taken with him. Smiley hooked his arm around my shoulders and posed me for the camera, but when I asked him to sign my autograph book he snarled, "I don't autograph nothing but the pictures for sale."

The second star on my life list was Tony Martin, the crooner who sang "There's No Tomorrow" and was married to Cyd Charisse. He came to town to publicize Tony Martin suits, which were manufactured by the Merit Clothing Company, the local factory where my mother worked. She and I went to the Hall Hotel and gawked at him as he got off the elevator. He was surprisingly short.

But from the time I was a child singers impressed me more than movie stars did. I listened to the radio constantly. Perry Como and Patti Page dominated the daytime airwaves in those days, but late on Saturday nights the radio blared out strange music: "John R here, way down South in Dixie, 1510 on the dial, fifty thousand watts of joy! WLAC, Nashville, Tennessee."

John R played raunchy, stomping-and-shouting blues numbers by black singers like Big Bill Broonzy and Memphis Slim and Little Junior Parker, Little Walter, T-Bone Walker, Elmore James, and Big Joe Turner. The theme song on John R's show was "Dig Those Blues," a slow, rolling piano blues. John R was white, but he sounded black. WLAC advertised mysterious products—Silky Strate, White Rose petroleum jelly, "lifetime" Bibles, and soul medallions. My parents and I stayed up late and turned the radio up loud, staring in amazement at our huge console, as big as a jukebox, as it blared out wild music. John R and another white disk jockey, Gene Nobles, who had a show earlier in the evening, played what they called "droopy-drawers songs" (the slow stuff) and "mean, low-down songs." The mean ones sounded dangerous. I could feel the power of big men stomping into their houses and dragging out their women when they'd been untrue. In the droopy-drawers songs, they cried their hearts out. John R talked through the songs: "Have mercy, baby! . . . Come on, honey. . . . Man, don't that tear you up?" Ruth Brown's "Mama, He Treats Your Daughter Mean" tore me up bad.

Gene Nobles specialized in bland white imitations of these risqué rhythm-and-blues songs—especially "cover" versions from Dot Records, owned by his sponsor, Randy's Record Shop in Gallatin, Tennessee. Randy's artists included Pat Boone and the Fontane Sisters. His star group was the Hilltoppers.

The Hilltoppers, I decided, represented everything I had ever felt and dreamed about my life. As I picked blackberries or hoed vegetables in the scorching morning sun, I longed to travel and see the world. The turbulent music on WLAC expressed my frustration, and the Hilltoppers made me feel there was an answer—some release from the cycle of the seasons, the planting and harvesting. (I didn't see the glamour in farm life then.) The Hilltoppers' style wasn't exactly Big Bill Broonzy and it wasn't rock and roll yet either—it was sort of like what would happen if Perry Como got hold of some Big Bill Broonzy material—but it grabbed me and shook me up like a religious vision, a calling. This was mainly because the group was from Kentucky. The Hilltoppers were students at Western Kentucky State College, in Bowling Green, where the sports teams were called the Hilltoppers. A Kentucky singing quartet had achieved national fame! The only famous person from Kentucky I had ever heard of besides Abraham Lincoln was Arthur Lake, who played Dagwood in the Blondie-and-Dagwood movies.

The Hilltoppers' first hit was "Trying," a ballad written by one of the

original members of the group, Billy Vaughn, and later on they were award-
ed a gold record for an old Johnny Mercer song, "P.S. I Love You." With the
arrival of rock and roll, they started recording livelier imitations of black
tunes—"The Door Is Still Open," "Only You," and Ruth Brown's "Tear-
drops from My Eyes." On some of the songs you could hear a rock-and-
roll saxophone or a boogie piano, and even a bass vocal "bum-bum-bum"
against the "do-do-do-do-do-do-do" background harmony. But their style
was born in an earlier time. Jimmy Sacca, the lead singer, had a strong, dis-
tinctive baritone that strained to be a tenor—a cross between matinée-idol
crooning and big-band swing. He was a dreamboat.

   I started a Hilltoppers fan club, and the day that the package of mem-
bership cards, autographed glossy eight-by-ten photographs, and buttons
("I AM A HILLTOPPERS FAN") arrived was the turning point of my life.
I advertised for members in Betty Burr's fan-club column in a New York
fan magazine, and for a time my whole life revolved around the mailbox
and the radio. I corresponded with a Hilltoppers fan on Long Island who
monitored all of New York's radio stations, flipping the dial ceaselessly
after school. She constructed elaborate charts, on graph paper, of Hilltoppers airplay. Over the next year, I diligently worked my way up through
the Hilltoppers' power structure, mostly by pestering the Hilltoppers' secretary in Gallatin and trying to impress her and the Hilltoppers with my
devotion so I could get to meet them, and at last became National President
of the Hilltoppers Fan Clubs. As National President, I wrote and mailed a
newsletter to three hundred fan-club chapters on an addressographed list—
mostly addresses in the exotic environs of New York City. One of my jobs
as National President was to conduct request campaigns to d.j.s. I wrote to
d.j.s in all the big cities:

   MEMO FROM THE NATIONAL HILLTOPPERS FAN CLUB
   To: ED BONNER, KXOK, ST. LOUIS
      Please play "Do the Bop," the new Hilltoppers record, on your
   show. It's a big hit! Thank you very much.
   —"Till Then"
   BOBBIE MASON, National President

("Till Then" was one of the Hilltoppers' early recordings.)
   I prayed for their records to be hits. After reading Norman Vincent

Peale, I applied the power of positive thinking to a tune called "Searching," so that the Hilltoppers might earn another gold record.

My memories of the Hilltoppers are vague. I actually got to know them very well, and if they walked into my house today they would be thoroughly familiar to me. I'm sure Jimmy Sacca would give me one of his big bear hugs and we would fall easily into joking conversation. We were friends. But even though I spent a lot of time with the Hilltoppers during my high-school years I knew very little about them. I didn't ask about their backgrounds—their parents, brothers and sisters, schooling, and the rest. Background had no meaning to me, because I hadn't been anywhere; where I was going was what counted. The Hilltoppers were stars, brilliant presences, and my function was to promote their fame, so that their glow would rub off on me, like the luminescent stuff from lightning bugs.

In *Hilltoppers Highlights,* the fan-club journal that I wrote and published, I reported what I knew of the Hilltoppers:

"Jimmy Sacca stands six-two and has black hair and brown eyes, loves steak, pizza, spaghetti (you can tell he's Italian!), and when time permits this ex-football player's hobby is miniature golf. He is also accomplished on the clarinet and saxophone. Jimmy comes from Lockport, N.Y.

"Blond, pug-nosed Don McGuire, the ladies' man of the Hilltoppers, surprises everybody with his deep bass voice. He went to Western Ky. on a basketball scholarship and became one of their star players. He planned to be a dentist until stardom beckoned. He hails from Hazard, Ky., is five-eleven, collects sports clothes, plays piano and drums.

"The clown of the Toppers, Seymour ('Sy') Spiegelman of Seneca Falls, N.Y., was Jimmy's roommate at college. He is five-eight, weighs 178, and has black hair and brown eyes. His hobbies are drawing and fishing, and he loves football, swimming, and tennis.

"Eddie Crowe, a friend of Jimmy's from Lockport, replaces Billy Vaughn, the original member of the group who penned their first hit, 'Trying.' Eddie lettered in four sports in high school. He's single, girls! In the Hilltoppers' show, he plays the trumpet and does comic impressions—James Cagney, James Stewart, Robert Mitchum."

In time, my mother and I travelled to Cincinnati to see the Hilltoppers perform. It was my first trip anywhere. The ride took sixteen hours, overnight, on a bus that jolted miserably around the curves along the Ohio River. I remember waking up at each stop and checking the town on the map, so I could say I had been there. I was so excited I couldn't eat, even though the group performing was not entirely the original Hilltoppers. While Don and Sy were in the Army (they'd been drafted, and this was just after the Korean War), Jimmy hired a series of replacements. The Hilltoppers were appearing with Barney Rapp's orchestra at the Castle Farms Ballroom in Cincinnati. It was a huge suburban dance hall that was packed with glamorous couples who drank liquor. Women smuggled in whiskey bottles under their wraps: I saw them do it. The Hilltoppers bounded onstage, wearing their red sweaters and beanies with "W" on them—the football sweaters and freshman beanies from their college. (I had ordered a beanie for myself from Western and had considered wearing it that evening, but it didn't go with my taffeta dress and borrowed rhinestone jewelry.) Their act was sensational. They sang all their hits, including "P.S. I Love You," "From the Vine Came the Grape," "I'd Rather Die Young," and my favorite, "Poor Butterfly." Their sound was principally Jimmy Sacca's lead backed up with a simple "doo-wah" harmony. In their sweaters and baggy gray flannels, they swayed from side to side in unison, sort of like cheerleaders. I learned later that their moves had been choreographed. At intermission, I was allowed to go backstage to meet my idols, and during their second show they introduced me proudly to the audience. In the second show, they wore tuxedos.

After the show, they bought my mother and me Cokes and potato chips. The Hilltoppers didn't drink, but they smoked and drove a Cadillac. They drove us back to the hotel in their sky-blue 1954 Fleetwood, and Jimmy Sacca gave me forty dollars to help operate the fan club.

At school, the Hilltoppers were my secret. I had few friends, because I lived out in the country, and also because I was shy and not interested in suntans and pajama parties. I read a lot: "The Search for Bridey Murphy," "The Practical Way to a Better Memory," "The Report on Unidentified Flying Objects."

The next time we saw the Hilltoppers was in Vincennes, Indiana. Mama and I were walking down the main street from Woolworth's to our hotel there when we spotted the Cadillac. It was the Hilltoppers, arriving in town for their show. I waved at them, and the Cadillac pulled over. Jimmy was driving.

"It's us again!" Mama cried. Jimmy hopped out and hugged us. While the other members of the group—more replacements—checked into the hotel, Jimmy took us to eat at a grill down the street. We sat in a booth and ordered pork chops with applesauce and French fries.

"Well, what did you think when you heard the news?" Jimmy asked us worriedly.

"I was shocked," I said lamely. I didn't know what to say. I had seen the newspaper: one of the various substitute Hilltoppers had been arrested for possession of marijuana. My mother and I had never heard of marijuana, so the news didn't really faze us.

"I was at the racetrack," Jimmy said. "And the P.A. system called my name. I had no idea he was using the stuff. I fired him so fast he didn't know what hit him."

"He wasn't one of the real Hilltoppers," I said loyally. I longed for the day when Sy and Don would rejoin the group. I knew I would like them, because they looked like such cutups in their pictures. Jimmy and Don and Seymour and Billy, the original group, were all family men, with wives and children.

After we finished eating, Jimmy lit up a Pall Mall, and Mama said, "If y'all come to Mayfield, I'll get you some free Tony Martin suits from the Merit."

"How will you do that?" I asked, surprised.

"Willie Foster will let me have them," Mama said confidently.

Willie Foster was the president of the Merit Clothing Company. We had been to his farm for the annual employees' picnic—fried chicken and roasting ears and washtubs of cold drinks. His farm was like a plantation—a magnificent place with acres of pasture and horses and a little lake with rowboats.

"We'd love to come to Mayfield," Jimmy said. "But you don't have to get us any suits."

"Well, you come, and I'll cook you up a big supper and get you some suits," Mama said. "I used to sew labels in coats, but the foreman told me to slow down because I was making more than the men. So I quit. I could make a dollar an hour, I was so fast." She laughed. "But with all the farm work I didn't have time to sew labels anyway."

"Well, since you quit, they won't let you have any free suits," I argued.

"Oh, Willie wasn't mad at me," Mama said. "Willie's good to his workers. And if the Hilltoppers wore his suits, that would be good publicity."

"Well, gee, Mrs. Mason," Jimmy said. "That would be swell."

He bought us strawberry sundaes and then we went to the show.

After that, Mama and I travelled many places to see the Hilltoppers. We went to Centralia, Illinois; Princeton, Indiana; Herrin, Illinois; Blytheville, Arkansas; and Cape Girardeau, Missouri, as well as St. Louis and Detroit. Daddy had to milk the cows and couldn't go. The Hilltoppers always welcomed us. Don and Sy got out of the Army and took their rightful places in the group. They were boyish, modest, and funny. I adored them. Being a groupie in the fifties was as innocent as the Girl Scouts. The Hilltoppers never even swore around me, except once—the day Jimmy forgot the words to "My Cabin of Dreams," which they lip-synced on Johnny Slagle's "Dance Matinee" on WXYZ in Detroit. They took a protective attitude toward me, and they were crazy about my mother, who didn't put on any airs just because she knew some stars. "I think it's nice they've got that Cadillac and ain't stuckup," Mama said. She still talked about those Tony Martin suits and how good the Hilltoppers would look in them.

During my years with the Hilltoppers, I met lots of stars: Buddy Morrow, Bill Haley and the Comets, Billy Ward and the Dominoes, the Fontane Sisters, the Four Lads, Ted Weems, Wink Martindale, Jaye P. Morgan, even Paul Hornung (the Green Bay Packer), and many others. In Memphis, I visited Vicki Woodall, the National President of Pat Boone's fan club, and a photo of me with Pat and Vicki appeared later in *16 Magazine*. (After she graduated, Vicki went to Hollywood to be Pat's secretary. Something like that was my ambition; the only alternative I could see was working at the Merit.) When the Hilltoppers played the Michigan State Fair, in Detroit, I appeared with the Hilltoppers on Soupy Sales' original TV show, and I was also interviewed by Robin Seymour and Don McLeod, major d.j.s on my request list. Johnnie Ray, whose big hits were "Cry" and "The Little White Cloud That Cried," stopped by the Hilltoppers' trailer at the fair one day. He flirted with me and seemed a little reckless, but his show was terrific. On the same bill was Eydie Gormé—before she married Steve Lawrence and they became Steve and Eydie. Eydie told me she admired my pixie haircut. Some weeks later, I saw her on TV and she had had her hair pixied. And at the Cotton Ball in Blytheville, Arkansas, I met Narvel Felts, a guy with a slick pompadour who said he was a singer in the style of Elvis. He asked for my autograph because I was a National President. More than twenty years later, I heard his name again, on the radio. He had finally made it. He had a hit record.

The day my mother and I drove to Blytheville and met Narvel Felts was the day the Russians sent up Sputnik. After the Hilltoppers' show, Don McGuire drove back to Mayfield with us in our Nash Rambler and then caught a bus to his home in Owensboro. As we rode through the night, listening to Chuck Berry and Little Richard and Elvis Presley on an after-hours show from New Orleans, we were aware of Sputnik spying on us. I noted the Sputnik launch in my diary:

> October 4. Blytheville, Ark. Cotton Ball. Hilltoppers and Jimmy
>    Featherstone Ork. Russian sattelite, Sputnik, launched.
> November 3. Sputnik II.
> November 7. 40th anniversary of Russian Revolution. President
>    Eisenhower's address to the nation. Senior rings.
> November 15. UFO sightings increase.
> December 11. English theme, "National Security," A+.

That fall, when I was a senior, a girl named Janine Williams went with my mother and me to see the Hilltoppers at a ballroom in a little town in Tennessee. Janine was popular at school, and she made a great impression on the Hilltoppers with her teasing, flirtatious personality. All the crinolines she wore under her dress made her look ready for flight, for a trip into outer space. "My brother went to Louisville to the basketball tournament last year," she told the Hilltoppers. "He won the tickets, and he flew up there in an airplane. And he stayed in the same hotel as the teams."

This was an outright lie—I didn't know why she told it—but the Hilltoppers didn't know the difference, so I didn't know what to say. I was happy, though, showing off the Hilltoppers to my friend. Jimmy introduced both of us to the audience at a special moment in the show before they sang "To Be Alone," in which Don did an Ink Spots–style monologue in his surprising bass voice and caused girls to squeal. (He had cherubic looks.) The Hilltoppers had a new record, "Starry Eyes," backed with "You Sure Look Good to Me," but they didn't sing it. I was disappointed. I was afraid it wasn't going to be a hit, and I was getting frustrated with the power of positive thinking. I hadn't told the Hilltoppers about the ESP experiments I had been trying (they involved sending telepathic messages to d.j.s to play Hilltoppers tunes). I was afraid the Hilltoppers would laugh. I wanted them to think I was normal. One of the fan-club presidents I had visited in Cape Girardeau, Missouri, had a deformed back and didn't even go to school. Another one I knew weighed about three hundred pounds, and her ambition was to be an actress. It was depressing.

"What do you think of Elvis?" Janine asked the Hilltoppers later. Elvis was singing "All Shook Up" on the radio of the Cadillac as Jimmy drove us out to a café for hamburgers.

"He's great," said Sy. "He has a fine voice."

"If I could wiggle like that, we'd make a million dollars," Jimmy said.

Don laughed. "Our manager had a chance once to manage Elvis, but he turned it down. He said nobody with a name like 'Elvis' would get anywhere."

"I like Elvis," Mama said. "He can really carry a tune."

For me, there was something as familiar about Elvis as our farm, with the oak trees and the cows and the chickens. It was as though Elvis were me, listening to WLAC and then coming up with his own songs about the way he felt about the world. I tried not to think too hard about Elvis. Janine had said to me, "If I got Elvis in a dark corner, I'd tear his clothes off."

Janine grew impatient with me and my obsession, and we didn't stay friends. She was going steady with a basketball player I had once had a crush on, and she had no interest in things like flying saucers and reincarnation. I had read "Reincarnation: A Hope of the World," and it impressed me. I was filled with philosophical questions and I wrote a paper for English class on agnosticism. My teacher, Miss Florence, summoned me to her office and accused me of plagiarism. "Young lady, you have no business entertaining ideas like this," she said. "Where did you get such an idea?"

I quaked. "I read about it. I read lots of philosophy," I said, which was only partly a lie. Reincarnation was philosophy, sort of. I told her I had read John Locke, which *was* a lie. But I hadn't plagiarized. I really believed it was possible that God did not exist, and furthermore it seemed likely that there was no way to know whether he did or not.

Miss Florence had lavender hair, and she kept a handkerchief tucked in her sleeve. Now and then she daintily plucked it out and snuffled into it. She was a terrifying woman, much admired by the whole town. Everyone since the thirties had been in her English class.

"Take my advice," she said, growing softer. "Give up these strange ideas of yours. Your field is mathematics. That's what you're good at. Stay away from these peculiar questions, because they're destructive. And stick with the Bible. That's all the philosophy you'll ever need."

I was silent, rigid with fury—too intimidated to speak.

"You have a lot of big ideas, but they will lead you astray," Miss Florence said in dismissal.

I immersed myself in my presidential duties, publishing my bimonthly newsletter, *Hilltoppers Topics*. In Mayfield, I was an outcast, but in the greater world I was suave and self-important. When d.j.s interviewed me, I spoke glibly in *Billboard* lingo. "Well, Ed, this new platter is slated to be a chartbuster," I said to Ed Bonner on KXOK. I had my own stationery, with a Hilltoppers logo. Running a fan club was expensive, but the Hilltoppers sent me ten dollars a week for expenses and fifteen dollars a week for myself. I saved all my money for college. I started hating math.

My mother had been serious about those Tony Martin suits. Shortly before my graduation, the Hilltoppers came to Mayfield, and Mama whisked them off to the Merit and got them measured for the suits. They picked out an off-white material with a subtle gray stripe in it. (Later, when the suits were finished, Mama went to the Merit and personally sewed in the labels.) That spring, I was a soda jerk at the Rexall drugstore in Mayfield, making fifty cents an hour, and after school that day I was drawing a Coke from the fountain for one of the regulars when all four of the Hilltoppers strolled into the drugstore. It was my big moment: I could show them off. A classmate of mine, one of those popular cheerleaders—an uptown girl who had made me feel like a shabby bumpkin—was testing nail polish at the cosmetics counter. I rushed over and told her I would introduce her to the Hilltoppers. "They're here," I said, pointing to the end of the counter, where I had served them Cokes.

"Oh, I don't think so," she said, flashing her cheerleader smile. "I wouldn't know what to say." With two fingernails painted Persian Melon, she hurried out the back door of the drugstore. The Hilltoppers scared her.

It was a triumph, sort of. I got off work early, and the Hilltoppers drove me home in the Cadillac. Mama made a huge catfish supper, with hush puppies and slaw and blackberry pie, and that evening my family and I all went to Paducah and saw the Hilltoppers sing at the National Guard Armory with Blue Barron's orchestra. It was a perfect day. "Your mother is an amazing woman," Don said to me.

The Hilltoppers were so conventional, such nice guys. I didn't know how to talk to them about the crazy thoughts in my head. I had just received a reply to my letter to George Adamski, the man who claimed in his book about UFOs to have been on a spaceship to Venus. He thanked me for writing and assured me that he had indeed been to Venus, but he failed to answer my questions about the spacecraft's interior and the landscape of Venus.

That summer, I picked blackberries in the early-morning dew with rock-and-roll songs like "Get a Job" by the Silhouettes and Eddie Cochran's "Summertime Blues" blasting in my mind, and in the afternoons I trudged down the dusty lanes through the fields with the dog to round up the herd of cows. In the evenings, I worked at the Rexall. I went out with boys—boys who wanted to settle down and work in the new factories—but I wasn't impressed. I was always dreaming. Our house was close to Highway 45, which ran straight south to Tupelo, Mississippi, where Elvis was born. I knew he had dreamed the same dreams.

Miss Florence refused to write me a recommendation to Duke University, where I wanted to study parapsychology with the famous Dr. J. B. Rhine, so in the fall I went away to the University of Kentucky, in Lexington, where I fell in love with a boy who was interested in UFOs and mind expansion. He wrote a column for the college newspaper and had a sense of humor that reminded me of Max Shulman's "Rally Round the Flag, Boys!" I neglected my fan-club duties and failed to get *Hilltoppers Topics* out on schedule. All the mysteries of the universe lay before me, and I couldn't learn fast enough. I read "Brave New World" and "1984" and "On the Beach" and "Mandingo" and "Elmer Gantry." I studied French and psychology and philosophy and volleyball. After hours, I still listened to John R jive-talking along with Ruth Brown and Little Walter and Jimmy Reed. Buddy Holly died that winter. Elvis was in the Army.

Earlier in the school year, before I fell in love, the Hilltoppers played at homecoming, and I went to the dance without a date—an unheard-of thing for a girl to do in those days. But I wouldn't have missed their show. I never tired of seeing it—even the old comic bit when the guys rolled up Don's pantlegs without his knowledge while he was singing the solo of "Ka-Ding-Dong." They always opened with something fast-paced, like "I Can't Give You Anything but Love" or "I've Got the World on a String," and sometimes they followed up with "Toot Toot Tootsie (Goo' Bye)"—which Jimmy sang as "Toot Toot *Tootie*"—before launching into their own numbers. Jimmy was noted for his clumsy introductions: "Ladies and gentlemen, and now we want to do the song that you made possible our being here with by buying those . . ." That night, as he always did when I was at their show, Jimmy introduced me to the audience, and the spotlight hit my face, momentarily blinding me. This time, I was embarrassed, because I thought everyone there would know I didn't have a date and would think I was peculiar. I felt as though I had just arrived from the moon.

The curfew was extended to 2 A.M. that night, because the Hilltoppers' show was late, and Sy walked me to my dorm. We sat in the parlor, surrounded by sorority pledges and their anxious dates. Some of them stared at us. Sy was the only one in the room in a tuxedo. I was the only one in the room who seemed to have a date with a member of the famous singing group that had just performed at the big dance. The lights in the parlor were bright, and the elderly housemother patrolled nervously. I got a fit of giggles when she looked at Sy suspiciously, as though he might be secretly organizing a panty raid. She had drilled the dorm residents in the horrors of panty raids, making them seem something like acts of terrorism.

A year later, I saw the Hilltoppers for the last time, at a night club in Louisville, where they were performing with Mel Tormé. I had driven over with some girls from U.K. The Hilltoppers' popularity had declined drastically. It wasn't my fault, though. They were being eclipsed by rock and roll. In their tuxedos or in their Tony Martin suits, they never really got the hang of it. That night in Louisville, I remember Don and Sy sitting at a table in a corner with me. They were as kind as ever—funny and generous, the way I always remember them. I had on a black cocktail dress with a taffeta balloon hem. "Those U.K. boys better watch out," Don said, teasing me.

Shyly, I told them about my boyfriend. By then, he was going with some other girl and my life was in ruins, but I didn't go into detail. I apologized for letting my club work slip. The newsletter was two months late.

Don smiled. "It's about time you forgot about the fan club," he said.

"No, it's not," I said loyally.

"You'll have other interests," he said. "You'll get married, and have your own family."

"I don't know." I knew I could never love anyone but that boy with the sense of humor. I would never get married.

"People change and go on to something else," Don said. "We won't stay with this forever. It's no way to live—one dinky ballroom after another. Travelling around all the time isn't what it's cracked up to be."

"Even in a Cadillac?" I asked.

"Even in a Cadillac," Don said, smiling again. "By the way, we'll drop you off in Lexington tomorrow."

"Thank you," I said. It was my last chance to travel in their Cadillac, I thought—a good way to end my national presidency. They had traded in the blue Cadillac for a newer, black model. I imagine it even now, rushing through the night, unrestrained in its flight, charging across America.

It was after midnight that night when Mel Tormé finished his set, but the band wouldn't quit. The crowd was wild. Jimmy took the microphone again. He sang "I Can't Get Started," a droopy-drawers sort of song. He had had a couple of drinks, and he was in mellow spirits. Then he eased into "St. James Infirmary." As the deep sadness of the song emerged, he suddenly became real to me, not a star. "St. James Infirmary" was slow and bluesy, but it wasn't a droopy-drawers song. It was the meanest, low-downest, saddest song I ever heard. I thought I would die. It was after hours, way down South in Dixie. It was 1959.

The Hilltoppers rode their behemoth Cadillac and played one-night stands only a while longer. Sy worked in a tobacco warehouse for a time, and then he and Jimmy became sales representatives for Dot Records. Don settled in Lexington. I lost touch with them. In the seventies, during the nostalgia rage, I heard that Jimmy Sacca was on the road again with a new Hilltoppers group. After college, in the sixties, I went to New York and got a job writing for a fan magazine—the same magazine that had once listed my fan club in its Betty Burr column. I found out that Betty Burr, who had once been an honorary member of my club, was only a name, like Miss Lonelyhearts. Part of my job at the fan mag was to write Betty Burr columns about fan clubs. I did that for about a year, and after that I left New York.

# Reading Between the Lines

Featured in the *Virginia Quarterly Review,* Spring 2014

When I was about ten, I received a five-year diary for Christmas. It was a small green leather-look book with a little lock and key. My grandmother, who had briefly kept a minimalist diary, insisted that I record the weather. In her diary she wrote things like "Wind in the north. Went down and helped Mrs. Hixon with her hog killing a while."

In high school, the habit of chronicling my life history seized me, probably at about the same time I was seized by a teenaged self-importance. Jottings from early 1957:

> Memorize 12 quotations from Emerson's "Self-Reliance"
> "30 Days to a More Powerful Vocabulary"
> Geometry theorems. Make 12-pointed star.
> Read "Oliver Twist"
> Tab Hunter on Steve Allen Show
> Elvis Presley "All Shook Up"
> "The Report on UFOs," E. J. Ruppelt

I'm still doing this. Since high school, I have kept a calendar diary, a brief account of each day. It is not a planner, where a schedule is set forth. And it is not a journal, for it is not really intimate. I've recorded only things I thought I wouldn't be embarrassed by—books, movies, trips, places, work.

The desk diaries are almost always visually appealing calendars, from museums perhaps. In recent years I have relied on the *New Yorker* desk diaries, because they offer more writing space and a pleasing format. The aesthetics of these notebooks is very important. They may be the only objects in my life that I treat with any specialness and reverence.

In high school, the little books were plain and I wrote sparely. The notation "5–8:30" simply meant that I worked at my regular job as a soda jerk at the drugstore during those hours. I didn't have to explain that to myself. In time, I scribbled more elaborate notes, yet never offered much clarity for a reader.

These notes were meant to trigger memories, but when I look back now I discover that many of the memories have vanished. For instance, during my second year in college I seem to have spent a *lot* of time hanging out with George Clooney's parents, but I hardly remember this. I knew some local DJs, including Nick Clooney. I remember Nick's fiancée, Nina, and I remember riding in Nick's red Corvette, which apparently now belongs to George. All I can say is that Nick was cuter than George is.

And I'm astonished to realize that I saw Miles Davis play at the Newport Jazz Festival in 1966. I like knowing that this happened, but how could I have forgotten even a moment of this?

I look back at these little daybooks rarely. But lately I have been perusing the annals of high school and college. I'm mortified! Most people have a grip on their past through memory and souvenirs—photos, home movies. My past is recorded in outline form. Normally we can fashion a narrative of our lives out of our murky memories, blocking out our callow youth, but I have *evidence*—record books—of it.

What stands out, ludicrously, is the ongoing list of movies I saw, sometimes juxtaposed improbably with my current reading.

*June 5, 1961*
Jerry Lewis, "Ladies Man"
Sartre, "Age of Reason"

*July 14, 1961*
"The Parent Trap," Hayley Mills
Joyce's "Portrait of the Artist"

Looking back at all the TV shows and movies, I cringe. Here is proof of my shallowness, misdirection, foolishness, vapid pastimes. There's more.

Some of the books I read in 1958, my last semester of high school and first semester of college: *The Hills Beyond, Ape and Essence, Brave New*

*World, All the King's Men, Mandingo, Gidget, Animal Farm, Forever Amber, Les Misérables, Crime and Punishment, On the Beach,* and *A Certain Smile.* Books I bought just before high-school graduation: *Philosophy Made Simple, Nineteen Eighty-Four, The Short Reign of Pippin IV, The Universe and Dr. Einstein, The Varieties of Religious Experience,* and *Teacher's Pet.*

I'm a product of a poor (criminally skimpy) grade-school education. For the first eight years I attended a country school in Cuba, Kentucky, a small school with no art, no languages, no music. There was no library! My mother bought me the Bobbsey Twins and Nancy Drew series books, and in sixth grade I discovered a copy of *Little Women.*

I remember now how hungry I was to learn, grasping for knowledge. What I wanted was an intense, intricate experience—like weaving a tapestry. Or reading novels! My mind was active, but I had few examples or role models. And no creative glimmer of possibility—only workbook rules. Not a scrap of creative encouragement. For art we colored outlined pumpkins and Santas. I was absorbed in coloring books and paint-by-numbers. I tried to write my own Nancy Drew–style mysteries.

By the time I got to high school, I was rebellious, headstrong. It was too late for guidance or role models. My artistic and intellectual development was stunted. My main outlet was music on the radio. No wonder I was drawn to DJs and kept tabs on Pat Boone's hit songs. The radio was my guide to the world. I plunged into an alternative life, ruled by the radio, and I spent my high-school years running the national fan club for a popular music group, the Hilltoppers. Pen pals, mail, and promotion projects filled my days.

I should have discovered language and literature, but it wasn't there for me.

My high school was good in science, math, and grammar, but literature was stuffy and remote. There was no art, music, or language except for Latin.

I was told that Latin was boring and dead, but secretly I loved it and only in retrospect do I realize it was my favorite subject. Miss Tossie Thorpe, the teacher, was a frail old woman, a little wren, making bird noises. Latin was purely strange, an adventure into the unknown, with cryptic clues (words that seemed like English) along the path.

I had no example of what you could do with learning—except for short-hand and typing (which I took, dutifully, forgoing the third and fourth years of Latin.) Any idiot can learn to type, and I've had no call for short-hand, but Latin has been my most useful subject, I see now, and I regret quitting halfway through.

I'm afraid to review my twenties and thirties. Will I discover that my whole life has been frittered away in jejune pastimes? Should I continue filling these little books? In my old age will I need to keep it up? Do I want anyone to read these little albums someday? My life is not a page-turner, please. I suppose that ultimately then the desk diary has an ending. I don't look forward to it. Will I be there to record it?

Although rereading my youth is embarrassing, I recognize that its limits turned out to hold some of my most precious resources, the details I would eventually draw on for fiction. They weren't the ones I wrote down then. But eventually the particulars of my country background, the vitality of farm people, and the language they spoke energized and defined the stories I began to write.

Floundering and misdirection are the basic methods of writing fiction. It is all done from scratch, without a pattern. Keeping a desk diary is a way of imposing a simple order on the stream of the day, but fiction demands something different—an openness to possibility, to what matters. It needs a fierce sense of urgency.

My mother kept a sort of journal during the last several years of her life. She wrote in notebooks and filled up the margins, so as not to waste any space. Like me, she attended to the main events of the day, but with a big difference: She made sentences. She used verbs! I can hear her voice, her laughter. She describes taking her dog, Oscar, out for a walk one cold day.

"He took me sailing down the hill, was about to mess. After he done that he was ready to come back home. It wasn't very windy but would cut you to the bone."

She was entertaining the events of the day, living a day fully enough to remark upon it, to feel it again through recollection. Ultimately, I learned the essentials from my mother. Life is process. Writing is process. With words we defy oblivion. I ponder my grandmother's little diary and a box-ful of my mother's notebooks, and it thrills me beyond words that I have been able to bring their stories out to the world. For all three of us, writing has been a response to a world that is rich in material even though bounded by farm fences.

I can imagine that in my last days I will still be writing down what happened. Maybe I will be studying Latin.

Wind in the north. *In ventum Aquilonis.*

*Tempus fugit.*

# FROM *Elvis Presley* (2003)

## Introduction

On August 16, 1977, when I learned that the King—Elvis Presley—was dead, I was vacationing in Nova Scotia. In the lounge at the inn where I was staying, the news came on TV. Stunned, I could only mumble some clichés. The bartender recalled the death of the actor Audie Murphy, a war hero of his generation. I felt far from home. Although I hadn't thought much about Elvis lately, I now sensed there was a great hole in the American cultural landscape. Elvis had always been there, hovering in the national psyche, his life punctuating our times—his appearances on *The Ed Sullivan Show,* his first movie, the death of his mother, the Army, his marriage, the 1968 "Comeback Special." It seemed inconceivable that Elvis—just forty-two years old—was gone.

For me, Elvis is personal—as a Southerner and something of a neighbor. I heard Elvis from the very beginning on the Memphis radio stations. Many parents found Elvis's music dangerously evocative, his movements lewd and suggestive—but when my family saw Elvis on *The Ed Sullivan Show,* singing "Ready Teddy," my father cried, "Boy, he's good!" We had been listening to rhythm-and-blues late at night on the radio for years, and we immediately recognized what Elvis was about. We had heard Arthur "Big Boy" Crudup and Little Junior Parker and Big Bill Broonzy and Wynonie Harris and Elmore James. In the daytime we listened to big bands, pop hits, country, the opera, everything we could find on the dial. On Sundays we sang in church along with the congregation, and we heard plenty of gospel music—especially the Blackwood Brothers, who influenced Elvis so much. Elvis listened to the same regional stew, seasoned by the far-ranging reach of the radio, so when he emerged with his own startling, idiosyncratic singing style, we recognized its sources.

150

Elvis was great, so familiar—and he was ours! I don't remember the controversy he stirred up because everything he did seemed so natural and real, and he was one of us, a country person who spoke our language. It was hard to grasp how revolutionary his music was to the rest of the world. And it was years before we could realize what a true revolution in American culture Elvis had ignited.

But now the King was dead. Two writer friends of mine dropped everything when they heard the news and rushed to Graceland, Elvis's Memphis home, to grieve with the multitudes of fans. One of the writers snitched a rose from a floral wreath and still has it displayed under glass on her wall. The other helped himself to the newspaper that had arrived at Graceland the day after Elvis died—the paper Elvis would have read if he had lived. Elvis, who was taken seriously in a wide variety of circles, inspired such a need for connection. He mattered deeply to many different kinds of people. After his death, the world absorbed the story—the utter loneliness of his life, his grasping for ways to ease his pain and sorrow. It was a sad—in some ways a sordid—story, hard to take. Then the grief gave way to a nervous national joke throughout the eighties. Elvis had been part of American life, and now it seemed people didn't quite know what to do about him. Elvis was ridiculed, reduced to a caricature in a sequined jumpsuit. In 1992, the post office held a contest to vote on the new Elvis stamp; we could choose between the young, pretty Elvis and the older, bejeweled Elvis. Of course we chose the pretty one.

Some people refused to accept the news of his death. Sightings were reported. He became a barometer of the culture, a sort of hillbilly voodoo doll. As in life, Elvis was both revered and reviled. In 1980, a scurrilous biography portrayed him as a redneck with savage appetites and perverted mentality, and of no musical significance to American culture. This character assassination undoubtedly helped promote the national joke. Many may have found it preferable to reduce Elvis to a symbol, because Elvis made them uncomfortable. For some, he represented the dark forces, a crude creature from the lower classes; for others, he represented innocence, and the destruction of innocence is an unbearable sight. Perhaps joking about him—transmogrifying him into a fat, drug-crazed hillbilly with gargantuan appetites—both alleviated the guilt and conveniently removed him as a subject for serious examination. But the nineties produced a steady stream of reconsiderations of Elvis. Peter Guralnick's thorough two-volume biography helped to rescue Elvis's reputation and restore an understanding of his music. Guralnick sympathetically portrayed a life that he called an American tragedy.

A few months after Elvis died, I visited the small two-room house in Tupelo, Mississippi, where he was born. It was now a museum, outfitted as it might have been when the Presleys lived there. It was furnished with flea-market antiques—Jesus figurines and heart-shaped pincushions, a wash-tub, a washboard, a pie safe, a kerosene lamp, and dishes that had come free in detergent boxes during the Depression. But what mesmerized me was the glitter poster—glitter spilled on felt paper, forming the shape of Jesus, with a Bible verse. I hadn't seen one of those since childhood. I remembered them from church. The poster evoked a powerful memory—this fake relic, this reminder of the innocent, religious rock-and-roll artist who became a superstar like the world had never seen before. In the glitter you could imagine the foreshadowing of the sequined jumpsuit. The glitter poster, once ubiquitous in the South, was a little bit of fancy in a drab world. And it embodied immense hope.

# V

# Family History

*Why do people write memoirs, anyway? I eschewed sensation and the penetrating exposé of the self. A good memoir ought to have a larger story, I thought, something beyond the typical personal saga of sexual awakening and the search for affirmation. I turned to history, the pioneers from the British Isles who moved down the Great Wagon Road to North Carolina and then westward.*

*My people, from a community called Clear Springs, were among those hardy travelers who stopped along the migration route and refused to budge or change much for several generations. My generation was the first since that perilous migration to embrace radical change. I discovered that I was a pioneer. In my childhood I spent summer afternoons sewing quilt pieces with my grandmother, who might have spent the morning picking shelly beans and drying apples in the sun, just as her mother and grandmother had done. But in a blink of an eye, I was off to a university. And just like that, I moved to New York City. Suddenly I was driving a Volkswagen through Europe. Then I was writing books, drawing upon my mother's good humor, perseverance, and way with words. My mother was the real center of this memoir, Clear Springs. When I told her it had been nominated for the Pulitzer Prize, she thought I said the Tulip Surprise. It was all the same to her. And really, that is so much better, so much more to the point, the heart and soul of writing.*

—BAM

# The Family Farm

FROM *Clear Springs* (1999)

It is late spring, and I am pulling pondweed. My mother likes to fish for bream and catfish, and the pondweed is her enemy. Her fishing line gets caught in it, and she says the fish feed on it, ignoring her bait. "That old pondweed will take the place," Mama says. All my life I've heard her issue this dire warning. She says it of willow trees, spiderwort, snakes, and Bermuda grass. "That old Bermudy" won't leave her flower beds alone.

The pondweed is lovely. If it were up to me, I'd just admire it and let the fish have it. But then, I'm spoiled and lazy and have betrayed my heritage as a farmer's daughter by leaving the land and going off to see the world. Mama said I always had my nose in a book. I didn't want to have to labor the way my parents did. But here I am, on a visit, wrestling with pondweed.

I'm working with a metal-toothed rake, with a yellow nylon rope tied to the handle to extend its reach. I stand on the pond bank, my Wal-Mart Wellingtons slopping and sucking mud. I fling the rake as far as I can, catch the pondweed, and then tug it loose. An island of it breaks off and comes floating toward me, snared by the rake. I haul it in and heave it onto the bank. The pondweed is a heavy mass of white, fat tendrils and a black tangle of wiry roots beneath the surface scattering of green leaves. Along with my rakeful of weed comes a treasure of snails, spiders, water striders, crawfish, worms, and insect larvae—a whole ecosystem, as in a tide pool. I haul out as much as I can lift—waterlogged, shiny leaves and masses of tendrils, some of them thick and white like skinned snakes. I rescue a crawfish. It wriggles back into its mud tunnel. As I work, the bank gets clogged with piles of weed. I am making progress. There is an unexpected satisfaction in the full range of athletic motion required for this job. I think about hard labor and wonder whether some of my fitness-minded friends with their rigid exercise routines could be talked into helping me out.

I've seen water lotus covering a lake, smothering it with plate-sized pads. Water lotus are giant lilies—double-story affairs that make gigantic seedpods resembling showerheads. Water lotus are a disaster if what you want is fish. Even without any lotus, this pond has seen disasters before— three fish kills: a fuel spill from the highway, warm-water runoff from a tobacco-warehouse fire, and a flood that washed the fish out into the creek.

In the early eighties, my father hired a backhoe to create the pond so that my mother could go fishing—her favorite pastime. He cut down a black-walnut tree so she could have a view of the pond across the field behind the house.

There used to be blackberries at the site of this quarter-acre pond— banks of berry bushes so enormous that we tunneled through them and made a maze. The blackberries were what we called tame. Back in the forties, my parents planted a dozen bushes to keep the fields from washing into the creek. The blackberries spread along all the borders. The berries were large and luscious, not like the small, seedy wild ones, but we never ate them with cream and sugar—only in pies or jam. Every July we picked berries and Mama sold gallons of them to high-toned ladies in the big fine houses in town. They made jelly. We got twenty-five cents for a quart of berries, a dollar a gallon. It took an hour to pick a gallon, and I could pick up to four gallons in a morning, before the sun got too hot, before I got chiggers implanted in the skin under my waistband. My fingers were full of thorn pricks and stayed purple all summer. The blackberries haven't disappeared, but they used to be more accessible, less weed-choked. They grew up and down all the creek banks, along the edges of all the fields, along the fencerows, along the lane. My father burned down masses of them before digging the pond.

The pond feeds into Kess Creek, which cuts across this farm—the place where I grew up, and where my mother still lives. The farm is fifty-three acres, cut into six fields, with two houses along the frontage. We are within sight of the railroad, which parallels U.S. Highway 45. We're on Sunnyside Road, a mile from downtown Mayfield, somewhere between Fancy Farm and Clear Springs, in Graves County. We are in far-western Kentucky, that toe tip of the state shaped by the curve of the great rivers—the

Ohio meets the Mississippi at Cairo, Illinois, about thirty-five miles north-west of Mayfield. To the east, the Tennessee and the Cumberland Rivers (now swelled into TVA lakes) run parallel courses. Water forms this twen-ty-five-hundred-square-mile region into a peninsula. It's attached to the continent along the border with Tennessee. Historically and temperamen-tally, it looks to the South.

There aren't any big cities around, unless you count Paducah (pop. 26,853), twenty-six miles to the north. The farm is typical of this agri-cultural region. A lane cuts through the middle, from front to back, and two creeks divide it crosswise. The ground is rich, but it washes down the creeks. The creeks are clogged with trash, dumped there to prevent hard rains—gully-washers—from carrying the place away. At one time this was a thriving dairy farm that sustained our growing family. It was home to my paternal grandparents, my parents, my two sisters, my brother, and me. There were at least eleven buildings along the front part of the farm, near the road: two houses, a barn, a stable, a corncrib, a smokehouse, two hen-houses, a wash-house, a milk house, an outhouse. I even had a playhouse.

The gravel-and-mud county road ran in front. Sometimes the school bus couldn't get through the mud. Before the road was paved and fast cars started killing our dogs and cats, we would sit on my grandparents' porch and say "Who's that?" whenever anybody passed. My grandparents' house was a large, one-story building with a high gabled roof—a typical farm-house. The other house, a small white wood-frame structure that my par-ents built when I was four, stood on a hill in the woods. When the road was paved, the roadbed was built up, so the house seemed to settle down to the level of the road. We still say the house is on a hill.

The farm is one field to the east of the railroad track that used to con-nect New Orleans with Chicago. The track runs beside Highway 45, an old U.S. route that unites Chicago with Mobile, Alabama. Highway 45 goes past Camp Beauregard, a Civil War encampment and cemetery, and leads toward Shiloh, a Civil War battlefield, and continues to Tupelo, Mississip-pi, where Elvis Presley was born. On this highway when I was about ten, my dog Rags was killed, smashed flat, and nobody bothered to remove his body. For a long time, it was still there when we went to town—a hank of hair and a piece of bone. It became a rag, then a wisp, then a spot. It's hard to explain the indifference of the family in this matter, for my heart ached for Rags. It had something to do with the immutability of fate. To my parents' way of thinking, there was nothing that could be done to bring Rags back to life, and besides they were behind on the spring planting or perhaps the fall corn-gathering. There was always something.

When I was in junior high, a motel opened up on the highway. It was the first motel in Mayfield. I could see it from my house. Marlene lived at the motel. I envied her. The allure of rootlessness—strangers passing through, stopping there to sleep—is a cliché, but if you live within sight of trains and a highway, the cliché holds power. Marlene's father built her a frozen-custard stand—to my mind the definition of bliss. It was a cozy playhouse on the side of the open road: a safe thrill. But Marlene was popular at school and grew too busy for any sidelines. Her father put an ad in the paper: "FOR SALE: Marlene's Frozen-Custard Stand. Marlene's tired."

Long before this, back in 1896, across the field in front of our houses, an amazing thing happened. Mrs. Elizabeth Lyon gave birth to quintuplets. For a brief time they were world-famous, until curiosity-seekers handled the babies to death. The quintuplets' house stood right beside the railroad track, and passengers from the train stopped to ogle. They were five boys— Matthew, Mark, Luke, John, and Paul. The names had come to Mrs. Lyon in a dream. President Grover Cleveland and Queen Victoria sent congratulations on the babies.

I am a product of this ground. This region is called the Jackson Purchase. In 1818, Andrew Jackson signed a deal with Chinubby, king of the Chickasaw Nation, and soon white settlers swarmed in, snatching up sweeps of prairie. Most of them came from Middle Tennessee, where the Cumberland Settlements had led to the founding of Nashville. One of the Cumberland pioneers was my great-great-great-grandfather, Samuel Mason. Several of his ten children headed for the Jackson Purchase, and four of them settled on Panther Creek, at Clear Springs, from whence all the relatives I have ever known sprang. In 1920, a century after my ancestors settled in Clear Springs, my grandparents boldly moved away from there, from the bosom of generations. The land had been divided up so many times that sons had to leave and find their own land. For Granddaddy, it was a long journey of eight miles. In 1920, he bought the fifty-three and one-tenth acres by the highway for five thousand dollars. The house, only six years old, was sturdy and attractive. The land was cleared and fertile, and it was only a mile from town, so trading at the town square or the feed mill would be an easy journey by buggy or wagon.

At one time, much of the land of the Jackson Purchase was covered with tall grass. The Chickasaws had apparently burned it periodically to create grassland for buffalo. When my father plowed in the spring, he turned up arrowheads. The land is not delta-flat, but it's not at all hilly either. It resembles rolling English farmland, both in the natural lay of the land and in the farming habits the farmers imposed upon it. It has small fields, and the fencerows are thick with weeds, vines, oaks, wild cherries, sumac, and cedars.

The landscape is still changing. On the highway, not far from our farm, are a tobacco-rehandling outfit, a John Deere business, and a chicken hatchery. The little frozen-custard stand, fallen to other uses and then to ruin, stood there until fairly recently, but the motel disappeared long ago. In its place is a collection of grim little buildings, including the House of Prayer. With the Purchase Parkway close by, industries have located near the interchange. My birthplace is now at the hub of industrial growth in the county, and the road in front of the houses is now a busy connector to highways and factories. When the cars rush by (ignoring the speed limit of thirty-five) on their way to work, or when a shift lets out, my mother sometimes stands at the kitchen window and counts them. "That's sixty-eight that have gone by in five minutes," she announces.

The farm now lies entirely within the Mayfield city limits. To the east, the subdivisions are headed our way. Behind the farm, to the south, we can glimpse an air-compressor factory. Just across the railroad, to the west, the four-lane bypass leads around town and to the parkway and to everywhere on the continent. Across the road, in a thirty-acre cornfield, which is like an extension of our front yard, is the landmark of the town.

I call it the chicken tower. It is the feed mill that processes feed for all the chickens that fuel Seaboard Farms, whose chicken-processing plant is on the other side of town. Construction workers came in 1989 and put up the tower in continuous twelve-hour shifts, while my father watched in fascination. The thing rose faster than hybrid corn shooting up. A chain-link fence girds the field. A deer was caught on the fence almost as soon as it went up.

The tower is a tall, gray concrete structure, without windows. It's a hundred and fifty-six feet high. If you see it at dawn, it's hard not to think about a space-shuttle launch. Adjoining the chicken tower are six cylindrical towers, attached like booster rockets. The architecture is unrelievedly functional. The word "Soviet" comes to mind. The tower has a framework of pipes crawling over it, and the six cylinders have earned the nickname "the concrete six-pack." These silos are a hundred and ten feet high. The mill hums, and big trucks come and go. It's like a huge refrigerator running. The chicken feed smells a bit like the mash of a whiskey distillery. The chicken industry, proliferating throughout the South, extravagantly promises prosperity, and many local farmers have grabbed the chance to raise chickens for Seaboard. The plant hatches the eggs and makes the feed, and the farmers raise the chicks in houses built at their own expense. Then low-wage workers cut up and package "poultry products" when the birds are six weeks old and sporting their first full plumage.

Beyond the chicken tower is the site where the Lyon quintuplets were born in 1896, and beyond that there's the feed mill where my mother's soybeans go, and beyond that is town. And then there's the wide world I eventually left home to see.

It's summer now. I am back again. With Oscar, the family dog, I'm visiting the pond on a warm evening, feeding fish. I'm flinging pellets of fish food out onto the water, trying to get it beyond the pondweed, which extends out all around the banks of the pond, except for the clearings I've made. When I pick up the empty fish-chow bucket—a plastic ice-cream tub—I find three crickets caught in it. They can't jump more than two or three inches straight up. There are two small ones and one large one. The smalls have striped backs like lightning bugs. They have feathery arms and legs and feathery feet. The large one has a long antenna it loops toward itself, then extends out tentatively, searching. The other antenna is grossly shortened—cut off by some vicious fighter-bug? Or did it come like that? Suddenly I realize that looking at crickets this way is the essence of what it was like to be a child here, immersed in the strange particulars of nature.

From the pond, in the green lushness of early summer, in three directions you see only fields of soybeans and corn, with thick fencerows and washed skies. A movie could be filmed here, a historical drama set in 1825, and it would seem authentic—except for the soundtrack: the noises of the highway, the air, the feed mill; the blare and thud of music from cars whizzing past. If you turned the camera in the other direction, toward the road, you'd get all the visual cues of the present day—the wires and poles, the asphalt, the Detroit metal, the discarded junk-food wrappers and beer cans thrown from cars that have "twentieth century" written all over them. You would also see a brown farmhouse with two rickety outbuildings, a red stable, and a small white house in a lovely woods that is mowed and trimmed like a park. And you would see the chicken tower, lord of the landscape.

Late September. The soybeans aren't quite ready to harvest. Some of the leaves are still green, but the pods are fuzzy and brown. The crop this year is full of weeds from outer space because the strongest herbicides have been banned. Something short of Agent Orange has been used this year, and the path to the pond is bordered with weeds, some a good ten feet tall.

Mama and I walk down this path to the pond. She uses her fishing rod to fight the weeds and snakes. Oscar trots along, thrilled to go with us. Miraculously, he never goes near the road.

"That's Johnsongrass," Mama says, pointing her rod at a clump of what looks like a trendy ornamental grass. "You can't ever get rid of that. Your Daddy used to cut it off and dig it up and dump it in the creek."

"What's that one?"

"Hogweed? Horseweed? I can't remember. But at the joint sometimes there's a big knot and inside is a worm that's good to fish with."

"It's horseweed," she says presently. "Not hogweed. Hogweed is what you call presley—pig presley I always called it. The hogs like it real well. It's got real tender leaves."

"Pig presley?"

"When we raised hogs I'd pull it up and give it to them, and Lord, they'd go crazy."

"What does it look like?"

"It grows along on the ground on a stem and has tender leaves. It looks rubbery."

"Purslane? Parsley?"

"I always called it pig presley."

"Is that one of your weeds that will take the place?"

"No, pig presley's all right. It's good."

We reach the pond just as a small heron escapes in a slow-motion flight over the creek. The pondweed has died back a lot, and the reflections in the pond are clear and still. The main house, inside its army of old oak and maple trees, is reflected in the pond. The chicken tower rises above the trees. The tableau is upside-down and innocently beautiful and abstract.

Mama gestures to the southeast and says, "If the wind is this way, I smell horse piss, and that way I smell cow mess, and over yonder it's tobacco curing, and from the north it's chicken feed." Her rod follows her directions. She laughs: her big, loud laugh. "If that don't beat a hen a-rootin'!" she says. Her laugh supposedly comes from her grandfather, "Jimmo" Lee, who had red hair and an Irish or Scottish burr in his voice. (Nobody remembers whether he was Irish or Scottish, but about half of the settlers were Scots-Irish, Protestants who came to America long before the Great Famine.) My mother uses idioms that are dying out with her generation, right along with the small family farms of America. Her way of talking is the most familiar thing I know, except maybe for the contours and textures of this land. Mama's language comes from the borderlands of England and Scotland and from Ireland, with some other English dialects thrown in, and it is mingled with African-American speech patterns acquired along the way. It is much like Mark Twain's language in *Huckleberry Finn*. It's spoken, with variations, in a band of the upper South stretching from the mid-Atlantic states across the Appalachians to the Ozarks. In the Jackson Purchase, this old dialect rested in the farmlands and changed with the weather and the crops and the vicissitudes of history as news filtered in from other places. Today there's a good chance you won't hear many people under sixty say, "If that don't beat a hen a-rootin'." It's an expression that comes from a deep knowledge of chicken behavior. Mama has contended with many a settin' hen. On free-range chickens, she's an expert.

Mama casts out a long rubber lure, a sort of Gummi Worm, and reels it in. She's casting for bass. "I'd rather fish for bream because they bite like crazy," she says.

The beanfields are leased out to a neighbor, and Mama frets about their proper cultivation. Dense growth from the creeks is creeping out into the fields. She hates weeds, insects, snakes, and bad weather. And she rails against the haphazard and violent methods of mechanized farming. A crop-spraying machine called a highboy straddles several rows, and the driver rides on tall wheels. One year, the combine missed so many soybeans that I imagine she was ready to go gather them up in a bucket and carry them to the mill herself. Another year, she chopped out all the pokeweed that had infiltrated a soybean field. She was afraid the pokeberries would stain the feed. "Them beans would have been purple by the time they went through the mill!" she said. "I don't know if hogs would appreciate purple feed. And pokeberries is poison."

Now it's winter. A tree is down, blocking the path across the creek. It has split, rotten at the center. I remember when that little tree hollow was a good hiding place for secret messages in fantasy girl-sleuth games—forty years ago. At the creek, a jumble of memories rushes out, memories of a period in my own lifetime which links straight back to a century ago, and even further: hog killing; breaking new-ground; gathering dried corn in the fall; herding cows with a dog; churning; quilting. I have a snapshot of myself as a child, sitting on a mule. I know the textures of all of these experiences.

What happened to me and my generation? What made us leave home and abandon the old ways? Why did we lose our knowledge of nature? Why wasn't it satisfying? Why would only rock-and-roll music do? What did we want?

With my family, the break started in 1920, when Granddaddy moved away from Clear Springs to find land, and we ended up living right on the edge of town. The stores around the courthouse square were tantalizingly near. Who wouldn't rather go shopping than hoe peas? And the radio told us that we weren't quite so isolated: we were in Radioland! The highway called us, too. Our ancestors had been lured over the ocean to America by false advertising—here was the promised land, literally—but once arrived, they had to clear rocks and stumps and learn to raise hogs. We inherited their gullibility. We wanted to go places, find out what was out there. My sisters and I didn't want to marry farmers; we were more interested in the traveling salesmen. By the time my brother—the youngest of us four, born too late—came of age, a family farm seemed to require more land and machinery than it once had in order to prosper. So again it was time to move on.

We didn't want to be slaves to nature. Maintaining the Garden of Eden was too much work—endless hoeing, fences to fix, hay to bale, and cows to milk, come rain or come shine. My mother, who knows more about wind and weather and soil and raising chickens than I ever will, approves of progress, even though she finds much of it scary and empty. The old ways were just too hard, she says wearily. She and my father expected better lives for their children. They knew we'd leave.

But I keep looking back to see where I've been. I am angry that my father died before I could ask him all I wanted to know about the life of a dairy farmer, because I think he knew all about the earth and the seasons.

The winter light is heavy and stark. Dim skies, silhouettes of black trees, mud. The pondweed lies dormant; the soybeans were recently harvested, and here and there stray beans have spilled out onto the soil. The dampness deepens these brown-and-black tones of the landscape. Oscar and I cross the creek and head out through the cornfield. The corn has been harvested by a big machine that gobbled up the stalks, moiled the shucks and spit them out, then glommed the kernels off the cob and spun them into a hopper. I recall the way dried corn comes off the cob when you do it by hand. You mash two cobs together hard and loosen a few of the kernels till they pop out like teeth. Then you can rub the cobs together more lightly and pop the rest of the kernels out of their sockets. I also recall shelling corn for the chickens with a corn sheller; it had a crank handle and an iron maw with teeth. Now I can hear corn being crumbled and gnashed in the tower.

The cedar trees on the fencerow along our western border have grown thick and tall and have lost their youthful prickliness. We always had a young, scraggly cedar from one of the fencerows for our Christmas tree. Now these are full of bluish berries and conelike cocoons made by some insect that shrouds itself with a dead cedar twig.

The chicken tower has a star on top for Christmas. From up there, you would see the lay of this farm, reduced in its significance, a small piece of the earth.

It is late afternoon, and the ominous winter light accents the trees. Then the harsh electric light of the chicken tower floods the area. It is never dark at night here the way it used to be, when there were just stars and moon.

There's a loneliness about the homeplace now. But the family straggles home each Christmas to renew itself, and the place returns to life. In the way of rural families, Mama doesn't invite us to come, but she expects us all to be there. And we always are. The family is small, only fifteen of us. Mama cooks a dinner for her four children, their three spouses, her five grandchildren, and two more spouses. She has turkey with cornbread dressing and giblet gravy, a ham, potato salad, dressed eggs, Jell-O salad, cranberry relish, her special Sunset Salad, broccoli casserole with cheese sauce, yeast-raised rolls. And from her freezer she may offer creamed corn, green beans, shelly beans, and brown field peas—all grown in her garden. Then she loads the table with fruit salad, boiled custard, her special uncooked fruitcake, coconut cake, German chocolate cake, peanut bars, decorated refrigerator cookies. She makes all this food herself because we don't really know how to do it and it is her joy to feed us amply. She makes enough for about thirty-six people. The feast seems always to be prepared for some imagined larger family.

This dinner defines the family and replenishes us for another year. We get here, regardless of what it costs us in money or trouble, or whatever difficulty with weather and flight delays. We're far-flung. We have not scattered simply to Paducah or Nashville or Louisville, places within reasonable reach. We didn't leave the farm for Pittsburgh or Hattiesburg or Racine. My sisters and I first headed to California, Florida, and New York—the meccas. One niece worked at Disney World; one sister works in special-effects computer graphics in Hollywood. The movies, Disney World, Manhattan. Those were the fishing lures that came over the airwaves and reeled us in. I stayed in the Northeast for many years, chasing literary dreams. Even my brother, who stayed closest to home, works for the quintessential American corporation, Coca-Cola.

We've been free to roam, because we've always known where home is.

Oscar and I turn back. As we approach the pond, a heron—a great blue one this time—takes off from the water, not far ahead of us. Its flight path cuts across the face of the chicken tower, which looms beyond the house and the bare winter trees. The dying pondweed is dissolving into the muddy murk of the pond. As I look into the reflections on the surface of the pond, I think about all the death on this soil: the oaks that Mama says were "barked up and skinned" by lightning; the hogs and cows and calves and chickens we've slaughtered for food; all the cats and dogs smashed on the road after it was paved; my grandparents; my father. Before my grandparents moved here, a farmer died of epilepsy, in the garden. I think about what a farmer knows up there on his tractor or walking along behind his mules—the slow, enduring pace of regular toil and the habit of mind that goes with it, the habit of knowing what is lasting and of noting every nuance of soil and water and season. What my father and my ancestors knew has gone, and their idioms linger like fragile relics. Soon my memories will be loosened from any tangible connection to this land.

I don't know what will happen to this piece of land eventually. Urbanization has hardly begun here in the Purchase. Kentucky is an agricultural state, ranking fourth in the nation in the number of family farms. The tension between holding on to a way of life and letting in a new way—under the banners of Wal-Marts and chicken processors—is the central dynamic of this area. There are no malls, no cinema complexes, no coffee bars here. But a Wal-Mart Supercenter is looming over the horizon like a UFO. The town is poised on the edge of the future.

As a family farm, this piece of land may be doomed. The family has fragmented. I live too far away to deal with a soybean crop. I wouldn't know how to make the ground say beans, the way Thoreau wanted it to, and would probably just prefer to read his musings on the subject. My nephew fantasizes a golf course; my brother dreams of building a minimart; someone has mentioned llamas. When land is spoken of these days, it's usually in an opportunistic tone. Someone sees a buck to be made. But the big bucks are usually made by someone else, not the people who know the land. I do not know what industrial or technological analogue of pondweed will take over this land. What is tame and what is wild seem to go through cycles of varying perspectives. I'm sort of wishing for a comeback of the blackberries. It's tempting to think of just holding on to the land while industries close in around. We could call the place a nature preserve. I think of those alligators and long-necked birds you see moving lazily in the foreground of a space-shuttle launch.

Our two houses face the chicken tower like cats staring at a stranger. My mother lives in my grandparents' old place, and the other house is unoccupied. It's the higgledy-piggledy house my parents kept adding onto periodically. I grew up in that house. The picture window is empty, and the shutters sag. The overgrown forsythia bushes reach the roof, and a mock-orange tree grows right smack atop the cistern. The house seems desolate, abandoned.

I own an oil painting of that house when it was in its prime—with trim green shutters, a white picket fence (which I once had to whitewash, like Tom Sawyer), a red-white-and-blue flower bed, a blue snowball bush, a pink climbing rose, and tall leafy trees hovering above the roof. My mother painted this scene; she painted one copy for each of her children and one for herself. It has been a long journey from our little house into the wide world, and after that a long journey back home. Now I am beginning to see more clearly what I was looking for.

# The Pond

FROM *Clear Springs* (1999)

October 4, 1996

*A couple of months after I went blackberry picking,*
*something unexpected happened. My mother told*
*me about it on the telephone. As usual, I asked*
*so many questions that she said, "Oh, you're*
*straining my little watery brain."*

It had been an unusually hot summer, and my mother had gotten out of the habit of stirring about, although she still drove to her garden at the farm each morning. When she lived at the farm, she had kept active all summer, but at the new house, she felt inhibited from going outside. There were so many houses around, with people to see her and make her feel self-conscious. She was stiffening up with arthritis, and her muscles were still weak from her stroke a year ago. The doctor told her she had severe osteoporosis, but he didn't seem to think that was unusual for someone her age—seventy-seven. Her daughters nagged at her about exercise. They went on and went on about muscle tone and skeletal support. It made her tired to listen to them.

Now that it was autumn, the weather was a little cooler, and she longed to go fishing. Her daughters had given her a new rod-and-reel for her birthday over a year ago, but she had hardly made use of it. She knew the fish were growing big. When Wilburn restocked the pond, just before he died, he had included two five-pound catfish.

One sunny day in early October, after her dinner at noon, she impulsively went fishing. Leaving the dirty dishes on the table and the pots and pans on the counter, she stowed her tackle box and her rod-and-reel in the car and drove to the farm. She parked the car in the shade by the stable, near her garden, and headed across the soybean field toward the pond. She knew the fish would be biting. She was quicker in her step than she had been lately, but she picked her way carefully through the stubbly field. The soybeans had been recently harvested, but she did not know if the men who leased the land had gathered the popcorn they had planted in the back fields. It had been several years since she had been across the creeks to the back acreage.

She was walking through the field behind Granny's house. Only one car was in the driveway, and she did not see any of the renters. The trampoline in the yard reminded her of a misshapen hospital cot. The black dog chained to the wash-house regarded her skeptically, pawed at the ground, and sat down lazily. With his chain, he had worn away her grapevine and turned the grass into a crescent of dirt. The old place had so much time and heart invested in it, too much to comprehend. Now it seemed derelict and unloved.

She was out of breath when she reached the pond, but she recovered quickly in the warm air. The leaves on the trees along the creek were beginning to turn yellow and brown. The pond was full and still. The pondweed had diminished somewhat this year because Don had released two grass-eating carp into the water. They were supposed to eat their weight in pondweed daily. She had told Don to make sure they were the same sex. She didn't want the pond overrun with carp, which could be a worse calamity than pondweed.

She felt good, eager to fish. She baited her hook with a piece of a chicken gizzard she had bought the week before. It was ripe, a piece of stink bait to lure a catfish. After wiping her hands on the grass, she cast out and reeled in slowly. It was pleasant to stand on the bank and watch the arc of her line fly out. She was standing at the deep bend of the pond, near the old lane. The water was exceptionally high, nearly reaching the rim of the pond. The wind was blowing from the east, and her floater drifted to the left. She reeled it toward her.

Lately she had been reviewing her life, reflecting on the hardships she had endured. She bridled at the way the women always had to serve the men. The men always sat down in the evening, but the women kept going. Why had the women agreed to that arrangement? How had they stood it? What if she had had an opportunity for something different? Wilburn, amazed by her paintings, once said, "Why, if you'd had a chance, there's no telling what you could have accomplished." She didn't know. The thought weighed her down, taunting her with something lost she could never retrieve, like a stillborn child.

After a while, she got a bite. Her cork plunged down and then took off. A fish was carrying the bait across the pond, against the wind, rippling the water, flying across. She reeled in and felt the fish pull steady. It was a big one, but she didn't allow her hopes to rise yet. It seemed heavy, though. She worked it back and forth, feeling the deep pleasure of hooking a fish. It grew lively then. It was a fighter. As it resisted, she gradually realized its strength. She was afraid her line wasn't strong enough to bring it in. She would have to play it delicately.

She had never felt such a huge fish pulling at her. With growing anticipation, she worked the fish for an hour or more. But time seemed to drift like a cloud. She thought of LaNelle's Lark at the bottom of the pond. Wilburn had sunk the dilapidated car at the high end of the pond to reinforce the levee. Its hulk would be like a cow's skeleton, she thought. She did not allow the fish to take her line near that area.

She thought she knew exactly which fish she had hooked. She had had her eye on it for years. It was the prize fish of the whole pond. She had seen this great fish now and then, a monster that would occasionally surface and roll. It would wallow around like a whale. Since the first time she'd seen it, she had been out to get the "old big one." Her quest had become legendary in the family. "Mama's going to get that old big fish," they'd say. But she hadn't imagined this would be the day. It was as though the fish had been waiting for her, growing formidably, until this day. It had caught *her* by surprise.

Slowly, the fish lost its strength. She could see its mouth as she drew it nearer, as it relaxed and let her float it in. The fish was gigantic, more immense than any fish she had ever caught. From the feel of it and now the glimpse of it in the murky water, she thought it might weigh thirty pounds. If only she could see Wilburn's face when she brought this fish in.

She had never landed a fish larger than eleven pounds. She had caught a ten-pound catfish at a pay-pond once, and she had hooked the eleven-pounder in this pond. She knew that landing this one would be a challenge. She would have to drag it out, instead of raising it and flipping it out of the water.

Finally, the fish was at the bank, its mouth shut on the line like a clamp-top canning jar, its whiskers working like knitting needles. It was enormous. She was astonished. It touched the bank, but without the smooth glide of the water to support it the fish was dead weight. She couldn't pull it all the way up the bank. She couldn't lift it with her rod, nor could she drag it through the weeds of the bank. She was more worn out than the fish was, she thought. She held the line taut, so that the fish couldn't slip back in the water, and she tugged, but it didn't give. The mud was sucking it, holding it fast. Its head was out of the water, and with those whiskers and its wide wraparound mouth, it seemed to be smiling at her. She stepped carefully through scrubby dried weeds and clumps of grass, making her way down the shallow bank toward the fish. Knots of pondweed bordered the water. Gingerly, she placed her left foot on a patch of dried vegetation and reached toward the fish.

The patch appeared solid. For a fraction of a second, the surprise of its give was like the strangeness of the taste of Coca-Cola when the tongue had expected iced tea. The ground gave way under her foot and she slid straight into the pond. It wasn't a hard fall, for her weight slid right into the water, almost gracefully. On the way, she grabbed at a willow bush but missed it. She still had hold of the line, even though her rod-and-reel slipped into the water. She clutched at dried weeds as she slid, and the brittle leaves crumpled in her hands. Then the fish was slipping back into the water, dragging the rod. She snatched the rod and felt the fish still weighting the end of the line. Quickly, she heaved the rod to the bank. She caught hold of the fish and held it tight, her fingernails studding its skin.

She was gasping at the chill of the water. She could not touch bottom. She was clutching the edge of the bank, and the water was up to her neck.

She hadn't imagined the pond was so deep next to the bank. The fish in her hands, she hugged the bank, propping herself against it with her elbows. She tried to get a toehold against the side of the pond, but as she shifted her weight, the solid matter fell away and her foot seemed to float free. She kept a tight hold on the fish, pointing its head away from her so it would not grab her fingers. Sometimes a channel catfish would grip bait and not let go, even after the fish was dead. It could bite a person's finger off.

She still couldn't touch the bottom, but she balanced herself against the side of the pond and held the fish's head out of the water. The water helped buoy the weight of the fish. The fish gaped, and the baited hook floated for a moment. The hook was not even sunk into its flesh. Then the fish clamped onto the hook again.

The fish was a fine one, she thought. It would make good eating. She was pleased, even amazed that she had caught it. It had lost much of its strength. She would have to wait for it to die. When the mouth stayed open, it would be dead, even if it still seemed to be breathing.

She managed to scoot it up onto the bank, inching it in front of her. She laid it in the ooze, placing it by the gills. Its gills were still working, its mouth loosened now. She held it down hard against the mud. The fish gaped, and she lessened her pressure. She floundered in the water, repositioning herself against the muck. She realized the water no longer seemed chilly.

The water was high, submerging the lower branches of the willow bushes. The willows were only a few feet away, but she did not want to get near those bushes. She was sure there were snakes around the roots of the willows. The snaky tendrils of the pondweed brushed her legs. She kicked and stirred the water while holding on to a tuft of grass.

To make her way to the shallow end, she would have to maneuver around the willows. But she would have to launch too far out into the pond to do that. She wasn't sure she could swim, yet her clothes did not feel heavy. She was wearing her old tan stretch-knit pants and a thin blouse and a cotton shirt and tennis shoes.

She noticed it was shady in the direction of the shallow end, so she decided to stay where she was, where she could feel the sunshine. She expected that someone would see her presently and come to help her out. With difficulty, she twisted her body toward the road, where cars were passing. She let out a holler. More cars passed. She hollered again. The cars were driven by the blind and the deaf. Their windows were rolled up tight.

"Hey!" She let out a yodeling sound, and then a pig call. "Soo-eeee!" She tried all the calls she knew, calls she used when she had to reach the men working in the fields, sounds that could carry across creeks and hollers. "Sook, cow!" she called, as if summoning a herd of milk cows.

There was no one at the house now, but she thought the renters would be there soon. The car she had seen was gone. Her car gleamed fire-red at the stable. In the smooth surface of the pond before her, stretching toward the soybean field and then the road, she saw the upside-down reflection of the chicken-feed mill. The sky was bright autumn blue, and the reflection of the tower was like a picturesque postcard, still and important-looking.

Balancing against the bank in the water up to her neck, she gazed across the field toward the houses and the road. In that panorama, her whole life lay before her—a rug at the foot of the feed-mill tower. She saw her own small house in the clump of trees. The bulldozer still had not come to demolish it. She was sure the house could be fixed up, if she could only tend to it. Leaving it vacant had caused it to deteriorate. The loss of her house probably hurt her more than anything about the farm. But she couldn't keep everything up. It was too much for her. She'd had the stable repainted—a clear red—but it needed more work. Her thoughts weighted her down with the heaviness of the farm's history. Her memories mixed together in a mosaic of hard bits, like chicken grit. She saw the calves, the horses, the corncrib, the gardens, the henhouses, and other buildings no longer there. She saw the onions and potatoes she stored in one of the stalls. She saw mules and tractors and bonfires of leaves. What she saw before her eyes now was the consequence and basis of her labor. Years of toil were finished now; sometimes she wondered what it had all been for.

She seized a clump of grass but could not nudge her weight onto the bank. It was like trying to chin herself on a high bar. She did not have the energy. Then the grass pulled loose. The fish gaped again, and she managed to push it farther up the bank. She avoided its mouth.

Time passed. For a while, she lay horizontal in the water, clutching grass; then she rested vertically against the sludge of the bank. When occasionally her grip loosened, she had to dog-paddle to keep afloat.

She was panting. She held herself steady until she gathered her strength, then she tried again to pull herself up. She could not. The water seemed quite warm now. She thrashed, to scare off snakes. If she could grab a willow branch, she was sure she could pull herself out, but the thought of snakes underwater around the willow roots made her tremble. Snapping turtles were there too, she felt sure.

The shade covering the shallow end had grown deeper and longer now. She needed to stay here in the sun.

A pack of coyotes could eat a person. Wilburn had said that was not true, but she believed it was. Last year, one of the neighbor women carried dinner to the farmhands at work in one of her back fields. She parked her car on a lane beside the field, and as she started toward the gate with the dinner she saw some coyotes running at her, a whole caboodle of them. She raced back to the car and slammed the door just in time. The coyotes clambered all over the car, sniffing.

Sometimes the siren of a passing ambulance started the coyotes howling. All along the creek, a long ribbon of eerie sound followed the siren. If the coyotes found her in the pond, she could not escape. They might smell the fish, she thought. That would draw them like bait. Her dread hardened into a knot. She thought she ought to pray. She hadn't been to church much lately. She had trouble hearing, now that they had a microphone. Its squealing hurt her ears.

Cars passed. She thought she saw her son's van under the trees. She thought he might be sawing wood. She hollered to the air. After a while, she could tell that what she had thought was the van was only some scrap metal glinting in the sun.

The soybeans had been harvested only a week before, and the combine had missed multitudes of beans. She could see clumps of them dotting the field. There was so much waste. It bothered her. The land itself was washing into the creek. She pictured herself in the pond, washing over the levee in a hard rain and then sweeping on down through the creek.

If Wilburn came along and saw her here, he would grin at her and say, "What are you fooling around in the pond for? Got time on your hands?" She wondered what it would be like to while away the hours in a country club swimming pool. She had never had time to idle like that. She did not know how people could piddle their lives away and not go crazy. She had stopped going on the senior-citizen bus tours because they wasted so much time at shopping malls. She told them she'd rather eat a worm.

She recalled falling into water before—it was familiar. She was a little thing, fishing in Panther Creek with her grandmother and aunt. Suddenly she slid off a log, down the bank, and into the water. Mammy Hicks and Aunt Hattie laughed at her. "You got wet, didn't you?" Hattie said, bobbing her pole. A whole life passed between those two splashings.

Her hands were raw. She thought she could see snakes swirling and swimming along the bank some yards away. She had never seen a cottonmouth at this pond, but a snake was a snake, poisonous or not. She shuddered and tightened her grasp on the grass. She kicked her feet behind her. Her shoes were sodden.

A pain jerked through her leg—a charley horse. She waited for it to subside. She did not know how much time had passed, but the sun was low. She was starting to feel cooler. Her legs were numb. She realized she could be having another stroke. For the first time, it occurred to her that she might really be stranded here and no one would know. No one knew she had come fishing.

She scrambled clumsily at the bank. Now she knew she had to get out. No one was going to come for her. She knew she should have tried earlier, when she had more strength, but she had believed someone would spot her and come to help her. She worked more industriously now, not in panic but with single-minded purpose. She paused to take some deep breaths. Then she began to pull, gripping the mud, holding herself against it. She was panting hard. Little by little, she pulled herself up the mud bank. She crawled out of the water an inch at a time, stopping to rest after each small gain. She did not know if she felt desperation. She was so heavy. Her teeth were chattering from the cold, and she was too weak to rise. Finally, she was on the bank, lying on her belly, but her legs remained in the water. She twisted around, trying to raise herself up. She saw a car turn into the driveway. She hollered as loud as she could. Her teeth rattled. After a moment, the car backed up and drove away.

The western sun was still bearing down. She lay still and let it dry her. As her clothes dried, she felt warmer. But her legs remained in the water, her shoes like laden satchels. She pulled and pulled and crawled until her legs emerged from the water. She felt the sun drawing the water from her clammy legs. But as the sun sank, she felt cooler. She crawled with the sun—moving with it, grabbing grass.

When she finally uprighted herself, the sun was going down. She stood still, letting her strength gather. Then she placed one foot in front of her, then the other.

She had to get the fish. Stooping, she pulled it onto the grass, but she could not lift it, and she knew she could not pack it to the car. It was dead, though its gills still worked like a bellows, slowly expanding and collapsing. It had let go of the hook. Leaving the fish, she struck out across the soybean field toward the car. No one was at the house. She reached the car. Luckily, the key had not washed out of her pocket while she was in the pond. In the dim light, she couldn't see how to get it in the ignition. For an interminable time, she fumbled with the key. Then it turned.

Instead of following the path around the edge of the field, she steered the car straight across the beanfield. She stopped before the rise to the pond and got out. As she climbed toward the pond, her feet became tangled in some greenbrier vines and she fell backwards into a clump of high grass. Her head was lower than her feet. She managed to twist herself around so that she was headed up the bank, but she was too weak to stand.

She lay there in the grass for some time, probably half an hour. She dozed, then jarred awake, remembering the fish. Slowly, she eased up the bank and eventually stood. When she reached the fish, it appeared as a silhouette, the day had grown so dark. She dragged the fish to the car and heaved it up through the door, then scooted it onto the floorboard behind the driver's seat. She paused to catch her breath.

The sun was down now. In the car, she made her way out of the field to the road. Cars were whizzing by. She was not sure her lights were working. They seemed to burn only dimly. She hugged the edge of the narrow road, which had no shoulders, just deep ditches. Cars with blazing headlights roared past. She slowed down. By the time she got into town, the streetlights were on. She could not see where to turn into her street. A car behind her honked. Flustered, she made her turn.

When she got home, the kitchen clock said 7:25. She had been at the pond for seven hours. She opened the back door, and Chester the cat darted in, then skidded to a stop and stared at her, his eyes bugged out. She laughed.

"Chester, you don't know me! Do I smell like the pond?"

Chester retreated under the kitchen table, where he kept a wary lookout.

"Come here, baby," she said softly. "Come on." He backed away from her.

She got into the shower, where she let hot water beat on her. Memories of the afternoon's ordeal mingled in her mind like dreams, the sensations running together and contorting out of shape. She thought that later she would be angry with herself for not pulling herself out of the pond sooner—she could have ventured into those willow bushes—but now she felt nothing but relief.

After she was clean and warm, she went to the kitchen. Chester reappeared. He rubbed against her legs.

"Chester," she crooned. "You didn't know me." She laughed at him again.

She fed Chester and warmed up some leftovers for her supper. She hadn't been hungry all those hours, and she was too tired to eat now, but she ate anyway. She ate quickly. Then she went out to the garage and dragged the fish out of the car.

She wrestled it into the kitchen. She couldn't find her hatchet. But she thought she was too weak to hack its head off now. Using the step stool, she managed, in stages, to get the fish up onto the counter. She located her camera. The flash didn't work, but she took a picture of the fish anyway, knowing it probably wouldn't turn out. She didn't know where her kitchen scales were—lost in the move somewhere. She was too tired to look for them. She found her tape measure in a tool drawer.

The fish was thirty-eight and a half inches long. It was the largest fish she had ever caught.

"Look at that fish, Chester," she said.

With her butcher knife, she gutted the fish into a bucket. The fish was full—intestines and pondweed and debris and unidentifiable black masses squished out.

She could feel herself grinning. She had not let go of the fish when she was working it, and she had gotten back home with the old big one. She imagined telling Wilburn about the fish. He would be sitting in front of the TV, and she would call him from the kitchen. "Just wait till you see what I reeled in at the pond," she would say. "Come in here and see. Hurry!" He would know immediately what she had caught. She had a habit of giving away a secret prematurely. Her grinning face—and her laughing voice—gave her away. When she had a surprise for the children, she couldn't wait to tell them. She wanted to see their faces, the delight over something she had bought them for Christmas or some surprise she had planned. "Wake up, get out of bed. Guess what! Hurry!"

# VI

# Nancy Culpepper

*Over the years, a character named Nancy Culpepper haunted my imagination. Her background was much like mine—country people in Kentucky. In the several stories and novella (Spence + Lila) in which she appears, I found she was closest to my own sensibility. She's not me, but in fiction I can play with her, trying out alternative paths and bestowing on her various qualities I wish I had.*

—BAM

# Nancy Culpepper

FROM *Nancy Culpepper: Stories* (2006)

When Nancy received her parents' letter saying they were moving her grandmother to a nursing home, she said to her husband, "I really should go help them out. And I've got to save Granny's photographs. They might get lost." Jack did not try to discourage her, and she left for Kentucky soon after the letter came.

Nancy has been vaguely wanting to move to Kentucky, and she has persuaded Jack to think about relocating his photography business. They live in the country, near a small town an hour's drive from Philadelphia. Their son, Robert, who is eight, has fits when they talk about moving. He does not want to leave his room or his playmates. Once, he asked, "What about our chickens?"

"They have chickens in Kentucky," Nancy explained. "Don't worry. We're not going yet."

Later he asked, "But what about the fish in the pond?"

"I don't know," said Nancy. "I guess we'll have to rent a U-Haul."

When Nancy arrives at her parents' farm in western Kentucky, her mother says, "Your daddy and me's both got inner ear and nerves. And we couldn't lift Granny, or anything, if we had to all of a sudden."

"The flu settled in my ears," Daddy says, cocking his head at an angle.

"Mine's still popping," says Mom.

In a few days they plan to move Granny, and they will return to their own house, which they have been renting out. For nine years, they have lived next door, in Granny's house, in order to care for her. There Mom has had to cook on an ancient gas range, with her mother-in-law hovering over her, supervising. Granny used only lye soap on dishes, and it was five years before Nancy's mother defied her and bought some Joy. By

181

then, Granny was confined to her bed, crippled with arthritis. Now she is ninety-three.

"You didn't have to come back," Daddy says to Nancy at the dinner table. "We could manage."

"I want to help you move," Nancy says. "And I want to make sure Granny's pictures don't get lost. Nobody cares about them but me, and I'm afraid somebody will throw them away."

Nancy wants to find out if Granny has a picture of a great-great-aunt named Nancy Culpepper. No one in the family seems to know anything about her, but Nancy is excited by the thought of an ancestor with the same name as hers. Since she found out about her, Nancy has been going by her maiden name, but she has given up trying to explain this to her mother, who persists in addressing letters to "Mr. and Mrs. Jack Cleveland."

"There's some pictures hid behind Granny's closet wall," Daddy tells Nancy. "When we hooked up the coal-oil stove through the fireplace a few years ago, they got walled in."

"That's ridiculous! Why would you do that?"

"They were in the way." He stands up and puts on his cap, preparing to go out to feed his calves.

"Will Granny care if I tear the wall down?" Nancy asks, joking. Daddy laughs, acting as though he understood, but Nancy knows he is pretending. He seems tired, and his billed cap looks absurdly small perched on his head.

When Nancy and Jack were married, years ago, in Massachusetts, Nancy did not want her parents to come to the wedding. She urged them not to make the long trip. "It's no big deal," she told them on the telephone. "It'll last ten minutes. We're not even going on a honeymoon right away, because we both have exams Monday."

Nancy was in graduate school, and Jack was finishing his B.A. For almost a year they had been renting a large old house on a lake. The house had a field-rock fireplace with a heart-shaped stone centered above the mantel. Jack, who was studying design, thought the heart was tasteless, and he covered it with a Peter Max poster.

At the ceremony, Jack's dog, Grover, was present, and instead of organ music, a stereo played *Sgt. Pepper's Lonely Hearts Club Band*. It was 1967. Nancy was astonished by the minister's white robe and his beard and by the fact that he chain-smoked. The preachers she remembered from child-hood would have called him a heathen, she thought. Most of the wedding pictures, taken by a friend of Jack's, turned out to be trick photography—blurred faces and double exposures.

The party afterwards lasted all night. Jack blew up two hundred bal-loons and kept the fire going. They drank too much wine-and-7-Up punch. Guests went in and out, popping balloons with cigarettes, taking walks by the lake. Everyone was looking for the northern lights, which were sup-posed to be visible that evening. Holding on to Jack, Nancy searched the murky sky, feeling that the two of them were lone travelers on the edge of some outer-space adventure. At the same time, she kept thinking of her par-ents at home, probably watching *Gunsmoke*.

"I saw them once," Jack said. "They were fantastic."

"What was it like?"

"Shower curtains."

"Really? That's amazing."

"Luminescent shower curtains."

"I'm shivering," Nancy said. The sky was blank.

"Let's go in. It's too cloudy anyway. Someday we'll see them. I promise."

Someone had taken down the poster above the fireplace and put up the picture of Sgt. Pepper—the cutout that came with the album. Sgt. Pepper overlooked the room like a stern father.

"What's the matter?" a man asked Nancy. He was Dr. Doyle, her Amer-ican History 1861–1865 professor. "This is your wedding. Loosen up." He burst a balloon and Nancy jumped.

When someone offered her a joint, she refused, then wondered why. The house was filled with strangers, and the Beatles album played over and over. Jack and Nancy danced, hugging each other in a slow two-step that was all wrong for the music. They drifted past the wedding presents, lined up on a table Jack had fashioned from a door—hand-dipped can-dles, a silver roach clip, *Joy of Cooking*, signed pottery in nonfunctional shapes. Nancy wondered what her parents had eaten for supper. Possibly fried steak, two kinds of peas, biscuits, blackberry pie. The music shifted and the songs merged together; Jack and Nancy kept dancing.

"There aren't any stopping places," Nancy said. She was crying. "Songs used to have stopping places in between."

"Let's just keep on dancing," Jack said.

Nancy was thinking of the blackberry bushes at the farm in Kentucky, which spread so wildly they had to be burned down every few years. They grew on the banks of the creek, which in summer shrank to still, small occasional pools. After a while Nancy realized that Jack was talking to her. He was explaining how he could predict exactly when the last, dying chord on the album was about to end.

"Listen," he said. "*There*. Right there."

Nancy's parents had met Jack a few months before the wedding, during spring break, when Jack and Nancy stopped in Kentucky on their way to Denver to see an old friend of Jack's. The visit involved some elaborate lies about their sleeping arrangements on the trip.

At the supper table, Mom and Daddy passed bowls of food self-consciously. The table was set with some napkins left over from Christmas. The vegetables were soaked in bacon grease, and Jack took small helpings. Nancy sat rigidly, watching every movement, like a cat stationed near a bird feeder. Mom had gathered poke, because it was spring, and she said to Jack, "I bet you don't eat poke salet up there."

"It's weeds," said Nancy.

"I've never heard of it," Jack said. He hesitated, then took a small serving.

"It's poison if it gets too big," Daddy said. He turned to Nancy's mother. "I think you picked this too big. You're going to poison us all."

"He's teasing," Nancy said.

"The berries is what's poison," said Mom, laughing. "Wouldn't that be something? They'll say up there I tried to poison your boyfriend the minute I met him!"

Everyone laughed. Jack's face was red. He was wearing an embroidered shirt. Nancy watched him trim the fat from his ham as precisely as if he were using an X-Acto knife on mat board.

"How's Granny?" asked Nancy. Her grandmother was then living alone in her own house.

"Tolerable well," said Daddy.

"We'll go see her," Jack said. "Nancy told me all about her."

"She cooks her egg in her oats to keep from washing a extry dish," Mom said.

Nancy played with her food. She was looking at the pink dining room wall and the plastic flowers in the window. On the afternoon Jack and Nancy first met, he took her to a junk shop, where he bought a stained-glass window for his bathroom. Nancy would never have thought of going to a junk shop. It would not have occurred to her to put a stained-glass window in a bathroom.

"What do you aim to be when you graduate?" Daddy asked Jack abruptly, staring at him. Jack's hair looked oddly like an Irish setter's ears, Nancy thought suddenly.

"Won't you have to go in the Army?" Mom asked.

"I'll apply for an assistantship if my grades are good enough," Jack said. "Anything to avoid the draft."

Nancy's father was leaning into his plate, as though he were concentrating deeply on each bite.

"He makes good grades," Nancy said.

"Nancy always made all A's," Daddy said to Jack.

"We gave her a dollar for ever' one," said Mom. "She kept us broke."

"In graduate school they don't give A's," said Nancy. "They just give S's and U's."

Jack wadded up his napkin. Then Mom served fried pies with white sauce. "Nancy always loved these better than anything," she said.

After supper, Nancy showed Jack the farm. As they walked through the fields, Nancy felt that he was seeing peaceful landscapes—arrangements of picturesque cows, an old red barn. She had never thought of the place this way before; it reminded her of prints in a dime store.

While her mother washes the dishes, Nancy takes Granny's dinner to her, and sits in a rocking chair while Granny eats in bed. The food is on an old TV-dinner tray. The compartments hold chicken and dressing, mashed potatoes, field peas, green beans, and vinegar slaw. The servings are tiny—six green beans, a spoonful of peas.

Granny's teeth no longer fit, and she has to bite sideways, like a cat. She wears the lower teeth only during meals, but she will not get new ones. She says it would be wasteful to be buried with a new three-hundred-dollar set of teeth. In between bites, Granny guzzles iced tea from a Kentucky Lakes mug. "That slaw don't have enough sugar in it," she says. "It makes my mouth draw up." She smacks her lips.

Nancy says, "I've heard the food is really good at the Orchard Acres Rest Home."

Granny does not reply for a moment. She is working on a chicken gristle, which causes her teeth to clatter. Then she says, "I ain't going nowhere."

"Mom and Daddy are moving back into their house. You don't want to stay here by yourself, do you?" Nancy's voice sounds hollow to her.

"I'll be all right. I can do for myself."

When Granny swallows, it sounds like water spilling from a bucket into a cistern. After Nancy's parents moved in, they covered Granny's old cistern, but Nancy still remembers drawing the bucket up from below. The chains made a sound like crying.

Granny pushes her food with a piece of bread, cleaning her tray. "I can do a little cooking," she says. "I can sweep."

"Try this boiled custard, Granny. I made it just for you. Just the way you used to make it."

"It ain't yaller enough," says Granny, tasting the custard. "Store-bought eggs."

When she finishes, she removes her lower teeth and sloshes them in a plastic tumbler on the bedside table. Nancy looks away. On the wall are Nancy's high school graduation photograph and a picture of Jesus. Nancy looks sassy; her graduation hat resembles a tilted lid. Jesus has a halo, set at about the same angle.

Now Nancy ventures a question about the pictures hidden behind the closet wall. At first Granny is puzzled. Then she seems to remember.

"They're behind the stovepipe," she says. Grimacing with pain, she stretches her legs out slowly, and then, holding her head, she sinks back into her pillows and draws the quilt over her shoulders. "I'll look for them one of these days—when I'm able."

Jack photographs weeds, twigs, pond reflections, silhouettes of Robert against the sun with his arms flung out like a scarecrow's. Sometimes he works in the evenings in his studio at home, drinking tequila sunrises and composing bizarre still lifes with lightbulbs, wine bottles, Tinkertoys, Lucite cubes. He makes arrangements of gourds look like breasts.

On the day Nancy tried to explain to Jack about her need to save Granny's pictures, a hailstorm interrupted her. It was the only hailstorm she had ever seen in the North, and she had forgotten all about them. Granny always said a hailstorm meant that God was cleaning out his icebox. Nancy stood against a white Masonite wall mounted with a new series of photographs and looked out the window at tulips being smashed. The ice pellets littered the ground like shattered glass. Then, as suddenly as it had arrived, the hailstorm was over.

"Pictures didn't used to be so common," Nancy said. Jack's trash can was stuffed with rejected prints, and Robert's face was crumpled on top. "I want to keep Granny's pictures as reminders."

"If you think that will solve anything," said Jack, squinting at a negative he was holding against the light.

"I want to see if she has one of Nancy Culpepper."

"That's *you*."

"There was another one. She was a great-great-aunt or something, on my daddy's side. She had the same name as mine."

"There's another one of you?" Jack said with mock disbelief.

"I'm a reincarnation," she said, playing along.

"There's nobody else like you. You're one of a kind."

Nancy turned away and stared deliberately at Jack's pictures, which were held up by clear-headed pushpins, like translucent eyes dotting the wall. She examined them one by one, moving methodically down the row—stumps, puffballs, tree roots, close-ups of cat feet.

Nancy first learned about her ancestor on a summer Sunday a few years before, when she took her grandmother to visit the Culpepper graveyard, beside an oak grove off the Paducah highway. The old oaks had spread their limbs until they shaded the entire cemetery, and the tombstones poked through weeds like freak mushrooms. Nancy wandered among the graves, while Granny stayed beside her husband's gravestone. It had her own name on it too, with a blank space for the date.

Nancy told Jack afterwards that when she saw the stone marked "NANCY CULPEPPER, 1833–1905," she did a double take. "It was like time-lapse photography," she said. "I mean, I was standing there, looking into the past and the future at the same time. It was weird."

"She wasn't kin to me, but she lived down the road," Granny explained to Nancy. "She was your granddaddy's aunt."

"Did she look like me?" Nancy asked.

"I don't know. She was real old." Granny touched the stone, puzzled. "I can't figure why she wasn't buried with her husband's people," she said.

On Saturday, Nancy helps her parents move some of their furniture to the house next door. It is only a short walk, but when the truck is loaded they all ride in it, Nancy sitting between her parents. The truck's muffler sounds like thunder, and they drive without speaking. Daddy backs up to the porch.

The paint on the house is peeling, and the latch of the storm door is broken. Daddy pulls at the door impatiently, saying, "I sure wish I could burn down these old houses and retire to Arizona." For as long as Nancy can remember, her father has been sending away for literature on Arizona.

Her mother says, "We'll never go anywhere. We've got our dress tail on a bedpost."

"What does that mean?" asks Nancy, in surprise.

"Use to, if a storm was coming, people would put a bedpost on a child's dress tail, to keep him from blowing away. In other words, we're tied down."

"That's funny. I never heard of that."

"I guess you think we're just ignorant," Mom says. "The way we talk."

"No, I don't."

Daddy props the door open, and Nancy helps him ease a mattress over the threshold. Mom apologizes for not being able to lift anything.

"I'm in your way," she says, stepping off the porch into a dead canna bed.

Nancy stacks boxes in her old room. It seems smaller than she remembered, and the tenants have scarred the woodwork. Mentally, she refurnishes the room—the bed by the window, the desk opposite. The first time Jack came to Kentucky he slept here, while Nancy slept on the couch in the living room. Now Nancy recalls the next day, as they headed west, with Jack accusing her of being dishonest, foolishly trying to protect her parents. "You let them think you're such a goody-goody, the ideal daughter," he said. "I'll bet you wouldn't tell them if you made less than an A."

Nancy's father comes in and runs his hand across the ceiling, gathering up strings of dust. Tugging at a loose piece of door facing, he says to Nancy, "Never trust renters. They won't take care of a place."

"What will you do with Granny's house?"

"Nothing. Not as long as she's living."

"Will you rent it out then?"

"No. I won't go through that again." He removes his cap and smooths his hair, then puts the cap back on. Leaning against the wall, he talks about the high cost of the nursing home. "I never thought it would come to this," he says. "I wouldn't do it if there was any other way."

"You don't have any choice," says Nancy.

"The government will pay you to break up your family," he says. "If I get like your granny, I want you to just take me out in the woods and shoot me."

"She told me she wasn't going," Nancy says.

"They've got a big recreation room for the ones that can get around," Daddy says. "They've even got disco dancing."

When Daddy laughs, his voice catches, and he has to clear his throat. Nancy laughs with him. "I can just see Granny disco dancing. Are you sure you want me to shoot you? That place sounds like fun."

They go outside, where Nancy's mother is cleaning out a patch of weed-choked perennials. "I planted these iris the year we moved," she says.

"They're pretty," says Nancy. "I haven't seen that color up North."

Mom stands up and shakes her foot awake. "I sure hope y'all can move down here," she says. "It's a shame you have to be so far away. Robert grows so fast I don't know him."

"We might someday. I don't know if we can."

"Looks like Jack could make good money if he set up a studio in town. Nowadays people want fancy pictures."

"Even the school pictures cost a fortune," Daddy says.

"Jack wants to free-lance for publications," says Nancy. "And there aren't any here. There's not even a camera shop within fifty miles."

"But people want pictures," Mom says. "They've gone back to decorating living rooms with family pictures. In antique frames."

Daddy smokes a cigarette on the porch, while Nancy circles the house. A beetle has infested the oak trees, causing clusters of leaves to turn brown. Nancy stands on the concrete lid of an old cistern and watches crows fly across a cornfield. In the distance a series of towers slings power lines across a flat sea of soybeans. Her mother is talking about Granny. Nancy thinks of Granny on the telephone, the day of her wedding, innocently asking,

"What are you going to cook for your wedding breakfast?" Later, seized with laughter, Nancy told Jack what Granny had said.

"I almost said to her, 'We usually don't eat breakfast, we sleep so late!'"

Jack was busy blowing up balloons. When he didn't laugh, Nancy said, "Isn't that hilarious? She's really out of the nineteenth century."

"You don't have to make me breakfast," said Jack.

"In her time, it meant something really big," Nancy said helplessly. "Don't you see?"

Now Nancy's mother is saying, "The way she has to have that milk of magnesia every night, when I know good and well she don't need it. She thinks she can't live without it."

"What's wrong with her?" asks Nancy.

"She thinks she's got a knot in her bowels. But ain't nothing wrong with her but that head-swimming and arthritis." Mom jerks a long morning glory vine out of the marigolds. "Hardening of the arteries is what makes her head swim," she says.

"We better get back and see about her," Daddy says, but he does not get up immediately. The crows are racing above the power lines.

Later, Nancy spreads a Texaco map of the United States out on Granny's quilt. "I want to show you where I live," she says. "Philadelphia's nearly a thousand miles from here."

"Reach me my specs," says Granny, as she struggles to sit up. "How did you get here?"

"Flew. Daddy picked me up at the airport in Paducah."

"Did you come by the bypass or through town?"

"The bypass," says Nancy. Nancy shows her where Pennsylvania is on the map. "I flew from Philadelphia to Louisville to Paducah. There's California. That's where Robert was born."

"I haven't seen a geography since I was twenty years old," Granny says. She studies the map, running her fingers over it as though she were caressing fine material. "Law, I didn't know *where* Floridy was. It's way down there."

"I've been to Florida," Nancy says.

Granny lies back, holding her head as if it were a delicate china bowl. In a moment she says, "Tell your mama to thaw me up some of them strawberries I picked."

"When were you out picking strawberries, Granny?"

"They're in the freezer of my refrigerator. Back in the back. In a little milk carton." Granny removes her glasses and waves them in the air.

"Larry was going to come and play with me, but he couldn't come," Robert says to Nancy on the telephone that evening. "He had a stomachache."

"That's too bad. What did you do today?"

"We went to the Taco Bell and then we went to the woods so Daddy could take pictures of Indian pipes."

"What are those?"

"I don't know. Daddy knows."

"We didn't find any," Jack says on the extension. "I think it's the wrong time of year. How's Kentucky?"

Nancy tells Jack about helping her parents move. "My bed is gone, so tonight I'll have to sleep on a couch in the hallway," she says. "It's really dreary here in this old house. Everything looks so bare."

"How's your grandmother?"

"The same. She's dead set against that rest home, but what can they do?"

"Do you still want to move down there?" Jack asks.

"I don't know."

"I know how we could take the chickens to Kentucky," says Robert in an excited burst.

"How?"

"We could give them sleeping pills and then put them in the trunk so they'd be quiet."

"That sounds gruesome," Jack says.

Nancy tells Robert not to think about moving. There is static on the line. Nancy has trouble hearing Jack. "We're your family too," he is saying.

"I didn't mean to abandon you," she says.

"Have you seen the pictures yet?"

"No. I'm working up to that."

"Nancy Culpepper, the original?"

"You bet," says Nancy, a little too quickly. She hears Robert hang up. "Is Robert O.K.?" she asks through the static.

"Oh, sure."

"He doesn't think I moved without him?"

"He'll be all right."

"He didn't tell me goodbye."

"Don't worry," says Jack.

"She's been after me about those strawberries till I could wring her neck,"
says Mom as she and Nancy are getting ready for bed. "She's talking about
some strawberries she put up in nineteen seventy-*one*. I've told her and told
her that she eat them strawberries back then, but won't nothing do but for
her to have them strawberries."

"Give her some others," Nancy says.

"She'd know the difference. She don't miss a thing when it comes to
what's *hers*. But sometimes she's just as liable to forget her name."

Mom is trembling, and then she is crying. Nancy pats her mother's
hair, which is gray and wiry and sticks out in sprigs. Wiping her eyes, Mom
says, "All the kinfolks will talk. 'Look what they done to her, poor helpless
thing.' It'll probably kill her, to move her to that place."

"When you move back home you can get all your antiques out of the
barn," Nancy says. "You'll be in your own house again. Won't that be
nice?"

Mom does not answer. She takes some sheets and quilts from a closet
and hands them to Nancy. "That couch lays good," she says.

When Nancy wakes up, the covers are on the floor, and for a moment
she does not remember where she is. Her digital watch says 2:43. Then it
tells the date. In the darkness she has no sense of distance, and it seems
to her that the lighted numerals could be the size of a billboard, only seen
from far away.

Jack has told her that this kind of insomnia is a sign of depression,
while the other kind—inability to fall asleep at bedtime—is a sign of anxiety. Nancy always thought he had it backwards, but now she thinks he may
be right. A flicker of distant sheet lightning exposes the bleak walls with
the suddenness of a flashbulb. The angles of the hall seem unfamiliar, and
the narrow couch makes Nancy feel small and alone. When Jack and Robert come to Kentucky with her, they all sleep in the living room, and in the
early morning Nancy's parents pass through to get to the bathroom. "We're
just one big happy family," Daddy announces, to disguise his embarrass-

ment when he awakens them. Now, for some reason, Nancy recalls Jack's strange still lifes, and she thinks of the black irises and the polished skulls of cattle suspended in the skies of O'Keeffe paintings. The irises are like thunderheads. The night they were married, Nancy and Jack collapsed into bed, falling asleep immediately, their heads swirling. The party was still going on, and friends from New York were staying over. Nancy woke up the next day saying her new name, and feeling that once again, in another way, she had betrayed her parents. "The one time they really thought they knew what I was doing, they didn't at all," she told Jack, who was barely awake. The visitors had gone out for the Sunday newspapers, and they brought back doughnuts. They had doughnuts and wine for breakfast. Someone made coffee later.

In the morning, a slow rain blackens the fallen oak branches in the yard. In Granny's room the curtains are gray with shadows. Nancy places an old photograph album in Granny's lap. Silently, Granny turns pages of blank-faced babies in long white dresses like wedding gowns. Nancy's father is a boy in a sailor suit. Men and women in pictures the color of café au lait stand around picnic tables. The immense trees in these settings are shaggy and dark. Granny cannot find Nancy Culpepper in the album. Quickly, she flips past a picture of her husband. Then she almost giggles as she points to a girl. "That's me."

"I wouldn't have recognized you, Granny."

"Why, it looks just *like* me." Granny strokes the picture, as though she were trying to feel the dress. "That was my favorite dress," she says. "It was brown poplin, with grosgrain ribbon and self-covered buttons. Thirty-two of them. And all those tucks. It took me three weeks to work up that dress."

Nancy points to the pictures one by one, asking Granny to identify them. Granny does not notice Nancy writing the names in a notebook. Aunt Sass, Uncle Joe, Dove and Pear Culpepper, Hortense Culpepper.

"Hort Culpepper went to Texas," says Granny. "She had TB."

"Tell me about that," Nancy urges her.

"There wasn't anything to tell. She got homesick for her mammy's cooking." Granny closes the album and falls back against her pillows, saying, "All those people are gone."

While Granny sleeps, Nancy gets a flashlight and opens the closet.

The inside is crammed with the accumulation of decades—yellowed newspapers, boxes of greeting cards, bags of string, and worn-out stockings. Granny's best dress, a blue bonded knit she has hardly worn, is in plastic wrapping. Nancy pushes the clothing aside and examines the wall. To her right, a metal pipe runs vertically through the closet. Backing up against the dresses, Nancy shines the light on the corner and discovers a large framed picture wedged behind the pipe. By tugging at the frame, she is able to work it gradually through the narrow space between the wall and the pipe. In the picture a man and woman, whose features are sharp and clear, are sitting expectantly on a brocaded love seat. Nancy imagines that this is a wedding portrait.

In the living room, a TV evangelist is urging viewers to call him, toll-free. Mom turns the TV off when Nancy appears with the picture, and Daddy stands up and helps her hold it near a window.

"I think that's Uncle John!" he says excitedly. "He was my favorite uncle."

"They're none of my people," says Mom, studying the picture through her bifocals.

"He died when I was little, but I think that's him," says Daddy. "Him and Aunt Lucy Culpepper."

"Who was she?" Nancy asks.

"Uncle John's wife."

"I figured that," says Nancy impatiently. "But who *was* she?"

"I don't know." He is still looking at the picture, running his fingers over the man's face.

Back in Granny's room, Nancy pulls the string that turns on the ceiling light, so that Granny can examine the picture. Granny shakes her head slowly. "I never saw them folks before in all my life."

Mom comes in with a dish of strawberries.

"Did I pick these?" Granny asks.

"No. You eat yours about ten years ago," Mom says.

Granny puts in her teeth and eats the strawberries in slurps, missing her mouth twice. "Let me see them people again," she says, waving her spoon. Her teeth make the sound of a baby rattle.

"Nancy Hollins," says Granny. "She was a Culpepper."

"That's Nancy Culpepper?" cries Nancy.

"*That's* not Nancy Culpepper," Mom says. "That woman's got a rat in her hair. They wasn't in style back when Nancy Culpepper was alive."

Granny's face is flushed and she is breathing heavily. "She was a real little-bitty old thing," she says in a high squeaky voice. "She never would talk. Everybody thought she was curious. Plumb curious."

"Are you sure it's her?" Nancy says.

"If I'm not mistaken."

"She don't remember," Mom says to Nancy. "Her mind gets confused."

Granny removes her teeth and lies back, her bones grinding. Her chest heaves with exhaustion. Nancy sits down in the rocking chair, and as she rocks back and forth she searches the photograph, exploring the features of the young woman, who is wearing an embroidered white dress, and the young man, in a curly beard that starts below his chin, framing his face like a ruffle. The woman looks frightened—of the camera perhaps—but nevertheless her deep-set eyes sparkle like shards of glass. This young woman would be glad to dance to "Lucy in the Sky with Diamonds" on her wedding day, Nancy thinks. The man seems bewildered, as if he did not know what to expect, marrying a woman who has her eyes fixed on something so far away.

# The Prelude

FROM *Nancy Culpepper: Stories* (2006)

Nancy was waiting in Windermere for Jack's train. With its grassy splendor, the Lake District was an ideal place for a marital reconciliation, she thought. She hadn't seen him in almost a year. He was flying from Boston to Manchester, then catching the train.

In the ladies' room at Booth's, next to the station, she fussed over her hair and her eye makeup in a way she never had when she and Jack started out together, in the sixties, when her hair was long and straight. Now she used hair mousse and eyeliner. She no longer knew how to interpret the face she saw in the mirror.

If it were 1967 again and she knew what she knew now, how would she behave? She liked to imagine herself as a young woman, going north to begin graduate school, but this time she would be carrying confidence and poise as effortlessly as wheeling ultralight luggage. If she had had a sense of proportion back then, would she have married Jack?

She bought a fat double-pack of Hobnobs. She remembered how much Jack had liked those oat biscuits when they were in the Lake District together, long ago—rambling amongst sheep and bracken through the Furness Fells. Now she was on a Romantic kick, she had told him on e-mail. She was tracing the footsteps of Coleridge and Wordsworth, trying to capture in her imagination the years 1800–1804, when the two poets were involved in a romantic upheaval in their personal lives. It was not true that Dorothy Wordsworth and her brother William had an incestuous love, Nancy thought; Dorothy was surely in love with Coleridge. Samuel Taylor Coleridge—a married man, peripatetic, unhealthy, an excitable genius. But Coleridge was obsessed with another woman. Dorothy, doomed never to know the love of a husband or a child, gathered mosses and made giblet pies and took notes for her brother's poems. That was the story that kept coming to life in Nancy's imagination, and once it had sparked in her mind, she couldn't stop it. When Nancy and Jack were young, pairings and commitments were casual and uncertain, and Nancy even wondered later if she had really been in love with Jack. But the passionate love triangles—and trapezoids—in the Lake District two centuries before seemed desperate.

Early in their marriage, when Nancy and Jack traveled to England, their passion was unadulterated. After arriving in London, jet-lagged, they collapsed in the afternoon, then awoke at 3 A.M. Not knowing what else to do, they made love, after dropping a shilling into a wall heater, as if it were some kind of condom dispenser. They always thought that their son, Robert, was conceived in England, perhaps on that occasion.

Or maybe it had been a few days later, here in northern England. Jack had an assignment to photograph cottages. Nancy, who had written a paper on the Romantic imagination for a history course, had brought along an anthology of Romantic poetry. But the poems seemed old-fashioned, with their hyperbole and exclamation points, and she read few of them. Jack was shooting landscapes, and throughout the trip he goofed around trying to sound as if he were from Liverpool, like the Beatles. Nancy had a cold, and she was hungry, but when they arrived in the town of Kendal late on a Sunday, there was no place to eat. They bought Hobnobs and overripe pears from a chemist, who directed her to a preparation on a dusty lower shelf—a fig syrup that was good for colds, an analgesic.

"It's a very old remedy," the chemist said. "We've used it for generations."

At a bed-and-breakfast on a hillside of houses with long front gardens, Mrs. Lindsay served an elaborate tea, with little sandwiches and biscuits, enough to call dinner. She sat by the fire chatting about her flowers, her youth, her son the stevedore in Cardiff. Nancy sat entranced, her slightly feverish warmth dissolving into a comfortable ease. Mrs. Lindsay was seventy-five—very old, Nancy thought, thinking of her frail, taciturn grandmother in Kentucky.

Upstairs with Jack, Nancy swigged fig syrup and blew her nose. The syrup made her sleepy, and she slept well in the deep feather bed with piles of fluffy coverlets. At breakfast downstairs, Nancy studied the lace curtains, the flowered wallpaper, the ornate china cupboard, while Jack wrote in his notebook.

"Did you see Dove Cottage, where Wordsworth lived?" Mrs. Lindsay asked as she poured hot milk into Jack's coffee.

"We're going today," said Nancy.

"When I was a wee one in Grasmere I heard the old ones talk about Mr. Wordsworth."

"You knew someone who knew Wordsworth!" Nancy was astonished. The Romantic period was ancient history.

Mrs. Lindsay set the coffeepot on the sideboard. "They remembered him walking over the hills, always walking, with that stick of his," she said.

Nancy's interest in the Romantic poets went dormant after that and didn't reawaken until the past year, after she and Jack sold their house in Boston and agreed to live apart for a time—until desire reunited them, they said. Alone in the Lake District, Nancy revived the image of Wordsworth and his stick. She carried it with her, supporting her thoughts of the friendship of Coleridge and Wordsworth, as she imagined the pair hiking in the surrounding landscapes. Her mind dwelled on those characters, seizing each clue to their reality. If Wordsworth was a steady walker, Coleridge was an intrepid pioneer trekker, the type of person who today would have written a Lonely Planet guide. In his fight against an opium addiction, he would trot out boldly into the wild, with his broomstick and his green solar spectacles, daring to walk the drug out of his system. On at least one occasion Coleridge hid out in an inn at Kendal, maybe on Mrs. Lindsay's street. He went to the chemist for his opium, a mixture called Kendal Black Drop. Nancy smiled to herself, remembering now the fig syrup, pushed to the back of the dusty shelf.

Nimble Jack bounded down from the train. When he saw her, he dropped his blue duffel. Still clutching his camera bag, he jumped up and clicked his heels in the air.

"I can still do it!" he cried.

Nancy burst into laughter. She loved the attention he attracted. Her husband—a grown man, a middle-aged man, a kid. His face was a little harder and thinner. Their embrace was long and tight, with embarrassed squeals and awkward endearments.

"I don't know how I got along without you," he said, holding her against the wall of the track shelter.

"We're both crazy," she murmured.

"What have you been doing up here?"

"Getting Hobnobs for you," she said, producing the package. He laughed. He probably hadn't thought of Hobnobs in thirty years, and maybe he didn't even recognize them, she thought.

In the taxi, Nancy gestured toward the glistening lake and the gentle green mountains, but Jack was chattering about his flight and his sister Jennifer's family in Boston. He had a nervous catch in his voice. Then he apologized for that.

"It's all right," Nancy said in a soothing tone. The tone was a bit new for her, she thought. She rather liked it. "We're going to be fine," she said.

"Thank God for e-mail," Jack said. "How did couples ever work out their differences in the past?"

"They went walking," Nancy said.

"Up here for the walking, are you?" the taxi driver, a woman in Bono sunglasses, asked. She said she was a native and had walked all over. "This is the best place in the world," she said. "I've just been to Spain and walked the Sierra Nevada. Really enjoyed that. But I wouldn't trade the Lakes."

As they neared the Ambleside, Jack began to consider the scenery. But the view now was throngs of tourists. Nancy had insisted they did not need a car. Cars were discouraged because of the traffic, she told him. She had been there for a week, walking miles every day, just as Dorothy Wordsworth did before she lost her mind.

The lobby of the hotel in Grasmere, where Nancy had been staying, was barely large enough for Nancy and Jack to stand together at the counter. Nancy could have afforded a posh hotel, but she had resisted, uneasy about spending her inheritance on luxuries her parents never had.

"Oh, is this your hubby?" the desk marm burbled, pronouncing it "hooby." She smiled pleasantly at Jack. "Enjoy your stay, luv."

As they climbed the soft-carpeted stairs, Jack said, "I brought my boots. You said we were going to climb a mountain a day. Do I need a walking stick?" He joked, "Maybe I need a cane."

"We're not old."

"If you say so," he said. "That reminds me. I've got some news."

"Oh, what?" She couldn't tell if he meant good news or bad. Jack had perfected an enigmatic expression.

"Robert and Robin took me to the airport. Robin sent you something. It's in my bag. But that's not the news."

"So is Robert going to marry that girl?"

Jack shook his head. "Who knows?" he said, with a slight flicker of a grin.

"She's nice. I like her."

Robert had been living with Robin for two years. Nancy thought Robin was an improvement over his ex-wife, the post-colonial feminist academic from Brattleboro.

In the modest room, Jack glanced around at the evidence of Nancy's life there—books, hiking boots, a periwinkle fleece neck gaiter—as if he was seeing a side of her he didn't know. Although he was still slim and athletic, she could see his face was older, but she was already getting used to it. His familiar face jumped back into place. Probably he saw the same aging in her, but he regarded her tenderly, as though he hadn't noticed the white down that in certain lights was beginning to show on her chin.

"I was afraid something would happen to you here, out walking alone," he said, hugging her once more.

"It's not dangerous here. Tourists, tourists everywhere."

"I still didn't like it."

"Tell your news?" she asked.

"We need to wait a little for a better moment."

"A Romantic moment?"

He grinned. "I get it."

"The poets have been keeping me company." She laughed.

"Aren't they a little old for you—dead, maybe?"

"Historians always get crushes on dead guys."

Nancy vowed not to bore him with her latest obsession. She was putting away her jacket, making a place for his luggage. She felt a bit flustered, as if she was going to entertain a near-stranger. They hadn't really kissed yet.

When Jack came out of the bathroom, she went in. Beside the sink she had made a wall display of Lake District scenes—Grasmere, Loughrigg, Derwentwater. Tourist postcards, not art. He probably disapproved, she thought. She hadn't always understood his photography. "What is it a picture *of?*" she always wanted to know, but he wouldn't tell. "History majors!" he would say. Yet she thought a photograph of knives laid in bomber formation lacked subtlety. Was it supposed to be a statement—about war, say—or was it the simple shock of surreal juxtaposition, as facile as a video on MTV? Even MTV was a generation ago, she thought now. She could hear the telly. Jack had turned on BBC 4.

She had once told him his pictures were cold, and that hurt him. He was actually warm and loving, much more so, than she was. Still, the pictures *were* cold somehow, she felt. But was that a good reason for the breakup of a marriage?

He was standing by the window, watching the swift, narrow rush of the River Rothay below. His hair was thinner, sandier, but not really gray. Her own brown hair had an auburn sheen, and in bright light she could still find individual rust-red hairs, as if they had been borrowed from Jack.

Turning from the window, he embraced her and they tripped around in a clumsy little circle on the thin floral carpet. She thought his news would be about his photographs, and she wanted to show affection, offer praise. She had been rehearsing. Never good at small talk, she had always found it difficult to issue congratulations or happy, encouraging words. She was often preoccupied; she was laconic; she didn't elaborate or waste words. It did not occur to her to say, "Good job, honey." She had never called him "honey." But of course, she had always loved him. He knew that.

Now Nancy, the grad student miraculously possessed of style and a sense of proportion, and ready with appropriate words, smiled. Jack had opened the curtain and was gazing across the fast-flowing water at the church tower. The Wordsworths lay in its shadow, in the graveyard.

"Robert and Robin—it's their news," Jack said, turning to her. "They're having a baby."

Nancy gasped. "Well, knock me down and call me Popeye!" It was something her mother might have said. The phrase shot foolishly through her newfound poise. She sank onto the bed. "Wow. I'm speechless."

"I was surprised. Bowled over. Thrown for a loop. You could have knocked me over with a feather. I'm agog. I'm stupefied. I'm—"

"You had time to rehearse that!" Nancy cried. Jack's trick of reeling out synonyms had always amused her. Now she started to cry.

"It's O.K.," he said, curling his arm around her shoulders. "Robin is a sweet girl. Robert's old enough to make us grandparents. Not that we're old! You just said that."

"Stop," Nancy said through her tears. "I'm not crying over that. I'm crying because of the synonyms."

"Want me to go on? I was dumbfounded. I was nonplussed. I was—"

"That's one thing I missed. I missed that so much."

"I begged Robert and Robin not to tell you yet, to let me bring the news, because it's *our* news too. I wanted to share it with you, to see the look on your face."

She smiled, but only slightly. She had a sense that she was somewhere off to the side, observing her happiness. She held back, for fear of ruining it.

The bed slanted downward, and the shiny duvet on the comforter made crinkly sounds. The bed was unfamiliar to their marriage. And the time of day was unusual, too. Robert, their child, was becoming a father. This was how it was done, she thought, as she and Jack reenacted the moment of creation. She couldn't get away from the surprise: a bit of her and a bit of Jack, combined once, now recombined with something else to initiate a new generation. The phrase "recombinant DNA" floated through her mind, although she wasn't sure what it meant.

Jack sat on the edge of the bed. "I'm sorry," he said. "I was slow. You used to call me 'Speedy.'"

Nancy patted him. "It's all right. We're out of practice." She smoothed the goose-down comforter in place. The thing was surprisingly warm. "Ejaculation," she said suddenly. "Jack off! I never thought of that before. People used to say ejaculation when they meant exclamation."

"They said erection too. Builders would call a house an erection." Jack pulled on his T-shirt. He said, "'My mighty erection,' he ejaculated slowly."

"Don't worry about it," Nancy said. She couldn't think of what else to say.

Soon after she left Jack, a year ago, she visited Northampton, Massachusetts, where they had first met. She drove her old history professor around the countryside. Professor Doyle—she still wanted to address him that way—was still passionate about the Transcendentalists. "I hate time!" he wailed. Nancy was unnerved. She remembered how in class he pumped his fist in the air for emphasis, making history come alive, as if it were a timeless possession in his mind.

Nancy pulled over in front of a post office across the road from the house where she and Jack used to live. The green saltbox, now painted brown, was for sale. The field where she and Jack once ran with their dog had sprouted a monochrome faux–New England housing development. Nancy entertained a quick fantasy of purchasing the house and moving in with Jack, starting over.

"History is imagination," Professor Doyle said, with a tinge of bitterness.

Jack napped while Nancy read snatches of Wordsworth's *The Prelude*, his long paean to Coleridge, in the light from the window. Wordsworth was reviewing his life, gearing up to write his magnum opus, not knowing that most of his great works were already behind him. She absorbed the fleeting scenes of youth, when the two poets had connived to whiplash the imagination. Wordsworth wrote about the eloquence of rustic people, who didn't use proper English and who toiled with bent bodies, people like those from Nancy's past. The poets, in their quest for what they called the sublime, thought nothing of walking the length of England. With Dorothy, they went for midnight rambles in the dead of winter. Nancy could not stop wondering about Dorothy's boots.

Robin's gift was a box of chocolate mice from Boston, and Nancy nibbled several down to their inedible tails. Jack seemed unusually tired, and she let him sleep.

The light was fading when he stirred. Nancy knelt by the bed and nudged him awake. "Come on, Jet-Lag Jack," she said. "You'll get your days and nights mixed up. It's time to go downstairs for dinner."

Jack groaned and sat up. "What time is it?"

"Eight-ten. You don't want to miss sticky-toffee pudding." She grinned as he grimaced.

Jack roused himself from bed, fumbled through his duffel bag, and found a wadded shirt. He began to change into it. Then he reached for Nancy, who was slipping into her black running pants and clogs—her dinner outfit.

"Actually there's more news," he said, holding her arm. "I have prostate cancer."

"*What?*"

"The prostate," he said.

"Oh, Jack!"

"They have to do some more tests, but they want to do surgery." Nancy realized she was now sitting on the floor, clutching the side of the bed. He sat on the side of the bed, and she raised herself to sit beside him. "Maybe it's not really cancer?"

"The doctor did a biopsy. I should have waited to tell you after I get all the results."

She recognized her numbness, the clicking into detachment mode. The news would not sink in for some time. She started to tell him that he was crazy to travel overseas instead of going for surgery right away. But she refrained.

She saw her emotions lying around her, in heaps, like children flung from a Maypole.

Holding her tightly, he told her the details. He had been worried for some time. Perhaps he had come back to her out of a need, she thought, but it was also possible that he knew there was no time for recriminations and separation. Now she was called upon to exert that confidence she had imagined in herself, to say the right things. But she didn't know exactly what. She was sitting in his lap, her head on his shoulder. Somehow they were now in the easy chair.

"I won't ever leave you again." The words didn't sound like hers. "I'm not just saying that," she said.

"I know. I'm not asking you to come back because of this."

"I wanted to come back anyway. You know I did."

"I was afraid to ask you, afraid it wouldn't be authentic."

"Let's not worry about the authentic. We've always pressured ourselves to be authentic. Let's just be ourselves."

He smiled. "Whatever that means." She rubbed his neck. "I missed you," he said.

"I'm glad."

He said, "I don't want you to come home if you don't really feel—"

"Home? We have no home." She ran her fingers through his hair. "You know, it doesn't necessarily mean doom. Some people just live with it."

"Unless I have the Frank Zappa kind."

Nancy reached for her fleece shirt, but she wasn't sure she was cold.

"Bopsy," Nancy said.

"What?"

"Mom pronounced it that way—when she had breast cancer. Biopsy. Bopsy."

"Bopsy, Mopsy and—Cottontail?"

She slid from his lap and stood. "You *know* I love you," she said. "It's *time* that I hate."

Jack's news hit her again. It was illogical, unreal.

She wondered if Mick Jagger ever worried about his prostate.

While Jack was in the bathroom, she roamed through a small paperback he had brought about the prostate. The walnut-sized gland—always described as a walnut, like something a squirrel would hide. The inconvenience of it, such a silly thing to harbor in one's body. A tumor in itself.

Her whole life with Jack was reconfigured in a couple of moments, its arc becoming a circle, like the circle implied in a rainbow or a sunrise.

The downstairs dining room, looking out on the river, was almost deserted. Their table for two was in a corner across from the sideboard of fruit and pudding. The table setting included three china patterns, Nancy noticed.

"The cuisine is strangely inventive here," she told Jack. "Nouvelle Borderlands."

She chose an Italian eggplant dish with cubes of smoked tofu and a pasta called orecchiette—fat blobs like collapsed hats. Jack ordered the plaice. The pasta came with roasted potatoes and carrots on the side, while the plaice had mashed potatoes, carrots and courgettes.

As they ate, Nancy talked rapidly, spilling out everything she had saved to tell Jack. They were ignoring his prostate, but her thoughts had adjusted like blocks of text rejustifying on a computer screen.

"Do you like the plaice?" she asked.

"It's fine—I guess what you always called a charming, cozy hotel."

"I meant the fish."

He grinned. "If I'd said the fish was good, you would have said you meant the hotel."

They laughed. "Maybe you know me better than I thought you did," she said.

In the gray morning they walked, in rain gear, under the soft, dim sky. Jack had slept through the night and declared his jet lag deleted. Dumped. Vanquished. Atomized. But his eyes still looked tired.

"The beans want sticking," Nancy said to Jack in the garden behind Dove Cottage.

"What?"

"Dorothy wrote in her journal, 'The Scarlet Beans want sticking.' It's the same way my grandmother talked. And my mother too. They grew scarlet runner beans, and they had to find sticks for the vines to hold on to. Dorothy wrote about William gathering sticks to stick the peas."

"You're still thinking about your past," he said, not unkindly.

Nancy was thinking of the time Coleridge stopped in at Dove Cottage, while Dorothy and William were away. Coleridge went into the garden, picked some peas, and cooked them. He dressed them, he wrote in his notebook. Nancy's mother used that word. She dressed eggs, dressed a hen. Nancy was pleased to find this cultural connection to her parents and grandparents, but she wouldn't mention that to Jack now. Nancy followed him down the cobbled lane past Dove Cottage, where he occupied himself with taking photos of some small-animal skulls displayed on the side of a stone house.

She said, "Did it ever occur to you that Wordsworth would have an accent, that he would have sounded like the Beatles?"

"Give me a line."

"'My heart leaps up when I behold a rainbow in the sky'?"

Jack tried it but didn't quite get it right. They laughed. She wondered if he was remembering their other trip to the Lake District, but she didn't ask.

A World War II–era Spitfire appeared suddenly, low in the sky over Grasmere. Jack fumbled with his zoom lens and took several shots. "Damn," he said. "I wanted to get it against that hill over there. I just got sky."

"There were fighter jets every day last week," Nancy said.

Early in their marriage, in their rural phase, Nancy grew vegetables. It seemed a moral obligation to grow something if there was good ground. But one night she found herself up at midnight preparing English peas for the freezer. And it occurred to her that she had left home in Kentucky to get away from the hard labor that had enslaved her parents. She was meant to use her mind. But her mind wandered, and she never had a successful career, because she shied away from groups, with their voluble passions. A career was more important to Jack, and she knew he sometimes felt a failure because he hadn't exhibited at the Museum of Modern Art.

Eventually they sold their place in the country. Jack craved the stimulation of artistic friends, and Nancy had grown restless. They moved to Boston, which Nancy loved for its history, and fell in with a set of articulate, intellectual dabblers. But she found something myopic in their ways, how they stirred and sifted the doings of the day as if they were separating wheat from chaff, passing judgments on everyone who came to their notice. Their gatherings, although bohemian, were little contests, a show of strained witticisms. They never made crude remarks or talked about sex or money, and they assumed that everyone in the nation knew who Susan Sontag was.

"I should have made a big pot of chicken-and-dumplings, complete with the yellow feet sticking up," Nancy told Jack once after a miserable dinner party when she had cooked fried chicken. "They would jump right in if it was Chinese. But if it's Southern, it's unacceptable."

Jack just sighed. "There you go again, Nancy. They ate."

"Don't laugh at me," she said.

Kentucky wouldn't release her. She wouldn't let it. She fought Jack on this, and he always accused her of being held back by her culture. She and Jack had often been apart for considerable stretches of time—her many trips to Kentucky; a former job that kept her on the road; and then a serious separation a decade ago. She went to England then, too, but that trip held no good memories. It was only a midlife crisis, she and Jack assured each other, when they reunited. Then a few years back, her parents died, in a ghastly six-month period—cerebral hemorrhage and massive stroke. Nancy broke from Boston then and began living part-time in Kentucky while she reconsidered herself and waited for her grief to subside. She supposed that 9/11 freed her from her own personal grief, but she never said so, for fear of sounding melodramatic. After her parents' farm was sold, that hard rural way of life that had endured for centuries passed away. Nothing held her there, except what Jack called the guilty-daughter syndrome, her conviction that she had betrayed her parents in a hundred ways and that she had never really explained herself to them.

Now Nancy stood in Dorothy's garden and gazed at the yew tree beside the house, a tree that had been there two centuries ago.

Her parents were gone. Their farm was gone. She was herself. It was the twenty-first century.

Heavy rain hit at lunchtime, but by afternoon it eased and the sky brightened slightly. They walked to Easedale, past Goody Bridge. The rain-swollen stream was rushing and high under the bridge. They walked along a board-walk with the water lapping at the edges, then crossed a sheep pasture to the rocky trail that ascended the mountain. Tall granite fences, the ancient work of farmers and shepherds, made hard lines up the mountain. The rock steps of the path were carefully laid, now worn smooth by generations of walkers. The ascent up to Sour Milk Gill was not difficult.

"Are you sure you're all right?" Nancy asked Jack.

"I'm O.K. Fine. Couldn't be better."

"Maybe we should have trekking poles," Nancy said, indicating a young couple with backpacks who were descending at a fast clamber, their metal-tipped poles clicking rapidly against the stones.

"I knew I should have brought a cane," Jack joked.

"We're not old," Nancy said.

They walked steadily for about a mile, Nancy following Jack's lead. They paused just before a steep ascent and drank some water. Nancy stood on a large, smooth rectangular stone that served as a small bridge over a streamlet. As she gazed across at the waterfall, she thought she glimpsed her own image, outsized, with a halo, in the mist above the water. She felt she was in one of Coleridge's "luminous clouds." The sudden sensation faded as she said all this aloud to Jack. "The poets called it a 'glory,'" she explained. "It's accidental, not something that can be forced. It just swoops in, like a bright-feathered bird landing inside your head."

"I've read about that," Jack said. "It's caused by a tiny seizure in the brain."

"Well, then, I'm having a tiny seizure."

The path veered close to the tumble of the waterfall, which was known long ago as Churn Milk Force. Nancy, watching the crash and spray of water, suddenly felt a rare burst of anger as she pictured the days lined up ahead, days that could descend into a dark tedium. Churning through her mind was an intolerable parade of flash-card images—a hospital corridor, a shrunken body, falling hair, a coffin. She would not be able to endure it.

"Stand still. I want to take your picture." Jack lifted his camera and pointed it at her. "I like the way your hair seems to be in motion."

He fiddled with his lenses, paused to let a hiker past, and began snapping.

"What are you thinking?" he said, shielding his camera in its case.

She hesitated, unzipping her jacket partway. She heard a sheep bleat. "I was remembering when we were in the Lake District before," she said. "In Kendal. Remember Mrs. Lindsay and how when she was small, the old people would tell about seeing Wordsworth walking around with his walking stick? Just think—we knew somebody who knew somebody who knew Wordsworth! I've never forgotten that."

"Only three degrees of separation."

"Isn't that amazing?"

"That's important to you?"

She heard the judgment in his voice. The "so what." But she sped along.

"Don't you remember Mrs. Lindsay? I'll never forget her."

"Vaguely."

"I counted forty-eight dishes and pieces of silverware on her breakfast table."

"What a thing to remember," Jack said. "You amaze me."

"Our minds are different."

He nodded, then zipped his camera into its pack. He moved away from the path and sat down on a large rock, his hand gesturing for her to sit beside him.

"I've done a lot of thinking in the past year," he said.

"Me too."

"We weren't paying attention to each other—for a long time."

"I know."

"Because our minds *are* so different," he said. "I get it now."

"We knew that."

"I know, but we were so busy going in different directions, we just didn't make time. You were always doing your puzzles—I mean your scholarly studies."

"Same thing."

"And I was translating everything into some formal meaning." He sighed. "What the hell am I trying to say?"

"You don't have to explain."

"I just mean that the tracks stopped crossing. And we forgot to say hello."

"It's pretty typical," Nancy said, then laughed. "I hate that. I hate to be typical."

"Let me tell you something that happened," Jack said, reaching for her hand. "I was in New Hampshire. Robert and I went to Franconia Notch. And I was overcome with a memory of when we went there years ago. Franconia Notch wasn't at all the way I remembered it."

"You and I were together there with Grover."

"Grover." Jack seemed about to blink out a tear. Grover had been his most beloved dog. "I remembered how we played hide-and-seek in the Flume. Grover and I hid from you. We had such a great time hiding from you. All those big boulders down there."

"The Flume was so narrow and dark," Nancy said. "And I remember a man gave me a hint—where you were hiding. I must have seemed lost. But I found you."

"God, that was such a great memory." Jack put his head in his hands. "And then I realized that all this time I've been hiding from you."

Nancy put her arm around him. "But it is a good memory. And Grover was at our wedding!"

"Life was grand then," he said.

"It was very heaven." Quickly she added, "Wordsworth."

At the top of the waterfall, the scene opened to the tarn, the small mountain lake leaking down the side of the mountain. The lake's surface was shiny and smooth, the reflections of the surrounding mountains sharp. Except for the half dozen hikers in view, there was no sign of the modern world. The mountains—erratic brown-and-gray walls—rimmed the setting.

"This is incredible," Jack said. His camera case dangled from its strap, as if at a loss for pictures, as Nancy was at a loss for words.

"Dorothy and William walked up here at night," she said presently. "They walked everywhere at night. Even in the winter. In the snow and rain."

"I hope they had Gore-Tex," said Jack.

As Nancy pulled Hobnobs from her pack, explosive sounds burst from above—a pair of jet fighters blasting through the sky above the tarn.

Jack scrambled for his camera. But the jets were gone.

The trickle of the river was loud through the open window.

"Let's call Robert," Nancy said.

"Good idea," Jack said, glancing at his watch. "He should be home now."

Robert and Robin were at the house in the White Mountains where Jack's family spent summers. Robert did research at Dartmouth in molecular biology, and he had already published a paper of some significance on cell signaling.

After Jack dialed a long series of numbers from his telephone card, Nancy took the phone. Robert answered on the second ring. Hearing her son's voice filled her with an anxious pleasure. She sensed that whenever she talked to him she turned into a slightly different Nancy, seeing herself as he saw her. Now she turned into a giddy grandmother, silly, talking to her son.

"Robin wants to keep her job," Robert was saying. "She can work at home."

"I hope you're happy," Nancy said. "I hope this is what you wanted." She wondered if they were still in love after two years of cohabitation.

"Dad told me some news too," he said.

"Oh?" Nancy sensed Robert's hesitation.

"He said you were getting back together."

"Did he know that?"

"You'd better ask him."

The coming together again seemed easy, she thought. Perhaps Jack's good news and bad news had canceled each other out, leaving them in limbo. While Jack spoke with Robert, Nancy examined her face in the bathroom mirror. More and more, she resembled her mother. This used to frighten her, but she had come to find the recognition pleasant. She would say a quiet hello. Now, as she gazed into her reflection, she could remember the stages of her growth in photographs—the tentative baby-faced first-grader; the saucy high-schooler; the college adventurer, with her brows darkened and thickened, her lipstick lustrous, her hair briefly beehived; her unadorned sixties personality (the "natural look," it was called); the thinner, more angular face as her son grew up and she weathered. She could see all her faces morphed together, each peeking out of the other, the guises through which she had acted out the scenes of her history. And, too, she saw her mother's turned-up nose and scared eyes; and her father's square jaw; and her grandmother's sagging jowls. She imagined other unknown faces of ancestors, and she saw her son, his mouth and warm coloring. And somewhere in her face was her grandchild.

She heard Jack winding up his talk with Robert. Again, she remembered that first trip to the Lake District with Jack, at Mrs. Lindsay's in Kendal. When Coleridge returned to England in 1806 from a long escape to Malta, he didn't want to see his wife. He had gone to Malta to forget a woman he loved—not his wife, and not Dorothy. He returned to England after two years, intending to ask for an official separation from his wife, but he couldn't bring himself to go home to the Lake District. He remained in London for months. And then when he did go, he delayed the reunion even further by stopping at an inn in nearby Kendal. After he invited Wordsworth to supper, people heard he was back. His family and friends rushed forth to see him, because he had been gone for two years, and they loved him. But he was afraid, afraid to go home.

Nancy could see him reaching far back on the dusty shelf for his opium mix. *Kendal Black Drop.* The words beat on her ears.


That evening after dinner, Nancy and Jack walked down Stock Lane to look at the stars. They wandered out into the soccer field. Tiny Grasmere was sleeping, but a faint stream of music and laughter seemed to emanate from the mountains, or maybe the moon. The moon was hornéd, as it was in *The Rime of the Ancient Mariner.* The hornéd moon, an image Dorothy had contributed.

Coleridge often walked the fourteen miles from Keswick to Grasmere to visit Dorothy and William. In her journal, Dorothy wrote that she and Coleridge took this very walk, along Stock Lane. They walked from the cottage to the church in the moonlight. She wrote of lingering in the garden later with Coleridge, after the others had gone to bed. To Nancy, the spare notations resonated with desire.

Nancy and Jack stood in the soccer field, gazing up into the night sky. Nancy's mind was busily adjusting the details from Dorothy's journal to this spot. She felt the sorrow of separation and unrequited love and romantic obsession—all of life's romance blowing like a cyclone through those lives two centuries ago, when they were innocent of time.

"I don't think I could live this far from a city," Jack said. "But I like this climate. I don't have any sinus trouble here."

"Good."

"What about your guys?"

"What?"

"The poets. Any sinus trouble?"

"Coleridge had to breathe through his mouth." She laughed. "But his worst trouble was his digestion." She paused, trying to remember one of his descriptions. She said, "He wrote in a letter that he had been bathing in the sea and it made him sick. He said, 'My triumphant Tripes cataracted most Niagara-ishly.'" She spoke slowly, to get the syllables right.

He laughed. "Your pals are starting to be real to me."

She squeezed his hand. "They're here, like ghosts." She could feel them, young people struggling with the future.

The air was damp but not biting. They crossed the road to Dove Cottage. The windows were dark. Nancy imagined Coleridge stopping there in the rain, wanting solace and comfort from his friends; arriving late, past midnight, he was wet and anxious after his long tramp over Mount Helvellyn in the rain. Probably he needed to spew out all his ideas and affections—the treasure trove of a young genius, thrust forth like a hostess gift. His was a mind that never stopped whirling and somersaulting. Nancy imagined the stone floor in the front room, wet with the rain Coleridge brought in, and the urgent glee of his voice slamming the walls and the low ceiling. A man whose voice was music.

In the dark, by the garden gate, Nancy and Jack huddled together, his arm tight on her shoulders. He had come across the ocean for her.

"I missed you," she said. "I want you back."

"I want you back," he said. "But where? Where will we live?"

"I don't know. Where *can* we live?"

# VII

# More Love Lives

*I am interested in how characters handle their limitations, especially those who glimpse unprecedented possibility. Anticipation, fear, anxiety, and gladsomeness merge at the thought of greener pastures, as seen through a knothole.*

*I don't have messages. I avoid issues, themes, and symbols. Those may be there, but they wouldn't be without the furniture and clothing of the story itself. More important to me is the sound of the language and the details. I am trying to get at what something is like—what it feels like, not what it means. Style and story should match, the dancer and the dance inseparable. A story is not reducible. Fiction is, above all, stories, not guidebooks or the ornamental takeaways of symbol and theme. Sometimes hearing a fly buzz means there is a fly in the room. And you need a fly swatter.*

—BAM

# Memphis

FROM *Love Life* (1989)

On Friday, after Beverly dropped the children off at her former husband's place for the weekend, she went dancing at the Paradise Club with a man she had met at the nature extravaganza at the Land Between the Lakes. Since her divorce she had not been out much, but she enjoyed dancing, and her date was a good dancer. She hadn't expected that, because he was shy and seemed more at home with his hogs than with people.

Emerging from the rest room, Beverly suddenly ran into her ex-husband, Joe. For a confused moment she almost didn't recognize him, out of context. He was with a tall, skinny woman in jeans and a fringed cowboy shirt. Joe looked sexy, in a black T-shirt with the sleeves ripped out to show his muscles, but the woman wasn't pretty. She looked bossy and hard.

"Where are the kids?" Beverly shouted at Joe above the music.

"At Mama's. They're all right. Hey, Beverly, this is Janet."

"I'm going over there and get them right now," Beverly said, ignoring Janet.

"Don't be silly, Bev. They're having a good time. Mama fixed up a playroom for them."

"Maybe next week I'll just take them straight to her house. We'll bypass you altogether. Eliminate the middleman." Beverly was a little drunk.

"For Christ's sake."

"This goes on your record," she warned him. "I'm keeping a list."

Janet was touching his elbow possessively, and then the man Beverly had come with showed up with beer mugs in his fists. "Is there something I should know?" he said.

Beverly and Joe had separated the year before, just after Easter, and over the summer they tried unsuccessfully to get back together for the sake of the children. A few times after the divorce became final, Beverly spent the night with Joe, but each time she felt it was a mistake. It felt adulterous. A little thing, a quirky habit—like the way he kept the glass coffeepot simmering on the stove—could make her realize they shouldn't see each other. Coffee turned bitter when it was left simmering like that.

Joe never wanted to probe anything very deeply. He accepted things, even her request for a divorce, without asking questions. Beverly could never tell if that meant he was calm and steady or dangerously lacking in curiosity. In the last months they lived together, she had begun to feel that her mind was crammed with useless information, like a landfill, and there wasn't space deep down in her to move around in, to explore what was there. She didn't trust her intelligence anymore. She couldn't repeat the simplest thing she heard on the news and have it make sense to anyone. She would read a column in the newspaper—about something important, like taxes or the death penalty—but be unable to remember what she had read. She felt she had strong ideas and meaningful thoughts, but often when she tried to reach for one she couldn't find it. It was terrifying.

Whenever she tried to explain this feeling to Joe, he just said she expected too much of herself. He didn't expect enough of himself, though, and now she felt that the divorce hadn't affected him deeply enough to change him at all. She was disappointed. He should have gone through a major new phase, especially after what had happened to his friend Chubby Jones, one of his fishing buddies. Chubby burned to death in his pickup truck. One night soon after the divorce became final, Joe woke Beverly up with his pounding on the kitchen door. Frightened, and still not used to being alone with the children, she cracked the venetian blind, one hand on the telephone. Then she recognized the silhouette of Joe's truck in the driveway.

"I didn't want to scare you by using the key," he said when she opened the door. She was furious: he might have woken up the children.

It hadn't occurred to her that he still had a key. Joe was shaking, and when he came inside he flopped down at the kitchen table, automatically choosing his usual place facing the door. In the eerie glow from the fluorescent light above the kitchen sink, he told her about Chubby. Nervously spinning the lazy Susan, Joe groped for words, mostly repeating in disbelief the awful facts. Beverly had never seen him in such a state of shock. His news seemed to cancel out their divorce, as though it were only a trivial fit they had had.

"We were at the Blue Horse Tavern," he said. "Chubby was going on about some shit at work and he had it in his head he was going to quit and go off and live like a hermit and let Donna and the kids do without. You couldn't argue with him when he got like that—a little too friendly with Jack Daniel's. When he went out to his truck we followed him. We were going to follow him home to see he didn't have a wreck, but then he passed out right there in his truck, and so we left him there in the parking lot to sleep it off." Joe buried his head in his hands and started to cry. "We thought we were doing the best thing," he said.

Beverly stood behind him and draped her arms over his shoulders, holding him while he cried.

Chubby's cigarette must have dropped on the floor, Joe explained as she rubbed his neck and shoulders. The truck had caught fire sometime after the bar closed. A passing driver reported the fire, but the rescue squad arrived too late.

"I went over there," Joe said. "That's where I just came from. It was all dark, and the parking lot was empty, except for his truck, right where we left it. It was all black and hollow. It looked like something from Northern Ireland."

He kept twirling the lazy Susan, watching the grape jelly, the sugar bowl, the honey bear, the salt and pepper shakers go by.

"Come on," Beverly said after a while. She led him to the bedroom. "You need some sleep."

After that, Joe didn't say much about his friend. He seemed to get over Chubby's death, as a child would forget some disappointment. It was sad, he said. Beverly felt so many people were like Joe—half conscious, being pulled along by thoughtless impulses and notions, as if their lives were no more than a load of freight hurtling along on the interstate. Even her mother was like that. After Beverly's father died, her mother became devoted to "The PTL Club" on television. Beverly knew her father would have argued her out of such an obsession when he was alive. Her mother had two loves now: "The PTL Club" and Kenny Rogers. She kept a scrapbook on Kenny Rogers and she owned all his albums, including the ones that had come out on CD. She still believed fervently in Jim and Tammy Bakker, even after all the fuss. They reminded her of Christmas elves, she told Beverly recently.

"Christmas elves!" Beverly repeated in disgust. "They're the biggest phonies I ever saw."

"Do you think you're better than everybody else, Beverly?" her mother said, offended. "That's what ruined your marriage. I can't get over how you've mistreated poor Joe. You're always judging everybody."

That hurt, but there was some truth in it. She was like her father, who had been a plainspoken man. He didn't like for the facts to be dressed up. He could spot fakes as easily as he noticed jimsonweed in the cornfield. Her mother's remark made her start thinking about her father in a new way. He died ten years ago, when Beverly was pregnant with Shayla, her oldest child. She remembered his unvarying routines. He got up at sunup, ate the same breakfast day in and day out, never went anywhere. In the spring, he set out tobacco plants, and as they matured he suckered them, then stripped them, cured them, and hauled them to auction. She remembered him burning the tobacco beds—the pungent smell, the threat of wind. She used to think his life was dull, but now she had started thinking about those routines as beliefs. She compared them to the routines in her life with Joe: her CNN news fix, telephoning customers at work and entering orders on the computer, the couple of six-packs she and Joe used to drink every evening, Shayla's tap lessons, Joe's basketball night, family night at the sports club. Then she remembered her father running the combine over his wheat fields, wheeling that giant machine around expertly, much the same way Joe handled a motorcycle.

When Tammy, the youngest, was born, Joe was not around. He had gone out to Pennyrile Forest with Jimmy Stone to play war games. Two teams of guys spent three days stalking each other with pretend bullets, trying to make believe they were in the jungle. In rush-hour traffic, Beverly drove herself to the hospital, and the pains caused her to pull over onto the shoulder several times. Joe had taken the childbirth lessons with her and was supposed to be there, participating, helping her with the breathing rhythms. A man would find it easier to go to war than to be around a woman in labor, she told her roommate in the hospital. When Tammy was finally born, Beverly felt that anger had propelled the baby out of her.

But when Joe showed up at the hospital, grinning a moon-pie grin, he gazed into her eyes, running one of her curls through his fingers. "I want to check out that maternal glow of yours," he said, and she felt trapped by desire, even in her condition. For her birthday once, he had given her a satin teddy and "fantasy slippers" with pink marabou feathers, whatever those were. He told the children that the feathers came from the marabou bird, a cross between a caribou and a marigold.

On Friday afternoon after work the week following the Paradise Club incident, Beverly picked up Shayla from her tap lesson and Kerry and Tammy from day care. She drove them to Joe's house, eight blocks from where she lived.

From the back seat Shayla said, "I don't want to go to the dentist tomorrow. When Daddy has to wait for me, he disappears for about *two hours*. He can't stand to wait."

Glancing in the rearview mirror at Shayla, Beverly said, "You tell your daddy to set himself down and read a magazine if he knows what's good for him."

"Daddy said you were trying to get rid of us," Kerry said.

"That's not true! Don't you let him talk mean about me. He can't get away with that."

"He said he'd take us to the lake," Kerry said. Kerry was six, and snaggletoothed. His teeth were coming in crooked—more good news for the dentist.

Joe's motorcycle and three-wheeler were hogging the driveway, so Beverly pulled up to the curb. His house was nice—a brick ranch he rented from his parents, who lived across town. The kids liked having two houses—they had more rooms, more toys.

"Give me some sugar," Beverly said to Tammy, as she unbuckled the child's seat belt. Tammy smeared her moist little face against Beverly's. "Y'all be good now," Beverly said. She hated leaving them.

The kids raced up the sidewalk, their backpacks bobbing against their legs. She saw Joe open the door and greet them. Then he waved at her to come inside. "Come on in and have a beer!" he called loudly. He held his beer can up like the Statue of Liberty's torch. He had on a cowboy hat with a large feather plastered on the side of the crown. His tan had deepened. She felt her stomach do a flip and her mind fuzz over like mold on fruit. I'm an idiot, she told herself.

She shut off the engine and pocketed the keys. Joe's fat black cat accompanied her up the sidewalk. "You need to put that cat on a diet," Beverly said to Joe when he opened the door for her. "He looks like a little hippo in black pajamas."

"He goes to the no-frills mouse market and loads up," Joe said, grinning. "I can't stop him."

The kids were already in the kitchen, investigating the refrigerator—one of those with beverage dispensers on the outside. Joe kept the dispensers filled with surprises—chocolate milk or Juicy Juice.

"Daddy, can I microwave a burrito?" asked Shayla.

"No, not now. We'll go to the mall after-while, so you don't want to ruin your supper now."

"Oh, boy. That means Chi-Chi's."

The kids disappeared into the family room in the basement, carrying Cokes and bags of cookies and potato chips. Joe opened a beer for Beverly. She was sitting on the couch smoking a cigarette and staring blankly at his pocket-knife collection in a case on the coffee table when Joe came forward and stood over her. Something was wrong.

"I'm being transferred," he said, handing her the beer. "I'm moving to Columbia, South Carolina."

She sat very still, her cigarette poised in midair like a freeze-frame scene on the VCR. A purple stain shaped like a flower was on the arm of the couch. His rug was the nubby kind made of tiny loops, and one patch had unraveled. She could hear the blip-blip-crash of video games downstairs.

"What?" she said.

"I'm being transferred."

"I heard you. I'm just having trouble getting it from my ears to my mind." She was stunned. She had never imagined Joe anywhere except right here in town.

"The plant's got an opening there, and I'll make a whole lot more."

"But you don't have to go. They can't make you go."

"It's an opportunity. I can't turn it down."

"But it's too far away."

He rested his hand lightly on her shoulder. "I'll want to have the kids on vacations—and all summer."

"Well, tough! You expect me to send them on an airplane all that way?"

"You'll have to make some adjustments," he said calmly, taking his hand away and sitting down beside her on the couch.

"I couldn't stay away from them that long," she said. "And Columbia, South Carolina? It's not interesting. They'll hate it. Nothing's there."

"You don't know that."

"What would you do with them? You can never think of what to do with them when you've got them, so you stuff them with junk or dump them at your mother's." Beverly felt confused, unable to call upon the right argument. Her words came out wrong, more accusing than she meant.

He was saying, "Why don't you move there, too? What would keep you here?"

"Don't make me laugh." Her beer can was sweating, making cold circles on her bare leg.

He scrunched his empty can into a wad, as if he had made a decision. "We could buy a house and get back together," he said. "I didn't like seeing you on that dance floor the other night with that guy. I didn't like you seeing me with Janet. I didn't like being there with Janet. I suddenly wondered why we had to be there in those circumstances, when we could have been home with the kids."

"It would be the same old thing," Beverly said impatiently. "My God, Joe, think of what you'd do with three kids for three whole months."

"I think I know how to handle them. It's you I never could handle." He threw the can across the room straight into the kitchen wastebasket. "We've got a history together," he said. "That's the positive way to look at it." Playfully he cocked his hat and gave her a wacky, ironic look—his imitation of Jim-Boy McCoy, a used-furniture dealer in a local commercial.

"You take the cake," she said, with a little burst of laughter. But she couldn't see herself moving to Columbia, South Carolina, of all places. It would be too hot, and the people would talk in drippy, soft drawls. The kids would hate it.

After she left Joe's, she went to Tan Your Hide, the tanning salon and fitness shop that Jolene Walker managed. She worked late on Fridays. Beverly and Jolene had been friends since junior high, when they entered calves in the fair together.

"I need a quick hit before I go home," Beverly said to Jolene. "Use number two—number one's acting funny, and I'm scared to use it. I think the light's about to blow."

In the changing room, Jolene listened sympathetically to Beverly's news about Joe. "Columbia, South Carolina!" Jolene cried. "What will I do with myself if you go off?"

"A few years ago I'd have jumped at the chance to move someplace like South Carolina, but it wouldn't be right to go now unless I love him," Beverly said. As she pulled on her bathing suit, she said, "Damn! I couldn't bear to be away from the kids for a whole summer!"

"Maybe he can't either," said Jolene, skating the dressing-room curtain along its track. "Listen, do you want to ride to Memphis with me tomorrow? I've got to pick up some merchandise coming in from California—a new line of sweatsuits. It's cheaper to go pick it up at the airport than have it flown up here by commuter."

"Yeah, sure. I don't know what else to do with my weekends. Without the kids, my weekends are like black holes." She laughed. "Big empty places you get sucked into." She made a comic sucking noise that made Jolene smile.

"We could go hear some of that good Memphis blues on Beale Street," Jolene suggested.

"Let me think about it while I work on my tan. I want to get in here and do some meditating."

"Are you still into that? That reminds me of my ex-husband and that born-again shit he used to throw at me."

"It's not the same thing," Beverly said, getting into the sunshine coffin, as she called it. "Beam me up," she said. She liked to meditate while she tanned. It was private, and she felt she was accomplishing something at the same time. In meditation, the jumbled thoughts in her mind were supposed to settle down, like the drifting snowflakes in a paperweight.

Jolene adjusted the machine and clicked the dial. "Ready for takeoff?"

"As ready as I'll ever be," said Beverly, her eyes hidden under big cotton pads. She was ruining her eyes at work, staring at a video display terminal all day. Under the sunlamp, she imagined her skin broiling as she slowly moved through space like that space station in *2001* that revolved like a rotisserie.

Scenes floated before her eyes. Helping shell purple-hull peas one hot afternoon when she was about seventeen; her mother shelling peas methodically, with the sound of Beverly's father in the bedroom coughing and spitting into a newspaper-lined cigar box. Her stomach swelled out with Kerry, and a night then when Joe didn't come back from a motorcycle trip and she was so scared she could feel the fear deep inside, right into the baby's heartbeat. Her father riding a horse along a fencerow. In the future, she thought, people would get in a contraption something like the sunshine coffin and go time traveling, unbounded by time and space or custody arrangements.

One winter afternoon two years ago: a time with Joe and the kids. Tammy was still nursing, and Kerry had just lost a tooth. Shayla was reading a Nancy Drew paperback, which was advanced for her age, but Shayla was smart. They were on the living-room floor together, on a quilt, having a picnic and watching *Chitty Chitty Bang Bang*. Beverly felt happy. That day, Kerry learned a new word—"soldier." She teased him. "You're my little soldier," she said. Sometimes she thought she could make moments like that happen again, but when she tried, it felt forced. They would be at the supper table, and she'd give the children hot dogs or tacos—something they liked—and she would say, "This is such fun!" and they would look at her funny.

Joe used to say to anyone new they met, "I've got a blue collar and a red neck and a white ass. I'm the most patriotic son of a bitch on two legs!" She and Joe were happy when they started out together. After work, they would sit on the patio with the stereo turned up loud and drink beer and pitch horseshoes while the steak grilled. On weekends, they used to take an ice chest over to the lake and have cookouts with friends and go fishing. When Joe got a motorcycle, they rode together every weekend. She loved the feeling, her feet clenching the foot pegs and her hands gripping the seat strap for dear life. She loved the wind burning her face, her hair flying out from under the helmet, her chin boring into Joe's back as he tore around curves. Their friends all worked at the new plants, making more money than they ever had before. Everyone they knew had a yard strewn with vehicles: motorcycles, three-wheelers, sporty cars, pickups. One year, people started buying horses. It was just a thing people were into suddenly, so that they could ride in the annual harvest parade in Fenway. Joe and Beverly never got around to having a horse, though. It seemed too much trouble after the kids came along. Most of the couples they knew then drank a lot and argued and had fights, but they had a good time. Now marriages were splitting up. Beverly could name five divorces or separations in her crowd. It seemed no one knew why this was happening. Everybody blamed it on statistics: half of all marriages nowadays ended in divorce. It was a fact, like traffic jams—just one of those things you had to put up with in modern life. But Beverly thought money was to blame: greed made people purely stupid. She admired Jolene for the simple, clear way she divorced Steve and made her own way without his help. Steve had gone on a motorcycle trip alone, and when he came back he was a changed man. He had joined a bunch of born-again bikers he met at a campground in Wyoming, and afterward he tried to convert everybody he knew. Jolene refused to take the Lord as her personal savior. "It's amazing how much spite Steve has in him," Jolene told Beverly after she moved out. "I don't even care anymore."

It made Beverly angry not to know why she didn't want Joe to go to South Carolina. Did he just want her to come to South Carolina for convenience, for the sake of the children? Sometimes she felt they were both stalled at a crossroads, each thinking the other had the right-of-way. But now his foot was on the gas.

Jolene was saying, "Get out of there before you cook!"

Beverly removed the cotton pads from her eyes and squinted at the bright light.

Jolene said, "Look at this place on my arm. It looks just like one of those skin cancers in my medical guide." She pointed to an almost invisible spot in the crook of her arm. Jolene owned a photographer's magnifying glass a former boyfriend had given her, and she often looked at her moles with it. Under the glass, tiny moles looked hideous and black, with red edges.

Beverly, who was impatient with Jolene's hypochondria, said, "I wouldn't worry about it unless I could see it with my bare naked eyes."

"I think I should stop tanning," Jolene said.

The sky along the western horizon was a flat yellow ribbon with the tree line pasted against it. After the farmland ran out, Beverly and Jolene passed small white houses in disrepair, junky little clusters of businesses, a Kmart, then a Wal-Mart. As Jolene drove along, Beverly thought about Joe's vehicles. It had never occurred to her before that he had all those wheels and hardly went anywhere except places around home. But now he was actually leaving.

She was full of nervous energy. She kept twisting the radio dial, trying to find a good driving song. She wished the radio would play "Radar Love," a great driving song. All she could get was country stations and gospel stations. After a commercial for a gigantic flea market, with dealers coming from thirty states, the announcer said, "Elvis would be there—if he could." Jolene hit the horn. "Elvis, we're on our way, baby!"

"There's this record store I want to go to if we have time," said Jolene. "It's got all these old rock songs—everything you could name, going way back to the very beginning."

"Would they have 'Your Feet's Too Big,' by Fats Waller? Joe used to sing that."

"Honey, they've got *everything*. Why, I bet they've got a tape of Fats Waller humming to himself in the outhouse." They laughed, and Jolene said, "You're still stuck on Joe."

"I can't let all three kids go to South Carolina on one airplane! If it crashed, I'd lose all three of them at once."

"Oh, don't think that way!"

Beverly sighed. "I can't get used to not having a child pulling on my leg every minute. But I guess I should get out and have a good time."

"Now you're talking."

"Maybe if he moves to South Carolina, we can make a clean break. Besides, I better not fight him, or he might kidnap them."

"Do you really think that?" said Jolene, astonished.

"I don't know. You hear about cases like that." Beverly changed the radio station again.

"I can't stand to see you tear yourself up this way," said Jolene, giving Beverly's arm an affectionate pat.

Beverly laughed. "Hey, look at that bumper sticker—'A WOMAN'S PLACE IS IN THE MALL.'"

"All *right!*" said Jolene.

They drove into Memphis on Route 51, past self-service gas stations in corrugated-tin buildings with country hams hanging in the windows. Beverly noticed a memorial garden between two cornfields, with an immense white statue of Jesus rising up from the center like the Great White Shark surfacing. They passed a display of black-velvet paintings beside a van, a ceramic-grassware place, a fireworks stand, motels, package stores, auto-body shops, car dealers that sold trampolines and satellite dishes. A stretch of faded old wooden buildings—grim and gray and ramshackle—followed, then factories, scrap-metal places, junkyards, ancient grills and poolrooms, small houses so old the wood looked rotten. Then came the housing projects. It was all so familiar. Beverly remembered countless trips to Memphis when her father was in the hospital here, dying of cancer. The Memphis specialists prolonged his misery, and Beverly's mother said afterward, "We should have set him out in the corncrib and let him go naturally, the way he wanted to go."

Beverly and Jolene ate at a Cajun restaurant that night, and later they walked down Beale Street, which had been spruced up and wasn't as scary as it used to be, Beverly thought. The sidewalks were crowded with tourists and policemen. At a blues club, she and Jolene giggled like young girls out looking for love. Beverly had been afraid Memphis would make her sad, but after three strawberry Daiquiris she was feeling good. Jolene had a headache and was drinking ginger ale, which turned out to be Sprite with a splash of Coke—what bartenders do when they're out of ginger ale, Beverly told her. She didn't know how she knew that. Probably Joe had told her once. He used to tend bar. Forget Joe, she thought. She needed to loosen up a little. The kids had been saying she was like either Kate or Allie on that TV show—whichever was the uptight one; she couldn't remember.

The band was great—two white guys and two black guys. Between numbers, they joked with the waitress, a middle-aged woman with spiked red hair and shoulder pads that fit cockeyed. The white lead singer clowned around with a cardboard stand-up figure of Marilyn Monroe in her white dress from *The Seven Year Itch*. He spun her about the dance floor, sneaking his hand onto Marilyn's crotch where her dress had flown up. He played her like a guitar. A pretty black woman in a dark leather skirt and polka-dotted jacket danced with a slim young black guy with a brush haircut. Beverly wondered how he got his hair to stick up like that. Earlier, when she and Jolene stopped at a Walgreen's for shampoo, Beverly had noticed a whole department of hair-care products for blacks. There was a row of large jugs of hair conditioner, like the jugs motor oil and bleach came in.

Jolene switched from fake ginger ale to Fuzzy Navels, which she had been drinking earlier at the Cajun restaurant. She blamed her headache on Cajun frog legs but said she felt better now. "I'm having a blast," she said, drumming her slender fingers on the table in time with the band.

"I'm having a blast, too," Beverly said, just as an enormous man with tattoos of outer-space monsters on his arms asked Jolene to dance.

"No way!" Jolene said, cringing. On his forearm was an astounding picture of a creature that reminded Beverly of one of Kerry's dinosaur toys.

"That guy's really off the moon," Jolene said as the man left.

During the break, the waitress passed by with a plastic bucket, collecting tips for the band. Beverly thought of an old song, "Bucket's Got a Hole in It." Her grandmother's kitchen slop bucket with its step pedal. Going to hell in a bucket. Kick the bucket. She felt giddy.

"That boy's here every night," the waitress said, with a turn of her head toward the tattooed guy, who had approached another pair of women. "I feel so sorry for him. His brother killed himself and his mother's in jail for drugs. He never could hold a job. He's trouble waiting for a ride."

"Does the band know 'Your Feet's Too Big'?" Beverly asked the waitress, who was stuffing requests into her pocket.

"Is that a song, or are you talking about my big hoofs?" the woman said, with a wide, teasing grin.

On the way back to their motel on Elvis Presley Boulevard, Jolene got on a one-way street and ended up in downtown Memphis, where the tall buildings were. Beverly would hate to work so high up in the air. Her cousin had a job down here in life insurance and said she never knew what the weather was. Beverly wondered if South Carolina had any skyscrapers.

"There's the famous Peabody Hotel," Jolene was saying. "The hotel with the ducks."

"Ducks?"

"At that hotel it's ducks galore," explained Jolene. "The towels and stationery and stuff. I know a girl who stayed there, and she said a bunch of ducks come down every morning on the elevator and go splash in the fountain. It's a tourist attraction."

"The kids would like that. That's what I should be doing down here—taking the kids someplace, not getting smashed like this." Beverly felt disembodied, her voice coming from the glove compartment.

"Everything is *should* with you, Beverly!" Jolene said, making a right on red.

Jolene didn't mean to sound preachy, Beverly thought. Fuzzy Navels did that to her. If Beverly mentioned what she was feeling about Joe, Jolene would probably say that Joe just looked good right now compared to some of the weirdos you meet out in the world.

Down the boulevard, the lights spread out extravagantly. As Beverly watched, a green neon light winked off, and the whole scene seemed to shift slightly. It was like making a correction on the VDT at work—the way the screen readjusted all the lines and spacing to accommodate the change. Far away, a red light was inching across the black sky. She thought about riding behind Joe on his Harley, flashing through the dark on a summer night, cool in the wind, with sparkling, mysterious lights flickering off the lake.

The music from the night before was still playing in Beverly's head when she got home Sunday afternoon. It was exhilarating, like something she knew well but hadn't thought of in years. It came soaring up through her with a luxurious clarity. She could still hear the henna-haired waitress saying, "Are you talking about my big hoofs?" Beverly's dad used to say, "Oh, my aching dogs!" She clicked "Radar Love" into the cassette player and turned the volume up loud. She couldn't help dancing to its hard frenzy. "Radar Love" made her think of Joe's Fuzzbuster, which he bought after he got two speeding tickets in one month. One time, he told the children his razor was a Fuzzbuster. Speeding, she whirled joyfully through the hall.

The song was only halfway through when Joe arrived with the kids—unexpectedly early. Kerry ejected the tape. Sports voices hollered out from the TV. Whenever the kids returned from their weekends, they plowed through the place, unloading their belongings and taking inventory of what they had left behind. Tammy immediately flung all her toys out of her toybox, looking for a rag doll she had been worried about. Joe said she had cried about it yesterday.

"How was the dentist?" Beverly asked Shayla.

"I don't want to talk about it," said Shayla, who was dumping dirty clothes on top of the washing machine.

"Forty bucks for one stupid filling," Joe said.

Joe had such a loud voice that he always came on too strong. Beverly remembered with embarrassment the time he called up Sears and terrorized the poor clerk over a flaw in a sump pump, when it wasn't the woman's fault. But now he lowered his voice to a quiet, confidential tone and said to Beverly in the kitchen, "Yesterday at the lake Shayla said she wished you were there with us, and I tried to explain to her how you had to have some time for yourself, how you said you had to have your own space and find yourself—you know, all that crap on TV. She seemed to get a little depressed, and I thought maybe I'd said the wrong thing, but a little later she said she'd been thinking, and she knew what you meant."

"She's smart," Beverly said. Her cheeks were burning. She popped ice cubes out of a tray and began pouring Coke into a glass of ice.

"She gets it honest—she's got smart parents," he said with a grin.

Beverly drank the Coke while it was still foaming. Bubbles burst on her nose. "It's not crap on TV," she said angrily. "How can you say that?"

He looked hurt. She observed the dimple on his chin, the corresponding kink of his hairline above his ear, the way his hat shaded his eyes and deepened their fire. Even if he lived to be a hundred, Joe would still have those seductive eyes. Kerry wandered into the kitchen, dragging a green dinosaur by a hind foot. "We didn't have any corny cakes," he whined. He meant cornflakes.

"Why didn't Daddy get you some?"

After Kerry drifted away, Joe said, "I'm going to South Carolina in a couple of weeks. Check it out and try to find a place to live."

Beverly opened the freezer and took chicken thighs out to thaw, then began clearing dishes to keep from bursting into tears.

"Columbia's real progressive," he said. "Lots of businesses are relocating there. It's a place on the way up."

The foam had settled on her Coke, and she poured some more. She began loading the dishwasher. One of her new nonstick pans already had a scratch.

"How was Memphis?" Joe asked, his hand on the kitchen doorknob.

"Fine," she said. "Jolene had too many Fuzzy Navels."

"That figures."

Shayla rushed in then and said, "Daddy, you got to fix that thing in my closet. The door won't close."

"That track at the top? Not again! I don't have time to work on it right now."

"He doesn't live here," Beverly said to Shayla.

"Well, my closet's broke, and who's going to fix it?" Shayla threw up her hands and stomped out of the kitchen.

Joe said, "You know, in the future, if we're going to keep this up, we're going to have to learn to carry on a better conversation, because this stinks." He adjusted his hat, setting it firmly on his head. "You're so full of wants you don't know what you want," he said.

Through the glass section of the door she could see him walking to his truck with his hands in his pockets. She had seen him march out the door exactly that way so many times before—whenever he didn't want to hear what was coming next, or when he thought he had had the last word. She hurried out to speak to him, but he was already pulling away, gunning his engine loudly. She watched him disappear, his tail-lights winking briefly at a stop sign. She felt ashamed.

Beverly paused beside the young pin-oak tree at the corner of the drive-way. When Joe planted it, there were hardly any trees in the subdivision. All the houses were built within the last ten years, and the trees were still spindly. The house just to her left was Mrs. Grim's. She was a widow and kept cats. On the other side, a German police dog in a backyard pen spent his time barking across Beverly's yard at Mrs. Grim's cats. The man who owned the dog operated a video store, and his wife mysteriously spent several weeks a year out of town. When she was away her husband stayed up all night watching TV, like a child freed from rules. Beverly could see his light on when she got up in the night with the kids. She had never really noticed that the bricks of all three houses were a mottled red and gray, like uniformly splattered paint. There was a row of vertical bricks supporting each window. She stood at the foot of the driveway feeling slightly amazed that she should be stopped in her tracks at this particular time and place.

It ought to be so easy to work out what she really wanted. Beverly's parents had stayed married like two dogs locked together in passion, except it wasn't passion. But she and Joe didn't have to do that. Times had changed. Joe could up and move to South Carolina. Beverly and Jolene could hop down to Memphis just for a fun weekend. Who knew what might happen or what anybody would decide to do on any given weekend or at any stage of life?

She brought in yesterday's mail—a car magazine for Joe, a credit-card bill he was supposed to pay, some junk mail. She laid the items for Joe on a kitchen shelf next to the videotape she had borrowed from him and forgotten to return.

# Midnight Magic

FROM *Love Life* (1989)

Steve leaves the supermarket and hits the sunlight. Blinking, he stands there a moment, then glances at his feet. He has on running shoes, but he was sure he had put on boots. He touches his face. He hasn't shaved. His car, illegally parked in the space for the handicapped, is deep blue and wicked. The rear has "Midnight Magic" painted on it in large pink curlicue letters with orange-and-red tails. Rays of color, fractured rainbows, spread out over the flanks. He picked the design from a thick book the custom paint-ers had. The car's rear end is hiked up like a female cat in heat. Prowling in his car at night, he could be Dracula.

Sitting behind the wheel, he eats the chocolate-covered doughnuts he just bought and drinks from a carton of chocolate milk. The taste of the milk is off. They do something weird to chocolate milk now. His father used to drive a milk truck, before he got arrested for stealing a shipment of bowling shoes he found stacked up behind a shoe store. He had always told Steve to cover his tracks and accentuate the positive.

It is Sunday. Steve is a wreck, still half drunk. Last night, just after he and Karen quarreled and she retreated to his bathroom to sulk, the tele-phone rang. It was Steve's brother, Bud, wanting to know if Steve had seen Bud's dog, Big Red. Bud had been out hunting with Big Red and his two beagles, and Big Red had strayed. Steve hadn't seen the stupid dog. Where would he have seen him—strolling down Main Street? Bud lived several miles out in the country. Steve was annoyed with him for calling late on a Saturday night. He still hadn't forgiven Bud for the time he shot a skunk and left it in Steve's garbage can. Steve popped another beer and watched some junk on television until Karen emerged from the bathroom and start-ed gathering up her things.

"Why don't you get some decent dishes?" she said, pointing to the splotched paper plates littering the kitchen counter.

"Paper plates are simpler," he said. "Money can't buy happiness, but it can buy paper plates." He pulled her down on the couch and tousled her hair, then held her arms down, tickling her.

"Quit it!" she squealed, but he was sure she didn't mean it. He was just playing.

"You're like that old cat Mama used to have," she said, wrenching herself away from him. "He always got rough when you played with him, and then he'd start drumming with his hind legs. Cats do that when they want to rip out a rabbit's guts."

Steve will be glad when his friends Doran and Nancy get home. Whenever Doran wrestled Nancy down onto the couch at Steve's apartment and tickled her, she loved it. Doran and Nancy got married last week and went to Disney World, and Steve has promised to pick them up at the airport down in Nashville later today. Doran met Nancy only six weeks ago—at the Bluebird Cocktail Lounge and Restaurant, over in Paducah. Doran was with Steve and Karen, celebrating Karen's twenty-third birthday. Nancy and another waitress brought Karen's birthday cake to the table and sang "Happy Birthday." The cake was sizzling with lighted sparklers. Nancy wore clinging sports tights—hot pink, with black slashes across the calves—and a long aqua sweatshirt that reached just below her ass. Doran fell in love—suddenly and passionately. Steve knew Doran had never stayed with one girl long enough to get a deep relationship going, and suddenly he was in love. Steve was surprised and envious.

Nancy has a cute giggle, a note of encouragement in response to anything Doran says. Her hips are slender, her legs long and well proportioned. She wears contact lenses tinted blue. But she is not really any more attractive than Karen, who has blond hair and natural blue eyes. And Nancy doesn't know anything about cars. Karen has a working knowledge of crankshafts and fuel pumps. When her car stalls, she knows it's probably because the distributor cap is wet. Steve wishes he and Karen could cut up like Nancy and Doran. Nancy and Doran love "The New Newlywed Game." They make fun of it, trying to guess things they should know about each other if they were on that show. If Nancy learned that grilled steak was Doran's favorite food, she'd say, "Now, I'm going to remember that! That's the kind of thing you have to know on the 'Newlyweds.'"

During those weeks of watching Doran and Nancy in love, Steve felt empty inside, doomed. When Karen was angry at him last night, it was as if a voice from another time had spoken through her and told him his fate. Karen believes in things like that. She is always telling him what Sardo says in the Sunday-night meetings she goes to at the converted dance hall, next to the bowling alley. Sardo is a thousand-year-old American Indian inhabiting the body of a teenage girl in Paducah. Until Karen started going to those meetings, she and Steve had been solid together—not deliriously in love, like Doran and Nancy, but reasonably happy. Now Steve feels confused and transparent, as though Karen has eyes that see right through him.

In his apartment, on the second floor of a big old house with a large landlady (gland problem), he searches for his laundry. Karen must have hidden his clothes. If he's lucky, she has taken them home with her to wash. The clipping about Nancy's wedding flutters from the stereo. He is saving it for her. "The bride wore a full-length off-white dress with leg-of-mutton sleeves, dotted with seed pearls." There's a misprint in the story: "The bridgeroom, Doran Palmer, is employed at Johnson Sheet Metal Co." Steve smiles. Doran will get a kick out of that. Before he and Nancy left for Florida, Doran told Steve he felt as though he had won a sweepstakes. "She really makes me feel like somebody," Doran said. "Isn't that all anybody wants in the world—just to feel like somebody?"

Steve's clothes are under his bed, along with some dust fluffs. From the television screen a shiny-haired guy in a dark-blue suit yells at him about salvation. There is an 800-number telephone listing at the bottom of the screen. All Steve has to do is send money. "You send *me* some money and I'll work on *your* soul," Steve tells the guy. He flips through all the stations on cable, but nothing good is on. He picks up the telephone to call Karen, then replaces it. He has to think of what to say. He cracks his knuckles. She hates that.

Steve stuffs all his laundry into one big bag, grabs his keys, and slams out of his place. As usual, the bag slung over his shoulder makes him think of Santa Claus. At the laundromat he packs everything into one machine. He pours powder in and rams in the quarters, pretending he's playing a slot machine. The laundromat is crowded. It's surprising how many people skip church nowadays. But it's good that there are fewer hypocrites, he decides. Catholic priests are dying from AIDS, and here in town half the Baptists are alcoholics. A pretty woman in purple jeans is reading a book. He considers approaching her, then decides not to. She might be too smart for him. He leaves his clothes churning and cruises past McDonald's and Hardee's to see if there's anyone he knows. Should he go over to Karen's? While he thinks about it, he pulls into the Amoco station and gasses up. Steve's friend Pete squirts blue fluid on Steve's windshield—a personal service not usually provided at the self-serve island. Pete leans into Steve's car and tugs the lavender garter dangling from the rearview mirror. "Hey, Steve, looks like you got lucky."

"Yeah." It was Nancy's, from the wedding. It was supposed to be blue, but she got lavender because it was on sale. Doran told Nancy that her blue-tinted contact lenses would do for "something blue." Nancy threw the garter to Steve—the same way she tossed her bridal bouquet to her girl-friends. He thought that catching her garter meant he was next in line for something. Something good—he doesn't know what. Maybe Karen could ask Sardo, but whatever Sardo said, Steve wouldn't believe it. Sardo is a first-class fake.

Steve has been banging on the pump, trying to get his gas cap to jump off the top. When it does, he catches it neatly: infield-fly rule. The gas nozzle clicks and he finishes the fill-up.

"Well, Steve, don't you go falling asleep on the job," Pete says as Steve guns the engine.

That's an old joke. Steve works at the mattress factory. The factory is long and low and windowless, and bales of fiberfill hug the walls. Steve steers giant scissors across soft, patterned fabric fastened on stretchers. After he crams the stuffing into the frame, Janetta and Lynn do the finishing work. The guys at the plant tease those girls all day. Janetta and Lynn play along, saying, "Do you want to get in my bed?" Or, "Let's spend lunch hour in the bed room." The new mattresses are displayed beneath glaring fluorescent lights—not the sexiest place to get anything going. But Steve likes the new-bed smell there. He likes the smell of anything new. The girls are nice, but they're not serious. Lynn is engaged, and she's three years older than Steve.

At the laundromat he transfers the soggy, cold load into a dryer and flips each dime on the back of his hand before inserting it. Two heads, two tails. He slides a dollar bill into the change machine and watches George Washington's face disappear and turn into dimes. He laughs, imagining George Washington coming back in the twentieth century and trying to make sense out of laundromats, Midnight Magic, and crazy women. The woman in the purple pants is still there, reading her book. He drives off, screeching loudly out of his parking spot.

Karen's apartment is above a dry cleaner's, next to a vacant lot. It's a lonesome part of town, near the overhead bridge that leads out of town. The parking lot has four cars in it, including her red Escort. An exterior wooden stairway with several broken steps leads to her apartment. There's a rapist in town, and he has struck twice in Karen's neighborhood. Now she sleeps with a knife beside her bed and a shotgun beneath it.

"Are you still mad at me?" he asks when she opens the door. She just woke up and her hair is shooting off in several directions.

"Yeah." She lets him in and returns to her bed.

"What did I do?" He sits down on the edge of the bed.

She doesn't answer that. She says, "When I came in last night I was too nervous to sleep, so I painted that wall." She points to the bedroom wall, now a pale green. The other walls are pink. The colors are like the candy mints at Nancy and Doran's wedding. "The landlord said if I paint everything he'll take it off the rent," Karen says.

"He ought to put bars on the windows," Steve says. Lined-up Coke bottles stand guard on the windowsills, along with spider plants that dangle their creepy arms all the way to the floor.

"If that rapist comes in through the window I'll be ready for him," she says. "I'll blast him to kingdom come. I mean it, too. I'll kill that sucker *dead*." She scrunches up her pillow and hugs it. "I need some coffee."

"Want me to go get you some? I can get some at McDonald's when I go get my clothes out of the dryer."

"I'll just turn on the coffeepot," she says, swinging out of bed. She's wearing a red football shirt with the number 46 on the front. Steve thumps his fist on the mattress. It's a poor mattress. He doesn't like sleeping with her here. He wanted her to stay with him last night.

Karen flip-flops into the kitchen and runs water into her coffeepot. She measures coffee into a filter paper and sets it in the cone above the pot, then pours the water into the top compartment of the coffee maker. He envies her. He can't even make a pot of coffee. He should do more for her—maybe get her a new mattress, at cost. Her apartment is small, decorated with things she made in a crafts club.

"You ought to move," he says.

She laughs. "Hey! I'm trying to lure the guy here. I want that five-thousand-dollar reward!"

"You could move in with me." He's never said anything like that before, and he's shocked at himself.

She disappears into her bedroom and returns in a few minutes wearing jeans and a sweatshirt. The dripping coffee smells like burning leaves, with acorns. Steve likes the smell, but he doesn't really like coffee. When he was little, the smell of his mother's percolator in the morning was intoxicating, but when he got old enough to drink it he couldn't believe how bitter it was.

"Did you find your clothes?" Karen asks after she has poured two mugs of coffee and dosed them with milk and sugar.

"Yeah, I had to haul 'em out from under the bed. Some fluffy little animals had made their nests in them." He reaches over and draws her near him.

"What kind of animals?" she says, softening.

"Little kittens and bunnies," he says into her hair.

She breathes into his neck. "I wish I knew what to do about you," she murmurs.

"Trust me."

"I don't know," she says, pulling away from him.

He starts playing with the can opener, opening and closing the handles.

"Don't do that," she says. "It makes me nervous. I didn't get enough sleep. I'm not going to get a good night's sleep till they catch that guy."

"Why don't you ask Sardo who that rapist is? Old Sardo's such a know-it-all."

"Oh, shut up. You never take anything seriously."

"I *am* serious. I asked you to move in with me."

She drinks from her coffee mug, and her face livens up. She says, "I've got a lot to do today. I'm going to write letters to my sister and my nephews in Tallahassee. And I want to alter that new outfit I bought and clean my apartment and finish painting the bedroom." She sighs. "I'll never get all that done."

As she talks, he has been playing air guitar, like an accompanying tune. He turns to box playfully at her. "Go to Nashville with me today to get Doran and Nancy," he says.

"No, I've got too much to do before tonight's meeting. It's about recognizing your inner strength." She stares at him, in mingled exasperation and what he hopes is a hint of love. "I have to get my head together. Leave me alone today—O.K.?"

Jittery on Karen's coffee but feeling optimistic, he drives back to the laundromat. He spends half his life chasing after his clothes. Traffic is heavy; families are heading home from church for fried chicken and the Cardinals game. People getting out of church must feel great, he thinks. He has heard that religion is a sex substitute. Karen told him Sardo is both sexes. "Double your pleasure, double your fun" was Steve's reply. Karen said, "Sardo says the answers are in yourself, not in God." On TV, the evangelists say the answers are in God. When people bottom out, they often get born again and discover Jesus. That's exactly what happened to Steve's father. He sends Steve pathetic letters filled with Bible quotations. His father used to live for what he could get away with, but now he casually dumps his shit in Christ's lap. Steve hopes he never gets that low. He'd rather trust himself. He's not sure he could trust anybody, especially Sardo—even if Sardo's message is to trust yourself. He's afraid Karen is getting brainwashed. He has heard that the girl who claims to be Sardo is now driving a Porsche.

At the laundromat, he finds his clothes piled up on top of the dryer, which is whirring with someone else's clothes. His laundry is still damp and he has to wait till another dryer is free. Fuming, he sits in the car and listens to the radio, knowing that his impatience is pointless, because when his laundry is finished, all he'll probably do is drive around and listen to the radio. "Keep it where you got it," says the DJ. "Ninety-four-five FM."

Through the window, he sees the woman in purple pants remove her laundry from the dryer he had used. He slouches out of Midnight Magic and enters the laundromat. Her laundry, in a purple laundry basket, includes purple T-shirts and socks and panties.

"Looks like you're into purple," he says to her as he wads his damp clothes into the vacated dryer.

"It's my favorite color, is all," she says, giving him a cool look. She grabs the panties in her laundry just as he reaches for them. She's quick.

"Do you want to hear a great joke?" he asks.

"What?"

"Why did Reagan bomb Libya?"

"I don't know. Why?"

"To impress Jodie Foster."

"Who's Jodie Foster?" she asks.

"You're kidding!" When Doran told Nancy that joke she got the giggles.

The woman folds a filmy nightgown into thirds, then expertly twines together a pair of purple socks. No children's T-shirts, no men's clothes in her pile.

"I just had some coffee and it makes me shake," he says, holding out his hand in front of her face. He makes his hand tremble.

"You oughtn't to drink coffee, then," she says.

"You really know how to hurt a guy," he says to her. "When you say something like that, it's like closing a door."

She doesn't answer. She hip-hugs her laundry basket and leaves.

The red light at the intersection of Walnut and Center streets is taking about three hours, and there's not a car in sight, so Steve scoots through. He drives back to Karen's apartment building and pulls in beside her Escort, trying to decide what to do. The small parking lot is wedged between Karen's building and the service entrance of a luncheonette. After business hours the place is deserted. Karen's windows look out on the roof of the luncheonette. At night the parking lot is badly lighted. He hates himself for letting her drive home alone last night, but he was too drunk to drive and she refused to let him. Last night, he suddenly remembers, he pretended to be the rapist. That was why she was so furious with him. But she didn't say anything about it today. Maybe he terrified her so much she was afraid to bring it up. "Don't do that again!" she cried when she broke free of his clutches last night. "But wouldn't it be a relief to know it was only me?" he asked. That was where tickling her on the couch had led. He couldn't stop himself. But it was just a game. She should have known that.

If he were the neighborhood rapist scouting out her apartment, he would hide in the dark doorway of the delivery entrance of the dry cleaner's downstairs, and when she came in at night, pointing the way with the key, he'd grab her tight around her waist. His weapon, hidden in his jacket, would press into her back. Catching her outside would be easier than coming through the window, smashing bottles to the floor and then being attacked by those spider plants of hers. Steve shudders. The rapist would simply twist her knife out of her hand and use it on her. He would grab her shotgun away from her, as easily as Steve pinned her on the bed last night.

Steve eases into reverse and creeps out of the parking lot. At a stop sign a pickup pulls around him, beeping. It's Bud.

"I found Big Red!" Bud yells. "He turned up at the back door this morning, starved." Big Red wobbles in the truck bed, his tongue hanging out like a handkerchief from a pocket.

"I knew he'd come back," Steve calls over.

"You didn't know that! Irish setters take a notion to run like hell and they get lost."

"Tell Big Red to settle down," says Steve. "Tell him some bedtime stories. Feed him some hog fat."

"Are you O.K., Steve?"

"Yeah, why?"

"You look like death warmed over." A car behind them blows. "Take it easy," says Bud.

Steve takes home a Big Mac and a double order of fries and eats in his kitchen, with a beer. The Cardinals game is just beginning. He feels at loose ends. Sometimes he has sudden feelings of desperation he can't explain—as if he has to get rid of something in his system. Like racing the engine to burn impurities out of his fuel line. He realizes a word has been tumbling through his mind all morning. Navratilova. The syllables spill out musically, to the tune of "Hearts on Fire," by Bryan Adams. Navratilova—her big arms like a man's. He imagines Nancy coming over—in her leg-of-lamb sleeves, her hot-pink tights. She's always in a good mood. He's sure she would be an immaculate housekeeper. Everything would be clean and pretty and safe, but she wouldn't mention how she slaved over it. Steve has noticed that most people feel sorry for themselves for having to do what they have actually maneuvered themselves into doing. His dad complaining about the food in jail. Bud moaning about his lost dog. Karen painting her wall. Or having to get her chores done so she won't be late to her meeting. When she had to get new tires, she fussed about the cost for weeks. He realizes he and Karen can never be like Doran and Nancy. There has to be some chemistry between two people, something inexplicable. Why is he involved with someone who follows the bizarre teachings of a teenager who says she's a reincarnated Indian? In a moment, he realizes how illogical his thoughts are. He wants something miraculous, but he can't believe in it. His head buzzes.

He finishes eating and surveys the damage. His place is straight out of Beirut. The waste can overflows with TV-dinner boxes and paper plates. In the oven, he finds a pizza box from last Sunday. Two leftover slices are growing little garden plots of gray mold. He locates a garbage bag and starts to clear out his kitchen. He's aware he's cleaning it up for Karen to move in; otherwise he wouldn't bother until it got really bad. If she moves in, she can have the alcove by the bedroom for her crafts table. He pops another beer. The Cards game is away, in a domed stadium. He can never really tell from TV what it would feel like to be inside such a huge place. He can't imagine how a whole ball field, with fake grass, can be under one roof. Playing baseball there seems as crazy as going fishing indoors. He picks up an earring beside the couch.

Then the telephone rings. It's Doran. "Steve, you crazy idiot! Where in Jesus' name are you?"

"I'm right here. Where are you?"

"Well, take a wild guess."

"I don't know. Having a beer with Mickey Mouse?"

"Nancy and me are at the Nashville airport, and guess who was supposed to meet us."

"Oh, no! I thought it was tonight."

"One o'clock, Flight 432."

"I wrote it down somewhere. I thought it was seven o'clock."

"Well, we're here, and what are we going to do about it?"

"I guess I'll have to come down and get you."

"Well, hurry. Nancy's real tired. She had insomnia last night."

"Are you still in love?" Steve blurts out. He's playing with Karen's earring, a silver loop within a loop.

Doran laughs strangely. "Oh, we'll tell you all about it. This has been a honeymoon for the record books."

"Go watch the ball game in the bar. And hang on, Doran. I'll be there in two and a half hours flat."

"Don't burn up the road—but hurry."

Steve puts the rest of the six-pack in a cooler and takes off. He heads out to the parkway that leads to I-24 and down to Nashville. He can't understand Doran's tone. He spoke as though he'd discovered something troubling about Nancy. Steve is miles out of town before he remembers he didn't pick up his laundry. He wishes Karen were along. She likes to go for Sunday drives in his car. He considers turning around, giving her a call at a gas station. He can't decide. On the radio a wild pitch distracts him and he realizes he's already too far along to turn around. The beer is soothing his headache.

Steve passes the Lake Barkley exits and zooms around a truck on a hill. The highway is easy and open, no traffic. As he drives, the muddle in his mind seems to be smoothing out, like something in a blender. Early in the summer he and Karen spent a Saturday over here at the Land Between the Lakes. At one of the tourist spots they saw an albino deer in a pen. Later, as they cruised down the Trace, the highway that runs the length of the wilderness, Karen said the deer was spooky. "It was like something all bleached out. It wasn't all *there*. It was embarrassing, like not having a tan in the summer."

"Maybe we ought to get Ted Turner to come here and colorize it," Steve said. "Like he's doing those movies."

Karen laughed. He used to be able to cheer her up like that before she got tangled up with Sardo. Before Sardo—B.S. Maybe he should become a cult-buster and rescue her. He has no idea how much money Sardo is costing her. She keeps that a secret.

Before long, he crosses the Tennessee line. Tennessee, the Volunteer State. For several miles, he tries to think of something that rhymes with Tennessee, then loses his train of thought. Suddenly he spots something lying ahead on the bank by the shoulder. It is large—perhaps a dead deer. As he approaches, he tries to guess what it is. He likes the way eyes can play tricks—how a giant bullfrog can turn out to be a cedar tree or a traffic sign. He realizes it's a man, lying several yards off the shoulder. He wonders if it's just a traveler who has stopped to take a nap, but there is no car nearby. Steve slows down to fifty. It is clearly a man, about twenty feet from the shoulder, near a bush. The man is lying face down, in an unnatural position, straight and flat—the position of a dead man. He's wearing a plaid shirt and blue running shoes and faded jeans. Lying out there in the open, he seems discarded, like a bag of trash.

Steve glides past the nearby exit, figuring that someone has probably already called the police. With beer in the car and on his breath, Steve doesn't want to fool with the police. They would want to know his license number, probably even bring him in for questions. If he stopped, he might leave footprints, flecks of paint from Midnight Magic. For all he knows, the mud flaps could have flung mud from Steve's driveway straight toward the body as he passed. But he's letting his imagination run away with him. He tries to laugh at this habit of his. He gulps some beer and tunes the ball game in over another station. It was fading away. Karen says to trust yourself, your instincts—know yourself.

"You don't need a thousand-year-old Indian to tell you that," he told her a few days ago. "I could have told you that for free."

The Clarksville exit is coming up. "Last Train to Clarksville" runs through his mind. The man lying out there in broad daylight bothers him. It reminds him of the time he fell asleep at lunch hour in the mattress room, and when he woke up he felt like a patient awakening after surgery. Everyone was standing around him in a circle, probing him with their eyes. Without really planning it, he curves onto the exit ramp. He slows down, turns left, then right. He pulls up to the side of a gas station, in front of the telephone booth. He leaves the motor running and feels in his pocket for a quarter. He flips the quarter, thinking heads. It's tails. There are emergency numbers on the telephone. The emergency numbers are free. He pockets the quarter and dials. A recorded voice asks him to hold.

In a moment, a woman's voice answers. Steve answers in a tone higher than normal. "I was driving south on I-24? And I want to report that I saw a man laying on the side of the road. I don't know if he was dead or just resting."

"Where are you, sir?"

"Now? Oh, I'm at a gas station."

"Location of gas station?"

"Hell, I don't know. The Clarksville exit."

"North or south?"

"South. I said south."

"What's the telephone number you're speaking from?"

He spreads his free hand on the glass wall of the telephone booth and gazes through his fingers at pie-slice sections of scenery. Up on the interstate, the traffic proceeds nonchalantly, as indifferent as worms working the soil. The woman's voice is asking something else over the phone. "Sir?" she says. "Are you there, sir?" His head buzzes from the beer. On his knuckle is a blood blister he doesn't know where he got.

Steve studies his car through the door of the phone booth. It's idling, jerkily, like a panting dog. It speeds up, then kicks down. His muffler has been growing throatier, making an impressive drag-race rumble. It's the power of Midnight Magic, the sound of his heart.

# Wish

FROM *Love Life* (1989)

Sam tried to hold his eyes open. The preacher, a fat-faced boy with a college degree, had a curious way of pronouncing his *r*'s. The sermon was about pollution of the soul and started with a news item about an oil spill. Sam drifted into a dream about a flock of chickens scratching up a bed of petunias. His sister Damson, beside him, knifed him in the ribs with her bony elbow. Snoring, she said with her eyes.

Every Sunday after church, Sam and Damson visited their other sister, Hortense, and her husband, Cecil. Ordinarily, Sam drove his own car, but today Damson gave him a ride because his car was low on gas. Damson lived in town, but Hort and Cecil lived out in the country, not far from the old homeplace, which had been sold twenty years before, when Pap died. As they drove past the old place now, Sam saw Damson shudder. She had stopped saying "Trash" under her breath when they passed by and saw the junk cars that had accumulated around the old house. The yard was bare dirt now, and the large elm in front had split. Many times Sam and his sisters had wished the new interstate had gone through the homeplace instead. Sam knew he should have bought out his sisters and kept it.

"How are you, Sam?" Hort asked when he and Damson arrived. Damson's husband, Porter, had stayed home today with a bad back.

"About dead." Sam grinned and knuckled his chest, pretending heart trouble and exaggerating the arthritis in his hands.

"Not again!" Hort said, teasing him. "You just like to growl, Sam. You've been that way all your life."

"You ain't even knowed me that long! Why, I remember the night you was born. You come in mad at the world, with your stinger out, and you've been like that ever since."

Hort patted his arm. "Your barn door's open, Sam," she said as they went into the living room.

He zipped up his fly unself-consciously. At his age, he didn't care.

Hort steered Damson off into the kitchen, murmuring something about a blue dish, and Sam sat down with Cecil to discuss crops and the weather. It was their habit to review the week's weather, then their health, then local news—in that order. Cecil was a small, amiable man who didn't like to argue.

A little later, at the dinner table, Cecil jokingly asked Sam, "Are you sending any money to Jimmy Swaggart?"

"Hell, no! I ain't sending a penny to that bastard."

"Sam never gave them preachers nothing," Hort said defensively as she sent a bowl of potatoes au gratin Sam's way. "That was Nova."

Nova, Sam's wife, had been dead eight and a half years. Nova was always buying chances on Heaven, Sam thought. There was something squirrelly in her, like the habit she had of saving out extra seed from the garden or putting up more preserves than they could use.

Hort said, "I still think Nova wanted to build on that ground she heired so she could have a house in her own name."

Damson nodded vigorously. "She didn't want you to have your name on the new house, Sam. She wanted it in her name."

"Didn't make no sense, did it?" Sam said, reflecting a moment on Nova. He could see her plainly, holding up a piece of fried chicken like a signal for attention. The impression was so vivid he almost asked her to pass the peas.

Hort said, "You already had a nice house with shade trees and a tobacco patch, and it was close to your kinfolks, but she just *had* to move toward town."

"She told me if she had to get to the hospital the ambulance would get there quicker," said Damson, taking a second biscuit. "Hort, these biscuits ain't as good as you usually make."

"I didn't use self-rising," said Hort.

"It wouldn't make much difference, with that new highway," said Cecil, speaking of the ambulance.

On the day they moved to the new house, Sam stayed in bed with the covers pulled up around him and refused to budge. He was still there at four o'clock in the evening, after his cousins had moved out all the furniture. Nova ignored him until they came for the bed. She laid his clothes on the bed and rattled the car keys in his face. She had never learned to drive. That was nearly fifteen years ago. Only a few years after that, Nova died and left him in that brick box she called a dream home. There wasn't a tree in the yard when they built the house. Now there were two flowering crab apples and a flimsy little oak.

After dinner, Hort and Cecil brought out new pictures of their great-grandchildren. The children had changed, and Sam couldn't keep straight which ones belonged to Linda and which ones belonged to Donald. He felt full. He made himself comfortable among the crocheted pillows on Hort's high-backed couch. For ten minutes, Hort talked on the telephone to Linda, in Louisiana, and when she hung up she reported that Linda had a new job at a finance company. Drowsily, Sam listened to the voices rise and fall. Their language was so familiar; his kinfolks never told stories or reminisced when they sat around on a Sunday. Instead, they discussed character. "He's the stingiest man alive." "She was nice to talk to on the street but *H* to work with." "He never would listen when you tried to tell him anything." "She'd do anything for you."

Now, as Sam stared at a picture of a child with a Depression-style bowl haircut, Damson was saying, "Old Will Stone always referred to himself as 'me.' '*Me* did this. *Me* wants that.'"

Hort said, "The Stones were always trying to get you to do something for them. Get around one of them and they'd think of something they wanted you to do." The Stones were their mother's people.

"I never would let 'em tell me what to do," Damson said with a laugh. "I'd say, 'I can't! I've got the nervous trembles.'"

Damson was little then, and her aunt Rue always complained of nervous trembles. Once, Damson had tried to get out of picking English peas by claiming she had nervous trembles, too. Sam remembered that. He laughed—a hoot so sudden they thought he hadn't been listening and was laughing about something private.

Hort fixed a plate of fried chicken, potatoes, field peas, and stewed apples for Sam to take home. He set it on the back seat of Damson's car, along with fourteen eggs and a sack of biscuits. Damson spurted out of the driveway backwards, scaring the hound dog back to his hole under a lilac bush.

"Hort and Cecil's having a time keeping up this place," Sam said, noticing the weed-clogged pen where they used to keep hogs.

Damson said, "Hort's house always smelled so good, but today it smelled bad. It smelled like fried fish."

"I never noticed it," said Sam, yawning.

"Ain't you sleeping good, Sam?"

"Yeah, but when my stomach sours I get to yawning."

"You ain't getting old on us, are you?"

"No, I ain't old. Old is in your head."

Damson invited herself into Sam's house, saying she wanted to help him put the food away. His sisters wouldn't leave him alone. They checked on his housekeeping, searched for ruined food, made sure his commode was flushed. They had fits when he took in a stray dog one day, and they would have taken her to the pound if she hadn't got hit on the road first.

Damson stored the food in the kitchen and snooped in his refrigerator. Sam was itching to get into his bluejeans and watch something on Ted Turner's channel that he had meant to watch. He couldn't remember now what it was, but he knew it came on at four o'clock. Damson came into the living room and began to peer at all his pictures, exclaiming over each great-grandchild. All Sam's kids and grandkids were scattered around. His son worked in the tire industry in Akron, Ohio, and his oldest granddaughter operated a frozen-yogurt store in Florida. He didn't know why anybody would eat yogurt in any form. His grandson Bobby had arrived from Arizona last year with an Italian woman who spoke in a sharp accent. Sam had to hold himself stiff to keep from laughing. He wouldn't let her see him laugh, but her accent tickled him. Now Bobby had written that she'd gone back to Italy.

Damson paused over an old family portrait—Pap and Mammy and all six children, along with Uncle Clay and Uncle Thomas and their wives, Rosie and Zootie, and Aunt Rue. Sam's three brothers were dead now. Damson, a young girl in the picture, wore a lace collar, and Hort was in blond curls and a pinafore. Pap sat in the center on a chair with his legs set far apart, as if to anchor himself to hold the burden of this wild family. He looked mean and willful, as though he were about to whip somebody.

Suddenly Damson blurted out, "Pap ruined my life."

Sam was surprised. Damson hadn't said exactly that before, but he knew what she was talking about. There had always been a sadness about her, as though she had had the hope knocked out of her years ago.

She said, "He ruined my life—keeping me away from Lyle."

"That was near sixty years ago, Damson. That don't still bother you now, does it?"

She held the picture close to her breast and said, "You know how you hear on the television nowadays about little children getting beat up or treated nasty and it makes such a mark on them? Nowadays they know about that, but they didn't back then. They never knowed how something when you're young can hurt you so long."

"None of that happened to you."

"Not that, but it was just as bad."

"Lyle wouldn't have been good to you," said Sam.

"But I loved him, and Pap wouldn't let me see him."

"Lyle was a drunk and Pap didn't trust him no further than he could throw him."

"And then I married Porter, for pure spite," she went on. "You know good and well I never cared a thing about him."

"How come you've stayed married to him all these years then? Why don't you do like the kids do nowadays—like Bobby out in Arizona? Him and that Italian. They've done quit!"

"But she's a foreigner. I ain't surprised," said Damson, blowing her nose with a handkerchief from her pocketbook. She sat down on Sam's divan. He had towels spread on the upholstery to protect it, a habit of Nova's he couldn't get rid of. That woman was so practical she had even orchestrated her deathbed. She had picked out her burial clothes, arranged for his breakfast. He remembered holding up hangers of dresses from her closet for her to choose from.

"Damson," he said, "if you could do it over, you'd do it different, but it might not be no better. You're making Lyle out to be more than he would have been."

"He wouldn't have shot hisself," she said calmly.

"It was an accident."

She shook her head. "No, I think different."

Damson had always claimed he killed himself over her. That night, Lyle had come over to the homeplace near dark. Sam and his brothers had helped Pap put in a long day suckering tobacco. Sam was already courting Nova, and Damson was just out of high school. The neighborhood boys came over on Sundays after church like a pack of dogs after a bitch. Damson had an eye for Lyle because he was so daresome, more reckless than the rest. That Saturday night when Lyle came by for her, he had been into some moonshine, and he was frisky, like a young bull. Pap wouldn't let her go with him. Sam heard Damson in the attic, crying, and Lyle was outside, singing at the top of his lungs, calling her. "Damson! My fruit pie!" Pap stepped out onto the porch then, and Lyle slipped off into the darkness.

Damson set the family picture back on the shelf and said, "He was different from all the other boys. He knew a lot, and he'd been to Texas once with his daddy—for his daddy's asthma. He had a way about him."

"I remember when Lyle come back late that night," Sam said. "I heard him on the porch. I knowed it must be him. He was loud and acted like he was going to bust in the house after you."

"I heard him," she said. "From my pallet up there at the top. It was so hot I had a bucket of water and a washrag and I'd wet my face and stand in that little window and reach for a breeze. I heard him come, and I heard him thrashing around down there on the porch. There was a loose board you always had to watch out for."

"I remember that!" Sam said. He hadn't thought of that warped plank in years.

"He fell over it," Damson said. "But then he got up and backed down the steps. I could hear him out in the yard. Then—" She clasped her arms around herself and bowed her head. "Then he yelled out, 'Damson!' I can still hear that."

A while later, they had heard the gunshot. Sam always remembered hearing a hollow thump and a sudden sound like cussing, then the explosion. He and his brother Bob rushed out in the dark, and then Pap brought a coal-oil lantern. They found Lyle sprawled behind the barn, with the shotgun kicked several feet away. There was a milk can turned over, and they figured that Lyle had stumbled over it when he went behind the barn. Sam had never forgotten Damson on the living-room floor, bawling. She lay there all the next day, screaming and beating her heavy work shoes against the floor, and people had to step around her. The women fussed over her, but none of the men could say anything.

Sam wanted to say something now. He glared at that big family in the picture. The day the photographer came, Sam's mother made everyone dress up, and they had to stand there as still as stumps for about an hour in that August heat. He remembered the kink in Damson's hair, the way she had fixed it so pretty for Lyle. A blurred chicken was cutting across the corner of the picture, and an old bird dog named Obadiah was stretched out in front, holding a pose better than the fidgety people. In the front row, next to her mother, Damson's bright, upturned face sparkled with a smile. Everyone had admired the way she could hold a smile for the camera.

Pointing to her face in the picture, he said, "Here you are, Damson—a young girl in love."

Frowning, she said, "I just wish life had been different."

He grabbed Damson's shoulders and stared into her eyes. To this day, she didn't even wear glasses and was still pretty, still herself in there, in that puffed-out old face. He said, "You wish! Well, wish in one hand and shit in the other one and see which one fills up the quickest!"

He got her. She laughed so hard she had to catch her tears with her hand-kerchief. "Sam, you old hound. Saying such as that—and on a Sunday."

She rose to go. He thought he'd said the right thing, because she seemed lighter on her feet now. "You've got enough eggs and bacon to last you all week," she said. "And I'm going to bring you some of that popcorn cake my neighbor makes. You'd never guess it had popcorn in it."

She had her keys in her hand, her pocketbook on her arm. She was wearing a pretty color of pink, the shade of baby pigs. She said, "I know why you've lived so long, Sam. You just see what you want to see. You're like Pap, just as hard and plain."

"That ain't the whole truth," he said, feeling a mist of tears come.

That night he couldn't get to sleep. He went to bed at eight-thirty, after a nature special on the television—grizzly bears. He lay in bed and replayed his life with Nova. The times he wanted to leave home. The time he went to a lawyer to inquire about a divorce. (It turned out to cost too much, and anyway he knew his folks would never forgive him.) The time she hauled him out of bed for the move to this house. He had loved their old place, a wood-frame house with a porch and a swing, looking out over tobacco fields and a strip of woods. He always had a dog then, a special dog, sitting on the porch with him. Here he had no porch, just some concrete steps, where he would sit sometimes and watch the traffic. At night, drunk drivers zoomed along, occasionally plowing into somebody's mailbox.

She had died at three-thirty in the morning, and toward the end she didn't want anything—no food, no talk, no news, nothing soft. No kittens to hold, no memories. He stayed up with her in case she needed him, but she went without needing him at all. And now he didn't need her. In the dim light of the street lamp, he surveyed the small room where he had chosen to sleep—the single bed, the bare walls, his jeans hanging up on a nail, his shoes on a shelf, the old washstand that had belonged to his grandmother, the little rag rug beside the bed. He was happy. His birthday was two months from today. He would be eighty-four. He thought of that bird dog, Obadiah, who had been with him on his way through the woods the night he set out to meet someone—the night he first made love to a girl. Her name was Nettie, and at first she had been reluctant to lie down with him, but he had brought a quilt, and he spread it out in the open pasture. The hay had been cut that week, and the grass was damp and sweet-smelling. He could still feel the clean, soft, cool cotton of that quilt, the stubble poking through and the patterns of the quilting pressing into his back. Nettie lay there beside him, her breath blowing on his shoulder as they studied the stars far above the field—little pinpoint holes punched through the night sky like the needle holes around the tiny stitches in the quilting. Nettie. Nettie Slade. Her dress had self-covered buttons, hard like seed corn.

# VIII

# Whimsy

*As a college student I wrote a humor column for the campus newspaper. And the impulse toward parody and wry commentary never left me. Eventually I had a chance to write some Talk of the Town pieces for the* New Yorker, *and several Shouts and Murmurs columns in that magazine.*

—BAM

# La Bamba Hot Line

Featured in the *New Yorker,* September 7, 1987

"Hello. La Bamba Hot Line."

"Is it true that 'La Bamba' is derived from the Icelandic Younger Edda, set to music by Spanish sailors and transported via the Caribbean to America in 1665?"

"No, not even close. La Bamba Hot Line. Go ahead, please."

"When is the next Louie Louie Parade scheduled?"

"You want the Louie Louie Hot Line. This is the La Bamba Hot Line."

"Oh."

"La Bamba Hot Line."

"This is Senator Sethspeaks in Washington, on the Committee for the Investigation of Obscene Rock Lyrics."

"State your business, please."

"Uh—I was wondering, just what are the words to 'La Bamba'?"

"Do you have the record?"

"Yes, I do."

"Well, listen to it."

"But I can't tell if the words are obscene or not."

"That's your problem. La Bamba Hot Line."

"My teen-age daughter has been acting funny lately. She refuses to eat, and she has frown lines on her face. She's become aggressive with her parrot and when you talk to her she just says everything is geeky. The doctor can't find anything wrong with her. What should I do?"

"I'm glad you asked. The La Bamba Hot Line has a special pamphlet dealing with problems of teen-agers. Just send a self-addressed stamped envelope to La Bamba Hot Line, P.O. Box 4700. But first, I'd have a heart-to-heart with that parrot."

"Much obliged."

"Likewise, I'm sure. La Bamba Hot Line."

"This is Phil Donahue. Is it true that the La Bamba Hot Line is having a lip-sync contest?"

"Absolutely. October the ninth."

"What do I have to do to win?"

"What do you think? Perform 'La Bamba' till your eyes bug out, do it like a rockin' fool, blow the house down."

"Do you think I've got a chance?"

"Everybody has a chance in life, Mr. Donahue."

You wouldn't believe the stuff I get on the La Bamba Hot Line. I work twelve to four. It's an intensive job and can burn you out quick. Two short breaks, while all the calls stack up. They get a message, "All the La Bamba Hot Lines are temporarily busy. Please try again." It's unfair that people have to keep calling and calling, dialing till their nails split in order to get the La Bamba Hot Line. We need help! We need somebody to handle the genuine emergencies, weed out the crazies. The things people want to know: they want to know are they going to get cancer, will the plane they have a ticket on for tomorrow crash, which stores are giving double coupons this week? We try to answer what we can, but I mean we're not God. I tell them play "La Bamba" thirty-two times in a dark room, then improvise thirty-two versions, then listen to it standing on their head. I tell them to walk down the street muttering "*Yo no soy marinero/Soy capitán.*" Count the number of people who recognize the lines and multiply by four, and whatever number that is, that's Ollie North's secret Swiss bank account. I mean, some things are so simple you wonder why anybody would bother calling up. We deal with a lot of that. Little kids call just to be funny, try to catch us off guard. Is your refrigerator running, that kind of thing. I'm on to them. I start screaming a wild, cacophonous sort of schizo "La Bamba." Blows them right out of the water.

But mostly it's scholars. Academic stuff. People wanting to know about roots, symbolism, the double-entendre of the *marinero/capitán* lines, etc. Idea stuff. I spend my mornings at the library just to stay even with these people. Man, they're sharp. One guy had a beaut—a positive beaut. The way he traced the Paul-is-dead hoax back to the lost Shakespearean sonnets, twisting it around and back through "Poor Ritchie's Almanac" straight up to the chord progressions of "La Bamba"—it was breathtaking. The switchboard was lit up like the stars in the open desert sky on a clear night while I listened and kept all those calls on hold. I was humbled right to my knees. Unfortunately, his spiel didn't get recorded and I didn't get the guy's name. But he'll call again. I'm sure he will.

Some of the ideas that come in are just junk, of course. Did Idi Amin record "La Bamba"? Of course not. But former President Jimmy Carter did. Some stuff you hear is so unbelievable. No, the Voyager is not carrying "La Bamba" out to the end of the universe. Don't I wish. That's sort of my job really, to carry "La Bamba" to the end of the universe.

My boyfriend is giving me a hard time. He says I take my work too seriously. We'll be watching "Washington Week in Review" and I'll say, "Look at those guys. Talk about serious. Don't they ever get down?" He says, "All day it's your La Bamba duties, your La Bamba research, your La Bamba outfits. You go off in the morning with your La Bamba briefcase. When are we ever going to talk about us?"

He says, "This La Bamba thing is going to blow over any minute. It may be blown over by Friday. Things are that fast these days."

"Don't say that!" I cry. "Buddy Holly. 'American Pie.' The Big Bopper. Elvis. Things last longer than you think."

We're going through crisis time, I guess. But we'll work it out. I have faith in that. Right now, my work is at a critical juncture. I'm talking demographics. Market potentializing. La Bamba aerobics, theme weddings, instructional software. We were represented at the harmonic convergence. We met on the boardwalk at Atlantic City, an overflow crowd of La Bamba regulars. We played the song over and over and concentrated on fibre optics, sending our vibes out all over the universe.

The special thing is, my boyfriend can sing "La Bamba." He's not allowed to enter the lip-sync contest because it would be sort of a conflict of interest. He doesn't just lip-sync. He sings it a cappella. He sounds so sincere when he sings it. He makes up the words—he's not a purist—but they sound right; he has the right tune. That is the secret of "La Bamba," inventing it as you go along. That is the true soul of La Bamba. La Bamba lives.

# Sheep Down Under

Featured in the *New Yorker,* May 4, 1987

From a young woman vacationing in New Zealand:

My friend Sharon and I are having a wonderful time. We're crazy about New Zealand! It's got everything: alps and tropical beaches and rain forests and fjords and the most wonderful, complicated hills, which look as though someone had draped a crazy quilt over a pile of oranges and rocks—the hills are very irregular, that is. The borders of the pastures on the hills are planted with "shelter belts," which are double rows of trees where sheep can huddle when it rains. I'll come back to the sheep in a minute.

The climate is temperate. It's fall now, and the leaves are turning. The people are very friendly, and they speak a fast, very British sort of English. Everyone in New Zealand says, "Ah, yeah!" Sometimes we can't understand them at all. Yesterday, when we were flying over Mt. Cook (12,349 feet, and New Zealand's highest mountain), I thought the flight attendant said there was a tea shop on Mt. Asparagus. Maybe she was talking about Mt. Aspiring, somewhere to the southwest. And Sharon thought a woman referring to the motorway said "mud whoopee." We keep getting the giggles—the giddiness of travel. We can't believe we're so far away. Did you know the moon is all turned around here? (Technically, I guess, *we're* turned around, in relation to you folks back home.) And a lot of other things here are turned around, too. The north is warm and the south is cold. They drive on the left. The racetracks go clockwise. (Our Maori guide took us to the speedway—he races sprint cars.) Even the numbers on the telephone dials are in reverse order. The hot and cold faucets are reversed (not always, though). And salt and pepper shakers are backward—one hole for salt, three holes for pepper.

I bought a sweatshirt depicting a mob of curious sheep surrounding a nonplussed kiwi bird. Sharon bought a T-shirt that said "New Zealand, Land of 70,000,000 Nuclear Free Sheep." I bought some "Footrot Flats" books. "Footrot Flats" is a national craze in New Zealand. It's a comic strip about a sheep farm, with a nameless dog and a farmer named Wal' and a neighbor and a possum and other animals. "Footrot Flats" is in all the stores—on coffee mugs, games, T-shirts—and there is even a "Footrot Flats" leisure park and a "Footrot Flats" movie. The line was too long at the movie.

The other day, we went to an amazing place called the Agrodome to see performing sheep. The stage had raised platforms for two rows of sheep to stand on. Each place had a nameplate below it and a feed cup on a stem. One by one, nineteen rams were let loose from the sidelines to trot up onto the platform and find their places while a taped voice lectured on sheep. When the sheep were all chained in place, they resembled two chorus lines, but they kept bumping into each other and stealing each other's feed. Of course, if the Rockettes had to wear heavy wool carpets they might have similar problems.

Up close, sheep look considerably different from the way they look scattered out on the hillsides. They come in assorted sizes and shapes and coat styles. The Merino, the largest in the mob at the Agrodome, occupied the star spot in the center of the stage. He had enormous curled horns, and his name was Prince. The English Leicester was very shaggy, with what seemed to be a kitchen mop hanging in his eyes. The bangs on the curly-fleeced Lincoln spilled down the center of his nose. The Corriedale, however, had short, neat bangs. The Suffolk had a black head and black legs, and the Hampshire had a black nose and black ears and black circles around his eyes. All the sheep were excited. The Border Leicester knocked down his feeding cup. The Perendale seemed to be doing a cha-cha-cha. The Dorset Horn broke his chain and had to be led back to his place. His horns curled around in front of his eyes like gigantic spit curls, and probably blocked his vision. Then the Merino folded his legs and sat down, front first. After licking their feeding cups clean, most of the others sat down, too. During the rest of the show, they sat there and chewed gum, it seemed.

While they watched, a man in a black wool singlet (traditional shearing garb) sheared a sheep—a female extra, not one of the stars. The shearer sat her down and pinned her by holding one of her forelegs between his knees. She was frightened, but he showed how you could touch certain pressure points to keep her in position, and she seemed relaxed. (I can do exactly the same with my cat.) The sheep got into the rhythm of shearing and allowed herself to be turned and twisted. The fleece came off in one piece, as if it had been unzipped. In seconds, the sheep was naked, and, looking embarrassed and sad, she scrambled off the stage.

Next, two sheep dogs hurled themselves onstage. Quickly and precisely, they responded to the man in the singlet as he whistled and spoke certain words ("Right," "Left," etc.) in a low tone. They were champions bred from border-collie mixes, and they were frisky and likable. They had short hair, shaggy tails, wide noses, and were much smaller than Lassie-style collies. They loved licking the sheep's faces. I used to have a collie, and these dogs reminded me so much of him it made me feel very sad but thrilled, too. I don't know why it always seemed an important point to me, but my dog was a full-blooded collie. His mother was the Lassie type, and his father was a border collie. People didn't believe my dog was a collie, though, because he had short hair and a wide nose, but those were his border-collie traits. He was never so happy as when he had the whole family rounded up, all in the same room. When one of the sheep dogs barked, it sounded just like my dog's welcome-home bark. There are two kinds of working sheep dogs: the huntaway dog, who drives sheep from behind with his strong bark, and the heading dog, or eye dog, who stalks the sheep and controls them with his eyes. My dog was definitely the huntaway sort. The dog in "Footrot Flats" is an eye dog.

Suddenly, the dogs onstage bounded across the backs of the sheep, using them for steps. The sheep shearer said that dogs often get from one side of the mob to the other in this manner. And Sharon said, "Hey, I just realized the joke at the end of 'Crocodile Dundee'! Remember when Crocodile Dundee is trying to get to the woman across the crowded subway platform after she's said she loves him? He walks right on top of the people—like a sheep dog! I bet nobody at home got that joke."

And then the man in the singlet invited people in the audience to come onstage and pat the big Drysdale sheep, the most huggable-looking sheep in the mob. (Sheep, you may have gathered by now, travel in mobs.) He had large, curled horns and long, shaggy wool that seemed to have been treated with mousse. Sharon and I took turns going onstage and photographing each other with this funny sheep. The sheep didn't move, but he sort of smiled. He felt like a big couch.

# Hot Colors

Featured in the *New Yorker,* September 1, 1980

At the Picasso retrospective at the Museum of Modern Art, the crowd one hot afternoon resembled a tropical garden of extravagant blooms and gay colors. It was as though in deciding how to dress for the heat everyone had been seized by Picasso's reckless willingness to try anything. We overheard someone say, "Form was to Picasso what color was to Matisse." Matisse, too, must have been involved in this scene, we thought—especially when it came to pink: neon pink, Day-Glo pink, hot pink, Shocking pink. We saw pink-flowered pants suits; pink trousers of velours; a glowing pink Picasso-signature T-shirt; pink plaid slacks; a very tiny woman in bright-pink pants and baby-size pink spike heels; a young man in jeans with a pink belt and red patent-leather shoes; a woman in pink plastic open-toed, backless heels; a trio of women in pants suits of the same flesh tones as "Les Demoiselles d'Avignon"; a girl in loud-pink basketball shoes with red laces; a man in rainbow-striped pants, a red shirt, and flamingo-pink shoes. One young woman was wearing an unobtrusive brooch in the form of a tube of paint with plastic paint oozing out. The tube was labelled, "Orange," but the color was more like that of a pinkish Elberta peach.

And green, a Cézanne-ish sort of green, was just about as popular as pink. It was Picasso's favorite green, the green of his "Still-Life with Hat (Cézanne's Hat)" and "Green Still-Life," from Avignon. A woman was wearing a tank top of this hue, and it was peeking out from her yellow seersucker jump suit, which had a dashing design of large jelly beans on it. Another woman's green sun dress exactly matched the green earplug of the museum tape-cassette tour she was carrying. But our favorite was a dress patterned with green frogs and pink strawberries.

Picasso's Blue Period was strangely somber—this group was wilder

264

than that. And in the gray Cubist rooms the colors were dancing: Hawaiian shirts, splendid purples, a black sun dress with palm trees on it, and a white skirt with purple birds flying across it. In the Garden Café, a woman in a red-and-white hibiscus-flowered muumuu and white gloves and marble-size beads was smoking a cigarette while standing in line to buy grapes and cheese—a Saran-wrapped still-life.

Picasso's harlequins had leaped out of the paintings. Most of the sun dresses that did not have flowers or birds on them had harlequin designs in flashy colors. One notable shirt had large pink and green diamonds. Even the plaid shirts were cut on the bias, making diamonds instead of squares, and one man's shirt, made from a patchwork-quilt top, imitated the wallpaper collage in "Women at Their Toilette."

For relief, the museum guards wore black and white, and one stationed in the Sculpture Garden sported reflecting sunglasses just like those of the prison guard in "Cool Hand Luke."

It was only a simple red, white, and blue, but our favorite blouse pictured twenties-style flappers standing on stair steps, and lists of names zigzagging beside them: Julie, Jeanne, Marcelle, Georgette, Germaine, Suzanne, Rose, Paulette, Camille, Blanche, Marthe, Thérèse, Agnès, Juliette, Claire.

Finally, before the gray agonies of the "Guernica," a startling sight: a woman in pumps of a linen fabric with a design like a Jan Brueghel still-life—one of those botanically impossible combinations of flowers. As she moved on, we tried to catch up with her, for it seemed as though she were the leader of all these mad expressions of the heat of summer, but she flitted away, her feet like birds of paradise.

# Sanctuary

*Featured in the New Yorker, October 5, 1981*

Letter from a woman in Pennsylvania:

On the first day that really felt like fall, Roger and I biked to a wildlife sanctuary in our community. Roger gets melancholy over autumn, and, besides, we had moved from a sixty-acre farm only a few months before, so the idea of going to a wildlife sanctuary in the middle of town at the beginning of fall had a promise of sadness in it. But we enjoyed our expedition.

At the entrance to the sanctuary, which covered seventy-five acres, a sign told us to leave pets at home and to "touch, not take." We picked up a brochure that said, "The silent observer sees the most. Take only memories, leave only footprints. Stay on the trails." It listed a woods-edge trail along the local river, an orchard trail, a tree-edge trail, and a woodland loop, offering varying "habitat experiences of stream, field, thicket, and forest." Most of the trails were carpeted with wood chips. Along the orchard trail, the rotting apples on the ground smelled like vinegar. The trail led to the bird blind, a three-sided six-foot barrier of woven strips of wood, painted red, with openings to look through at several feeders. People had written on the bird blind "You saw somethin' else didncha?" and "I'm Free." On a clipboard you could record the birds you saw at the feeders. Billy Zaboroush had seen a pigeon three days before. I watched for pheasants and wild turkeys, but the only creatures I got a good look at were some chipmunks skittering about and a sparrow—whose markings resembled a chipmunk's—nibbling leaves and cheeping like a day-old chick. Roger was sitting on a bench reading a book called "Two Acre Eden," which he had brought along. He whispered to me that the book said you can try to keep rabbits out of your garden by putting spices on the vegetables but that in fact rabbits are crazy about cabbages sprinkled with chili powder. Around us, the invisible birds were an orchestra tuning up: there was crying and trilling and clucking, led by the teasing mew of a catbird. Now and then, we heard the huff and swish of horses in the shade of the apple trees. When I spotted a robin, Roger told me that his book said a robin gets so single-minded about wild cherries that once it spies one it will fly through a cat's whiskers, if necessary, to get it. All at once, I caught sight of a bird that I thought was an extinct heath hen, but it flew away before I could even guess its real identity. Heath hens had been on my mind since I saw an ad in the "Antiques" classifieds in the *Times* for "extinct heath hens, male and female, mounted on extinct American cedar ($250,000. Call Tom)." I wrote down "Robin" under Billy Zaboroush's pigeon.

We followed the thicket path through reddened poison ivy and raspberries. Everything had a dried-up look about it except a village of white mushrooms in the path. The brightest thing in the woods was the scattered butter-yellow leaves of the tulip poplar. On many trees, patches of leaves had turned brown. We found a large wire cage, its door swinging open. Inside were two hutches, a large feeding pan, and a climbing branch. Outside, on the doorstep, was a hard, yellow cucumber. Fifty feet away, we stumbled across these small gravestones: "Peckie, Loveable and Playful," "Buster, A Cuddly Lovable Puppy," "Fritz, Rebellious Puppy, Lovable Dog," and "Bozo, A Lovable Rogue." I suddenly thought how odd it was that we had to go to a special place, a sanctuary—a refuge, with a sort of religious connotation—for a ritual farewell to nature, because in becoming town dwellers we had already said goodbye.

And then, just down the wood-chip path, we made an unexpected find—bladdernut shrubs. These gracefully bending little trees, up to eight feet high, lined the path, arching to meet overhead. We seemed to be on an endless trail of bladdernut shrubs (*Staphylea trifolia*), all waving reluctant goodbyes. Their clusters of seed packets—some green, some crisp brown—were hidden beneath the highest leaves. The green pods made me think of limp, wrinkled party balloons that have hung too long, and the brown withered ones were almost as tough as cocoons. The seeds rattled inside like a baby's rattle. The seeds were the size and color of lentils but more spherical, and some of them peeped out—surprised eyes.

The hanging "cocoons" made me think of butterflies and caterpillars, and I thought that perhaps this grove was the showcase of the sanctuary, a kind of special exhibit of nature's metamorphosis, a hopeful but ironic insistence that, despite appearances, not everything was going to end up in graveyards, parks, or zoos.

As we biked home, a gust of wind pushed a dried leaf alongside me for half a block.

# All Shook Up

Featured in the *New Yorker,* March 4, 1994

Scream sightings have been popping up all over the place ever since the famous Munch painting was stolen from the National Art Museum in Norway. The Scream was first spotted at the Olympics, and then at a Starbucks in Santa Barbara. It was glimpsed on a frozen shoulder of I-95 just south of Waterville, Maine, trying to hitch a ride, and it turned up on the same morning in the crowd beside the batting cage in Sarasota where Michael Jordan was making his first swings of the day. It has been seen driving a big-rig, walking a Rottweiler, and lurking around mini-marts, laundromats, and factory outlets. But these are all bogus reports. I know where the Scream really is. It's right here in front of me, in my kitchen. How the universal totem of complaint materialized at my house in the Heartland is a good question.

I had already been screaming a lot over assorted recent tribulations (ruckus on the Richter scale; Tonya Harding's bodyguard; Oliver North's olive-drab hat flying into the ring; Lillehammer-like winter weather everywhere), and a friend who has one of those inflatable four-foot Screams tethered in her dining room sent me an eighteen-inch Scream, Jr., of my very own. My husband, Roger, blew it up and set it on a paddle of the ceiling fan. It looked terrified. He put it on the floor, where the cats gave it a good sniffing over, and the Scream looked as if it were holding its breath in the expectation of a fatal puncture. Then Roger placed the Scream in the arms of our lifesize plush Koko the Gorilla: nothing doing. Everywhere he put it was worse than the last, from the Scream's timid-looking perspective.

Then something happened. Roger set the Scream in front of our Elvis. (More than one vanished icon has found a new place to dwell here, but I can't go into that.) Our Elvis, a sexy ceramic collectible, entertains on top of a cabinet between the sun space and the stairs. He's decked out in one of his caped Aztec-sun-god suits, which is missing a few sequins. There in the light, he really appears to be a sun god—or at least one of the sun god's buddies. I like to think of him as Orpheus, the original rockabilly who plucked the lyre in a band with Apollo, Hermes, and Big Boss Man Pan. They say Orpheus could charm rocks, but Elvis could charm the pants off a snake.

Now the King of Rock and Roll and the official spokesperson of angst stand face to face, their mouths hanging open. It is as if they were meeting down at the end of Lonely Street, one block over from Valhalla. Their confrontation is timeless, yet full of moment.

"Eeeeee," says the Scream.

It shakes Elvis up. What is this? The Scream looks about a hundred years old and is as bald as a monk. Bless my soul, what's wrong with me, Elvis wonders. He starts itching like a man on a fuzzy tree. He's acting white as a bug. His insides are shaking like a leaf on a tree.

"You ain't nothin' but a hound dog," Elvis cajoles, trying to shush the Scream. "Cryin' all the time." He croons, "Are you lonesome tonight?"

"EEEEEE," says the Scream.

"Hey, baby," Elvis says. "I ain't askin' much of you. No no no no no no no no. Don't be a stingy little mama. You 'bout to starve me half to death. Just a big-a big-a big-a hunk o' love will do."

The Scream is fixing to scream again, so Elvis tries a different tack. He says, "Bugsy turned to Shifty, and he said 'nix nix!'" Elvis's knees begin to roll; then his pelvis begins its customary swivel, his left leg working like a bit brace. "Everybody let's rock!" he cries.

Slowly, the Scream begins to undulate. Its lips are like a volcano when it's hot. It feels its temperature rising, higher and higher, burning through to its soul. Its brain is flaming. It doesn't know which way to go. It's burning, burning, and nothing to cool it. It just might turn to smoke. The flames are now licking its body. It feels like it's slipping away. It's hard to breathe. Its chest is a-heaving. Its burning love is lighting the morning skies. It's just a hunk-a hunk-a burning love.

The Scream reaches for the scarf around the King's neck.

"EEEEEEEE!" it says.

"I'm proud to say that you're my buttercup," Elvis gasps.

I am smiling. If rock and roll will never die, can spring be far behind?

# Hear My Song

Featured in the *New Yorker,* March 20, 1995

> It wasn't the books that I didn't read,
> It wasn't the teachers who tried to teach me,
> It wasn't that varsity baseball coach
> Who kept on telling them locker-room jokes.
> It was Bobbie Ann Mason, back in high school.
> She was way too cute, she was way too cool.
> How was I gonna get an education
> Sittin' right in back of Bobbie Ann Mason?
>
> —Rick Trevino, singing on
> Columbia Records' *Looking for the Light*

O.K. How many people do *you* know with their own theme song? How many people have you even heard of whose full names are also song titles? John Wesley Harding? Pretty Boy Floyd? Joe DiMaggio and Mickey Mantle did have songs named for them, but not many other folks get to have a song of their own, the way I do. Well, I guess from now on you'll have to look at me through smoked glass: don't use the naked eye.

The writer Lee Smith is the only person I actually know who has come close to having her own song. Bruce Hornsby, of Bruce Hornsby and the Range, once called her up and said, "Hi, this is Bruce Hornsby." She said, "Bruce who?" Later, she told me, "He was a big star, but I didn't know it." He said he was a fan of her novels, and he invited her to his concert. These days she's a big Bruce Hornsby fan and belongs to his fan club. One of her novels inspired his song "The Road Not Taken."

Now along comes Rick Trevino, ambling down the same little-used road. He's a big country star, but I didn't know it. His new album includes a song called "Bobbie Ann Mason." I'm not sure he's singing about me, but I won't argue. Ditty immortality is mine. That's me, no mistake. My name. On my birth certificate. Social Security card. The works. And I'm a real person, unlike Norma Jean Riley. Or Johnny B. Goode. Or sad Eleanor Rigby, who keeps her face in a jar by the door.

Of course, plenty of *first* names have been song titles: Alison, Elvira, Gloria, Layla, Maybellene. But those gals have no last names. They don't even have middle names. They have a kind of broad-spectrum immortality. Too vague for Rick Trevino—he likes to be specific.

Actually, I'm reduced to a perfect nonplus. Rick Trevino is *way* too young to be singing about me back in high school, years ago. But that's O.K. I'll take it. How well he knows me! This song is a high-school-vindication dream, the wallflower's revenge. Carrie returns! I was voted "most studious," an accolade meaning "Homecoming queen? In your *dreams,* Mason!" My time has come.

> Well, Bobbie knew her history. Bobbie knew her French.
> Bobbie knew how to keep the boys in suspense.
> She teased with a touch. She teased with a kiss.
> I was three long years being teased by pretty Miss
> Bobbie Ann Mason, back in high school.
> She was way too cute, she was way too cool.

I hope Rick will play my song when he comes to Rupp Arena, here in Lexington, this spring. Rupp Arena is the home of the University of Kentucky Wildcats. At first, I had Rick Trevino mixed up with Rick Pitino, the Wildcats coach. Did Rick Trevino confuse me with somebody else? Maybe Rick doesn't even know I'm real. Back in high school, I didn't know *he* was real. He wasn't born yet. Reluctantly, I checked into this. It turns out that Rick didn't write the song. The guy who wrote it just liked the way my name sounded. He wrote the song for an old girlfriend whose name wouldn't fit the melody, so he plugged in mine. Does this mean I wasn't cute after all? To tell the truth, I didn't know a soupçon of French.

The trouble with this song is that it's so catchy it grabs that little gizmo in your brain that runs a tape loop. Or it does in mine, anyway. I'm being throttled by my own name, but at least I won't ever forget it. It's like an ad jingle, a singing logo, a talking T-shirt. Everybody should have a theme song. Hey, if you've got five syllables in your name, you can borrow my song! Hillary Clinton, take it for the weekend.

Of course, once you get your own song, your name is liable to enter the fuzzy realm of myth, like Stagger Lee or Jumpin' Jack Flash or Louie Louie. But what I want to know is how did Dede Dinah feel when she first heard her song on the radio? And what did she do when she found out it was really written for Peggy Sue?

# Terms of Office

Featured in the *New Yorker,* July 26, 1993

Q: Mr. President, in a recent news conference you used the rather colorful expression "He doesn't know me from Adam's off ox." Senator Dole alleges there is no such term and says you employed this "pseudo-colloquialism" (he also called it a "Gergenism") as a calculated attempt to sound "down-home" in order to woo back Southern Democrats who have deserted you. Would you care to comment, sir?

A: Yes, Brit, I'd be glad to clarify that allusion. In a team of oxen, the "off" one is the one farther away from the driver—that is, to the right. So if our ancestor Adam is far back in memory his off ox is even farther away—but maybe not as far right as Senator Dole. When I left Arkansas to attend Oxford as a Rhodes Scholar, people back home would ask my mother where I was, and she would tell them I was off. Off at Oxford. I could have said he didn't know me from Adam's hatband, or Adam's pet monkey, Adam's brother, his brag dog, his chief communications officer—whatever. We use lots of these sayings in Arkansas, but you don't know split beans from coffee about Arkansas, do you?

Q (follow-up): Sir, isn't this another example of what your critics call Slick Willie waffling—claiming to be both an Oxonian and a good old boy?

A: Brit, let me say that "Adam's off ox" is heard chiefly west of the Appalachians, according to the Dictionary of American Regional English. In the Northeast, there are only two lonely spots where the D.A.R.E. maps the usage of "Adam's off ox"—one in upstate New York and one in Massachusetts.

We have a language gap. Let me point out that I wouldn't naturally say, "He doesn't know me from Adam's off bull." When I was coming up in Hope, we didn't say "bull" in mixed company. We said "he-cow." A bull

274

was a gentleman cow, or a male cow, or a top cow. Up here inside the Beltway, you call a bull a bull, and you call bull "bull." In the South, we have an expression for people who do that. We say, "He's a person who says what he thinks." And it's not necessarily a compliment.

What you call "waffling" is just good manners back home. I was taught to say "he-cow." And we didn't say "rooster." We said "chicken," or "he-chicken." Schoolteachers would speak of "the he" and "the she" and "girl birds" and "boy birds." People never said "cock" in public. Any word with "cock" in it was taboo. They'd say "hoe handle." Why, some Southerners still won't say "the clap." They say "the collapse." Some old-timers back home still can't bring themselves to say my brother's name, Roger. "Roger" used to be a dirty word. A verb.

But yesterday's gone. Now you can say "bullshit," and it doesn't even mean anything. Let me just say this: The trait of being inoffensive in mixed company is a major strength of this Presidency. You see, the whole world now is mixed company. It's an advantage that the President of the United States is in the habit of spontaneously blurting out obscure regional metaphors that wouldn't make ladies blush a century ago. I expect to do more of it.

Hey, I just got here and I've got a lot to learn. I know the Presidency is more than knitting cat fur into kitten britches. That reminds me—I could have said, earlier, "He doesn't know me from Adam's house cat." And it might interest you to know that Adam's house cat was called Nethergarment. A polite term for britches. Why, I know folks who won't even say the word "socks."

## IX

# Fiction and History

*In 1988, I heard about a woman who had given birth to quintuplets in my hometown a century before and had become a worldwide sensation. Surprisingly, this had occurred just across the field from the house where I grew up. I don't know why I had never heard the story before, but once I did, I knew it was mine. Within the afternoon I realized I was going to write a historical novel, a long one. I knew the basic situation, but I didn't know the story. Who was this hapless family? What was it like to be a celebrity at the beginning of the twentieth century? It was necessary to imagine Christie Wheeler and her family and their community. I expected it would be a challenge to go back to the world of 1900, the turn of the century, which happened with all the hysteria and foreboding that accompany such milestones. But I soon realized that 1900 was hardly the past. As William Faulkner famously noted, "The past is never dead. It's not even past." Indeed, the world of charlatans, miracle cures, lurid journalism, and celebrity culture flourished at the end of the nineteenth century, just as now. But also it was very much the world of my early childhood, when mules and horses worked the farm, when women cooked on a wood stove. My parents still spoke the language of that time, so I slid easily into the country talk of the Wheeler family in* Feather Crowns. *A pair of drawers might be "plumb full of holes" or someone might not have "the sense God gave a tomcat." Talk like that doesn't die out quickly.*

—BAM

# FROM *Feather Crowns* (1993)

## CHAPTER 1

Christianna Wheeler, big as a washtub and confined to bed all winter with the heaviness of her unusual pregnancy, heard the midnight train whistling up from Memphis. James was out there somewhere. He would have to halt the horse and wait in the darkness for the hazy lights of the passenger cars to jerk past, before he could fly across the track and up the road toward town. He was riding his Uncle Wad's saddle horse, Dark-Fire.

The train roared closer, until it was just beyond the bare tobacco patch. Its deafening clatter slammed along the track like a deadly twister. Christie felt her belly clench. She counted to eight. The pain released. The noise of the train faded. Then the whistle sounded again as the train slowed down near town, a mile away. The contractions were close together now. The creature inside her was arriving faster than she had expected. The first pain had been light, and it awakened her only slightly. She was so tired. She dreamed along, thinking it might be no more than the stir and rumble she had felt for months—or perhaps indigestion from the supper James's Aunt Alma had brought her.

"You have to eat," Alma had told her. "That baby'll starve, though by the looks of you I reckon he could last a right smart while. You've got fat to spare."

"I can't eat butter beans," Christie said. "They're too big."

Alma hooted. "The beans is too big? You keep on with them crazy idies and we'll have to carry you off to the asylum."

"Good," said Christie, making a witch face.

In late December, when the doctor advised Christie to stay in bed, they talked about moving her back up to Alma's house, where the women could take care of her more easily, but Christie wouldn't go. She had had enough of that place—too many people under one roof. She said she didn't want her children to be in their way. And she didn't want to be waited on like James's Uncle Boone, who wheezed and didn't work. He believed he had TB.

She tried to turn, expecting the pain to come back, but her stomach felt calmer now. Dr. Foote probably wouldn't want to come out this late, she thought, when the clock began to strike midnight.

Alma burst through the back door a few moments later. She hurried through the kitchen into the front room where Christie lay.

"Lands, here I am again." Alma wore enormous shapeless shoes and a big bonnet with a tiny gray-leaf figure that resembled mold seen up close. A woman in a blue bonnet followed her into the room. "Hattie Hurt's here," Alma said. She grunted—her laugh. "It's just like James to run off after the doctor when Hattie was right near. Why, Hattie can dress that baby."

"Babies like to meddle with our sleep right off," said Hattie cheerily. "They don't want to come in the middle of the morning like civilized company." She dropped her leather satchel on a chair and hurled off her coat all in one motion. Then she unbuckled the satchel. "Where's Mrs. Willy?" she asked. "She always beats me to a birthing."

"She went to Maple Grove to see her daughter and grandchillern and didn't say when she'd be back," Alma said.

"Mrs. Willy told me to take calomel when the pains commenced, but I didn't," Christie said.

"You'll feel better when you get this baby out, Christie," said Hattie soothingly.

"It's not a baby."

"She's talking foolishness again," said Alma.

Christie tried to sit up. She was in her front room, or Sunday room. The bed, directly across from the fireplace, was sheltered from the front door by the closed-in stairway to her right. To her left was the kitchen. The door was swung back all the way against the kitchen wall so that the two roofs joined into one. Christie leaned over to the bedside table for a rag, and Alma ran over to help her. Alma was rarely this attentive. Christie didn't want to depend on her, but she was helpless. She had been helpless for weeks, and the condition had made her angry and addled. The children seemed scared of her lately.

"Alma, reach me a drop of water. My lips is parched."

"You done flooded the bed," Alma mumbled. She brought Christie a cup of water and a wet rag, then turned to the kitchen stove to tend the fire. "This water's going to take awhile to boil," Alma said.

"We've got time," said Hattie, busy with her jars and tools. Her apron was freshly starched. It gleamed white as new teeth.

Christie's belly was tight. It needed to loosen up. She tried to knead it, to make it pliable. She thought it might explode. She ran her hands around the expanse—the globe of the world, James had joked. She hadn't needed a doctor for her other babies. It seemed that each time she had a baby her belly stretched and could accommodate a larger one. The second boy had been a pound heavier than the first, and then Nannie was so big she caused a sore that didn't heal for weeks. But what Christie had in her now was more than twice as large as any of the others. She had a thing inside her that couldn't be a baby—it was too wild and violent.

Hattie Hurt had visited several times during the winter, even though they hadn't been able to give her anything more than a ham and some green beans Christie had put up in jars. Dr. Foote was sure to charge more money than they could pay, but James said he'd sell a hog.

"Let me take a look at what's going on down there," said Hattie. "Can you get them drawers off?"

Christie's stomach was quiet now. She loosened her clothes and pushed down her step-ins, one of three enormous pairs she had sewed this winter. James had joked about those too, but she thought he was trying to hide his concern.

Hattie Hurt had strong hands and a gentle, reassuring voice. Her voice reminded Christie of her grade-school teacher, Mrs. Wilkins. Christie still remembered the teacher leading a recitation of short a's: march, parch, starch, harsh, marsh, charm, snarl, spark. She remembered how Mrs. Wilkins moved her jaws in a chewing motion to stress the sound.

Hattie poked around, feeling Christie's abdomen. She examined the place between Christie's legs. "You're pooching out some," she said. "Now just lay back and wait real easy. We don't want to force it too soon."

While Alma worked at the stove, the children still slept. Christie could see Clint and Jewell in the loft, above the kitchen, on a feather bed. She heard them stirring. Nannie was sleeping on a pallet in the corner between the fireplace and the kitchen wall. This winter, because of her pregnancy, Christie and James had shut off their north bedroom and slept close to the brick fireplace in the front room. Ordinarily, the children weren't supposed to enter the front room except on Sundays, but this winter they had all moved in. The front room contained Christie's best furniture, the almost-new cabbage-rose carpet, and her good Utopian dishes in an oak china-safe. James had made their furniture when they started out together in Dundee. When they moved to Hopewell, they stored it in Christie's parents' stable in Dundee until their own house was ready. When the furniture final-ly arrived, it had some mouse stains, but Christie had never seen anything so lovely. She sanded it down and oiled it. Now her weight had broken two of the slats in the bed, and the corn-shuck mattress beneath the feather bed sagged through the hole in the slats. It almost reached the floor, until James put a hassock under the bed for support.

"Is it time for breakfast?" Nannie asked. She was standing beside the bed, twisting the hem of her muslin nightdress across her face.

Christie pulled the dress away and patted her child. "No, hon. Go back to sleep."

"I want to get in with you. Where's Papper?"

"He's outside." She started to make room for Nannie in the bed, but her belly contracted then and she cried out involuntarily.

"You hurt me," said Nannie. "You hurt my fingers."

Christie released her. Alma came over from the stove and steered her back across the soft carpet to her pallet. "Go look for your dreams, child," she said. "They'll get away from you." Turning back to the kitchen, she said to Christie, "I told Mandy to get on down here and carry the chillern up yonder to the house, but where is she?" Alma cupped her ear to listen. "The moon's shining big as a Sunday communion plate, so I don't know what she'd be scared of."

"Hoboes from the train," said Christie. "And devils behind bushes."

"She ain't got the sense God give a tomcat."

Amanda was Alma's sister-in-law, married to Alma's brother, Wad Wheeler. Alma bossed everybody in the household, but she bossed Aman-da the most. She believed Amanda thought herself too good for ordinary work.

"I wonder if Mrs. Willy's back yet," said Christie.

"Oh, I don't think she knows a woman's behind from a jackass, to tell you the truth," Alma said, scowling till Christie imagined Alma's loose-jawed face drooping all the way down to her apron.

Christie couldn't help laughing, although it jiggled her stomach uncomfortably. During the winter, she had grown so fat she had to enter the narrow door of the springhouse sideways. Her ankles swelled and her feet ached. She made clumsy padded house-shoes out of double thicknesses of burlap, folded and stitched on top and gathered around and tied with twine at the ankles. She shuffled through the house, skirting the ashy hearth. For several weeks, she thought she must have miscalculated her time. She kept thinking the baby was due any moment. But the storm inside her kept up, at an ever more frantic pace. And now her time had come, the full time since the heat of last June when she and James had lain in the steamy night without cover, their bodies slippery as foaming horses, while the children slept out on the porch. She recalled that the midnight train had gone by then, too, and that she had imagined they were on the train, riding the locomotive, charging wildly into the night.

Christie screamed and grabbed Hattie's arm. A sharp pain charged through her like the train. Hattie held Christie's hand throughout the agony, while the thing inside tore loose a little more.

Alma said, "The water's about to boil and Mandy ain't here. I've a good mind to go up there and give her what-for."

The hurting passed. Christie sank into her feather bolster and pulled the cover up to her neck. Hattie wiped Christie's face.

"Bring me that likeness of my mama, please, Hattie," said Christie.

Hattie handed her the silver-framed photograph from the mantel. In the small portrait, Mama had a large smile, as though she had been caught by surprise.

"She looks right young," said Hattie.

"Yes, but she'd look old if I was to see her again. It's been two years since I was home." Christie touched the bleached-out image, wishing it would come to life under her fingertip. "I never oughter left Dundee," she said.

"You need your mama," said Hattie soothingly. "A woman always needs her mama at a time like this. But we'll do the best we can, Christie."

On the very day Christie and James married, her Aunt Sophie told her,

"It's nine months from the marriage bed to the deathbed." At the time, Christie had dismissed the words as the careless remark of an old maid— Aunt Sophie had been to a female seminary and was thoughtlessly outspoken—but lately Christie had dwelt on the thought. She hadn't mentioned it to James, not wanting to worry him. But she was afraid she would die. No woman could pass a child this big. The commotion inside her felt like a churn dasher, churning up crickets and grasshoppers. Christie had thought she might be carrying twins, but the doctor hadn't encouraged that idea. Christie never felt sorry for herself, but this pregnancy had been different—hard and spiteful, as if something foreign had entered her body and set up a business of a violent and noisy nature. Almost from the beginning, it seemed she could feel the thing growing oddly inside her. At first, the sensation was only a twinge, like a June bug caught on a screen door. Then it grew into a wiggly worm, then a fluttering bird. Sometimes it was just kittens, then it would be like snakes. It kept changing, until the commotion inside her was almost constant, and terrifying. One day a clerk at the grocery where they traded showed her some jumping beans from Mexico. The beans were somehow electrified, jerking as though taken by fits. She had something like that in her. She imagined there were devils in her, warring over her soul. And even at calm, peaceful moments, she knew something was not right. The baby drained her strength, and now she could barely eat. Even though her breasts had grown huge and firm, she was afraid her milk wouldn't make.

"I know you want your mama," said Hattie. "Believe me, I know how it is."

Hattie worked busily, clipping Christie's hairs and washing her with a clear, sweet-smelling liquid. She laid out the contents of her bag on the small bedside table—shiny scissors, a slender knife, cotton wool, tubing, twine, soap, a device for expelling milk, bandages, small cotton cloths, blue bottles of liniment and alcohol and calomel, a variety of ointments in tiny round tins. As she worked, Hattie repeated a story Christie had heard before, how her husband had had his teeth pulled one day and the next day was kicked in the face by a mule. He said he regretted having paid the dentist to do what the mule would have done for free.

Steps sounded on the back porch, and Alma's brother Wad entered the kitchen. He never knocked on a door. Behind him was his wife, Amanda,

Christie's only real friend on the place. Amanda was pretty, with soft gray eyes and a warm smile. Even though it was the middle of the night, she had put on a clean dress and had pinned her hair up under her fascinator just as though she were going someplace important.

"Well, fine time you picked," yelled Wad across the kitchen to Christie.

"Don't let Wad in here," Alma said to Amanda. "And shut that door. You're letting the cold night air in."

Amanda pushed her husband out and closed the door. Christie could hear him out on the back porch stomping his boots in the cold. He was many years older than Amanda—his second wife.

Amanda crossed the kitchen to Christie's bedside. She said, "Wad sent Joseph to get Mrs. Willy. That's how come we didn't get here so quick."

Joseph, one of Wad's grown sons by his first marriage, lived down the road a short piece.

"I thought Mrs. Willy was gone to Maple Grove," Alma said.

"Joseph said he saw her driving her buggy uptown yesterday evening peddling eggs," said Amanda, pausing over Nannie, who had gone back to sleep on her pallet. "I'll gather up the younguns and take 'em up to our house to get them out of the way. Come on, precious."

Clint and Jewell were awake now, their puzzled faces peering down from the loft. Clint, the older boy, had been suspicious for some time about his mother's condition, but Christie didn't want James to tell him where babies came from yet. Clint was still too young, and he should see it in cows and horses first.

"Where are we going?" said Jewell, scrambling sleepily down the stairway.

Christie heard Amanda cooing to the children, saying that their papa had gone to get a surprise for them. "It's like Christmas and we have to go away and close our eyes for the rest of the night so in the morning we can see the surprise—if we're real good." Amanda always took time to talk to the children. She turned even everyday events into stories. She had a way with all the children on the place, maybe because she seemed like such a child herself, although she was three years older than Christie and had two daughters.

Amanda was hurriedly wrapping the children in their coats.

"Get your caps, boys," she said. "Tie your shoes, Clint."

"It's a baby," said Clint.

"Papper's gone to get a baby," said Jewell. He reached out and pulled Nannie's nightdress, and she jerked it away from him. "You're a baby," he said. "Nannie's a baby."

"Stop that," said Alma, slapping Jewell. "This ain't no time for such foolishness. Get on out of here."

"Wait," said Christie. "Come here and give me a kiss."

She hugged each one of her children till they squirmed. Then, as Amanda whirled them away, the pain came again—a wave like the long, growling thunder that sometimes rolled through a summer sky from end to end. She was washed with pain, but she didn't feel how deep it went because she was seeing her children's faces go out the back door, one by one.

CHAPTER 2

It had been a hard winter, the coldest in Christie's memory. It was too cold for the roosters to crow. Alma beat icicles off the bushes, and the children collected the large ones for the springhouse. When the men stripped tobacco out in the barn, their hands were nearly frost-bitten. The winter wheat was frosted like lace, and the ponds and the creek were frozen solid. Some of the children went sliding across the pond on chairs. Christie couldn't see their fun from the house, but she recalled chair-sliding when she and James were courting back in Dundee and her father's pond froze over. James pushed her hard and fast, and she flew freely across to the other side, laughing loud and wild. That was the only time in her life the pond had frozen solid enough to slide on, but this winter James reported that six cows were standing on Wad's pond.

Amanda had told everybody it would be a hard winter. The persimmons said so, she believed. She broke open persimmon seeds for the children. Inside each one was a little white thing, the germ of the seed. Amanda said, "Look at that little tiny fork. That means a hard, hard winter's a-coming! If it was drawn like a spoon, it would be a sign of mild weather; and if it was a knife, it would mean a lot of frost, but not too thick for the knife to cut. But the fork is the worst."

When James and the boys stripped tobacco, Alma had to wash their smoke-saturated clothes. Christie gazed outside helplessly at the bare black trees, the occasional birds huddling inside their fluffed feathers, and the cows chomping hay beside Wad's barn, making a picture of color against the dusting of snow that had come overnight. Wad's mercury had gone down to naught on ten different nights that January and February. A snow in early January, after the ice storm, lasted till the end of the month. None of the farmers around had ever seen such weather—but then they always said that, Christie noticed. They'd never seen it so warm, or so cold, or so changeable, or so much rain to follow a cold spell. This year, everybody said the cold winter had something to do with the earthquake that had been predicted for New Year's.

Livestock froze: a cow who freshened too early; then her calf, stranded across the creek; then another cow who was old and stayed out in the storm. Wad and James worked to repair the barn so they could keep the cows in at night. They spread hay for insulation, piling bales in front of some of the largest cracks in the walls. The breath of the cows warmed the barn like woodstoves. Christie felt like a cow inside her tent dress and under the layers of cover on the bed. Her bulk heated up the bed so much that many nights James thrashed himself awake. They couldn't let the fireplace go cold—the children needed its warmth—but Christie felt as if she were carrying a bucket of hot coals inside her. In the past, she had been comfortable with pregnancy because of the privacy of it. It was her secret even after everyone knew. They didn't really know the feeling—a delicious, private, tingly joy. The changes inside her body were hers alone. But this time the sloshing, the twinges, the sensation of blood rushing, the bloating, the veins in her legs popping out—all were so intense it was as if her body were turning into someone else's. Walking from the stove to the dishpan—barely four steps—was a labored journey, her legs heavy like fence posts.

As she grew larger, she felt as though she were trying to hide a barrel of molasses under her dress. She was used to sleeping on her back, but when she gained weight, lying like that seemed to exert enough pressure to cut off the flow of blood to the baby. When she sat, she couldn't cross her legs. Her hip joint seemed loose, and it was painful to bend or stoop or turn her foot a certain way. The right leg seemed longer, and she walked in a side-to-side motion. She learned to minimize the painful motion, and her right leg grew stiff.

At night, James stroked her belly so sensuously she feared the baby might be born with unwholesome thoughts. As the season wore on and she grew still heavier, she retreated from James and wouldn't let him see her belly. She didn't want him to see the deep-wrinkled, blind hollow of her navel turning inside out. It made her think of the apron strings she made by pushing a safety pin through a tunnel of material and reversing it so the seam was inside. He seemed proud and happy about the baby, but she didn't think he would care to know that the baby was kicking—flutters and jabs inside. Men were afraid of babies. There was so much you didn't tell a man; it was better to keep things a mystery. One night as she was falling asleep, she felt a sharp jolt, unmistakably a foot jamming the elastic of her womb. The kick was violent, as though the little half-formed being had just discovered it had feet and was trying to kick its way out.

Sometimes a small event would soar through her heart on angel wings: the train going by, the frost flowers forming on the window light, flour sifting down onto the biscuit board, a blackbird sailing past the window in a line parallel to the train. For a moment, then, she thought she was the blackbird, or that she had painted the frost flowers herself, or that she was setting out carefree and young aboard the train. One day she heard a flock of geese and went outside bareheaded to watch them tack across the sky. The lead goose would go one way and the others would fall out of pattern, and then he would sway the other way and they would all follow, honking. The stragglers seemed to be the ones yelling the loudest. She felt like one of those stragglers, trying to keep up but finding the wayward directions irresistible. It wasn't just her condition. She had always felt like that. She was hungry at odd times, and she would fix herself a biscuit—cold, with sorghum and a slice of onion. In the henhouse one day, gathering eggs, she leaned against the door facing, breathing in the deep, warm fumes. She cracked an egg against the door and slid the contents down her throat. Then she laughed, like somebody drunk. Several boys had been drunk and torn up some hitching posts on the main street in town not long ago, she had heard. She wondered what it was like to be drunk. It would probably mean laughing at the wrong times, which she did anyway.

Back before she took to her bed, James had a spell of sleeplessness that made him drag for several days. A farmer couldn't afford to lose sleep, and she blamed herself for waking him up when she got up in the night to use the pot. One Saturday just before Christmas, he had hardly slept all night.

He made his weekly trip to town as usual, but he didn't stay long. He came home and slept the rest of the morning. He had never done that in his life, he said, annoyed with himself.

That was the day Mrs. Willy came visiting. Mrs. Willy, who lived by herself in a little white house, lost her husband in a buggy wreck soon after they married. She raised a daughter alone. Now she helped out women and sewed.

"Come in, Mrs. Willy," Christie called. "Clint, get Mrs. Willy a chair. Get her that mule-eared setting chair." But she was in no frame of mind for company. She had ironing to do.

Mrs. Willy stepped across the floor as tenderly as if she feared her weight would break a board, although she was slender and pigeon-boned. Alma had remarked that Mrs. Willy hung around pregnant women like a starved dog around the kitchen door.

She settled down in the chair Clint had pulled out from the back porch.

"Go on out and see if you can help Papper," Christie said to Clint. The other children were gathering hickory nuts with Amanda. James was in the barn rubbing down horse leather.

"I've got a splinter," Clint said, holding up his thumb.

Christie felt her apron bib for a needle she kept there. Holding the boy by the daylight through the window, she picked at the splinter until it shot out. She kissed the dirty little finger.

"I didn't cry," he said proudly.

"Now go on. Papper needs you."

Clint slipped out the back door. Christie had been heating an iron on the stove. She spit on it now to test it. It hissed. She started ironing a shirt.

"I need to do my arning," Mrs. Willy said. She leaned toward Christie with hungry eyes. "What's that baby up to in there today?"

"Growing." Christie didn't want to talk about her pregnancy. She didn't want to satisfy the woman's curiosity.

"And how's your man holding up?"

"He don't sleep good," said Christie, aiming her iron down a sleeve.

"Witches might be bothering him."

"Witches?"

"Here's what you do," said Mrs. Willy, untying the strings of her splint bonnet. "Make him sleep with a meal sifter over his face. When the witches come along they'll have to pass back and forth through ever hole in that sifter, and by the time they get done he'll have had enough sleep."

Christie laughed until she had to catch hold of her side.

"Don't you believe that?" asked Mrs. Willy. She was unsmiling, her face like a cut cabbage.

"I can't see James sleeping with a meal sifter on his face," Christie said through her laughter. "Anyway, I wouldn't want witches working in and out of a meal sifter so close to my face while I was sleeping. I'd rather be wide awake."

Christie felt her laughter shrink like a spring flower wilting, as Mrs. Willy retied her bonnet strings.

"You've got to get used to waking up through the night," Mrs. Willy said. "That's the Lord's way of getting you used to being up with the baby in the night."

"Does the Lord carry a meal sifter?" Christie asked.

"Why, what do you mean?"

"Oh, sometimes I can't tell witches from devils," Christie said. "Reckon it was witches that made our mule go crazy last summer? And what about that swarm of bees that got after Wad one spring?" Christie paused to tighten a hairpin. She cast a glance at the ceiling. "And that he-cow that busted out of his stall last week? Witches?"

"Christianna Wheeler!" said Mrs. Willy disapprovingly, realizing she was being mocked. "If you act ill towards people, that baby will have a ill disposition."

"I can handle any witches that get in my house," said Christie, pushing her iron forcibly up the back of the shirt.

"Well, Christie, when you went to camp meeting down yonder at Reelfoot, Alma said you got enough religion to get you through to your time. I hope so."

Christie didn't want to think about Reelfoot. There was a lull, while the fire in their voices died down into embarrassment. Christie finished the shirt and lifted a sheet from the wash basket.

Mrs. Willy said, "You need some new domestic. That sheet's plumb full of holes."

"This sheet's old. I'm aiming to tear it up into diapers."

Christie was glad when the woman left. She made Christie nervous, watching her iron and waiting for a crumb of personal detail. Christie wouldn't tell Mrs. Willy about the particular sensations—the way the blood flowed, the way all those creatures turned somersets in her stomach, the way she jolted awake. One night she had awakened after dreaming that her little sister Susan was alive again. In the dream, Nannie had been tugging on her nipple, but Nannie was Susan. The rhythm of the sucking had words, like words to a song. One of Susan's first words was moo-moo, her word for milk. Awake, Christie remembered the time her mother made a pinafore for Susan, starching the ruffles and working the fine lace. But the dogs tore it off of Susan, chewing it to tatters. Mama had worked on that pinafore for most of one winter.

A few days after Mrs. Willy's visit, James came in unexpectedly from the barn, slamming the kitchen door. He said, "I heard you was nasty to Mrs. Willy."

Christie was standing at the stove, stirring cream corn. "Mrs. Willy?" She turned away from James and reached for a bowl on the shelf. Her heart pounded.

James said, "Her sister's telling how you laughed at her and hurt her feelings."

Christie set the bowl on the table and dumped the corn in it. She said, "Some people like to talk."

For a second James's face looked as hard as clay dirt baked in the sun. "We have to live with all kinds," he said. "You can't just laugh to a person's face, Chrissie."

Christie bent her head down. She was conscious of her swollen breasts, her own, not his or anyone else's. James had never talked to her like this.

"When we moved here, we promised we was going to get along with everybody," he said. "You remember that."

Christie nodded. She was tired. She put her hands on her stomach, and she felt it move. James rarely got upset with her. He usually turned everything into a joke, he was so easy.

"Since you and Mandy went down to Reelfoot, it's like you come back a different woman," James said. "I don't know what's got into you, Christie. You're making my heart ache."

She turned, and her skirt tugged against her middle.

James's face softened a little then. "That baby's coming sooner than we thought," he said, touching her stomach. He seemed shocked to realize her girth.

In bed that night, Christie couldn't get comfortable. She felt monstrously heavy, as if with the weight of opinion. When she got up to relieve herself, she took the pot into the kitchen and tried to hit the side to muffle the sound. Afterward, she reached inside the warming box of the stove for a chicken wing. She gnawed the chicken, then searched for a piece of liver, the grease congealed with the crust. In the dark, she nibbled like a mouse, as quietly as possible, chewing breathlessly. She felt better. She heard Nannie stir on the pallet.

But the pregnancy dragged on, like the winter. Her mother couldn't come from Dundee on account of her bronchitis. And Mama was afraid of the earthquake. Christie had to be helped back to her feet when she sat in her rocking chair. She was afraid of falling. She had to struggle up the steps to the porch. On New Year's Day, she managed to cook field peas and turnip-greens-with-hog-jaws for good luck, but the cornbread burned. She hated being fat. She remembered an old woman in Dundee who told Christie's mother, "I had a fat place to come on my leg, just like a tit." The woman said, "The doctor mashed it up real good and then drawed that fat out through a little hole."

Christie fell asleep early at night, curving away from James. She couldn't sleep comfortably in any position except on her side, with a knee pulled up to support her belly. She curled her body around the baby, holding it as closely as possible—hooked to it from heartbeat to heartbeat, her blood flowing into her child.

# X

# Literary Meanderings

## NABOKOV

*For me, literary criticism is a foreign language, and I haven't made a habit of it. Writing fiction is more inviting than writing nonfiction, which demands a logical mind and a fidelity to fact. I usually approach essays and reporting much as I do fiction—as organic, intricately involved designs rather than as straightforward journalism—and I usually find that the design doesn't want to be that literal.*

*I wrote my graduate dissertation on Vladimir Nabokov's* Ada, or Ardor. *The novel was new at the time, and only reviewers had picked at its dense fabric. John Updike in his review said it would be good fodder for some graduate student, and I grabbed the challenge. It was a great pleasure trying to track down the hundreds or thousands of literary allusions, obscure words, and intricate patterns in this seemingly abstruse novel. My youthful earnestness ran roughshod over the delicacy and exquisiteness of Nabokov's novel, and I apologize for the excesses of the misdirected scholar that I was then.*

*Luckily, my scholarly pursuits more or less ended there, but I still urge the reader to delve into the magic of Nabokov's writing, including the dazzle and dance of his poetic novel* Ada.

## MARK TWAIN

*I wrote about Mark Twain's humor and language for an introductory essay to one of his novels,* The American Claimant, *in the Oxford series of facsimiles of Twain's books.*

*Mark Twain's parents migrated from Kentucky to Missouri. Twain's dia-*

*logue could have been a transcription of my grandparents talking. It was the language I used for the novel* Feather Crowns, *as it channeled through my parents and grandparents.*

—BAM

# The Universe of *Ada*

FROM *Nabokov's Garden* (1974)

John Updike, in his *New Yorker* review of *Ada*, chides Nabokov—whom he otherwise admires greatly—for taking his characters off the planet Earth and fabricating a science-fiction wonderland for otherwise earthly beings. He says: "I confess to a prejudice: fiction is earthbound, and while in decency the names of small towns and middling cities must be faked, metropolises and nations are unique and should be given their own names or none. I did not even like it when Nabokov, in *Pale Fire,* gave New York State the preempted appellation of Appalachia." By suggesting that Updike has made a mistake about Nabokov's setting, I hope to settle some business the discussion to follow has no time otherwise to pursue, but which would be useful to bear in mind. The action of *Ada* ostensibly occurs on the planet Antiterra, a mirror-image of our possibly microscopic Terra; and there is a time lag between the two planets, as well as a relentless distortion of Earth geography on Antiterra. The late 1800s on Antiterra have a modern earth-time superimposed on them, with Coca-Cola and motorcars and planes and movies; and Russia and America are blurred together. The reversal of time and the distortion of geography are often tedious and teasing for the reader used to expecting a replica of his own planet in the fiction he reads.

However, Updike surely would not object to a first-person novel about a character who does not tell his story straight: we have many of these. And, I submit, this is exactly the case in *Ada*. Van Veen, the narrator of the novel—who is obsessed with his sister Ada and wants to recreate in his chronicle the Ardis, or paradise, of his youth with her—is given to exaggeration, as well as self-delusion, romanticizing, and (both conscious and unconscious) distortion and manipulation of memory. He is so unable to face the real world head-on that he goes so far as to fantasize that his story

295

did not take place on the planet Earth, where human beings live and die, but on Antiterra, subtitled Demonia, a hell which he argues he must escape through the private, self-reflecting act of incest: a delicious and erotic flight from the deadly claims of the world around him. Van, I suggest, invents Antiterra to justify his own departure from reality: for him Demonia is the planet ruled by his father Demon and others of his ilk (tabooists with conflicting sets of standards). If the world is such a place, then, Van congratulates himself on trying to construct a more nearly perfect world: his private Ardis, or Eden. And this act of escape from Antiterra is, in effect, Van would argue, an escape to Terra—to the earth, to nature, and to a normalized geography. But this is all Van's rationalizing: he has a monstrous ego, as Updike is correct in emphasizing; and Van's incest with Ada, as I will argue, is unnatural and wrong, within the terms of the book. Hence, Van's fantasy: his effort to distort things in such a way that he is justified in his incest.

Van points out that he is not alone on Antiterra, that everyone is trying to get away from it, and that some go mad in the attempt, for Terra the Fair is a hoped-for heaven, knowledge of which is obtained through the visions of madmen. Some people on Antiterra—including Van, himself a madman of sorts—take these visions to be true evidence of the existence of Terra.

When Van writes about his adolescence, Ardis—the garden/paradise of his youth—appears as a fanciful jumble of aristocratic old Russia and modern America, with servants on an old country estate as well as flying carpets (a misplaced fantasy Arabia) and central heating. Van's motivation here is the creation of a perfectly delightful world for himself to dwell in in memory—one which combines the best of two worlds (such as the two spheres which Nabokov himself has inhabited and unites in his own experience—but, as I will argue, Van and Nabokov should not be confused with one another in reading the novel). However, as Van grows older and goes away from Ardis, more conventional, earthlike realities intrude upon his consciousness—bothersome mockeries of his youthful dream: the rise of modern hotels, wars, "sham art," the advent of electricity and self-service elevators.

Van Veen, as I shall attempt to show, tries to blame the disastrous consequences of his affair with his sister upon his heritage, upon his corrupt and luxurious family, and upon a demonic planet with narrow-minded conventions. But Van, in spite of his attempt to portray the naturalness and delightfulness of incest, is tormented by guilt and fear that his behavior was unnatural.

The use of the sibling planets Terra and Antiterra is a reflection—among many others in the book—of the incest theme. *Ada* is about incest, and, as incest is treated in the book, it is virtually synonymous with solipsism. Van and Ada Veen, siblings, resemble each other like twins and love each other passionately, but their love essentially is like masturbation before a mirror. Van narrates the story in an attempt to capture forever the essence of that childhood "paradise" with Ada in the bushes and to rationalize away his guilt.

In effect, Van Veen attempts to opt out of life, with its changes and surprises and calamities, by arresting it and trying to patrol his one narrow nook—his book, which contains his memories, as he has reworked and romanticized them into his immortalized Ardis, a bright and beautiful world besieged by the dark forces of Antiterra. He fails, as his narrative reveals, because realities continually intrude, and Van never is able to face them straightforwardly—nature, Ada's needs, mortality, even the geography of the planet, which he twists mercilessly in the process of his self-justification.

In his review, Updike kindly invites the graduate student to "spend many a pleasant and blameless hour unstitching the sequined embroidery of Nabokov's five years' labor of love." Thank you for the invitation, Mr. Updike: here is the first tangle of thread, but, of course, there is "much, much more."

# FROM Mark Twain's
## *The American Claimant*

### Introduction to the 2004 Edition

In most of the places I've lived, Mark Twain has left his mark. When I lived near Elmira, New York, I went to movies at the Twain Theater and shopped at Langdon Plaza, built on the site of Twain's Elmira-born wife's family home. The octagonal study in which he wrote *Adventures of Huckleberry Finn* sits on the campus of Elmira College like a misplaced steamboat's pilothouse. I peeked through the windows once, expecting to see cats. I've supped at the Mark Twain Hotel in Elmira.

When I lived in Connecticut, I frequently drove past Twain's gaudy mansion but never took the tour. As a Southerner undergoing the culture shock of moving north to graduate school, I was too disoriented to imagine I had anything in common with Samuel Langhorne Clemens' own long-ago journey from the heartland to Hartford.

We have a claim on Mark Twain in Kentucky, where I'm from. His parents grew up there and got married in Lexington. His mother was born in Adair County; her cousin, Major James J. Lampton, the original of Colonel Mulberry Sellers in *The American Claimant,* lived in Hopkinsville. Colonel Henry Watterson, editor of the *Courier-Journal* in Louisville, was also some sort of distant cousin of Twain's. And then there's Cousin Jesse Madison Leathers, from Mercer County—more on him later.

Twain's native Missouri is our neighbor. The Mark Twain National Forest is just across the Mississippi River from western Kentucky, where I grew up. And Dawson's Landing of *Pudd'nhead Wilson* is somewhere out there. Cairo, which figures so big in *Huckleberry Finn* and *Life on the Mississippi,* is nearby. I married a man born in Missouri. My father-in-law is even from Hannibal.

I'm sure I'm not the only admirer of Mark Twain who feels his presence all over the place. Mark Twain got around. He is part of the American landscape, always underfoot. He's very contemporary, I think, because in his time he saw so far ahead, as if he were looking right at us. And so we're reminded of him everywhere. His white-haired image was ingrained in us in childhood when we played the card game Authors. Today he's known to the public at large through impersonators. There are few figures in American history who lend themselves so frequently to impersonation: Mark Twain, Abraham Lincoln, and Elvis Presley. Twain was America's first superstar. And he knew it, too. He created his own persona—the unsmiling man in dazzling white, a clever icon designed to last. And for all I know, he had it copyrighted.

My own feeling for Mark Twain is grand and large. He's dear to my heart for a number of reasons, not least of which was his love for cats. Maybe my infatuation has something to do with the photograph I saw of him years ago—the one without a shirt. All that hair on his head and chest is resplendent. The photograph is shocking because he seems so real, so physical, not some stuffy, overly clothed portrait from another century. We don't expect Victorians to be sexy.

For me, the feeling for Twain is close to home. I claim Samuel Clemens–Mark Twain for my own personal heritage, as regional kin. I'm a descendant of the Clemenses' neighbors, more or less. Those pioneer families who crossed the Cumberland Gap and settled along the Cumberland River through Kentucky and Tennessee, and across the Mississippi River into Missouri, had much in common. Twain heard the same stories my forefathers did, talked the talk that was and still is pervasive in that stretch of country. My great-great-grandfather, John P. Mason, might have swapped some tales with John Marshall Clemens, Twain's father. They were about the same age and in the same vicinity at the same time. (Such wheedlings out of the murk of history are the sideline stuff of the genealogy craze.)

Mark Twain's original boyhood language, the deepest source of his artistic energy, is familiar to me. The varieties of dialect in *Huckleberry Finn* are quite particular. In general, though, the language—not just the idiom but the intonations and rhythms and cadences—is the way my grandparents and parents talked, and it's a language that is still spoken throughout the mid-South from the Appalachians through the Ozarks. I'm partial to a culture that uses the phrase "telling a story" to mean "lying." (When she caught me in a lie, my mother would say, suspiciously, "Are you telling me a story?") And I'm thrilled to read any writer who has the audacity to put the word "pudd'nhead" in a title and who uses the word "sqush" a lot. The "whang" in Huckleberry Finn's voice is as familiar to me as the speech of my parents. They would say "chimbley" and "dust-rag" and "fair-to-middling" and use fishing-worms for bait and bark their shins, and they would say "curious" to mean "peculiar." They have even called me "pudd'nhead"—with affection, of course, the same way they'd say somebody "needs killing." They didn't really mean it the way it sounded.

This language has a certain higgledy-piggledy quality, which accounts for Huckleberry Finn's outlandish way of talking—Twain's exaggeration of the actual speech of a young boy. It's a language that functions through its potential for inventiveness just as the necessities of the frontier called for ingenious solutions—making do with what was at hand. I call it rigged-up language. You can rig up phrases and invent words when you don't have more precise words at hand, the way you might rig up a makeshift lock for a door, or knock together a stile to get over a fence. That's how Twain came up with "spider-webby," "waffle-iron face," "premature balditude," "googling out," "ring-streaked-and-striped," etc. He took advantage of this creative potential in the language he learned as a youth. This way of talking often uses more words—and especially a lot of prepositions and adverbs and intensifiers strung together, each deeply meaningful and particular—but that's the fun of words. Instead of "forsythia," my grandmother might say "them yaller bushes up yonder around to the back of the barn." Or she might say, "Go get me that jar—the one that did for your last-summer lightning-bug catcher—down from up off of that board that's tacked up all antigodlin out yonder in the smokehouse. It's way back in the back." Having to piece scraps of words together keeps the brain active and the ear lively.

The idioms and sounds of Twain's boyhood speech make a colorful, expressive language that may seem to meander but gets directly to the heart of a matter. Twain's journalistic background helped shape his blunt, bare-to-the-bone style. That plain style assaulted the wordy romantic rubbish of his day. "Flowery writing" still means full of too many big, unfamiliar and empty words. Flowery language has given literature such a stigma that even now people who feel they aren't educated enough to read literature are intimidated by it, afraid it will be above their heads. They expect it will be flowery. For generations, many people who can read quite well have been steered away from literature by this strange notion. Twain was one of the first writers in America to deflower literary language. He grabbed stigma, pistil, stamens and all. One of James Fenimore Cooper's major crimes was that his characters talked in a flowery way. (Once in a while we need to go back to Twain's attack on Cooper's literary offenses to get our bearings.)

Cooper had a tin ear. But Twain demanded that dialect be authentic. He annotated his editions of Bret Harte's works with notes on accuracy of dialect and seemed not to have been concerned about Harte's sentimentality and other literary shortcomings. Mark Twain, the man who filled his autobiography full of lies and could turn anything into a tall tale, nevertheless wanted the way his characters talked to sound just right. The dialect had to suit his ear, match his memory of voices heard from his childhood in Missouri. It didn't always have to be literal, but the sound had to be real. That was sacred; those voices were the music that came from his soul.

This language that could be stretched and accommodated and made to fit every circumstance depended absolutely on sound. By artfully working the rhythms and sounds of real speech into his writing, Twain emphasized the dignity and complexity of people often dismissed as illiterate. Their heritage is an oral tradition, based on sound and not print, so the language has nuances and textures that formal written English lacks. The language is biblical, historical, musical, close to elemental experience. Twain's genius enabled him to plow this language into other forms of expression: standard English, literary English, even medieval and Shakespearean English. He plowed it in, turned it under, and allowed it to fertilize the growing American language. He brought the storytelling art from the frontier into the written language in such a bold way that American literature was defined by it.

A hundred years ago, Mark Twain was the most popular man in America. As we approach the end of the century, I'm thinking about him as lecturer, storyteller, music lover. I wish I could hear his voice from the stage right now. I imagine him in his white suit as he pets his cat, waves his magic wand, and orchestrates a work that reverberates down to our own time.

His voice and image loom as the major character—the artist—in his works. He seems so real; there are so many photographs, so many places around the world we know him from. He is so often quoted. It's as if the reports of his death were indeed exaggerated. We imagine him through Hal Holbrook's *Mark Twain Tonight!* (But did he really sound like a ninety-five-year-old man?) There are so many impersonators because he sprang from an oral culture and he was a stage performer. The oral culture is speeding along at present, replete with superstars and high-tech spectacles. Now, in our feverish *fin-de-siècle* CAT scans and ultrasound studies of the American heart and soul, it seems fitting to read Twain, especially *The American Claimant*, a neglected work that he published in 1892, near the end of his own century.

*The American Claimant* is enormous fun. I'm here to celebrate the mad energy of this strange novel. In it we have the pleasure of seeing Mark Twain's imagination go berserk. The story rolls along like a tumbling tumbleweed, except faster. Twain himself woke up in the night laughing over his creation. He seems to have been on an acid trip during much of it. (Critics of this work mention loss of control.) The humor hurtles beyond tall tale into simon-pure absurdity—antics and situations that would seem right at home today on the BBC with *Monty Python* and *The Goon Show*. It may have been too farfetched for Twain's time. In *Huckleberry Finn*, Tom Sawyer's regulation by-the-books imagination (prisoners are supposed to have rope ladders and pirates have to kill their victims) contrasts with Huckleberry Finn's spontaneous, genuinely creative imagination; when he's in a fix, Huck can invent an elaborate story on the spot—with setting, background, characters, intricate relationships. But in *The American Claimant,* the inventions spill out merrily, and none of them are required to make sense. Twain seems free to go along on a wild amusement park ride with Colonel Sellers, his mad scientist and huckster, and not notice the patches and lapses in the narrative flow. Twain is having too good a time to find fault with the outing.

The novel is a comedy of mistaken identities and role switches—familiar goods in Twain's works—all revolving around a serious debate about whether aristocracy or democracy is superior. At the time, awareness of British nobility was still warm in American memory, democracy was still a new experiment, and the question of which would win out was still being argued. Can you become somebody, or are you just who you are by birth?

Colonel Mulberry Sellers, who first appeared in *The Gilded Age* (as Eschol and later Beriah, not Mulberry), is the American claimant to the Earl of Rossmore's title, held blissfully for generations in England by a line of alleged usurpers. Colonel Sellers is irrepressible. He is effusively, buoyantly optimistic, full of limitless possibility. He is also seriously deluded, brimming with harebrained ideas. Nothing is impossible for him. His scheming mind runs a mile a minute. He lives on the edge. When he learns he might be an earl, he can manage that, too. No problem. He can be an American entrepreneur by day and an English earl by night, with receptions at Rossmore Towers—otherwise his "rat-trap" of a house. He's totally loopy.

"He's all air, you know—breeze you may say—and he freshens them up; it's a trip to the country they say. . . . [He's] as popular as scandal" (42). That's Sellers' wife, Polly, talking. She's a great talker, and good at clearing the fog. Colonel Sellers' voluble wackiness leaves you reeling. He is the only Perpetual Member of a Diplomatic Body. He's "a Materializer, a Hypnotizer, a Mind-Cure dabbler" (28). He's a gadget freak, but his devices don't work. The telephone on the wall is fake, though he sometimes talks on it. He rings a bell for a servant, but it has no wire, so he boasts that he told Graham Bell "in theory a dry battery was just a curled darling" (80). The book is full of marvelous schemes that prefigure DNA cloning, fax machines, copiers. Colonel Sellers invents the Cursing Phonograph, which stores up profanity for use at sea (sailors have to be cursed at during storms), and the decomposer, which saves up sewer gas and recycles it for illumination. These could be *Goon Show* plots.

Colonel Sellers struts along a bridge between *Frankenstein* and *Star Trek*. His plan to materialize dead people to use as an automaton labor force reminds me of the duplicator box in the *Calvin and Hobbes* comic strip. Calvin's duplicator is a cardboard box that creates doubles and triples of six-year-old Calvin, who reasons that the replicas can do his homework. Colonel Sellers bubbles, "We live in wonderful times." But in those post-slavery times, if everybody is free, with an equal chance to strike it rich, who does the labor? Colonel Sellers' scheme is a wishful solution to the wrenching question of social class in a democratic society.

He was originally modeled, as I've said, on Major James J. Lampton, a cousin from Twain's mother's side of the family. The Colonel Sellers in *The American Claimant* also owes a debt to Twain's older brother, Orion Clemens, a gentle man with a good heart and boundless energy and eccentric notions. He fooled around trying to invent a flying machine until Twain put a stop to it. (Twain's business sense was notoriously cockeyed.) Colonel Sellers draws on Twain's father, too. John Marshall Clemens had a fanciful hope that his investment in some Tennessee land would be a legacy for his children. (The Tennessee land shows up in *The Gilded Age* and seems to have been a guiding principle for many of Twain's aspirations.) And Jesse Madison Leathers, a distant cousin, plagued Twain for years to help him track down the family lineage and reclaim the estate of the Earl of Durham, which he believed was theirs. In Twain's novel, Colonel Sellers inherits his earldom claim from the previous claimant, Simon Lathers. The Leathers-Lathers Clemens-claimant interplay of fiction and fact is one of the seesaw games Clemens-Twain always enjoyed.

Not only does Colonel Sellers seem to reflect so many of Twain's own kinfolks, but he is also an American type. After the success of *The Gilded Age,* William Dean Howells (who subsequently collaborated with Twain on a Colonel Sellers play) had encouraged Twain to write more about Sellers, whom he saw as the quintessential American character. And so he is, in his pragmatism, opportunism, good-naturedness. And of course to this day there are actually people like Colonel Sellers who compulsively tell their mad stories, and really believe them. They often call themselves "Colonel." One of the characters says that in the South everybody's a colonel. In Kentucky, it is an institution to be named a Kentucky Colonel, an honorific. There are thousands of them (I'm one).

Colonel Sellers also reflects a side of Twain himself. When Twain wrote this novel, he was in financial difficulty with his ill-fated investment in the Paige typesetting machine. Like the colonel, Twain was always investing in some invention, trying to make a killing. In 1891, when he started *The American Claimant,* he was also working on a history game he had devised. At the time, a silly maze-and-marbles game called Pigs in Clover was sweeping the nation. It was the Rubik's Cube of its day. It turns up in *The American Claimant* as a trifling game Mulberry Sellers tosses off the top of his head and doesn't expect success from, but to his amazement it turns out to be a big hit and he makes "stacks of money." Twain must have felt at least a little envious about the pig-game fad. He had patented a few inventions himself—a dry-mounting scrapbook and a garment-fastening device—but he had little success with any of his investments. "Pigs in clover" was an expression meaning "rich people who behave indecently." The original expression was "happy as pigs in shit."

The language in this novel shines. There are wonderful names. Two of the main characters, Sellers and Hawkins, are selling and hawking their way through the age of tycoons that Twain dubbed "the Gilded Age." There's a girl called Puss, and a One-armed Pete, as well as Simon Lathers and Colonel Mulberry Sellers. (Greenberry and Littleberry were popular first names in the nineteenth century, and Twain may have stretched Mulberry and Huckleberry out of those.) A name gets in the way of the romance between Sally Sellers and Viscount Berkeley, alias Howard Tracy and One-armed Pete and Spinal Meningitis Snodgrass—the latter a perfect blend of the ridiculous and the snooty and the horrifying.

The Sellers family is a bunch of first-rate storytellers. Sally, Polly, and Mulberry Sellers: all those *l*'s in their names spring up from the soil of the oral tradition. Twain loved the sound of words and he knew how to string them by sound, like different shades of one color: "The earl's barbaric eye," "the Usurping Earl," "a double-dyed humbug," "a slouchy dabster." He was always doodling around with words: "a splendid flunkey, all in flamed plush and buttons and knee-breeches as to his trunk, and a glinting white frost-work of ground-glass paste as to his head, who stood with his heels together and the upper half of him bent forward, a salver in his hands" (22).

Twain relied on the punch of plain words. The undercutting, deflating power of hard Anglo-Saxon words was essential to tone and attitude and meaning. The vigor of plain language had texture and substance: "a plaided sack of rather loud pattern," "pauper-shod as to raiment," "lewd American scum," "his brother never was worth shucks." "Hatchments" is a choice word. It means a panel bearing the coat of arms of a dead person, and Colonel Sellers nails "a couple of stunning hatchments" (55) to the front of his house. Because it's not a commonly used word, yet is presented as if it is common as shucks, it's a grabber. The British Earl of Rossmore "drew the line at hatchments."

"The escritoire in our boudoir" (63) is high-toned, but set in a low-toned context. As an utterance of Colonel Sellers in his earl mode, the French phrase crashes right down off of its pedestal. Twain's humorous use of literary English punctuated with informal phrases is not just facile; in this novel he had a particular opportunity to experiment with language, by contrasting freewheeling American expressive idiom with the carefully poised empty utterances of the English nobility. Twain weaves together strands of standard English, highfalutin earl speech, idiomatic American speech, and snatches of amalgamated mid-South dialect—into an intricate fabric. This is no simple patchwork quilt. It's more of a tapestry, fluid in its texture. Or maybe it's a crazy quilt that has transmogrified into a tapestry, since a quilt is a rigged-up job, like Twain's native speech. Twain blithely weaves the raggedy-looking bits together.

When Colonel Sellers puts on his Earl of Rossmore airs, his wife is likely to say "Oh, scat!" And when he shifts back and forth between the two forms of talk, we're seeing his imagination totter between the illusion of being an earl, with unearned riches, and the dream of achieving success through his own efforts. Those efforts are always aimed at get-rich-quick schemes. In either case, wealth is the goal, and with it comes status; therefore, according to one of the characters, it stands to reason that anyone would be a fool to turn down a free earldom, whether he believed in democracy or not. Nobility may be un-American, but if it's up for grabs, take it. That's both American and human nature.

The story is built on this paradox, and the intricately blended language accommodates it, an organic resolution to the enigma of democracy versus aristocracy. The center of the resolution is based on a bit of wordplay: "Yes, he could have his girl and have his earldom, too." If you can have it both ways, that means the matter can't be split in two. Like the three baskets of ashes (thought to contain variously the young viscount) that can't be separated into three distinct sets of remains, the ideological positions can't be separated and labeled.

A happy romance can resolve any paradox. That's the simple popular metaphor for resolution, but beneath the girl and the earl is a more complex grasp—woven into the nuanced language—of truth and human nature. Nothing is one or the other. It's not Clemens *or* Twain, Hartford *or* Hannibal, earl *or* girl, but some of each. Good-hearted Colonel Sellers won't pursue his claim if it means alienating his daughter's new family; besides, she gets to marry an earl, usurper earl or not. And Colonel Sellers is distracted by another moneymaking challenge. His notion to use sunspots to reorganize the world's climates seems to suggest that one might as easily mastermind the weather as mess with human nature. But Colonel Sellers goes out on a hopeful note, intending to do something about that weather. (Twain had said everybody always complained about it but never did anything about it. So he hires the colonel.)

With Twain's writing, and *The American Claimant* is no exception, the reader often has the feeling that his artistic judgment was so mixed up with his life that he couldn't see the difference between what would make a great work and what would make money. But this is Colonel Sellers all over again. This naiveté, a basic characteristic of the yokel, which the yokel-gentleman never quite gets rid of, is both strength and handicap. The Colonel Sellers inside him allowed Twain to astound the world with his fresh voice but may have prevented him from finding his proper sense of self.

It makes most sense to read this entertaining novel in an autobiographical light. The claimant theme runs through Twain's writings, and he was in a way a claimant himself all his life, coming from a Virginia planter-class family that once had aristocratic pretensions, before the lure of the frontier taught the necessities of making do. Much has been made of the deep division in Twain's personality. He questioned whether he was a humorist or a literary writer, Samuel Clemens or Mark Twain, prince or pauper. To my mind, the most significant split was between his early life west of the Mississippi River and his later life in the Northeast. I'm awed by his heroic struggle to tame his uncouth background in order to become a cultivated Victorian gentleman and crash the literary scene of the Northeast. That culture was at odds not only with his Western/journalist/sagebrush-Bohemian/riverboat-pilot identities but also with his Southern heritage. (His people and the settlers of Hannibal were Southern, with large numbers from Kentucky.) I imagine that many of the contradictions and paradoxes in Twain's life and writing come down to that mile-wide-Mississippi gap between his formative experience and the land of his aspirations. I don't think a person ever truly transcends his background, and so I feel keenly the contradictions of the irreverent but hopeful claimant Samuel Clemens of Hannibal and points west arriving in the drawing rooms of Hartford society. He must always have suspected he was a pauper in princely garb, something of a fraud. He tried to conform to the behavior of polite society and give up his bad habits, but couldn't—and wouldn't—entirely. I'm pleased that he couldn't keep from draping his legs over the sofa arms, and tickled that Mrs. Thomas Bailey Aldrich found him so boorish and that she was appalled by his fabulous sealskin outfit. I recognize the need to hide one's insecurity by acting and dressing outrageously. It's a way of keeping something of yourself and rebelling against what you've agreed to join. He was a parvenu, they said sneeringly in Hartford. I think about the gap between Olivia Langdon and Samuel Clemens—how he could never really share the South with her.

So it seems to me that any division in his identity has most to do with his exile from his past and his adoption of a new identity in a new place. I recognize the exile mentality. When you try to become a new person in a new place, you sense that one of the two identities must be a fraud. But which one? You or the twin who died at birth? Which one are you? Parvenu or subversive? Entering the official literary culture of the Northeast with doddering Ralph Waldo Emerson at the helm, Twain may have felt insecure, but he also staked his claim there as if it were the Comstock Lode. The division between mere humorist and man of letters was a chasm he had to straddle. That he had one foot in each culture was his great success. His genius was in bringing the literary world the brash idiom and humorous storytelling energy of the America of discovery, can-do, and rigged-up solutions. In *The American Claimant* we hear that song.

Twain was an original. He was a visionary who struggled against his era and crossed regional and class lines with a fresh style that made him stand out as an oddity, someone exotic. Henry James called him "quaint." Twain joined the official culture and played by its rules to the extent that it allowed him a subversive power. It was with the creation of art that he balanced his past and present and mingled the complex contradictions of his vision into an original whole. He rigged up a singular persona, the gentleman in the angelic-white outfit, a disguise for his dark side.

Twain's preoccupation with duality and role switches is characteristic of exile. The Russian émigré Vladimir Nabokov, like Twain, was fascinated with the double theme. Nabokov reached for the English language to turn his Russian memories into the dappled sun-shade fabric of art. His true home was in the life of art, the refuge of the exile. Twain, a willing exile, used the language of his Hannibal past in the service of his new adopted class and culture. Like Twain, Nabokov was also fond of wordplay. Vladimir Nabokov worked the letters of his name around to get "Vivian Dark-bloom." I've discovered that Mark Twain yields up "A Twin Mark," as well as "Twin Karma"—whatever we are to make of that. Perhaps it means that Colonel Sellers has dressed himself up in Mark Twain's white rigging and beamed himself up to our century to become Colonel Sanders, the Kentucky Fried Chicken king, both tycoon and inventor, hawking his secret formula of seventeen herbs and spices.

Finally, and this is not entirely tangential, there's the matter of cats. There are seventeen casual mentions of cats in *The American Claimant,* including the cat-sneeze "Oh, scat!" Twain once called himself an author-cat. (God purrs, he wrote in *Letters from the Earth.*) Twain had a cat's wise and wary eye and skill at pretense. A claimant has to answer to a cat; in *Puff'nhead Wilson* he wrote, "A home without a cat—and a well-fed, well-petted, and properly revered cat—may be a perfect home, perhaps, but how can it prove title?" Twain's self-deceptions and disguises are cat behavior. Nabokov, of course, pretended cats were irrelevant and would not admit that his omnipotent paw was in the birdhouse. When Twain, as lecturer and entertainer, told his famous scary hark-from-the-tomb story about the Golden Arm and sprang the punch line on the unsuspecting girl in the first row, he was just like a cat pouncing on a mouse. ("Who's got my Golden Arm?"—(pause)—"YOU'VE got it!")

To see and hear Twain tell that story out loud now would be worth an earldom. The desire to hear his voice is enough to send one to a séance. As the century draws to a close, I'll bet there's a secret yearning in Mark Twain circles for him to materialize. Where is Colonel Sellers when we need him?

# XI

# Atomic Fact and Fiction

*When the* Washington Post *reported on plutonium contamination at a uranium-processing plant in my home region in western Kentucky, once again I seized on a story that had a personal connection. First, I wrote a nonfiction piece for the* New Yorker *about the fallout from the nuclear fears suddenly stirred up in Paducah, Kentucky. And then, feeling the limits of journalism, I wrote a novel inspired by this situation so close to home. Yet I deliberately set the novel,* An Atomic Romance, *not in Kentucky but in an indeterminate place in the heart of the country, in order to suggest that nuclear mischief could take place anywhere in America. It is a threat that affects us all. I didn't want it to be dismissed as something out in the boondocks.*

*But the novel is a romantic comedy. It's all about dancing, I think. Spinning, whirling, and dancing are central images: flocks of birds, centrifuges, minds and moods, the Artie Shaw big-band tune "Dancing in the Dark." The title* An Atomic Romance *is a celebration of the life force in the face of indeterminacy and chaos. That's dancing in the dark, one of the most exciting phrases I know.*

—BAM

# Fallout

Featured in the *New Yorker,* January 10, 2000

On the national radar screen, Paducah, Kentucky, is a provincial town with a funny name, but here in the western end of the state it was never an inconsequential place. I grew up on a farm near the small town of Mayfield, and Paducah was so far away—twenty-six miles—that we went there only on special occasions. It was the city, the Mecca for several counties of farmland. It had department stores, fine ladies' shops, movie theatres. I was dazzled when, as a child in the nineteen-forties, I went shopping with my grandparents on a Saturday. We dressed up and wandered through the riverfront Market House, where exotic produce—even oysters—arrived by train. On the way into Paducah, we passed the railroad repair shop, with huge locomotives squatting in the yard—an impressive sight that made me think important industry occurred here, something that linked our area to the whole world.

Downtown Paducah was ritzy. In high school, I attended a dance at the swank pseudo-Tudor Hotel Irvin Cobb, named for a novelist and humorist who had appeared in a movie. He won the O. Henry prize for the best short story in America in 1922. But Paducah's true star was Alben W. Barkley, who was born in a log house and worked his way up in society and politics through a long career in Congress, eventually becoming Vice-President under Harry S. Truman. After President Truman dropped atomic bombs on Japan to end the Second World War, Barkley—Paducah's favorite son—contrived to bring one of the nation's first atomic plants to his home turf. Everybody called it the bomb plant, even though it didn't really make bombs; it processed and enriched the fuel for them. Paducah, Barkley argued, had just the location—the site of the Kentucky Ordnance Works, which had manufactured explosives for conventional bombs during the last war. It was a logical shift to the new technology that America's defense depended on. And, in a gesture of pork-barrel politics gone nuclear, Barkley bequeathed a lasting gift to his hometown—uranium.

The Paducah Gaseous Diffusion Plant began enriching uranium fuel in 1952. This top-secret business was something like increasing the octane in gasoline—putting the oomph in the bomb. Helping to create A-bombs was a giddy, lucrative endeavor, and Paducah began to change. The first apartment buildings I ever saw shot up while the plant was being built, in the early fifties. Twenty thousand construction workers jammed the town, and local people rented out spare rooms and barn stalls—any available nook—for the newcomers to sleep in. At a time when "The Walt Disney Story of Our Friend the Atom" was a popular book, and Nikita Khrushchev's name was on every tongue, and Sputnik was terrifyingly in orbit above us, Paducah was called upon to be alert—and secretive—in exchange for good jobs and the chance to beat the Russians. It wasn't afraid. Doomsday wasn't going to happen in Paducah, not as long as the plant helped supply the nation with its friendly atomic arsenal. Today, the plant enriches uranium for nuclear-power reactors instead of atomic bombs, but workers still affectionately call it the bomb plant. License-plate holders from the nineteen-seventies show Paducah's namesake, Chief Paduke, on the left and an atomic cloud on the right, framing the words "Paducah, the Atomic City."

Last summer, Paducah's deal with atomic energy seemed to be exposed as a bargain with the Devil. The news was packaged in one explosive bundle in the Washington *Post,* on August 8th: radioactive-waste dumps, safety violations, bureaucratic lies, cancer, environmental pollution. Whistle-blowers, in a sealed lawsuit filed in June (it has since been opened), charged that former operators had defrauded the government by covering up knowledge of widespread radiation contamination, without regard for the safety of the workers. The *Post* reported stories of nuclear waste being treated lackadaisically—as if it were no more dangerous than kitchen compost. Workers routinely breathed heavy black uranium dust and some said that supervisors sprinkled it on the cafeteria food—to prove that the dust was harmless. Workers handled so much of a uranium compound called greensalt that their skin turned green, like the Jolly Green Giant's. Their bedsheets at home were stained green.

Even worse, the *Post* reported that many workers had also unwittingly handled plutonium—for decades. Plutonium, which is deadly and cancer-causing, was never supposed to be at the Paducah plant. It had arrived during the Cold War along with other highly radioactive fission by-products, as an impurity in shipments of used uranium. And it remained in the plant, like an unwelcome guest, dirtying up the place. The plutonium was in the uranium dust that the workers breathed.

The workers never made much fuss about safety conditions, although the plant was becoming its own toxic-waste dump—tons of radioactive scrap metal and cylinders of depleted uranium were piling up with nowhere to go. Toxic trash was tossed over the fence into an adjoining wildlife area, and local wells had become contaminated. Then plutonium was detected in a ditch outside the fence. And a radioactive, technetium-tainted underground plume of water was inching toward the Ohio River. Paducah, exemplary heartland town, where people went to church and gave the time of day to strangers, thought it had been spared such modern ills. The local press—the Paducah *Sun*—had downplayed the dangers. Until the Washington *Post* showed up, it was as though all the toxic trash were just part of the furniture—the price Paducah paid to have a thriving economy, the price paid to help win the Cold War.

Plutonium is heavy and it doesn't move fast, but, when I heard that it was present at our local nuclear-fuel refinery, I felt as if a plutonium-polluted plume were headed toward me. This wasn't Chernobyl—a nuclear power plant run amok. It was personal. My sister had worked at the bomb plant for several years during the late seventies. I emailed her in Florida, where she now lives. "I guess I was exposed," she answered. "But don't worry. If you got it you got it, and there is nothing that can be done—but maybe it can for the next generation." She reminded me how good the plant had been to its employees. The salaries were the highest around, and the benefits were off the scale. Besides, she told me, everything was so secret there. Nobody talked. You felt you were doing something important, something good for the country.

It was late in the dust-bowl summer, and dust from the desiccated fields sifted onto my car when I drove to Paducah from my home in central Kentucky. I was trying to think of a reasonable synonym for "freaked out," which was just about how I felt. The guy who pumped my gas said there was too much else to worry about in this world for him to be concerned about loose isotopes or technetium seepage. Wars, earthquakes, and such.

From Paducah, I continued west to Future City, where construction workers were housed when the plant was being built. Now it was just a crossroads, with a grocery and a barbecue eatery. The bomb plant was nearby, and just up a parallel road was Heath High School. The school had been the site, in 1997, of one of the first of the string of school shootings. A fourteen-year-old boy gunned down three of his classmates in a prayer meeting in the lobby. I remembered the responses and the television crews descending on the place like paratroopers, and I imagined that Paducah must feel jinxed now. The atomic-waste scare was bringing the news crews rushing back. The same barbecue joint fed both frenzies. I came to a halt at the crossroads. I was reluctant to look at either of these scenes—the plant or the school—and I didn't know if it was from fear or from sadness. I drove back to Paducah.

Dottie Barkley has been a family friend for twenty years. When she was seven years old, she was a guest on "I've Got a Secret," one of the old TV quiz-game shows. Her secret was that her grandfather was Vice-President Alben W. Barkley, Paducah's local hero. On another occasion, she was taken to the Plaza Hotel in New York where she pitched a fit because the Palm Court didn't serve catfish. She cried, "If I can't have catfish, then I don't want anything!"

We were sitting in Dottie's backyard among morning glories and gourd vines. Seven cats and Winnie, a chow-shar-pei mix, crowded around us. "This is outrageous," Dottie said, fuming about the local coverage. "The other Sunday, the Louisville *Courier-Journal* had a big front-page story about plutonium in Paducah, but there wasn't a peep about it in the Paducah *Sun* until the next day. Most of Paducah didn't even know about this!"

Did she think people felt betrayed? I asked.

"Hell, most people don't really care," she said. "Everybody at the plant knew they were working with dangerous stuff. Maybe they didn't all know it was plutonium, but they knew. Now people don't want to talk about it. They don't want to lose their jobs."

To visualize Dottie, imagine Marilyn Monroe—outfitted by the Limited—with a pickup truck. She is glamorously bohemian, with a blond heap of curly hair. And, as Alben Barkley's granddaughter, she holds a unique social position in Paducah, even though she avoids the cocktail-party carrousel of the local big dudes, where she might rightfully belong—not her style. She works at the Party Mart ("Paducah's Most Interesting Store").

She explained how the plant got here. "Granddaddy just muscled it through. He was best friends with Speaker of the House Sam Rayburn. And it was such an exciting thing when the plant came! The plant gave people good jobs. It kept a lot of people from starving. And now look what's happened. There's so much good—and so much horror." She shuddered. "Granddaddy couldn't have imagined this. He couldn't have known how it would turn out. Could he?"

A cat named Dinah Shore jumped into my lap. "Dear Hearts and Gentle People"—the song by the real Dinah—ran through my mind. I thought of the fifties, when a war-weary nation quelled its fears of the bomb by listening to songs like this, or to Doris Day's "Que Será, Será."

Dottie said, "The people out at the plant were so innocent back when it started. They used to handle uranium with their bare hands!" She bent over briefly to hug her dog. "You know, you should talk to my ex-husband Joe. He's worked at the bomb plant for twenty-six years, and he can tell you what it's like. They're like a big family out there, and he's been exposed to just about everything."

As I was leaving, I noticed a photograph in the dining room of Dottie with her parents and her grandfather, taken when Barkley Airport was dedicated, in 1948. Dottie, a child in a shiny taffeta dress with a cross-sash, has a missing front tooth.

"Look at me in my queen outfit," Dottie said, laughing at herself in the picture. "Get Joe to take you out to the bomb plant. It's so eerie."

A different Joe, Joe Harding, had known about the dangers years ago. He died in 1980, of stomach cancer. He began working at the plant in 1952, and his jobs included flushing impurities out of the processing pipes. Apparently, a residue of all kinds of radioactive things—plutonium, neptunium, and other contaminants—remained in the system once the processing was completed. Even today, there is a residue clinging to the pipes, like what's left in the skillet after you cook onions. Harding was chronically ill, but when he declared that he had radiation poisoning no one believed him. He had weird toenail-like growths coming out of his elbows and kneecaps, but people only laughed. The management said his illnesses were caused by eating too much country ham. His disability benefits and insurance claims were denied. A few years after his death, lawyers representing his widow ordered that his body be exhumed, and his bones revealed a level of uranium hundreds of times above normal.

Normal? Radiation is good for you; it boosts the immune system, according to a local engineer in an August 23, 1999, *Sun* column. "Radiation . . . may benefit the health of those exposed . . . a low dose of radiation actually increases immunity," he wrote. The plant's neighbors must glow with good health, then, because radioactive technetium-99 has turned up in the gardens—in banana peppers and turnip greens. Traces of plutonium were found in deer in the wildlife sanctuary—not enough to hurt you, officials said. To be in any kind of danger, "You would have to eat the whole deer," the Kentucky state health commissioner insisted on TV last summer—his remark delivered with the fervor of a political stump speech. Why, I wondered, do people always seem to be telling us that we can eat radioactive waste?

Downtown is "Historic Paducah"—antique stores, funky shops, and Saturday-night street parties. Like many other towns, Paducah is energetically reclaiming itself from the mall, and you can almost imagine the main street in its heyday. Tourists from the Mississippi Queen and the Delta Queen stream in through gates in the flood wall, which is being painted with murals depicting the history of the city. The showpiece of downtown is a quilt museum. Paducah is morphing from the Atomic City to the Quilt City. You might think that quaint old quilts are a clever atomic-age coverup, but the museum is on the cutting edge. Its quilts are postmodern.

I was headed for the Paducah Public Library. I had been mulling over the phrases "acceptable risk" and "eat the whole deer." ("I can't believe I ate the whole deer!") And for that matter, just what is a "trace"? What is an acceptable number of picocuries of plutonium? How many would you want to have settle in your brain, your lungs, your islets of Langerhans?

Plant managers claim that the amount of plutonium that came to Paducah was only twelve ounces—a piddling amount. Neptunium may be a worse problem. It is less radioactive than plutonium, but forty pounds of it were brought to the plant in the ill-fated uranium shipments. Plutonium and neptunium are transuranics, metals that are heavier than uranium. They are artificially created radioactive elements. They don't occur in nature; they pop up when atoms are split. I knew that plutonium is a hundred thousand times as radioactive as uranium, with a half-life of twenty-four thousand years—longer than civilization has existed. A beeline to the encyclopedia revealed to me what no one was admitting: twelve ounces is a lot. Theoretically, that much plutonium contains as much energy as nearly six thousand tons of TNT. More to the point, it's incredibly toxic, even in microscopic amounts. The "safe" dose for a human being is 0.13 micrograms. Thus twelve ounces is enough to provide a maximum legal limit of ingested plutonium for about two and a half billion people, or nearly half the world.

Around town, though, people didn't seem worried. There were virtually no letters to the editor of the Paducah *Sun,* and few people seemed willing to voice any fear of atomic pollution—as though talking about radioactivity might be enough to shut the plant down. TV NewsChannel 6 (which is owned by the *Sun*'s parent company) seemed more alarmed by weather scares than by radioactive-waste dumps or the presence of plutonium in the food chain.

I chatted a while with Iris Garrott, one of the librarians, and she reminded me that that was how folks were around here. "There's a sense that they took the risk for the jobs," she said. "They went along with it. People here are concerned about personal and emotional things—like the shooting at Heath. That's when everybody gets in a stir, when it touches you personally." Iris, who had three flashy earrings in her left ear and one in her right, leaned forward. She said, "But the news is sinking in. Every day, something new comes out. Everybody's on edge, I think. They're just waiting."

"For what?"

"They're waiting for somebody big to come to town—Energy Secretary Bill Richardson, Tom Brokaw. If Tom Brokaw came, then it would be real."

Joe Gorline, Dottie's ex-husband, loves working at the bomb plant, as his father did. From the start, Joe's father told him, "This stuff is not good," and Joe has been careful. His father died from chlorine-damaged lungs, but Joe has been loyal to the plant and to its important secret work.

He looks strong and healthy. He is tan and muscular, somewhat large in the middle, and has a long gray ponytail fastened at intervals with colored rubber bands. He lives with his pit bull–Rottweiler, Baba Ram Dass (Bubba, for short). In his house are a Finnish 20-mm. antitank rifle and a Second World War German MG 34, and a safe filled with his gun collection.

Joe repairs equipment in what's called the cascade—a six-hundred-mile complex of pipes which comprises the enrichment system. Uranium hexafluoride gas, or $UF_6$, is sieved repeatedly in the cascade to get a richer concentration of uranium—a panning-for-gold procedure. Joe might replace joint seals or weld pipes that carry $UF_6$. For such work, he wears a safety suit with a respirator. "I call it my banana suit," he told me. "It's yellow, with yellow rubber boots, orange gloves."

Orange gloves? I asked.

"It's a statement," he said with a grin. "Accessories are everything."

Doesn't he get hot in that suit?

"Oh, I'm used to the heat. But it's noisy! It's like being in the crankcase of your car. I haven't heard a bird chirp in years." He laughed and cupped his ear. "I listen to the machines. My job is to keep things running. After a while, you want it to run. You develop pride in your work."

Wasn't he afraid of radioactivity?

"There's nothing out there now that scares me. The safety has improved. But if anybody got big doses I did. Fifteen years ago, the same place I'd go now in my banana suit, I went in with coveralls. We'd get covered with black oxide dust and it would be all over us, and then we'd go to the cafeteria and wallow around. I got $UF_6$ and black oxide in my mouth and eyes." He laughed. "It tastes terrible!"

He showed me a small crater on the side of his nose, where he was burned by fluorine. "It would condense on a vent and drip over the door. One day, a guy went out the door and something dripped on his nose. He went nuts. He thought he'd been burned until we yelled, 'No, that's just pigeon shit!' But it dripped on me one day. My nose started smoking on the end. When you start smoking, you have to go to the dispensary. One guy's nose was worse than mine. It was flat."

I knew I ought to see the plant, but I wasn't sure I wanted to go. I'm health-conscious. I consume antioxidants, count fat molecules, pick organic turnip greens. Did I really need to go on a treasure hunt for transuranics? Should I carry a Geiger counter? Wear throwaway shoes?

I rode to the plant with Joe in his old Chevrolet truck. He flicked his cigarette discreetly out the cracked-open window. Paducah's urban sprawl is westward, toward the plant. Around the mall are the typical clusters of ugliness which deface America. In the subdivisions, Ten Commandments signs had sprouted in people's yards. The tall houses in the extravagant new developments looked overpriced and too close together, but I was glad that at least they weren't usurping all the fine farmland. Just past Future City, we turned onto a road that led to the plant, lined with small farms and modest homes. The corn was dying.

"The soybeans are strangely green," I said.

"It's plutonium that does it," Joe said. "All that radiation."

Sometimes you have to take what Joe says with a grain of greensalt.

The plant, which occupies a fenced-in area nearly the size of Central Park, is a sprawling gray complex. The architecture resembles the back end of a shopping mall. Right away, I noticed what was stored in the front yard—the blue cylinders of depleted uranium, rows and rows of them. Each of these cylinders—there are thirty-seven thousand of them—weighs between ten and fourteen tons. They made me think of a stockpile of pods from "Invasion of the Body Snatchers." The cylinders will be there until someone figures out an economical way to recover the last traces of valuable uranium in them. In the meantime, everyone hopes that they won't rust, or leak—or explode.

As we drove around the outskirts of the plant, I glimpsed some of the "hot spots" the Washington *Post* had written about—small areas where toxic waste had been spilled or buried or dumped. They were roped off and low to the ground, with little warning signs. At one time, five hundred picocuries of plutonium were detected on the plant grounds—thirty-three times what the government deemed an acceptable standard at blast sites in the South Pacific. Some of the buildings are so heavily contaminated that they have been abandoned, and, unfortunately, wildlife now live in them.

The plant itself is not a reassuring image: it's aging and corroding. There are six processing buildings, and they are all hooked together with pipes—long, unsupported, seemingly precarious overhead pipes. I was trying to grasp the way the plant worked, the way the gas was pumped through a network of compressors and converters—the cascade. It was such a mysterious concept—waterfalls, something beautifully flowing—that for a moment I almost wanted to see it. My sister saw it once when she worked in the safety department. A supervisor took her inside one of the big buildings which housed part of the cascade. He wanted to show her what their work was all about.

We turned north, on a gravel road alongside the chain-link fence, and spectacular waste dumps came into view: the rusty scrap heap, the old cylinders, the giant mound of crushed fifty-five-gallon drums (Drum Mountain, it's called). Uranium, radionuclides, "uranium daughters" (a phrase that captured my fancy), and transuranics infused these collections like mildew in damp clothes. Neptunium, plutonium, technetium, old kitchen sinks—it all seemed to be here in the scrap piles, as common-looking as a junk yard of wrecked cars. In a way, the scene seemed normal. It's a time-honored rural practice to save your trash in the yard—what won't fit on the porch. You dam the creeks with old mattress springs and broken refrigerators, to stop soil erosion. An earthquake on the dreaded New Madrid fault could turn this region, embraced by the Ohio, Mississippi, Tennessee, and Cumberland Rivers, into mush. Where would all this irradiated trash wind up then?

The plant had been built on a thirty-four-hundred-acre federal property, where the old munitions plant—the original Kentucky Ordnance Works, or the K.O.W., as it was called—operated during the Second World War. Most of the land that surrounds the plant is the wildlife area and extends almost to the Ohio River. Joe was driving through this wilderness now. I know that there were still toxic chemicals from the ordnance works in the ground. (The K.O.W. had manufactured TNT.) And now radioactive pollution had spread through this area. The Washington *Post* said that two dozen radioactive rubble piles from the bomb plant dotted the landscape, but I didn't see any. Radioactivity was an invisible, ghostly presence.

"Over there's a great pond for frogs," Joe said. "I used to frog gig there a lot with my son."

We passed other ponds, where recently the fish had been killed so that nobody would eat them. People have hunted and fished here for decades; no one wants to throw back a good catch. I was aware that this wildlife area is virtually sacred. People feel so deeply about hunting here that they would be up in arms, so to speak, if the area were condemned because of mere toxic waste. We twisted and turned down gravel roads; then we were in the scrubby fields, on what were just old worn paths that Joe said he knew by heart.

"I love this old truck!" he burst out gleefully as we bounced over a bump. The tracks ran beneath thick weeds and tall grass. We were in a labyrinth of ancient trails. In a clearing, we passed a group of teenagers slouching around a pickup truck, playing hooky. This park is where kids come to party, Joe told me, and schoolchildren have picnics in these fields, where, over the years, thirty tons of uranium were flushed into the streams, saturating the earth, and recently an unmarked pile of contaminated railroad crossties was discovered.

We passed a pair of sirens on poles, with signs—what to do if the siren sounds. (Basically, run for at least two miles.) A concrete water tower loomed ahead, then another and another. We were among the ruins of the ordnance works—concrete hulks. Vines crawled over the gray shapes. Even though nature was taking over, the landscape itself was a ruin, shriveled by the drought, the sumac and sassafras reddening prematurely.

I had lost my sense of direction, and I didn't fancy crawling through scrubland fertilized by uranium or TNT, but Joe wasn't worried. It was a hot day. He had a jug of water and a cooler of Cokes. I clutched my bottle of water from France. We got out of the truck and waded through tickseed and ironweed, then down a gravel path. Joe, sockless in sandals, reminisced about youthful outings here as we peered inside some of the dank old buildings. They were dark, with graffiti-covered walls. A disintegrating couch, its stuffing spewing, sat beneath some lingering asbestos that hung from the ceiling like a Spanish moss.

I was either in a gothic romance novel or in an apocalyptic Italian movie. I faced a wall, spray-painted with a message: "Live in Fear, the End Is Near."

I felt suddenly uncomfortable to be in a place that had an unhealthy obsession with bombs and guns and other insidious things that kill people. I saw the K.O.W. as the ancestor of the bomb plant, and I knew the plant was creating its own ineradicable legacy. The sins of the past—uranium daughters—lay strewn over the landscape and in the water and under the earth. From TNT-based weaponry in the Second World War to the first atomic bombs and the nuclear stockpiles of the Cold War, the wartime urgency left a habit of mind and a profusion of poisons.

Dottie had shown me a photograph Joe took of her out here. She was standing in an open window in one of these ruined buildings, and in the photo the light had created an apparition above her head, merging with her bright hair. She said it looked like a dove, but its glaring whiteness remind- ed me of an atomic blast.

On another day, screwing up my courage, I returned to the plant alone, determined to see the cascade for myself—heat and noise and all. It was a bleak, gray, rainy day, but after the drought I was glad to see it. I was in my rain gear, with bright-yellow boots. I wished I had Joe's banana suit.

My guide wore a thermoluminescent dosimeter, a radiation-monitoring badge, but she said that I didn't need one, since I wouldn't be allowed anywhere in the plant where there might be radiation. I was a little disap- pointed but mostly relieved. I was allowed into the control center, a round domed concrete building. Inside, on the curved wall, was an immense dia- gram of pipes and compressors and converters and electric motors. It was fifties technology, intricate but decidedly pre-Microsoft. It was like the cockpit of Captain Video's spaceship. The diagram on the wall, with lots of red and green lights and dials, mimicked the cascade. The system has never been shut down since it started, in 1952. If it were shut down, the gas would cool and turn into a solid, and the cascade would clog up like a cholesterol-choked artery. A gauge on the wall—like a big clock—had a dial indicating the gas level.

I was left to imagine the mighty cascade. It was like a Rube Goldberg cartoon version of the human circulatory system—the crudest technology for something as mysterious as a beating heart. The heart of the mystery of atomic energy, its deadly magic, was a mundane industrial process. Some- how, I could picture Lucy and Ethel in here, running this thing.

The onset of autumn brought a startling revelation: an accidental uncon- trolled nuclear chain reaction was theoretically possible in the plant. Pa- ducah jumped out of its time warp, crashing into the twenty-first century. People were confused and scared. Energy Secretary Richardson visited and promised the moon. He apologized for the plutonium. The plant was buzz- ing with investigators. Joe E-mailed me, "During the day the plant is a hotbed of activity, auditors everywhere. They don't know whether to shit or go blind." In September, a ten-billion-dollar class-action lawsuit was filed against former contractors, including Union Carbide and Lockheed

Martin, claiming, among other things, mental distress and "unjust enrichment." Joe wouldn't join it, and he had no kind words for whistle-blowers.
"If I get cancer, I don't even want to know," he told me.

I've been trying to put my finger on why, for so long, Paducah remained
passive in the face of danger, something I feel I know intuitively as an insid-
er but which seems to befuddle outsiders. Why did the workers trust some
of the government contractors that ran the plant? Did they really believe
that giant corporations would look out for their well-being? How could
they have been so innocent? Is that how those contractors got their colos-
sal abuses?

These are post-Vietnam questions. The same people who are asking
these questions seem a bit wistful about the virtues of small towns. All I
can say is that such things exist. People here haven't yet plunged into the
frantic greed frenzy of the big time. They're independent, proud people—
agrarian, basically. They don't want to be told what to do—like "don't
hunt on the wildlife refuge"—but once a bargain is made and a trust is
built, as it was with the plant from the beginning, they will honor it and
they will do as they are asked. It was more than high-paying jobs. Neigh-
borliness, not litigiousness, has always been the norm around here, and
the social contract meant getting along by going along. The problem was
that the plant had been a good neighbor. It was good to its workers, who
kept the secret well.

I'm drawn again to Future City. At the intersection, it seems that the
future is nuclear fallout in one direction and guns in the schools in the other. I turn north, toward Heath High School. Driving up, I see kids across
the road at band practice. A banner outside the entrance of the school
reads, "Rising to the Challenge." Inside, in the lobby, fourteen-year-old
Michael Carneal opened fire on the prayer group two years ago. The Paducah Gaseous Diffusion Plant—a good neighbor—contributed generous-
ly to the memorial fund for the three dead girls.

I recall that, for some of the students, the instinctive reaction to the
massacre was forgiveness. They painted banners that said "We forgive
you, Michael" and "We love you, Mike."

And that's the heart of the story. This turning the other cheek, the
strange embrace of sudden horror, startled outsiders. The students' anger
came later, when grief had set in and the lawyers showed up, but their ini-

tial acceptance—their passive non-resistance—was not so surprising in an agricultural region, where farmers forgive the forces they cannot control. Droughts and pestilence are risks the farmer takes at every planting time in every hopeful spring.

# FROM *An Atomic Romance* (2005)

Reed Futrell still went camping in the Fort Wolf Wildlife Refuge, but he no longer brought along his dog. One spring evening, after his shift ended, he raced home, stuffed his knapsack, loaded his gear onto his bike, and headed for the refuge. He was in one of the enigmatic moods that clobbered him from time to time, and when it struck—the way a migraine hammered some people—his impulse was to hop on his hog and run. Last fall, when one of these moods grabbed him, he rode hundreds of miles, to Larimer County, Colorado, where—in a hot-tub at a spa—he came to his senses and felt like turning back home.

"Good boy, Clarence," he had said to his collie-shepherd combo as he left the fenced yard and fastened the gate. "Lay low now. And be sweet—unless anybody tries to break in. You know what to do, killer."

During the five-mile ride, he ignored the industrial scenery and the suburban tableaus and the trailer havens. He escaped the desolation of the outskirts quickly, pretending his hog was a Thoroughbred stallion. As he approached the wilderness, Reed tried to imagine that he was seeing the place for the first time, as if he were entering the unfolding present of the opening of a movie. He was watching, curious to see what might happen.

What anyone notices first about this vast, flat landscape is the fantastical shapes of rising white clouds—plumes and balloons and pillows of cloud, like fleecy foam insulation blown from a hose. When Hollywood filmed a frontier drama here, the source of the clouds remained just outside the frame of the Cinerama panoramas. A radiant green extended for miles, and the great mud and might of the river seemed unlimited. Even now, if you saw this landscape from a sufficient distance and you didn't know better, you might imagine an untouched old-growth forest. The billowy puffs seem innocent. They are so purely white, it's as though only dainty, clean ladies' drawers could have been set aflame to produce them.

But now as the camera zooms in closer, you see that the green is criss-crossed by linked electric towers leading to a set of old gray buildings of assorted sizes—including Quonset huts and prefab mobile units. They are unprepossessing except for the largest two, which appear ample enough to house a fleet of C-5 transport aircraft. These two buildings, in chorus, emit a low roar, like the sound of a waterfall.

Now, the close-ups. The row of gleaming scrap heaps. The gate with the DANGER signs. The small building brightly decorated with yellow signs and festooned with yellow tape. One rusty pile of smashed barrels and girders and coils staggering to the height of a two-story building. From this mountain of metal, a ditch threads into a lagoon, where the still water is green and shiny. Other small lagoons are outlined with yellow ribbon.

A parking lot is filled with large metal canisters painted a pretty aqua color. They resemble gargantuan Prozac capsules. Thousands of them line the pavement. They are parked in geometric rows, like patient pupae wait-ing to become worms. Beyond the six-pack of cooling towers and the twin smokestacks, two tall construction cranes rise from a clearing on the edge of the wilderness, where a scrim of temporary fencing conceals a new act in an ongoing drama.

Reed's motorcycle plugs along a gravel road, skirting the security pe-rimeter, passing the tall scrap heap, then leaving the gray, humming village and easing into the solace of the woods, where campers and hunters, with their dogs and deer rifles and picnic coolers, have pursued the natural life for years. Boy Scouts have their roundups and jamborees here. Coon-dog clubs hold their field trials.

The wilderness sprawls toward the river. The road leads into the heart of this sanctuary, away from the string of high-voltage towers and the dancing plumes. Even the crash and gurgle of the invisible waterfall grows distant. But the luminescence of the place remains, brightening with the growing dusk.

Reed Futrell wound through a labyrinth of gravel roads, stirring up a dust-ing of memories. He had been coming to this place all his life. His uncle Ed taught him to fish here in the large ponds, long before the water be-gan to turn strange colors. He killed his first—and only—buck here. He hunted squirrels with his cousins. He went on church picnics, although he belonged to no church. He probably had camped in this woods three hundred times.

He decided to camp near the levee, where he could hear the blasts from the tugboats towing barges of iron ore and coal. Leaving his bike near a clearing, he lit out through a stand of river birches. He followed his glimpses of the immense metal bridge that spanned the river. At the top of the levee, he squatted and let the last of the sunset happen, imagining it was coming out of him, that he had the power to make the sun go down. If the sun, flaming orange, was like the inferno inside him, the burning blaze of fear and desire, then perhaps he could drop it over the horizon as casually as a basketball. He rose to attention as the sun's top rim sank. A haze of thin clouds spread above the horizon. A cool tinge in the air brushed his skin. A coal barge was gliding along, and he could see the tugboat captain on his perch. Reed had considered that way of life for himself at one time, a means of living without moorings.

At the levee, he was always aware of his maternal grandfather, who had worked with the Army Corps of Engineers building the levees and preparing the way for the marching towers of electricity that fed the gaseous-diffusion plant. Somewhere along the levee, Boyce Reed had been working on an erosion project, laying willow matting along the banks, when he fell ill with pneumonia. Whenever Reed came here, he was gripped by the vision of his grandfather suffering from fever and congestion while lying in his tent by the riverbank. He had been in the tent for three days before anyone realized how sick he was. He died in 1951, before Reed was born. Reed knew little about him, a pale man in a portrait on his mother's mantel, so coming here was like a ritual connection. Reed did not have a line of men he was close to. His father, Robert Futrell, had died young, in 1964, when Reed was only six, in an accident at the plant. It was up to his uncles to teach him how to be a man. "This is the way your daddy always baited his hook," they would say. Or, "He was the champion when it came to muzzle loading." And "The Almighty broke the mold after he made Robert Futrell." Reed felt he couldn't live up to his father's reputation, and it took years for him to realize that his uncles meant nothing personal.

In the growing darkness, he hiked briskly through the woods back to the spot where he had left his bike. He made his camp methodically, laying out one of his tarps on the ground and stringing the other among some tree branches for an overhead shelter. Then he smoothed off a place for his tent. Slamming the pegs with satisfaction, he anchored the base corners, then wormed the aluminum tubes through their little fabric tunnels. His pup tent sprang open like a flower unfolding on high-speed film.

He constructed a small fire and heated some beans, then unwrapped a chicken focaccia sandwich and snapped open a can of beer. He ate, watching the fire swell and turn colors. The warmth was pleasant. The air still held the mellow spring daytime smells of bloom and decay. The light from the plant blotted out much of the night, but he could see a faint smattering of the Milky Way and a few of the brighter stars. He thought he could make out Sirius. He liked to imagine dying stars, their enormous fires imploding or exploding. He tried, as he often did, to grasp the idea that the present moment did not exist in some star a million light-years off. It was not now there. Not even on Mars was it now. If that was true, it could be reversed, he thought. He and his fire and his tent did not exist from the vantage point of the star, or on Mars, at this moment—whenever that might be.

Viewing the stars, he always felt privileged to witness ultimate mystery, to be in it. The universe tantalized and affronted him, ripping him out of his own petty corner. As he ate, hypnotized by the fire, he listed in his mind all the things in his life that were good. His kids had jobs and weren't in trouble, his ex-wife was satisfied, his mother was nestled in a senior citizens' home. His dog didn't have fleas.

But he had not seen Julia in six weeks. She came out here with him a couple of times, most recently on a freakishly fair day on the last of February. They picnicked in a meadow beside the ruins of Fort Wolf, the old munitions factory that had operated during World War II. It was one of his favorite places. The hulks of the ragged concrete walls were like the forlorn remnants of a castle. Two water towers, their brick and mortar crumbling, stood like bookends without books to hold. He cavorted with her, half-naked, shouting, "It can't get any better than this!" In the sunny afternoon they wallowed around lazily on a flannel blanket. At night they snuggled in the pup tent (his double-pup tent, he told her when she questioned its size) and shook up the wilderness with riotous sex.

Still gazing at the fire, his sandwich now gone, he wandered into a reverie about Julia, trying to create a Top Ten list of sex-dates with her. But none of them could be relived in his mind. He couldn't remember what she was wearing the last time he saw her. She said, "I can't loiter. I've got an immunogenetics seminar to go to." And after that, she did not answer the telephone messages he left.

Julia, who worked at a cytopathology lab, planned to save the world from sinister infectious diseases like Ebola and anthrax. Early in their relationship, not realizing how ambitious she was, he had suggested she go to nursing school. She good-humoredly dismissed his idea.

"I can stick people," she said. "But I'd rather be in charge of a mental hospital than have to do a Foley or a rectal."

"You'd rather hear about their cracked minds than look at their cracks," he said.

She thought for a moment. "A cracked mind—I like that."

Julia was from Chicago. He loved to hear her talk. Her sweet Scandinavian-Irish-Polish twang. Her sharp, precise sounds, her back-slanted A's and rounded O's. He missed her vowels. He missed her lip gloss. She used flavored lip gloss habitually and sometimes smeared it straight across, instead of following the natural lines, so that her mouth was a wide, glistening swath.

He would get his blood tested if she could be the one to stick him. He hadn't had a complete physical in five years. He was a notorious procrastinator—with tinnitus and a thrumming lust that ran like a refrigerator, kicking on and off automatically.

The tree frogs were peeping a cacophony, in which he heard raucous machines and anxious melodies. He draped a blanket around him and fed the fire little twigs. He picked a tick from his scalp and dropped it into the flame. The sky was gathering clouds, and the stars were fading. The clouds moved swiftly. He couldn't even see the Dippers. He had been to the Smoky Mountains one August during the Perseid meteor shower; it was dazzling, like fireworks, like the Big Bang. He tried to remember it now, but it was like trying to remember sex; you had to be there then. If there was no now there now, then there would be no then there now either.

Inside his tent, he sidled in and out of sleep, dreaming that Julia was with him. He dreamed that she telephoned a pizza parlor, and a machine voice told her, "Your call is important to us. Please stay on the line."

A sound penetrated his sleep. In his semiwakefulness he thought he heard himself fart—a muffled, explosive blat that projected over toward the levee, as if his bowels were practicing ventriloquism. But he hadn't heard himself fart that loudly in years. As a gentle rain began to fall, he sank back into sleep, with the soothing and hypnotic shush of the raindrops on the leaves.

In his dream, a car pulls up nearby and the engine shuts off. The head-lights go off, but an interior light stays lit. The car seems to huddle between the shadows of the ancient water towers. The moon climbs high, but the driver of the car does not emerge. With spring peepers screaming out their courtship messages, the night seems welcoming. Hours pass. Then, near midnight, the car door opens once briefly, and a woman—indistinct in the dim light—slips out of the seat, shuts the door, and squats on the ground for a few minutes. Then she reenters the car, starts the engine and lets it run. Radio music blares. The car does not move from its spot in the shad-ows. The engine keeps running, with the dome light shining and the music playing until the car runs low on gas and begins to sputter. The engine dies. The light goes out. And the blast of the gun splinters the night calm. In a while, rain begins to fall softly.

Reed tries to awaken, but he feels paralyzed. He struggles fitfully, and then eases deeper into dream as his muscles release and he floats toward the car. He glimpses the ice-blue metal, burning like candles, between the water towers. He approaches cautiously, noticing that it is a luxury sedan, a nice city car, not the kind of vehicle a camper or hiker would be driving. Slopping his way through puddles, he reaches the car.

He stares through the broken window at the shattered face. She has fallen toward the wheel, but he can see half her face is ripped away, leaving a reddish-brown spaghetti sauce. She must have hit her temple at a slant. He does not need to open the door. He can see the revolver on the floorboard, a .38 special, its handle decorated with floral decals.

On the dashboard, fastened with tape, are pictures of children. Two boys and two girls. All of them little, smiling, in Halloween costumes, the least one in a bunny outfit, with long, erect ears.

Moaning, Reed reels away. He streaks through the woods—crazed, stupid with disgust and horror. He calls out. He runs and runs, but he feels he is traveling at the speed of a shrimp trawler, which he imagines as a slow boat to Ethiopia. But then the shrimp trawler zooms across the Gulf of Mexico, where he awakens, in a sea of sweat.

His mind had given him a private screening of a horror film. Who was the woman? Why would she come out here to kill herself? He could not fathom a woman killing herself when she had four small children to care for. He turned and stretched in his musty, oversized sleeping bag. Was it so simple to go mad and kill yourself? He didn't believe it. What if she wanted to spare her children from something? An illness. Maybe the woman believed herself inadequate to the task of raising them. He wondered if her husband would ask the same questions he was asking. Over and over he heard the shot muffled by the rain, saw the faceless woman, someone he would never be able to recognize. The Halloween costumes raced ahead of him as he relaxed again into sleep.

Rain awoke him at the brink of dawn. The dripping rain made a sound like someone pounding in a fence post. Leaving his camp undisturbed, he pulled on his slicker and zipped up his tent. Guided by his flashlight, he began slogging his way through overgrown brambles and wet vines toward the shimmering light of the plant, until he spotted a certain metal scrap heap some two hundred yards away. He didn't go closer. He could see eerie blue flames licking the metal junk, with tongues of fire nearly a foot high. In a gentle rain like this one, mysterious blue flames often erupted, flickering delicately like a gas fire on artificial logs. The flames were lovely yet terrible, another of those elusive phenomena—like a solar storm, a starburst—that you strive to grasp but can't. They made him think about quasars, those distant blue lights in the firmament.

The rain was slacking up. He tramped a different route back to his camp, following dirt-bike paths and small lanes, avoiding the briar patches. The ruins of the munitions factory lay ahead. He reached the clearing where in his dream he had found the dead woman. In the dream the setting was visually more of a museum than a wilderness, but his mind had placed it in this space. It was the exact spot where he had romped with Julia among the slag heaps and ruined buildings. They had played hide-and-go-seek in the bunkers, chasing each other around the towers. That was before she accused him of betrayal.

When he reached his camp, he quickly collapsed his tent, rolled up his wet tarps, and crammed his gear into the carrier. Then he kicked the motor to life.

Women were always after him to get a cell phone. If Reed had really needed to call the police about the dead woman, it would have taken him half an hour to find a telephone. The dream had been so real that as he swerved through the back roads, he seemed to be dreaming still. He imagined going to the police station to report what he had seen. He harbored a slight worrisome thread of paranoia. What about his footprints at the site? And did he touch the window? No. He knew nothing. She was a stranger.

The scene had been so desolate. No one had heard the woman's last utterances; she was like a tree falling in the forest with no one around to hear. His own ears were nearly dead from the decibels at work.

Reed was normally a confident guy, given to bursts of pleasure and celebratory blasts of energy. He wasn't afraid of much, he knew how to protect himself, he could deal with almost anything. Being neighborly, he once rushed into a burning house to save a ninety-seven-year-old invalid. "Slow down," his former wife, Glenda, had often said to him. "You'll burn yourself out." Now in his forties, he still aimed to charge through life with youthful zeal. But for the last couple of years, a deep pain welled inside him occasionally and confused him. He supposed it was simply chemical—if chemistry was ever simple. But as bitter as his moods had sometimes been, he had never entertained a suicidal thought. The dead woman couldn't have represented Glenda. She was too much of a schemer, a master of coupon organization. And the dead woman was definitely not his mother. Although she had high cholesterol and arthritis, her life force had the strength of the Saturn V.

And she wasn't Julia. In no way was she Julia.

He skirted the construction site east of the plant. It seemed forsaken without the row of blue portable toilets, which were removed the day construction was halted. The cranes posed for still lifes.

Reed rode all day, through several counties, following no particular route. The dream wouldn't fade out. If he had really found a dead woman, people at work would approach him, curious and agog. They would want to hear his story over and over. It would be like receiving congratulations for something extraordinary he had done. Over and over he thought of her last hours. The way she lined up the photos on the dashboard—how long did she stare at those pitiful pictures? Did she talk to them? Did she put off her act until she had said everything she wanted to say?

He let the wind fly through his hair as he swirled around the narrow roads, the sun winking through the leaves like a strobe light. He loved the patterns of sun and shade in the woods on either side of him. Wildlife fled from his mighty engine. Reed Futrell did not know where he was going. He rode along a precipice. He was a mechanized Road Runner, rushing along, but watching himself too, knowing that if he leaned too far in one direction or the other he would pancake down a canyon. His fatalism annoyed Julia.

"I've been living with that stuff so long my insides would be neon green if you opened me up," he had told her. "If I've got it, I've got it."

"But if you don't, wouldn't it be a relief to know?"

"Can't you do the blood test for me?"

"No, it's against the rules. The paperwork would screw you up."

"Won't you stick me, honey?" he said, running his hand down her back. "Can't do."

"I'd like to stick you," he said.

Julia could not know his work history. He hadn't told her. He wouldn't.

His mind always meandered while on the road, or lying on the tarp in the woods, or inside the patched pup tent he'd hauled around for years. But now he observed that he was surveying his whole life as though it had a pattern, passions and frailties that connected together.

Reed had grown up reading the *Encyclopedia Americana* and listening to big bands. He always had dogs. He loved shooting targets. He loved women. He loved being married for the first fifteen years, before he and Glenda began fighting. He realized that when they married, they didn't understand each other, that they were too young to understand their own natures, or their differences. Glenda had always been picky, and then she sometimes demeaned him by calling him boorish and overly macho. Their counselor began harping on passive aggression, which Reed understood to mean that Glenda blamed him for her own bad behavior. She said she had to go away so she could grow as a person; Reed said that was ironic for a person always on a diet. The divorce was simple, and she finished raising the kids, Dalton and Dana. Now his children were young adults whom he saw only once in a while. They treated him decently. They seemed normal. He was lucky.

His kids bounced along with the scary optimism of youth. Dalton, with ambitions of becoming an architect, worked at a design company in North Carolina. And Dana, who didn't quite finish college, worked with a producer on Music Row in Nashville. She sent him CDs, sickly pop stuff that you would call gruel if it were food, Reed thought. One of the songs Dana was so proud of had a line, "Carry the gospel to them all," which Reed persisted in hearing as "Carry the gospel to the mall." He often kidded her about that song, even singing it on her answering machine.

In a titty bar somewhere on the edge of a river town, Reed ordered a beer. A jejune band was playing country-pop drivel, and he had to listen to half a dozen songs before the girls came on, swinging their fringed anatomies—fringe flying from their tits, fringe hanging between their legs like a collie dog's skirt.

Reed kept himself fit. Every day he stretched and pumped and jacked up his heart rate. He considered himself sexually attractive and had no trouble getting women. He enjoyed women, made new conquests easily, flirted shamelessly. He'd tuck his finger inside a woman's blouse and playfully tug her bra strap, or he'd reach down and play with the hem of her short skirt. He would do that even before he knew their names, and they would giggle and swoon. Reed had a certain cockiness, and the way he moved seemed to thrill women. He had simple urges—always present, it seemed, throbbing like a hurt toe and keeping him on high alert, like those power lines humming into the plant.

Sitting at a table near the door, he stayed through two beers, but he did not tip these girls. Tonight he did not feel like folding a five-dollar bill and tucking it under a G-string. He left the titty bar and whisked through the night.

As he crossed the bridge over the river, his mood shifted. He gunned his bike, knowing that just a little slip on a pebble could send him flying. He was eager to check his telephone messages.

His street was quiet and the moon was high when he arrived at his old bungalow, a relic from the 1940s with a pyramid roof and a pillared porch. He left his bike and gear in the garage and went to the backyard where Clarence was in an uproar. The dog was overjoyed to see him, nearly knocking Reed over as he entered the gate. Clarence lunged into the house with him, and Reed hugged him and let him slobber on him.

"Yes, that's exactly what I'm saying," Reed said to Clarence. "Woof woof. We're in total agreement."

The answering machine held nothing significant, nothing from Julia. He sat on the dog-abused sofa with Clarence and read the newspapers, to see what had happened in the world during his absence. Same old thing, he learned quickly. More commotion at the plant, troublemakers demanding more investigations. The wider world in chaos. Clarence rested his head on Reed's lap and ate corn chips with him.

"Clarence, it says here the cops found five bags of marijuana at a yard sale." Reed laughed. "Probably antiques."

He was glad to be home. It was comfortable here now with Clarence. Reed read the obituaries, noting the ages. On the page of personal funeral notices, a guy named Jack, a construction worker, had died at age sixty-eight. Reed said, "Come see Jack in the box, visitation two to four p.m. Sunday." Reed laughed. Jack could have waited all his life for such a moment and then missed it.

The telephone rang. "Go, killer," Reed said, opening the back door and shooing Clarence out. He answered the telephone.

"Hey, Reed. This is your Prayer Warrior, calling with your ten o'clock prayer." It was Burl, his best pal since high school. "Hey, man, are you up?"

"Up? Why wouldn't I be up? Do you mean Big Reed or Little Reed?"

"No, man, wake up. Listen. This is urgent."

"What?" Reed settled himself against the wall.

"A while ago I had a heavy, heavy notion, Reed, that you were in need of prayer. I need to pray for you."

"Pray away, Burl." Burl could be a Prayer Warrior or a pagan dancer. It was all the same. Inevitably, he was drunk.

"Are you all right, Reed? Was your little trip good?"

"Yeah. I saw the blue flames again."

"No shit! I wish I'd seen them."

"Next time."

"But you shouldn't hang out at that place."

"I was way over by the river. That's O.K."

Reed told Burl in some detail his dream about the dead woman. "It was so vivid," he said. "I'm still thinking about it."

"Write that down, Reed. You could win the Pulitzer Prize."

"Win what? The tulip surprise?"

Burl chortled. "You need a hearing aid, Reed. I said *Pulitzer Prize!*"

"You don't have to yell! I was making a joke."

"I'm praying for you, Reed."

"O.K."

"That business out at the plant is like the butterfly effect," said Burl. "One thing leading to another."

"Sure." What *wasn't* involved with the fucking butterfly effect?

"Did you get that test yet?"

"Oh, Burl, go on back to Xanadu, and let me get some sleep. I'll see you tomorrow."

"O.K., but I'm praying for you."

"That's nice, Burl. Thank you. I'll pray for you too."

There was no way to pray for Burl, even if Reed were a praying type. Burl was like an asteroid that made periodic close encounters, but never quite came to earth.

Although Reed was tired, he sat down at his computer. As usual, he had a hard time getting past his screen savers, a dazzling variety of galaxies and nebulae, photographs from the Hubble telescope, gliding silently toward him, changing at twenty-second intervals. They shifted before him, unbelievable, colorful close-ups of outer space—galactic clusters, hot clumps of nebulosity, supernovas, spiral galaxies. The universe. When he stared at these pictures, his mind seemed to empty out. He changed the pictures frequently in order to retain that fresh astonishment.

Finally, he checked his e-mail. He wished Julia had e-mail, but she refused to waste her time with it. He found dozens of new answers to a personal ad he had placed on the Internet. Curious, and with a pleasing sexual stirring, he ran through the responses. His ad had been simple: "Strong, good-looking guy looking for smart, sensitive woman with sense of humor and curiosity. Sex not a requirement. Let's just hang." He left his zip code and moniker, "Atomic Man."

He dumped all the messages with distant zip codes. He read the remaining one, from a zip code near his own, someone calling herself Hot Mama.

"Your ad is too vague. You don't reveal anything about yourself. Why should I be interested? Your ad seems intended to reel in all women indiscriminately. Who would confess to being insensitive, without humor or curiosity? Sex? Screw you."

"Goddamn," Reed said aloud. "I can't deal with you tonight, Hot Mama."

He stared at the message until his screen saver came on; the shifting images of the cosmos were hypnotic, and he began to feel sleepy.

Exhausted, he fell into his stale sheets. Sleep wouldn't come. He was too tired to sleep. He rose and dashed off a message to Hot Mama. "I'm sensitive, with a sense of humor, and I'm loaded with curiosity. I don't stick to the everyday. I fool around with the *cosmos*. My favorite poem is 'Kubla Khan.' I have a scar on my wrist that resembles a rat's ass. Why am I telling you all this?"

He sent the message, felt better, then went easily to sleep.

# XII

# Zigzagging

*For a long while, the short stories I wrote zigzagged among longer works of fiction. Stories came sporadically, and that was best, for they offered more surprise and possibility. A story grows not from an idea, or a plot outline, but rather from a buildup of creative energy that seizes an image or a sound. I never know what might burst forth, but it is good to be there to catch it.*

*—BAM*

# With Jazz

FROM *Zigzagging Down a Wild Trail* (2001)

I never paid much attention to current events, all the trouble in the world you hear about. I was too busy raising a family. But my children have all gone now and I've started to think about things that go on. Why would my daughter live with a man and get ready to raise a baby and refuse to marry the guy? Why would my son live in a cabin by the river and not see a soul for months on end? But that's just personal. I'm thinking of the bigger picture, too. It seems a person barely lives long enough to begin to see where his little piece fits in the universal puzzle. I'm not old but I imagine that old people start to figure out how to live just when it's too late.

These thoughts come up at my weekly neighborhood group. It started out as a weight-reducing club, but we kept meeting even after we all got skinny. Now on Fridays after work a bunch of us get together at somebody's house and talk about life, in a sort of talk-show format. Although we laugh a lot, for us it's survival. And it helps me think.

It's so hard to be nice to people. It's something you have to learn. I try to be nice, but it's complicated. You start feeling guilty for your own failures of generosity at just about the same point in life when you start feeling angry, even less willing to give. The two feelings collide—feeling gracious and feeling mean. When you get really old, they say, you go right back to being a child, spiteful and selfish, and you don't give a damn what people think. In between childhood and old age, you have this bubble of consciousness— and conscience. It's enough to drive you crazy.

After our group session last Friday, I went up to Paducah, across the county line, hoping to see this guy I know. He calls himself Jazz, but his real name is Peter. He always hated that name. Kids in school would tease him. "Where's your peter?," "Oh, you don't look like a peter," etc. Some kids from my distant past used the word "goober," the first name I ever heard for the secret male anatomy. I thought they were saying "cooper." That didn't make any sense to me. Then I learned that the correct word was "goober." I learned that in the fourth grade from Donna Lee Washam, the day she led me on an expedition to a black-walnut tree on the far edge of the playground. She came back to the classroom with two black walnuts in her panties and giggled all afternoon as she squirmed in her seat. Across the aisle and a couple of seats up, Jerry Ray Baxter sometimes took his goober out and played with it. He couldn't talk plain, and after that year he stopped coming to school.

Jazz was at the Top Line, where I thought he'd be. He was lounging at the bar, with a draught beer, shooting the breeze. When he saw me he grinned slowly and pulled a new brassiere out of his pocket, dangling it right there between the jug of beet-pickled eggs and the jug of pickled pigs' feet. Ed, the bartender, swung his head like he'd seen it all. "There you go again, Jazz, pulling off women's clothes."

Jazz said, "No, this is my magic trick."

I stuffed the bra in my purse. "Thanks, Jazz. I guess you knew my boobs were falling down."

He came from down in Obion, Tennessee, and grew up duck hunting around Reelfoot Lake. Now he goes to France and brings back suitcases full of French underwear. He sells it to a boutique and occasionally to friends. It's designer stuff and the sizes are different from here. His ex-wife gets it at cost from a supplier in Paris where she works. He goes over there once a year or so to see his kids. Jazz works construction and saves his money, and then he quits and lights out for France. I've got a drawerful of expensive bras he's given me—snap-fronts, plunges, crisscrosses, strapless—all in lace and satin.

"That's a special number," he said, moving close to me. "Scalloped lace and satin stretch. Molded cup, underwire. I'll want to check the fitting later."

I grinned. "We'll see about that, Jazz. Tonight I feel like getting drunk."

"You're gonna be a granny again in a few months, Chrissy. Is that how an old granny's supposed to act?" he teased.

"But I'm happy, damn it! I feel like I'm in love."

"One of these days I'll make you fall in love with me, Chrissy."

I ordered a bourbon. What Jazz needed, I thought, was a woman who felt romantic about him. But he'd never make a claim on a woman he cared about. He'd always step aside and let the woman go fall in love with some clod who jerked her around.

Glancing up at a TV newsbreak—a local update on water pollution—I said, "All the mussels in the lake are dying. It's all those pesticides."

"I heard it was last year's drought," said Jazz. "That's natural."

"Here I am celebrating a new baby coming into the world—for what? To see a dead lake? And air not fit to breathe?"

Jazz touched my shoulder, to steady me. "World's always had trouble. No baby ever set foot in the Garden of Eden."

I laughed. "That's just like you to say that, Jazz."

"You think you know me, don't you?" he said.

"I know you well enough to feel sorry I always treat you so bad."

Ed set my drink before me and I took it eagerly. I said to Jazz, "Why don't you ever get mad at me, tell me off?"

He punched my arm, buddy style. "You should never go away mad at a person, because one of you might get killed on the way home."

The regular crowd was there at the Top Line—good old boys who worked at the plants, guys wandering around loose on a Friday night while their wives took the kids to the mall. A tall man entering the bar caught my eye. He walked like he had money. He had on an iridescent-green shirt, with a subtle paisley design that made my eyes tingle. His pants had cow-boy-style piping on the pocket plackets. Over the shirt he wore a suède vest with fuchsia embroidery and zippered pockets.

"That's Buck Joiner, the radio guy," Jazz said, reading my mind.

Buck Joiner was the D.J. I listened to while I was getting ready for work. His "Morning Mania" show was a roaring streak of pranks and risqué jokes and call-in giveaways. Once, he actually telephoned Colonel Qad-dafi in Libya. He got through to the palace and talked to some official who spoke precise English with a Middle Eastern accent.

As soon as I felt I'd had enough bourbon, I marched over to Buck Join-er's table, wielding my glass.

"I listen to you," I said. "I've got your number on my dial."

He seemed bored. It was like meeting Bob Dylan or some big shot you know won't be friendly.

"I called you up once," I went on recklessly. "You were giving away tickets to the Ray Stevens show. I was trying to be the twenty-fifth caller. But my timing wasn't right."

"Too bad," he said, deadpan. He was with a couple of guys in suits. Blanks.

"I've got to work on my timing." I paused, scrambling for contact. "You should interview my Friday-afternoon talk group."

"What's that?"

"We're a group of ladies. We get together every Friday and talk about life."

"What about life?" Out of the side of his face, he smirked for the benefit of the suits.

"The way things are going. Stuff." My mind went blank. I knew there was more to it than that. Right then, I really wanted him to interview our group. I knew we sparkled with life and intelligence. Rita had her opinions on day care, and Dorothy could rip into the abortion issue, and Phyllis believed that psychiatrists were witch doctors. Me, I could do my Bette Davis imitations.

"Here's my card," I said, whipping one out of my purse. I'd ordered these about a month ago, just for the privilege of saying that.

"It's nice to meet a fan," he said with stretched lips—not a true smile.

"Don't give me that, buddy. If it weren't for your listeners, you wouldn't be sitting here with all that fancy piping scrawled all over you."

I rejoined Jazz, who had been watching out for me. "I'd like to see Oprah nail him to the wall," I said to Jazz.

Of course, I was embarrassed. That was the trouble. I was lost somewhere between being nice and being mean. I shouldn't drink. I don't know why I was so hard on the D.J., but he was a man I had depended on to start my day, and he turned out to be a shit. From now on I'd listen to his show and think, Stuck-up turdface. Yet there I was in a French bra and with an unusual amount of cleavage for this area. I didn't know what I was getting at. Jazz was smiling, touching my hand, ordering me another drink. Jazz wore patience like adhesive tape.

In bits and pieces, I've told this at the Friday talk group: My first husband, Jim Ed, was my high-school boyfriend. We married when we were seniors, and they didn't let me graduate, because I was pregnant. I used to say that

I barely understood how those things worked, but that was a lie. Too often I exaggerate my innocence, as if trying to excuse myself for some of the messes I've gotten myself into. Looking back now, I see that I latched on to Jim Ed because I was afraid there'd never be another opportunity in my life, and he was the best of the pickings around there. That's the way I do everything. I grab anything that looks like a good chance, right then and there. I even tend to overeat, as if I'm afraid I won't ever get another good meal. "That's the farm girl in you," my second husband, George, always said. He was an analytical person and had a theory about everything. When he talked about the Depression mentality of our parents' generation he made it sound physically disgusting. He had been to college. I never did go back and get my high-school diploma, but that's something I'm thinking about doing now. George couldn't just enjoy something for what it was. We'd grill steaks and he'd come up with some reason why we were grilling steaks. He said it went back to caveman behavior. He said we were acting out an ancient scene. He made me feel trapped in history, as though we hadn't advanced since cavemen. I don't guess people have changed that much, though, really. I bet back in caveman times there was some know-it-all who made his woman feel dumb.

After a while, I didn't pay any attention to George, but then my little daughter died. She had meningitis, and it was fairly sudden and horrible. I was still in shock a month later, when George started nagging at me about proper grief displays and the stages of grief. I blew up. I told him to walk. What we really should have done was share the grief. I'm sure the most basic textbook would say that. But instead he's lecturing me on my grief. You can't live with somebody who lectures you on your grief. I'll have my grief in peace, I told him. Kathy wasn't his daughter. He couldn't possibly know how I felt. That was so long ago he doesn't seem real to me. He still lives around here. I've heard that he married again and that he raises rabbits and lives out in the country, out near Bardwell—none of which I would have ever imagined. But, you know, as small as this place is, I've never laid eyes on him again. Maybe he's changed so much I just don't recognize him when I see him.

"How did you just happen to have that bra in your pocket, Jazz?" I wanted to know, but he only grinned. It was like carrying around condoms in case of emergency, I thought. The bra was just my size. I'd put it on in the rest-room. The one I had worn was stretching out, and I left it in the trash can. Let people wonder.

At first, I thought Kathy just had the flu. She had a fever and she said her head was splitting—a remark so calm that she might have said her hands were dirty in the same tone. It was summer, a strange time for flu, so I hurried all the kids on out to their grandmother's that Sunday, like always, thinking the country air would make Kathy feel better. Don and Phil kept aggravating her because she didn't want to play in Mama's attic or go out to the barn. She lay around under one of Mama's quilts, and I thought later, with a hideous realization, that she somehow knew she was going to die. You never know what a child is thinking, or how scared they might be, or how they've blown something up in their imagination. She was twelve, and she'd just started her period a couple of months before. I thought her sickness might be related to that. The doctor just laughed at me when I brought that up. Can you imagine the nerve? It's only now that I've gotten mad about that. But I hear that that doctor has had a stroke and is in a nursing home. What good do bad feelings do when so much time has passed? That's what Jazz says.

George blamed me for taking her out to Mama's that day. He was gone to an engineering convention in Nashville; he was a chemical engineer at Car-bide then. He said there was no reason a child shouldn't recover from menin-gitis. He wagged a book in my face, but I refused to read what he had found on the disease. I thought it would kill me to know her death was my fault. I guess George wasn't such a bad guy. He just had his ways. I think we all do and none of us knows how to be sensitive enough, it seems. He probably just didn't know how to deal with the situation. It occurred to me recently that maybe he felt guilty for being away at the time, just as I felt guilty for not noticing how quiet and withdrawn she was, as though she was figuring it all out for herself. Kathy was in 4-H, and that year she was working on a Holly Hobbie display for the fair—the little girl hiding her face in the calico bon-net. Kathy sewed the clothes herself, and she was making a little stuffed dog and decorating a flower basket for the scene. I still have that unfinished Holly Hobbie scene—in the closet in a stereo box. I should probably get rid of it, because if Kathy had lived she would have grown out of that phase, but all I have is those little scraps of the way Kathy was, the only reality she ever had.

Don and Phil grew up and left as soon as they got cars. Can you believe anybody would name their sons after the Everly Brothers? I reckon I'd still do something that silly. But I never told them we named them for the Everly Brothers. Jim Ed, the father of all my children, loved the Everly Brothers, and he used to play them in his truck, back when eight-track tape decks were a new thing. Jim Ed was loose about a lot of things, and he never criticized me the way George did. I don't know if he blamed me about Kathy. I have a feeling that if we'd stuck it out we could have learned to love each other better. But he was restless, and he couldn't hang around when we needed him most. He moved over to Cairo and worked on the riverboats— still does. I guess he has some kind of life. The boys see him. Don's wife ran off with one of the riverboat guys and Don lives in a cabin over there. I don't see him very much. He brought me a giant catfish, a mud cat, on Mother's Day. Catfish that big aren't really good to eat, though. He sets trotlines and just lives in the wilderness. I doubt if he'll ever marry again. Phil is the only one of my children who turned out normal. Now, what is there to say about that? A wife with a tortilla face and bad taste in clothes, spoiled kids, living room decorated with brass geese and fish. I go there and my skin breaks out. There's no pleasing me, I guess.

Last week, Laura—my other daughter, the baby—wrote me that she was pregnant. She's barely divorced from this museum director she met at school—he restored old pieces of pottery, glued them together. He made a good living but she wasn't satisfied. Now she's going to be tied down with a baby and a man, this Nick, who does seasonal work of some sort. They're living in his home town, a little place in Arizona, in the desert. I can't imagine what would grow there.

Laura, on the telephone this past Sunday, said, "I don't want to get married again. I don't trust it anymore. And I want to be free of all that bureaucratic crap. I trust Nick more than I trust the government."

"You need the legal protection," I said. "What if something happened to him? What if he ran off and left you? I can tell you exactly how that works."

"I'd have to murder Nick to get him out of my life! Honestly, he's being so devoted it's unbelievable."

"I guess that's why I don't believe it."

"Come on, Mom. Just think, you're going to be a grandma again! Aren't you going to come out when the baby's born? Isn't that what mothers do?"

Laura was five when Kathy died. We didn't take her to the funeral. We told her Kathy had gone off to live with Holly Hobbie in New York. If I could undo that lie, I would. It was worse when she found out the truth, because she was old enough then to understand and the shock hurt her more. I thought my heart would break when I saw Jim Ed at the funeral. I saw him alone only once, for a few minutes in the corridor before the service started, but we couldn't speak what we felt. Jim Ed was crying, and I wanted to cling to him, but we could see George in the other room, standing beside a floral display—a stranger.

Jazz said, "Ever notice how at night it's scary because you feel like your secrets are all exposed, but you trick yourself into thinking they're safe in the dark? Smokey bars, candlelight—that's what all that atmosphere shit is about."

"That's what I always say," I said, a little sarcastically. Sometimes Jazz seemed to be fishing around for something to say and then just making something up to sound deep.

We were driving to see my son Don out at his cabin by the river. It was Jazz's idea, a crazy notion that seized him. He said he felt like driving. He said I needed some air. He didn't let me finish my last drink.

I met Jazz a year ago, in traffic court. We'd both been in minor fender benders on the same road on the same day, at different times. We'd both failed to yield. I remember Jazz saying to me, "I hope that's not a reflection on my character. Normally, I'm a very yielding guy." That day Jazz had on a plaid flannel shirt and boot-flared jeans and a cowboy hat—the usual garb for a man around here. But it was his boots I loved. Pointy-toed, deep-maroon, with insets of Elvis's photograph just above the ankles. He'd found the boots in France. That night we went out for barbecue and he gave me some peach-blush panties with a black lace overlay. We had been friends since then, but we never seemed to get serious. I thought he had a big block of fear inside him.

The cab of his truck was stuffy, that peculiar oil-and-dust smell of every man's truck I've ever been in. I lowered the window and felt the mellow river breeze. Jazz chattered nonstop until we got deep into the country. Then he seemed to hush, as though we were entering a grand old church.

We were traveling on a state road, its winding curves settled comfortably through the bottomland, with its swampy and piney smells. There were no houses, no lights. Now and then we passed an area where kudzu made the telephone poles and bushes look as though they were a giant's furniture covered up with protective sheets. At a stop sign I told Jazz to go straight instead of following the main road. Soon there was a turnoff, unmarked except for an old sign for a church that I knew had burned down in the fifties. We saw an abandoned pickup straddling the ditch. When the road turned to gravel, I counted the turnoffs, looking for the fourth one. Jazz shifted gears and we chugged up a little hill.

"Reckon why he lives way off out here?" Jazz said as he braked and shut off the engine. There were no lights at the cabin, and Don's motorbike was gone. Jazz went over into the bushes for a minute. It was a half-moon night, the kind of night that made you see things in the silhouettes. I thought I saw Don standing by the side of the cabin, peering around the corner, watching us.

Jazz reached through the truck's open window and honked the horn.

I heard an owl answer the horn. When I was little I thought owls were messengers from the preachers in charge of Judgment Day. "Who will be the ones?" I remember our preacher saying. "Who?" Even then I pictured Judgment Day as an orchestrated extravaganza, like a telethon or a musical salute. I never took religion seriously. I'm glad I didn't force my children into its frightful clutches. But maybe that was the trouble, after all.

We stood on the sagging porch, loaded with fishnets and crates of empties—Coke and beer bottles. The lights from the pickup reflected Jazz and me against the cabin windows. I tried the door, and it opened into the kitchen.

"Don?" I called.

I found the kitchen light, just a bulb and string. The cord was new. It still had that starched feel, and the little metal bell on the end knot was shiny and sharp. It made me think of our old bathroom light when Jim Ed and I first married. It was the first thing I'd touch in the morning when I'd get up and rush to the bathroom to throw up.

The table was set for one, with the plate turned face over and the glass upside down. Another glass contained an assortment of silverware. A little tray held grape jelly and sugar and instant coffee and an upside-down mug.

The cabin was just one room, and the daybed was neatly made, spread with one of my old quilts. I sat down on the bed. I felt strange, as though all my life I had been zigzagging down a wild trail to this particular place. I stared at the familiar pattern of the quilt, the scraps of the girls' dresses and the boys' shirts. Kathy had pieced some of the squares. If I looked hard, I could probably pick out some of her childish stitches.

"This is weird," said Jazz. He was studying some animal bones spread out on a long table fashioned from a door. "What do you reckon he's aiming to do with these?"

"He always liked biology," I said, rising from the bed. I smoothed and straightened the quilt, thinking about Goldilocks trespassing at the three bears' house.

The table was littered: bones, small tools, artist's brushes and pens, a coffee cup with a drowned cigarette stub, more butts nesting in an upturned turtle shell, some bright foil paper, an oily rag. Jazz flipped through a tablet of drawings of fangs and fishbones.

"He must be taking a summer course at the community college," I said, surprised. "He talked about that back in the spring, but I didn't believe it."

"Look at these," Jazz said. "They're good. How can anybody do that?" he said in amazement.

We studied the drawings. In the careful, exact lines I saw faint glimpses of my young child, and his splashy crayon pictures of monsters taped to the kitchen wall. Seeing his efforts suddenly mature was like running into a person I recognized but couldn't place. Most of the pictures were close-ups of bones, but some were sketches of fish and birds. I liked those better. They had life to them. Eagerly, I raced through two dozen versions of a catfish. The fish was long and slim, like a torpedo. Its whiskers curved menacingly, and its body was accurately mottled. It even looked slippery. I stared at the catfish, almost as if I expected it to speak.

I jerked a blank sheet of paper from the tablet of drawings and worked on a note:

Dear Don,

It's 10:30 P.M. Friday and I came out here with a friend to see if you were home. We just dropped by to say hello. Please let me know how you are. Nothing's wrong. I've got some good news. And I'd love to see you.

Love,
Mom

"It doesn't sound demanding, does it?" I asked as Jazz read it.

"No, not at all."

"It almost sounds like one of those messages on an answering machine—stilted and phony."

Jazz held me as if he thought I might cry. I wasn't crying. He held my shoulders till he was sure I'd got the tears back in and then we left. I couldn't say why I wasn't crying. But nothing bad had happened. There wasn't anything tragic going on. My daughter was having a baby—that was the good news. My son had drawn some fishbones—drawings that were as fine as lace.

"Me and my bright ideas," Jazz said apologetically.

"It's O.K., Jazz. I'll track Don down some other time." As we pulled out, Jazz said, "The wilderness makes me want to go out in it. I've got an idea. Tomorrow let's go for a long hike on one of those trails up in Shawnee National Forest. We can take backpacks and everything. Let's explore caves! Let's look for bears and stuff!"

I laughed. "You could be Daniel Boone and I could be Rebecca."

"I don't think Rebecca went for hikes. You'll have to be some Indian maiden Daniel picked up."

"Did Daniel Boone really do that sort of thing?" I said, pretending to be scandalized.

"He was a true explorer, wasn't he?" Jazz said, hitting the brights just as a deer seemed to drift across the road.

Jazz thought he was trying to cheer me up, but I was already so full of joy I couldn't even manage to tell him. I let him go on. He was sexiest when he worked on cheering me up.

It was late, and I wound up at Jazz's place, a sprawling apartment with a speaker system wired into every room. His dog, Butch, met us at the door. While Jazz took Butch out for a midnight stroll, I snooped around. I found a beer in the refrigerator. I had trouble with the top and beer spewed all over Jazz's dinette. When he returned, I started teasing him about all the women's underwear he owned.

"Put some of it on," I urged.

"Are you nuts?"

"Just put it on, for me. I won't tell. Just for fun."

I kept teasing him, and he gave in. We couldn't find any garments that would fit. We hooked two bras together and rigged up a halter. With his lime-green bikini briefs—his own—he looked great, like a guy in a sex magazine. It's surprising what men really wear underneath. I searched for some music to play on Jazz's fancy sound system. I looked for the Everly Brothers but couldn't find them, so I put on a George Winston CD. To be nice, I never said a word about Jazz's taste in music. Exhilarated, I sailed from room to room, following the sound, imagining it was "Let It Be Me" instead. I suddenly felt an overwhelming longing to see Jim Ed again. I wanted to tell him about Don going to school, drawing pictures, making contact with the world again. I wanted to see the traces of Don's face in his. I wanted the two of us to go out to Arizona and see Laura and the baby when it came. We could make a family photo—Jim Ed and me and Laura, with the baby. The baby's father didn't enter into the vision.

It occurred to me that it takes so long to know another person. No wonder you can run through several, like trying on clothes that don't fit. There are so many to choose from, after all, but when I married Jim Ed it was like an impulse buy, buying the first thing you see. And yet I've learned to trust my intuition on that. Jim Ed was the right one all along, I thought recklessly. And I wasn't ever nice to Jim Ed. I was too young then to put myself in another person's place. Call it ignorance of the imagination. Back then I had looked down on him for being country, for eating with his arms anchored on the table and for wiping his mouth with the back of his hand. I'd get mad at him for just being himself at times when I thought he should act civilized. Now I've learned you can't change men, and sometimes those airs I'd looked for turn out to be so phony. Guys like Jim Ed always seemed to just be themselves, regardless of the situation. That's why I still loved him, I decided, as I realized I was staring at Jazz's reflection in the mirror—the lime green against the shimmering gold of his skin and the blips of the track lighting above.

Jazz followed me into the bedroom, where we worked at getting rid of our French togs. I was aware that Jazz was talking, aware that he was aware that I might not be listening closely. It was like hearing a story at my little neighborhood talk show. He was saying, "In France, there's this street, rue du Bac. They call streets *rues*. The last time I left Monique and the two kids, it was on that street, a crowded shopping street. The people over there are all pretty small compared to us, and they have this blue-black hair and deep dark eyes and real light skin, like a hen's egg. I waved good-bye and the three of them just blended right into that crowd and disappeared. That's where they belong, and so I'm here. I guess you might say I just couldn't *parlez-vous*."

"Take me to France, Jazz. We could have a great time."

"Sure, babe. In the morning." Jazz turned toward me and smoothed the cover over my shoulders.

"I love you," Jazz said.

When I woke up at daylight, Jazz was still holding me, curled around me like a mother protecting her baby. The music was still playing, on infinite repeat.

# Charger

FROM *Zigzagging Down a Wild Trail* (2001)

As he drove to the shopping center, Charger rehearsed how he was going to persuade his girlfriend, Tiffany Marie Sanderson, to get him some of her aunt Paula's Prozac. He just wanted to try it, to see if it was right for him. Tiffany hadn't taken him seriously when he had mentioned it before. "Don't you like to try new things?" he asked her. He would try anything, except unconventional food. But she seemed more interested in redecorating her room than in revamping her mind.

He cruised past the fast-food strip, veered into the left-turn lane, and stopped at the light. He stared at the red arrow like a cat waiting to pounce. He made the turn and scooted into a good spot in the shopping-center parking lot. At the drink machines in front of the home-fashions store where Tiffany worked after school, he reached into his work pants for a couple of quarters. He needed to wash himself out. He felt contaminated from the chemicals at work. He fed the quarters into a machine, randomly selecting the drink he would have chosen anyway—the Classic. He wondered if there was any freedom of choice about anything.

Tiffany wanted to get married in June, right after her graduation. He had not proposed, exactly, but the idea had grown. He was uneasy about it. His mother said he was too young to marry—nineteen, a baby. She pointed out that he could barely make his truck payments and said Tiffany would expect new furniture and a washer and dryer. And Charger knew that Tiffany's fat-assed father disapproved of him. He said Charger was the type of person who would fall through the cracks when he found out he couldn't rely on his goofy charm to keep him out of trouble. Tiffany's father called it "riding on your face." Charger was inclined to take that as a compliment. He believed you had to use your natural skills to straddle the cracks of life if you were going to get anywhere at all. Apparently he gave the impression that he wasn't ready for anything—like a person half-dressed who suddenly finds himself crossing the street. Yet he was *not* a fuck-up, he insisted to himself.

Tiffany appeared in front of the store, a bright smile spreading across her face. She wore tight little layers of slinky black. She had her hair wadded up high on her head like a squirrel's nest, with spangles hanging all over it. She had on streaks of pink makeup and heavy black eyebrows applied like pressure-sensitive stickers. She was gorgeous.

"Hi, babe," she said, squinching her lips in an air kiss.

"Hi, beautiful," Charger said. "Want something to drink?" Then she raised her hand and he saw the bandage on her thumb. "Hey, what happened?" he asked, touching her hand.

"I mashed my thumb in the drill press in shop."

"Holy shit! You drilled a hole in your thumb?"

"No. It's just a bruise. It's not as bad as it looks."

"How did it happen?" He held her hand, but she pulled it away from him.

"I was holding a piece of wood for Tammy Watkins? And we were yakking away, and I had my thumb in too far, and she brought the drill press right down on my thumb. But not the drill, just the press part."

"I bet that *hurt*. Does it still hurt?"

"It's O.K. I'm just lucky I didn't lose my dumb thumb."

As they walked down the sidewalk, she repeated the details of her accident. He gulped some Coke. His stomach burned. He could hardly bear to listen as he imagined the drill press crunching her thumb. He whistled in that ridiculous way one does on learning something astounding. Then he whistled again, just to hear the sound. It blotted out the image of the drill going through her thumb.

"I might lose my thumbnail, but it'll grow in again," Tiffany said.

"I wish I could kiss it and make it all better," he said. His throat ached, and he itched.

"No problem," she said. "Didn't you ever mash a finger with a hammer?"

"Yeah. One time when I was cracking hickory nuts."

A young couple carrying a baby in a plastic cradle emerged from the pizza place. The woman was mumbling something about rights. The man said, "I don't give a damn what you do. *Go* to Paducah for all I care."

Charger guided Tiffany by the elbow through the traffic into the parking lot. She said, "I asked Aunt Paula about her pills, and she said I didn't need one." Tiffany swung her bandaged hand awkwardly in his direction, as if she were practicing a karate move. She laughed. "And I can't open her pill bottle and sneak one out with this thing on my thumb."

"It looks like a little Kotex," he said.

She giggled. "Not exactly. How would you know?"

"Did you tell Paula the pill was for me?"

"No." Her voice shifted into exasperation. "If you want one, go ask her yourself."

"Man, I gotta get me one of those pills." He struck a theatrical pose, flinging the back of his hand against his forehead. "I'm so depressed, I'm liable to just set down right here in the parking lot and melt into that spot of gop over there. I get depressed easy." He snapped his fingers. "I go down just like that."

They reached his truck, and he slammed his hands on the hot hood. Then he realized that Tiffany was holding up her thumb like a hitchhiker, waiting for him to open the door for her. She said, "Charger, you're not depressed. I don't believe that. It's just something you've heard on TV."

"When do I hear TV? I don't even watch it." They were talking across the hood.

"*I* don't get depressed," said Tiffany. Her hair seemed to lift like wings, along with her spirit. "I always say, if I've got my lipstick on, nothing else matters."

"I know, Miss Sunshine."

"Why would you get depressed anyway? You've got a decent job at the bomb plant. You've got a truck with floating blue lights. You've got a fiancée—me. You've got nothing to complain about."

Charger didn't answer. Stepping around to her side, he opened her door and boosted her in. The fun of having a high-rider was helping girls in, cupping their rear pears in his eager paws. Yet he had not tried out this automotive technique on many girls, because he started going with Tiffany soon after he bought the truck. She always squealed with pleasure when he heaved her in. Charger had fallen for Tiffany when she stole the YARD OF THE MONTH sign from someone's yard and ran naked with it down the street at midnight. He had dared her to do it, while he waited in his truck at the end of the street. It was a street where big dudes lived, people who spent piles of money on yard decorators and had swimming pools behind fences. Now he loved her, probably, and he wanted to have sex with her every day, but he had trouble telling her his deepest thoughts. He didn't want her to laugh at him. He wasn't sure he *was* depressed, but he was curious about Prozac. It was all the rage. He had heard it was supposed to rewire the brain. That idea intrigued him. He liked the sound of it too—Prozac, like some professional athlete named Zack. "Hi, I'm Zack. And I'm a pro. I'm a pro at everything I do. Just call me Pro Zack."

Tiffany had told him that her aunt Paula took Prozac because she was worried about her eyelids bagging. Her insurance wouldn't cover a facelift or an eye tuck, but it would pay for anti-depressants if she was depressed about her face—or about her health coverage. Prozac seemed to give her a charge of self-esteem, so that she could live with her baggy eyes. "I feel good about myself," Paula was fond of announcing now.

That was what Charger was interested in, a shift of attitude. Bad moods scared him. He didn't know where they came from. Sometimes he just spit at the world and roared around like a demon in his truck, full of meanness. He had actually kicked at his father's dog, and the other day he deliberately dropped his mother's Christmas cactus, still wrapped in its florist's foil. His father had disappeared in December, and now it was May. Months passed before they heard from him. His mother pretended indifference. She didn't even call the police or report him missing. "He'll come back with his tail between his legs," she said. Charger believed that she knew where his father was and just didn't want him to know.

Charger answered the telephone when his father finally called, in April, from Texas. He had left the day before Christmas and just kept driving; once he got out of Kentucky, he couldn't turn back, he said. Might as well see what there is to see, he said. He hadn't had a chance to call, and he knew Charger's mother wouldn't worry about him.

"Are you coming back?" Charger wanted to know.

"Depends on what the future holds," his father said vaguely.

"What do you mean by that?" Charger said, thinking that his father wouldn't be happy even if he did come back. He realized how sad-faced and thin his dad had been. He was probably having a better time where he was, out looking at skies. "I never knew about skies before," his dad had said in a mysteriously melancholy voice. He started singing a song, as if the telephone were a microphone and he had grabbed a stage opportunity. "Ole buttermilk sky, can't you see my little donkey and me, we're as happy as a Christmas tree." In a hundred years, Charger would not have imagined his dad bursting into song.

Charger sometimes looked at his life as if he were a spy peering through a telescope. The next afternoon he could see himself and Tiffany as though he were watching from the other side of town. He saw a carefree young couple frolicking at Wal-Mart together. At least, that was how he tried to picture himself with Tiffany—as beautiful people in a commercial, scooting around having fun. They played hide-and-go-seek in the maze of tall aisles, piled to the ceiling with goods. He whistled "Buttermilk Sky," and she followed the sound from aisle to aisle. She caught him in lingerie, where the canyons of housewares gave way to prairies of delicate flowers.

"I win!" she cried, taunting him with a pair of pink panties on a hanger.

A country-western star was at the store that day, signing pictures to promote his new album. He was a young heartthrob named Andy or Randy something. He was sitting at a table next to a shopping cart full of his CDs. Charger didn't trust the guy. His shirt was too fancy.

"Bet he didn't buy them duds here," Charger said to Tiffany.

"He doesn't have to," Tiffany said, her breath trailing like gauze. "Oh, I've *got* to get his autograph."

Charger stood waiting in line with Tiffany, feeling ridiculous. Tiffany had on snake pants. Her legs looked like two sensational boa constrictors. They were attracting comments. A woman and a little girl were standing in line behind Charger and Tiffany. The woman—overdressed in beads and floral fabric—was eyeing Tiffany.

"She's going on his tour," Charger told the woman impulsively. "She's a singer."

"Oh," the woman gasped. "Do you know him?"

"Yes, as a matter of fact," Charger told the woman. He felt his orneriness kicking in. He couldn't help himself when opportunities like this arose. "We're in his entourage. What do you need to know about country's newest sensation, Randy what's-his-name?"

"Andy," Tiffany said, elbowing him.

The woman said, "I'm a lounge pianist and former gospel artist? I've been trying for months to get my tapes to Andy." She had the tapes in her hand. "I know he'd love them. Our hearts are on the same wavelength. His songs tell my life story." She jerked her head to the left. "Get back here, Reba," she yelled to the little girl, who had spun off down the cosmetics aisle. She reeled the child in and continued at some length. She said her life was a Barbara Mandrell kind of story, involving a car wreck and a comeback. The woman wore a country-music hairdo—a mountain of frizz and fluff that looked to Charger as though it had sprung out of a jack-in-the-box.

A number of young girls in the line—pre-babe material, Charger thought—had long frizzed and fluffed hair too.

"Your story is an inspiration," Charger said to the woman.

Tiffany whispered to Charger, "You're embarrassing me."

The gospel-lounge singer heard and frowned at Tiffany. Charger imagined the woman sticking out her tongue.

Charger said, "If you give me your name and number, I'll have you on television inside a month."

"Here's my card," the woman said. "You'll put in a word to him about my tapes, won't you?" She took her child's hand. "Come on, Reba. Stay in this line or I'm going to skin your butt."

The little girl clutched one of Andy's CDs and a box of hamster food.

"I like hamsters. I had hamster for supper last night," Charger said, making a face at the child.

Tiffany made the same face at Charger. "Why do you do things like that?" she said. "It irks me."

"Irk? I *irk*? Well, pardon me all over the place." He flapped his arms like a bird. "*Irk. Irk.*" Teasingly, he nudged Tiffany with his knee, and then he pinched her on the rear end. "I'm a hawk. *Irk.*"

"Cool."

Afterward, as they drove out of the crowded parking lot, Tiffany was engrossed in her autographed picture of the cowboy warbler. As she traced her finger along the signature, her bandaged thumb seemed to erase his face. She had grown quiet when it was her turn to meet the star. She had said to him, "All I can say is, 'Wow.'"

"He probably never heard anything so stupid," she said now, as Charger turned onto the main drag. "I was so excited I couldn't think of what to say!"

"I'm sure what you said is exactly what he wanted to hear," Charger said. "He eats it up. Isn't he from Atlanta? He probably thinks we're just dumb hicks here."

Tiffany said excitedly, "Oh, let's go to Atlanta this weekend."

"And blow my paycheck?"

"We can manage."

Charger braked at the red light. He stared at Tiffany as if he had just picked up a hitchhiker. Sometimes he felt he didn't know her at all. Her snake legs squirmed—impatient to shed their skins, he thought.

On Friday after work Charger decided to go straight to the source. He thought that Tiffany's aunt might give him some of her Prozac if he caught her in the right mood. Paula was O.K. She covered for them when Tiffany spent the night with him. Paula said that her sister, Tiffany's mother, would die if she knew about the little overnight trips in Charger's truck.

Paula hadn't expected him, but she seemed pleased to see him at the door. She brought him through the living room into the kitchen. "Don't look at this garbage," she said.

She had school projects—flags and Uncle Sam dolls and Paul Revere hats—scattered around. She taught fourth grade.

Charger noticed that her eyelids drooped down onto her eyelashes, but her face had few wrinkles. He wondered how long Tiffany's eyelids would hold up. She resembled her aunt—the same smidgen nose and whirlpool curls.

Paula handed him a glass of ice and a two-liter Coke. He poured, and the Coke foamed over onto the kitchen counter. He sat numbly on a stool, embarrassed. While she wiped up the spill, she said, "This morning I dressed in the dark and put on one blue sock and one green sock?" She laughed. "At school I got a citation for a fashion violation. At school we get citations for bad hair, static cling, leopard-skin underwear beneath white pants, color clash, sock displacement. The fashion police sentenced me to work in the beehive section of the fashion salon."

"You've still got on a blue sock and a green sock," Charger said. He wondered how her fourth-graders dealt with her high-pitched babbling.

"Do you want a mayonnaise sandwich?" she asked.

"No. Do you eat kid food, being's you're a teacher?"

"I have to have at least a teaspoon of Miracle Whip a day or I'll blow my brains out," she said. "Bill won't eat anything at lunch but crackers. I get mad at him because he won't eat the food I leave for him. He won't eat fruits and vegetables. I said, 'There are some grapes on the counter.' He said, 'Are they washed?' I said no. He said, 'I don't have to wash crackers.' But he's sure slim and trim on the cracker diet. I'll give him that."

"Give that man a Twinkie!" Charger said, jumping off the stool in what he thought was a dramatic gesture. "You don't have to wash Twinkies."

"I don't know if he ought to eat Twinkies."

"Well, if that don't work, give him a Ding Dong." He grinned.

"He's already got a ding-dong."

"Then give him a Little Debbie."

"But I don't want him to have a little Debbie."

Charger laughed. "Little Debbies are my favorite."

"Charger, you're such a great kidder." She laughed with him, shaking her head. "And you're such a baby."

When Charger finally got around to mentioning Paula's Prozac, she didn't seem surprised that he wanted to try the drug.

"I need to reprogram my head," he said.

"Why not go to church? Or take piano lessons?"

"Why don't *you?*"

Paula opened a cabinet above the toaster and chose a vial of pills. "You don't really need these pills, Charger. You just need to believe in yourself more."

"My *self* doesn't have that much to do with it."

"Maybe you just haven't found it yet. You've got a deep soul, Charger. Tiffany doesn't see it yet, but she will, in time."

She shook the pill bottle in his face like a baby rattle. She said, "One of the side effects of these little numbers is that they can make you nonorgasmic. But I've tested that thoroughly, and it's not true for me. I don't have that side effect!" She laughed loudly. "I don't think you want one of these, Charger."

"It might be just what I need to relax my sex machine. It's running away with me." He winked.

She turned serious. She put the pills back in the cabinet and said, "Charger, I believe you're scared. You don't act like you're ready to settle down and have a family. Have you given any thought to what you would do if you and Tiffany had a baby?"

"She's not pregnant, is she?" he asked, alarmed.

"Not that I know of. But it's something you have to be ready for."

He *had* thought about it. He wasn't ready for it. The idea was all wrong. Some guys he knew were working hard to feed their kids. They were not much older than he was, but they seemed years older. He couldn't imagine being a father yet. He knew he didn't have much chance of rising above the loading dock, at minimum wage. How could he feed a kid? He tried to shake off the thought. That was the distant future.

Charger and Tiffany didn't get away until after eight o'clock that night, after he had changed his oil and worked on his carburetor. They were going to Nashville instead of Atlanta. Tiffany's mother was having a family dinner on Sunday for Tiffany's cousin's birthday, and Tiffany had decided that Atlanta was too far away for them to get back in time. She said she wanted to go to a store in Nashville called Dangerous Threads.

On the drive Charger drank a can of beer. He glanced at Tiffany. She had on her snake pants again. They sort of gave him the creeps. He slid his hand down her thigh. The pants had a slinky, snaky feel that startled him every time he touched them. He moved his hand in little circles over her inner thigh. His hand moved like a computer mouse, tracing the snaky terrain beneath it.

"Do you think I've been acting funny?" Charger asked.

"No. Why?" She was picking at the closure on her bandage. It made a scratchy sound, like a mouse in a wall.

"You don't think I'm moody, or liable to jump up and say the wrong thing or throw a flowerpot on the floor? You're not scared to cross the state line with me? You don't think I'm weird?"

"No, I think you're just super-sexy. And you're fun-loving. I rate that real high." Twisting in her seat to reach him, she touched his cheek with her bandaged thumb. It was splinted for protection.

"What do you want to do in Nashville besides shop?" he asked.

"Go to that new mall, and maybe get into a good show at Opryland, and stay in a big hotel."

With her quick enthusiasm, she was like a child in Santa's lap. "Motel Six is more like it," he said.

"Well, that's all right. I just think we ought to have our fling before we get married and can't run around so much."

Charger was passing a long-haul truck. He returned to the right-hand lane. The truck was far behind, like an image in slow motion. "Let's go to Texas instead of Nashville," he said.

"It's too far. And we're headed in the wrong direction."

"We could drive straight through."

She didn't answer. In a moment she said, "If you're thinking about your daddy, you know you can't find him just by driving to Texas for the weekend."

"I know, but I wish I could." He glanced at the rearview for cops and chugged some beer. "When Daddy called from Texas this spring, I was about two french fries short of happy," he said. "And then the feeling just wound down, and I thought I could sort of see why he did what he did, and I could see me doing it too." He shuddered. "It gives me the bummers."

He was afraid Tiffany wasn't listening. She was pulling at a strand of her hair, twirling it around her finger. But then she said, "I was just thinking about your dad. I was wondering what he was doing out there. And why your mother didn't make more of a fuss about him going off."

"She was probably glad he was gone," Charger said. He belched loudly. "*Irk!*" he said, to be funny. He made her laugh.

They stopped for gas, then kept driving and driving. They sped past the Cracker Barrel. Usually they stopped there and ate about eight pounds of rosin-roasted potatoes and big slabs of ham. He so often overdid things, he thought sorrowfully. He had gotten his nickname years earlier from his childhood habit of charging into things without thinking. Recently he had dared himself to drive up the bank side of the clay pit; he was trying out his new used truck. The road wound around the clay pit, ascending steeply on one side. The dirt was loose. He wasn't scared. He thought, I can do this. He steered very carefully and inched up the winding trail.

"I can do this," he said now, in a barely audible voice.

Tiffany patted his arm affectionately. She said, "Charger, I know you don't know what you want to do with your life. And you don't make a whole lot. But we have plenty of time. I know we're going to be real happy."

She spoke as though she had worked that up in her mind for the past two hours. Then she switched gears again, back to her usual self. She said, "See the moon? I am just thrilled out of my mind to see that moon. I love seeing the moon. I love going to church. I love work. I love driving at night. I love getting sleepy and snuggling up to you."

The moon was rising, a pale disk like a contact lens. The bright lights in the other lane obscured the path in front of him. He hit his brights and could see again. The stretch of highway just ahead looked clean and clear. Tiffany made everything seem so simple—like his father bursting into song about sky-watching. Was love that easy?

He ran his hand along her leg, up the inseam. Then he turned on the radio. A song ended, followed by some unidentifiable yapping. He hit the SEEK button. Tiffany screeched. "That's Andy! Turn it up. I just love that voice of his."

"Personally, I think he's full of himself," Charger said.

"Oh, you just wish *you* could carry a tune." With her left hand she slapped her leg along with the song.

The singer sounded like a cranky old crow, Charger thought. It was an odd voice for such a young guy. Charger had no special talents. He had never had any encouragement from anybody in his life other than Tiffany. She wanted him to take a computer course, because everything was computers now. But he knew he couldn't sit still that long. That was the trouble with high school. He liked his present job at the bomb plant O.K., because he got to joke around with a bunch of people he enjoyed. He called it "the bomb plant" because it produced fertilizer. He felt lucky to have such an attractive girlfriend. But he was aware that his mother, too, had been cute when she was young. Now she was overweight and had a hacking cough. His father had worked at the tire plant for twenty-five years, and his mother was a nurse's aide at the hospital. She emptied bedpans. They lived in a tacky, cramped house that she took little pride in. They did not go on vacations. His father watched television every evening. He used to watch a regular lineup. But when they got cable and a remote, he couldn't stick to his old favorites. He cruised the airwaves, lighting here and there. Five afternoons a week Charger's mother cooked supper for the family, left it on the table, and went off to work. She grew heavy and tired from being on her feet long hours. She was forty-four years old. Her eyelids drooped, but she didn't even seem to know it. Maybe when Tiffany was that age, she would accept baggy eyes as gracefully as she regarded her injured thumb. He shuddered.

Driving down the interstate, Charger contemplated his life. He was nineteen years old and still lived with his mother, but already he was thinking ahead to the middle of his life. Since his father disappeared, Charger had been catapulted forward. Something about his mind wouldn't let him be young, he thought. He saw too far ahead. He wanted to rewire his brain. He wanted to plunge into the darkness and not be afraid. Being in love ought to seem more reckless, he thought. Tiffany was napping, her head nestled in a yellow pillow in the form of a giant Tweety Pie. It did not look like a comfortable position, but she seemed relaxed. Her snake legs were beautiful. They seemed almost to glow in the dark.

When they reached Nashville, Charger impulsively turned down I-40 toward Memphis. He thought Tiffany wouldn't mind if they headed west. He felt like driving all night. He thought he could reach the Texas border sometime tomorrow. Then he could get his bearings. Tiffany kept sleeping, tired from school and work. He played the radio low, a background for his thoughts. He finished a Coke he had bought at the gas station. He had to keep his head open for the road. In the dark the road seemed connected to his head, like a tongue.

Just before two he pulled off the interstate at a cheap-looking motel. Tiffany woke up but didn't seem to notice where she was. He guided her into the lobby. Clumsily she struggled with her purse and the heavy satchel she had brought with her. Charger pressed a buzzer on the wall to awaken the night clerk. He could hear noises from the back room, like someone swatting flies. Tiffany studied her bandage as they waited at a pine-paneled counter. She squirmed restlessly. "I have to pee so bad," she said. Charger wondered how she wriggled out of those tight snake pants.

A thin middle-aged man in sweatpants and an oversized Charlotte Hornets jersey appeared. He wore thick glasses. Silently he took Charger's credit card and ground it through a little press. The man grunted as he presented the paper slip. The room was thirty-two dollars—less than Charger had feared. Pleased, he signed the slip with a grand flourish, as if he were endorsing an important document. The clerk ripped out the yellow copy, wrapped it around the key, and handed the little package to Charger.

"I'm going to get muscles in my left arm," Tiffany said as she hoisted her satchel. She held her bandaged thumb ahead of her, like a flashlight.

From the truck Charger retrieved the other bag she had brought and his own bag, a weathered Army duffel of his father's. The room was 234, up an exterior flight of concrete stairs. A light rain had started. Below, a car pulled in, and a woman got out with a screaming child clutching a pink-plush pig. Charger heard a door slam.

The room smelled stale. The bedspread looked heavy and dark with dirt and smoke and spills. Charger set the bags down and clicked on a light. Then the telephone rang. Tiffany gasped, but Charger thought it seemed normal to get a phone call here. He picked up the phone.

"Your Nellie-babe dropped a scarf on the floor down here," the night clerk said.

"You dropped your scarf," Charger said to Tiffany, who was tugging at her zipper. "I'll be right down," he told the clerk. He hung up the phone. Nellie-babe?

"Wait. I have to pee and I need a little help with these pants," Tiffany said, reaching for him. "I feel ham-handed."

"You can do it. How did you manage at that gas station?"

"Why I dropped my scarf is, I couldn't tie it around my neck with this clumsy thumb."

"I'll go get it." Charger slipped out of the room and bounded down to the desk, leaving Tiffany to work herself out of her snake pants. She whined when she was tired.

"Some britches your Nellie's got on," the night clerk said in a friendly voice.

"How am I supposed to take that?" Charger demanded. "And what do you mean—Nellie? Is that something I'm supposed to know from television?"

The skinny guy retreated an inch or two, and his lip quivered. Charger felt gratified. The clerk said, "Hey, man. I didn't mean nothing. I mean you're a lucky guy. No offense. I was just commenting on them snakes." He grinned. He had big teeth, chinked with food. "I mean, I wouldn't want to get tangled up with a lady wearing snakes. I looked at those, and they threw me for a minute. Man, I hate snakes. Did a snake bite her on the finger?"

Charger snatched Tiffany's scarf from the counter. It was a long banner, shimmering blue like a lava lamp. He went to the door and stood gazing at the parking lot. The winking motel sign had a faulty bulb. DUNN'S MO-TEL. DUNN'S MOTE. DUNN'S MOTEL. DUNN'S MOTE. The inter-state traffic was sparse, just lights moving like liquid. Charger saw the faint glow of Memphis in the west. He saw a gray car cruise by the motel slowly and then head down the service road. He turned and surveyed the lobby. The TV was blank. The coffeepot was clean and ready for morning. The clerk opened a hot-rodding magazine.

"Can't face them snakes, can you, buddy?" The guy smirked.

"That's none of your business," Charger said, coming back to the counter.

"What's private anymore?" the clerk said, with a burst of bitterness like chewing gum cracking. He set down his magazine and smoothed the cover with his palm, as if he were ironing. "Nothing's a secret. All them numbers we've got nowadays? Why, I could take your credit-card number and use it if I was of a mind to. It's all in the computers anyway. The government knows everything about everybody. It's not enough to take your taxes. They want to keep up with the news on you too. And *we* pay for their meddling. They can peep into them computers and find out anything they want to."

Charger decided to humor the guy. Somehow, he didn't want to go back upstairs just yet. "If they're that good, they could find my daddy," he said.

"Is he on the FBI list?" The clerk seemed impressed.

Charger shrugged. "No, he took a wrong turn and he just kept going."

"If they want to find him, they'll get him. They've got their ways. They come in here on stakeouts all the time. Them black helicopters that come over? They have computers right on board that plug into a global network."

"Bullshit," Charger said. "*Irk, irk,*" he muttered to himself.

The clerk looked angry, ready to pounce at him. He had a belligerent gleam in his eye. Then he seemed to steady himself. "Matter of fact, right before you came in, I checked in an escaped convict," he said in a superior tone. "He's in the room right next to you."

Charger felt his stomach flip. But he was on to the guy, he thought. He was a fruitcake. More bullshit, Charger decided. He stared the guy in the eye—magnified by the bottle-bottom glasses—until the clerk looked away.

"If he's in his room, he won't hurt nobody," Charger said. "He's probably tired. He probably couldn't get a wink of sleep in jail."

The clerk opened a newspaper. "Look at this picture. That's him."

The photograph showed a dark-haired guy with a receding hairline who wore a prison work shirt and had a serial number on his chest. The headline read PRISON ESCAPEE SOUGHT IN THREE STATES.

"He signed his name 'Harry Martin' when he checked in," the clerk said. "But the guy in the newspaper is named Arthur Shemell. Look." He punched the newspaper with his finger. "Didn't fool me!"

Charger felt his confidence ebb a little. "Well, call the police, then."

"Oh, I don't want to bother them tonight. I've had them out here on so many cases—drug busts and kidnappings. Sometimes they don't appreciate my efforts. I don't owe them any favors." The clerk shook the newspaper.

"I know what you mean," Charger said. "Been there, done that."

"Dittos."

"Been there, done that," repeated Charger, testing the sound.

The clerk folded the newspaper to display the escapee's picture. "I don't believe he's Harry Martin *or* Arthur Shemell. He's the spittin' image of Clarence Smith, this guy back in high school I used to know. He used to sneak into the girls' locker room and steal their basketball bloomers. He had one eyebrow that went all the way across. Them's the guys to watch out for. And their ears stick out too far. His whole family was like that, and they were *all* bad; one time the big-daddy busted out of the house with a hatchet and swung it at his uncle's wife's daddy—for no good reason. He split his head right open like a watermelon. That happened half a mile from my house—in 1938."

The clerk rattled the newspaper in Charger's face so quickly that Charger jumped. The guy's own ears were airplane wings, he thought.

"I hear you, buddy," Charger said, trying to calm him. He wasn't afraid of any escaped convict, but the nut behind the counter was a different story. Charger drummed his fingers loudly on the counter. I can do this, he thought.

"Well, if we've got an escaped convict here, we better get the cops on him," Charger said. "Or do you think that would be government interference? Maybe everybody should just go free. Is he a serial killer or what?"

"Bank robber, gas-station holdup, attacked his brother with a jigsaw, stole a thousand dollars from his sister—her trousseau money. Bad, bad, bad."

Charger breathed once and talked fast. He said, "Hey man, I'm busy. I've got a girl upstairs about to pee in her pants if I don't get up there. But it looks like we need to call the law on this old pal of yours, whatever his name is." Charger grabbed the portable telephone and dialed 911. Tiffany's scarf fell to the floor.

"You don't need to do that," the clerk said, reaching across the counter.

"Hey," Charger said. "No problem." He trotted a few steps out of reach.

Nine-one-one answered. Charger said, "This is the night clerk at Dunn's Motel off of exit forty-eight." He made his voice low and conspiratorial. "We've just checked in that escaped convict that was in the paper. He's your guy, folks. Come on out to our crummy little motel next to the BP off exit forty-eight. I'll hold him for you." He punched the OFF button and returned the phone to the counter with a bang. "It's all yours, buddy. Now I'm going to go get some sleep. Thanks for the opportunity to serve." He picked up the scarf.

The clerk was trembling. "Stay here with me till the cops get here," he said. "Please."

Charger rolled his eyes. "Sorry, buddy. Gotta get back to my Nellie-babe." At the door he said, "So long. If he's really a convict, they'll get him. Be sure to tell about them basketball bloomers."

The clerk stared, bug-eyed.

The blue scarf flying from his fist, Charger ran up the concrete steps like a fugitive. He imagined blue lights flashing in the distance. He heard rain spatters on the asphalt. But he felt a spurt of elation. He plunged into the room and bolted the door.

"What's going on?" Tiffany asked. She was standing in the bathroom doorway, holding a towel around her. "I was afraid something had happened to you."

"It's O.K. I got your scarf."

Tiffany retreated into the bathroom. Charger turned out the lamp by the chair and then the lamp by the bed. He heard water running in the shower. The bathroom door was ajar, and the crack of light was like a beam from a projection booth. He watched out the window from behind the edge of the drapes. Several minutes passed. Then a cruiser floated in quietly, its roof light making blue patterns on the concrete-block wall in front. Only one cop was in the car. The cop got out slowly, adjusting his heavy belt. Charger could see him and the night clerk in the doorway of the lobby. Their arm gestures seemed to suggest that the two were acquaintances. The cop shook his head knowingly, as though listening to a speeder's excuses. Finally, he waved and returned to his cruiser. The night clerk rolled up the newspaper and beat his leg. Charger kept looking, as if something more were supposed to happen.

"Is there some kind of trouble down there?" Tiffany said, moving toward him. She was wrapped in towels. By now the cruiser was gone, and the clerk had retreated into his back room.

"I'll be ready in a minute," Charger said, his voice muffled by the drape.

All he wanted was to get to Texas, Charger thought, to see those skies. He glanced up into the light-shimmering drizzle. If he got an early start on what his father had gone to see, maybe he would not mind what was to come later. It would be a way to fool destiny. "My little donkey and me," he murmured, turning and reaching for her.

# XIII

# Another War

"Behind the Book" FROM *The Girl in the Blue Beret* (2012)

*My father-in-law was a pilot. During World War II, he was shot down in a B-17 over Belgium. With the help of the French Resistance, he made his way through Occupied France and back to his base in England. Ordinary citizens hid him in their homes, fed him, disguised him, and sheltered him from the Germans. Many families willingly hid Allied aviators, knowing the risks: They would have been shot or sent to a concentration camp if they were discovered by the Germans.*

*In 1987 the town in Belgium honored the crew by erecting a memorial at the crash site, where one of the ten crew members died. The surviving crew was invited for three days of festivities, including a flyover by the Belgian Air Force. More than three thousand Allied airmen were rescued during the war, and an extraordinarily deep bond between them and their European helpers endures even now.*

*My father-in-law, Barney Rawlings, spent a couple of months hiding out in France in 1944, frantically memorizing a few French words to pass himself off as a Frenchman, but his ordeal had not inspired in me any fiction until I started taking a French class. Suddenly, the language was transporting me back in time and across the ocean, as I tried to imagine a tall, out-of-place American struggling to say* bonjour. *Barney had a vague memory of a girl who had escorted him in Paris in 1944. He remembered that her signal was something blue—a scarf, maybe, or a beret. The notion of a girl in a blue beret seized me, and I was off.*

*I had my title, but I didn't know what my story would be. I had to go to France to imagine the country in wartime. What would I have done in such*

*circumstances of fear, deprivation, and uncertainty? What if my pilot charac-*
*ter returns decades later to search for the people who had helped him escape?*

*Writing a novel about World War II and the French Resistance was a chal-*
*lenge both sobering and thrilling. I read many riveting escape-and-evade ac-*
*counts of airmen and of the Resistance networks organized to hide them and*
*then send them on grueling treks across the Pyrenees to safety. But it was the*
*people I met in France and Belgium who made the period come alive for me.*
*They had lived it.*

*In Belgium, I was entertained lavishly by the people who had honored*
*the B-17 crew with the memorial, including by some of the locals who had*
*witnessed the crash landing. I was overwhelmed by their generosity. They*
*welcomed me with an extravagant three-cheek kiss, but one ninety-year-old*
*man, Fernand Fontesse, who had been in the Resistance and had been a POW,*
*planted his kiss squarely on my lips.*

*In a small town north of Paris I met Jean Hallade. He had been only fifteen*
*when Second Lieutenant Rawlings was hidden in a nearby house. Jean took a*
*picture of Barney in a French beret, a photo to be used for the fake ID card he*
*would need as he traveled through France over the next few months, disguised*
*as a French cabinetmaker.*

*And in Paris I became friends with lovely, indomitable Michèle Agniel,*
*who had been a girl guide in the Resistance. Her family aided fifty Allied avia-*
*tors, including Barney Rawlings. She takes her scrapbooks from the war years*
*to schools to show children what once happened. "This happened here," she*
*says. "Here is a ration card. This is a swastika." She pauses. "Never again,"*
*she says. The characters in* The Girl in the Blue Beret *are not portraits of ac-*
*tual people, but the situations were inspired by very real individuals whom I*
*regard as heroes.*

—BAM

# FROM *The Girl in the Blue Beret* (2011)

## CHAPTER 1

As the long field came into view, Marshall Stone felt his breathing quicken, a rush of doves flying from his chest. The landscape was surprisingly familiar, its contours and borders fresh in his memory, even though he had been here only fleetingly thirty-six years ago. Lucien Lombard, who had brought him here today, knew the field intimately, for it had been in his family for generations.

"It was over there beside that tree, *monsieur*," Lucien said, pointing toward the center of the field, where an awkward sycamore hovered over a patch of unruly vegetation.

"There was no tree then," Marshall said.

"That is true."

They walked through the furrowed field toward the tree, Lucien's sturdy brown boots mushing the mud, Marshall following in borrowed Wellingtons. He was silent, his memory of the crash landing superimposed on the scene in front of him, as if there were a small movie projector in his mind. The Flying Fortress, the B-17, the heavy bomber the crew called the *Dirty Lily*, had been returning from a mission to Frankfurt.

"The airplane came down just there," said Lucien as they neared the tree.

Lucien was elderly—probably in his eighties, Marshall thought—but he had a strong, erect physique, and he walked with a quick, determined step. His hair was thin, nearly white, his face smooth and firm.

"Normally a farmer would not permit a tree to thrive in his field," he said. "But this tree marks the site."

Unexpectedly, Marshall Stone began to cry. Embarrassed, he turned his face aside. He was a captain of transatlantic jumbo jets, a man who did not show weakness. He was alarmed by his emotion.

Lucien Lombard nodded. "I know, *monsieur*," he said.

In Marshall's mind, the crumpled B-17 lay before him in the center of the field. He recalled that the plane had been lined up with the neatly plowed furrows.

The deep, rumbling sound of a vast formation of B-17s roared through Marshall's memory now. The steady, violent, rocking flight toward target. The sight of Focke-Wulf 190s—angry hornets darting crazily. The black bursts of flak floating like tumbleweeds strewn on a western highway. The fuselage flak-peppered. Slipping down into the cloud deck, flying for more than an hour unprotected. Over Belgium, hit again. The nose cone shattering. The pilot panicking.

Marshall, the co-pilot, took the controls and brought the *Dirty Lily* down. A belly landing on this foreign soil. There was no time to jettison the ball turret. Only as they were coming down did Marshall see that Lawrence Webb, the pilot, was unconscious. The Fort grazed the top of a tall hedgerow and slid in with a jolt, grinding to a hard stop. The crew scrambled out. Marshall and the flight engineer wrestled Webb's slack body from the plane. The navigator's face was torn, bloodied. The fuselage was burning. Machine-gun rounds were exploding at the gun stations. Marshall didn't see the tail gunner anywhere. The left waist gunner lay on the ground, motionless.

Marshall had been just twenty-three years old then. Now he was nearly sixty, and he had come to see this place again at last. He was crying for the kids in the B-17, the youngsters who had staked their lives on their Flying Fortress. He hadn't known he had pent up such a reservoir of emotion, even though he probably thought about the downing of the B-17 every day. He willed his tears to stop.

Lucien Lombard had seen the plane come down near the village, and he rushed to help the crew, but Marshall didn't remember him.

Now Lucien said, "It is like yesterday."

Marshall toed a weed-topped clod of dirt. "The worst day of my life," he said. "Some bad memories."

"Never mind, *monsieur*. It had its part."

Several people were crossing the field, headed toward them. They had arrived in a gray van with the name of a hardware store on the side.

"Everyone from the village has heard of your visit," said Lucien. "You are a hero."

"*Non.* I did very little." Marshall was ashamed.

Lucien introduced him to the group. They were all smiling at him and speaking rapidly. When Marshall could not follow some of their thickly accented French, Lucien explained that everyone there remembered the crash. Three families had sheltered members of the crew, and Dr. Bequet had treated the wounded.

"I'm very grateful," Marshall said, shaking the doctor's hand.

"It was necessary to help."

More introductions and small talk followed. Marshall noticed two men scanning the ground. Lucien explained that people still found pieces of metal there—bullet casings, rivets, and once even a warped propeller blade. Marshall thought of how he had torn up the field when he came zigzagging down that day.

A man in a cloth cap and wool scarf stepped forward and touched Marshall's arm.

"*Oui*, it is sad, *monsieur*," the man said. He regarded Marshall in a kindly way and smiled. His face was leathery but younger than Marshall's. He seemed familiar.

"You were the boy who helped me!" Marshall said, astonished.

"*Oui. C'est moi.*"

"You offered me a cigarette."

The man laughed. His taut, weathered cheeks seemed to blush.

"*Bien sûr.* I would never forget that day. The cigarettes I had obtained for my father."

"That was my very first Gauloises," Marshall said.

"You were my first *Américain*," the man said, smiling. "I am Henri Lechat."

They shook hands, the younger man first removing his glove. "You warned me that the Germans were coming," Marshall said.

Henri nodded. "It is true. You had no French then, and I had no English."

"But I knew. We communicated somehow."

Marshall's voice broke on the word *communicated*.

"We will never forget, *monsieur*."

"You told me to run," Marshall said, recalling how he had stowed the cigarette in the inner pocket of his leather jacket. Now he felt his tears well up again.

Henri tugged on his scarf. "I told you to hide in the woods, and you comprehended."

Recalling the boy's urgency, Marshall tried to laugh. Henri had raced up, calling a warning. Pointing back the way he had come, he cried, "*Les Allemands! Les Allemands!*" Then, pointing to the woods in the other direction, he shouted, "*Allez-y!*" Marshall did not see any Germans, and he would not leave until all the crew was out. The bombardier was wounded in the shoulder, and the navigator had a shattered leg. The tail gunner appeared; he had hopped out easily. The left waist gunner was unconscious and had to be pulled from the fuselage window. Marshall was relieved to see the ball-turret gunner, who was limping toward the church with a man carrying a shovel. Someone said the right waist gunner had parachuted. The pilot was lying on the frozen ground, his eyes closed. Fire was leaping from the plane.

Marshall knelt by Webb, trying to wake him. Nothing. Someone squatted beside Marshall and opened Webb's jacket.

"*Docteur*," the woman said, pointing toward the village. She pointed in the opposite direction, toward the woods, and said, "Go."

Marshall stood. The flight engineer appeared at his side. "Let's go," he said. "Everybody's out."

Several of the villagers were making urgent gestures toward the road. German troops would be here in moments. Marshall knew that they converged on every fallen plane, to arrest the Allied aviators and to salvage the wrecked metal for their own planes. The German fighter that had downed them was circling low overhead. Marshall began running toward the woods.

*Had the Germans shot anyone from the village for helping the American flyers?* Marshall wondered now, but he did not want to ask. He had tried to be sure all the crew were out, and then he left the scene. In the years after, he didn't probe into the aftermath. He lived another life.

"We were so thankful to you, *monsieur*," one of the men was saying. "When your planes flew over we knew we would be liberated one day."

Marshall nodded.

A stocky woman with gray, thick hair and a genial, wrinkled face said,

"The airplanes flying toward Germany in those days—there were hundreds of them. We rejoiced to see them crossing the sky."

Henri kicked dirt from his leather boot. "I didn't know at that age everything that was understood by the adults. But I knew the deprivation, the difficulties, the secrecy. Even the children knew the crisis."

Cautiously, Marshall asked, "Did the Germans arrest anybody for helping us?"

"*Oh, non, monsieur.*" Henri paused. "Not that day."

Lucien Lombard clasped Henri's shoulder and said, "The father of this one was killed—shot on his bicycle, on his way home after convoying one of your *aviateurs* across the border to France."

Henri said, "I had to grow up quickly. I had the responsibilities then for my mother and my sisters."

Lucien said, "His family hid that *aviateur* in their barn for a time."

Marshall recoiled. He could see the waist gunner lying motionless across the furrows. He saw himself running into the woods. He saw the boy's face. The plane was on fire.

Marshall had decided to return to this place finally, knowing it was time to confront his past failure. He had expected to be alone in the field, and he had not thought anyone would remember. The news of the death of the boy's father jolted him. He had never heard about that. In all these years, he had thought little about the people who had come running to the downed airplane. He had felt such a profound defeat in the war that he had not wanted to return here. During the war, more than anything, he had wanted to be heroic. But he was no hero. He had felt nothing but bitter disappointment that he didn't get to complete his bombing missions against Nazi Germany. And what happened later, as he skulked through France, was best forgotten, he had thought.

Marshall was a widower. His wife, Loretta, had died suddenly two years before, and the loss still seemed unbelievable, but now he began to feel his grief lift, like the morning fog disappearing above a waiting airport.

CHAPTER 2

Dazed by his brief visit to the muddy field in Belgium, Marshall spent the last hours before his flight home walking around Paris. It was a mellow spring day.

He had always enjoyed this city. He bid for Paris flights several times each year, and when he became senior enough, he got them. Climb out of JFK in the evening, fly above the invisible Atlantic during the hours of darkness, and arrive in Paris under a bright sun.

He thought tenderly of Loretta, who had always refused to believe he was anything less than heroic. He wished she could have been with him on this trip.

He watched children on skates zooming alongside the Luxembourg Gardens, near the crew hotel. He thought about the boy in Belgium who had helped him, and he thought about the boy's father—shot for convoying a gunner from the *Dirty Lily*.

On his layovers, Marshall had rarely gone to museums or tourist attractions, but he enjoyed the bustle and anonymity of a city that still had a feeling of intimacy—unlike New York. Or London. He liked being able to understand conversations he overheard. After the war, he had taken courses in French, and over the years he had become fluent enough to get along. He liked to read novels in French.

By the time he reached the Louvre, he realized that during his walk he hadn't been seeing Paris as it was now, 1980. He had been resurrecting 1944. Ghostly images overlaid the scene before him. At the Tuileries, his gaze followed the magnificent view through the gardens and on up the Champs-Elysées to the Arc de Triomphe. Over this sight now he superimposed his memories of being there long ago, when there were hardly any vehicles. He saw images from newsreels and photographs: Hitler's hordes marching in perfect lockstep; later, Churchill and de Gaulle triumphant.

To Marshall's right, somewhere along the rue de Rivoli, was a Métro stop. He and a brash bombardier named Delancey had stumbled up from the Métro, scared, towering like Lombardy poplars among the crowd of much shorter Frenchmen. If they missed their contact, they would be stranded—lost amidst the Germans, circulating around them in their menacing gray-green uniforms.

She was there. He saw her first, sitting on a bench reading a timetable. There was a quietness to the crowd, as if people were on their best behavior. Marshall had doubted that a mere schoolgirl would be sent as their contact, but there she was, sitting with a book satchel and earnestly consulting a timetable.

The agent's directions had been precise. *Find the girl in the blue beret. She will have a timetable and a leather school bag.*

Marshall remembered that moment vividly. She was waiting there, her blue beret standing out like a flower against the barren winter gardens of the Tuileries.

There was still a bench in that area. Not the same bench, he thought, but it was in approximately the same place.

But no, he was wrong. When he saw her on the bench, Delancey hadn't been with him. He and Delancey had first seen her at the train station. Why did he meet her in the Tuileries? Then he remembered.

As he neared the place de la Concorde, he thought of the Concorde—the SST. He wished it would fly over, a happy coincidence, tying history in a knot. Moments of history entwined here—Marie-Antoinette lost her head; the Egyptian obelisk replaced the guillotine; Napoléon dreamed the triumphant arch. Marshall felt his own history emanate from him, as if he had been holding it condensed in a small spot inside himself. Reviewing his past was new for Marshall, something that had started as he approached his sixtieth birthday—and retirement. Tomorrow was his final flight.

For years, Marshall had dreaded retirement. Mandatory premature retreat, he called it, infuriated at the federal law. He hated being forced out. He was perfectly healthy, and he had stopped smoking ten years ago. Asking a pilot to stop flying was like asking a librarian to burn books. Or a pianist to close the lid forever. Or a farmer to buy a condo in the city. His mind entertained new metaphors every day.

Retirement would be like the enforced passivity he had endured during the war, after the crash landing. Then, he was a caged bird.

The airline didn't want rickety, half-blind ancients at the controls. *Screw the airline*, he thought now. Roaming Paris, he composed the thousandth rebuttal he would never send in: *Since being let go on account of advanced age and feebleness, I've been forced to adopt a new career. Henceforth, I shall guide hikers up Mont Blanc, and on my days off I'll be going skydiving.*

The pilots Marshall hobnobbed with might talk about investments, or summer homes, or time-share condos, but none of them really cared about anything except flying. One former B-24 pilot golfed, and an ex-fighter jock intended to sail his deep-draft sloop around the world someday, but Marshall thought their pastimes were half-hearted substitutes. He was interested in everything to do with aviation, and he was always reading, but he thought hobbies were silly. Collecting swizzle sticks or crafting model airplanes—he couldn't imagine. Whenever he thought of what to do with his retirement, he drew a blank. Pushing the throttles forward, racing down the runway, feeling the wings gain lift, pulling the yoke back and aiming high into the sky—that's what his pilot friends really wanted. That's what he wanted.

Marshall wandered down a street of five-story apartment buildings. This was the lovely, proportionate architecture he remembered.

The people who had helped him in Paris during the war would be retired now, he thought. The French retired young. Robert? *Rohbehr.* Marshall didn't recall the young man's last name, but he would never forget him. Robert and his clandestine missions. He remembered Robert appearing in the small hours of the morning with an urgent message. He remembered Robert letting his rucksack fall to the floor, then reaching in like a magician to produce cigarettes or a few priceless eggs. Once, he pulled out an actual rabbit, skinned and purple. From inside the lining of his coat came thin papers with secret messages. Whatever happened to him after the war?

. . .

## Chapter 17

Back in his Paris hotel, alternating between insomnia and waking dreams, he could hear Annette Vallon's singsong French, her playful teasing. During those three weeks in 1944 he thought he saw the soft baby fat of her cheeks grow thinner. Her mother insisted on giving him the largest portions of food. "You are large, *monsieur,*" Mme Vallon told him. "We do not need so much."

"I don't want this," Annette said, moving a carrot on her plate. "You may have it."

Perhaps she still needed the nourishment of milk, he thought. She needed meat. The milk ration, for children only, was for her younger sister, Monique. Food had been more plentiful in the country, on the farms and in Chauny with the Alberts.

He remembered the way Annette and her mother hugged so casually. He could see in them a happiness that persisted despite the hardships of wartime. Mme Vallon had embraced him too. She was small, and she had to reach up, but her warmth momentarily blotted out the war. He thought of his own mother, when she was a young woman, before she got sick.

Marshall had hardly ever paid attention to cooking, but in Paris food was so scarce it became a fixation. He watched Mme Vallon practice her art. With a small piece of chicken, a dab of saved butter, and some elaborate fussing with the pots on the wood-stove, she made a terrine, a sort of chicken Jell-O with a yellow layer at the bottom. She flavored it with bits of dried herbs.

"You need your strength for your journey," she said, giving him a second helping.

He didn't know when the journey would be, or how.

He offered them some francs from his escape kit. He had two thousand francs, oversized bills like pages from a book. The portrait of the woman in a helmet was Joan of Arc, he learned years later.

They would not take his money. "We do this gladly," Mme Vallon insisted. "It is our necessity."

"But you could buy a rabbit and some eggs," he argued.

One evening she cooked a pot of tripe—the only item the butcher had left, she said. Marshall was revolted when he saw her scrubbing and soaking the hog's entrails that afternoon. He ate sparingly, but M. Vallon treated the dish as a delicacy, making soft groans of appreciation.

"With more butter and some cream, this would be almost divine," he said, but everyone knew he was pretending.

Annette nibbled. Monique did not speak at the table. Marshall hardly remembered her. A child of eight or ten?

They spoke English with him. Annette listened carefully when the adults spoke. Then she tried to offset the anxiety in their voices with her own girlish chatter. Her mother indulged her, he thought. He could see in her mother's face what Annette would become. Mme Vallon wore her hair swept up, with long hairpins holding a pile of it. In the corner of the sitting room she sometimes brushed Annette's hair, twirling it with her fingers. Annette's hair was medium length, dark brown with curls framing her face. She wore no lipstick. Her clothing hung loosely on her thin frame.

On Sundays she washed and ironed her blue smock for the school week. It was what the girls wore to protect their clothing, she explained, and it was a sort of uniform.

He remembered her sitting at a table, working with the buckles of her cowhide school bag, which she called her *vache*. She placed her books and papers inside purposefully—like a pilot packing his brain bag, he thought now.

In the morning, Mme Vallon went to the market early, and M. Vallon left soon after for his office. Marshall did not remember now where Monique had been.

"Time for your French lesson," Annette announced.

The large apartment was cold, and Marshall was wearing three sweaters.

"Pronunciation, *s'il vous plaît*," he said. "I'm lost."

"My English teacher thinks I have a 'bad' accent," she told him. "She tries to teach the way they say in England. Tomato—we say *tuh-maht*, they say *tuh-MAHT-oe*; that's easy. But you say *toe-MAY-toe*. I have fear that my teacher will recognize where I am getting an American accent!"

She made him a tea of herbs, plentiful because the Germans detested herbs and had not appropriated all of them. She rubbed a piece of leftover bread with some mint and a little oil and warmed it on the stove. He had built a small fire with some chips of coal and paper so that her mother could make coffee, a substitute made of acorns—or perhaps cockleburs and birdseed. Marshall didn't know.

"Perhaps Maman will bring an egg. I will cook it for you in this fragrant oil."

"*Mais non.* You and your mother should have it."

"No, you have half, and Maman and I share half." She wiped the pan with a lump of bread she had saved. She smiled. "Perhaps Maman will bring some butter. And cinnamon."

"And cornmeal."

She didn't understand, and when he explained she turned up her nose.

"One doesn't eat that," she said. "Food for the animals."

"Then maybe she will bring some more of those delicious pig guts we had last night!"

"*Les tripes! Mmm. Bonnes. Bonnes.*"

They laughed.

She made him pronounce all the words they had discussed. The words for corn and cinnamon and butter. Eggs. Bread.

"Perhaps I make us too hungry," she said apologetically, reaching to pull up her limp white sock that was sagging into her shoe.

"It's all right to talk about food," he said. "I think about food every day!"

"We should speak of other things," she said emphatically. "Now, let's learn flowers."

"Do I need to know flowers? I was never any good with botany. *Botanique?*"

"Well, then, trees. It is necessary to know *les arbres.*" She led him through a list of trees, then some animals. "At our summer house in Normandy, we had geese and chickens. We could have stayed there since the beginning of the war, when everyone suddenly left Paris, but we returned. Maman insisted we were in more danger there than here. My father had to be here, and I must be here to do what I can to help," she said.

"Do your parents hide many aviators? How do you feed them?" He wasn't supposed to ask his helpers questions, so the Krauts couldn't force anything out of him if he got caught.

She shrugged. "We manage."

"And what do you do?" He knew she went somewhere Friday afternoons after school.

"You are not to know." She smiled. "The Germans, if they are on the bus, I put my books beside me and occupy as much space as possible. I enjoy making inconvenience for them. Also, it is amusing to drop my books at their feet. In a way they are gentlemen. 'Oh, mademoiselle, I must assist you!' and in another way they are ready to make the arrest. But they do not, not the schoolgirls. So they think they are kind and helpful, but we are laughing at them. Every little bit of trouble we can cause, innocently—'Oh, it is only the schoolgirls'—is a way to express our frustration."

"Should you be provoking the Germans?" he asked. "It sounds dangerous."

"I know. But how can one resist?"

Mme Vallon was at the door, with her groceries, mostly rutabagas.

"Your usual catch," Marshall said, but he could not make the expression understood.

"If this war ever ends, I will never touch another rutabaga!" Mme Vallon said, depositing the bags on the kitchen table.

"Did you find anything else?" Annette asked, poking into the smaller bag.

"I have ten grams of butter—very precious. I have the sugar. We must get along without even ersatz coffee. Tomorrow, they said. No bread, of course. All the farina is going to Germany. Maybe our men working at the factories will get some of it." Mme Vallon rummaged deeper in the bag. "One cheese ration."

"Let me imagine," Annette said. "Tonight, baked rutabaga with cheese. A soupçon of butter."

"A tiny pinch of sugar with the butter," her mother said with a smile. "I have some herbs."

They warned him to stay away from the dining room window, which gave onto the street, but he could watch from a side angle through the lace curtains. He saw only an occasional vehicle—a Kübelwagen or a Mercedes-Benz flying a small flag with a swastika on it. The building was on a corner, and his bedroom overlooked a small side street. The blackout curtains at night cocooned him. He heard few traffic noises. People were out in the mornings and flocking home late in the day, after dark. He watched them, did exercises to keep his muscles from cramping with inactivity, and studied French. For months as a pilot trainee he had studied mechanical manuals: hydraulic pressures, lift angles. In January he had been keeping house in his barracks, writing lovesick letters to Loretta, trying to squelch suspense over the next mission. During the day he attended lectures and flew trial runs, and ten times in two months he had been out on wild sky rides, lugging bombs. A few times he had visited the villages near the base, and once he had been to London. Now, he was trying to talk French and reading Verlaine. He was almost twenty-four years old. He had stepped into an alternate life, like Alice in Wonderland, down a rabbit hole—but without his Bugs Bunny jacket.

There was hardly anything he could do to help Mme Vallon. He envied Robert, the good-humored young guy who came by bringing fresh meat wrapped in paper. He brought cigarettes. Marshall listened for his bicycle, arriving in the downstairs foyer. Robert was slender but powerfully built, with thick hair and dark eyes. He always seemed to be on urgent business.

Marshall imagined him as a daring Resistance agent out gathering intelligence or transporting explosives, while Marshall himself sat out the war behind lace curtains.

Annette teased Marshall for lolling around the house while she worked so hard at school. She teased him for his efforts at French, even while she patiently coached him. And she teased him for the rude outfits he had to wear—the layers of old sweaters, the too-short pants, the rough socks, the cloth slippers with the seams loosened to make room for his huge toes.

At the table the family managed to make their meager dinners last for hours, regaling one another with jokes at the Germans' expense and family stories that Marshall thought must have been often told.

"The wine makes us convivial," said Mme Vallon. "We forget the difficulties."

M. Vallon did not speak of his work at the city hall, but Marshall observed that he came home with extra ration books.

"If they fail to account for the number, who is to know?" Marshall overheard M. Vallon say—but in French, so Marshall wasn't sure.

Once M. Vallon said to Marshall, "I am an honest man. I have always been an honest man. It is for honor, for patriotism, that we take care of the *aviateurs*."

"We are not violent," said Mme Vallon. "But we can do this."

"The Germans were a people of culture," M. Vallon said sadly. "I do not permit myself to believe that every German connives in this conquest."

"We are ancient enemies," Mme Vallon said.

From time to time, hints of despair broke through the Vallons' determined tranquility. But they quickly assured themselves that de Gaulle and his Free French troops would liberate Paris soon. Any day the *débarquement* of the Allies would begin. In the evenings the family played card games and conversed. At nine o'clock, Annette's parents tuned in to the BBC on the wireless for the news of France. *Chut!* Shh!

One night, they were awakened by explosions followed by sirens. In the chilly dark they were all out of bed, peeking from behind the curtains.

"It is not far," said Mme Vallon. "The smoke is across the park."

"Whatever happens, I will not consent to leave Paris again," said her husband. "The exodus in 1940 was shameful. We will not descend to that again."

# The Real Girl in the Blue Beret

Featured at newyorker.com, Page Turners, May 18, 2013

I didn't know if Michèle Moët-Agniel was still alive. She would be over eighty by now. I had written her a letter—in painstaking French—in August, 2007, and it was now January, 2008. I mailed another copy of the letter with an updated note. I told her I was coming to Paris in the spring and very much wanted to meet her because I was writing a novel about the war years, when she was a teen-ager in the French Resistance.

I studied the photo of her with my father-in-law, Barney Rawlings, taken in 1993 at a reunion of Allied aviators and the Europeans who had helped them escape from the Germans during the Second World War. (Barney was one of these former airmen.) I regretted that I had not been there to meet her then. In the photo, she looked attractive in a short-sleeved yellow dress, and she had the air of someone energetic and fun-loving. A firecracker. I knew that my in-laws had celebrated a D-Day anniversary with her in France, but they are dead now, and all I had was her address.

Barney, a B-17 copilot, at twenty-three, had been shot down near the French border with Belgium, and he spent several weeks hiding in safe houses before being sent to Paris by the Resistance. Michèle, then a girl of seventeen, guided him from Gare du Nord to an apartment where he was hidden. Later she led him on the Metro from her home in Saint Mandé to the Photomaton near the Louvre to make a photo for a fake I.D. He remembered her as the girl in the blue beret. He was supposed to follow her, and they were not to acknowledge each other.

Michèle and her parents had worked with the Bourgogne network, one of many secret networks of ordinary citizens who wanted to participate non-violently in the Resistance. These networks, the best known of which was the Comète line, returned over three thousand Allied aviators to safety—

across the English Channel or over the Pyrenees. Ominous posters through-out Paris warned citizens against helping stranded airmen—men would be shot, women sent to concentration camps.

I had begun my novel with little more than the title, "The Girl in the Blue Beret," and the notion that a retired airline captain decides to return to France to find the people who had helped him during the war after his bomber crash-landed. I didn't know what he would find when he got to France, but I knew that he would be searching for the girl in the blue beret. I especially wanted to find a Frenchman who could inspire a character. I made plans to travel to France.

Finally, I received a letter from Michèle Moët-Agniel. Although she had done few interviews, she agreed to meet me because of the link to my father-in-law. I knew that she and her parents had been arrested and deported in 1944 for helping aviators. She and her mother were sent to Ravensbruck, and her father had died at Buchenwald. I could not match these facts in my mind with the vivacious woman who greeted me so warmly.

She was a widow. Her small apartment near the Bois de Vincennes was filled with massive old furniture. The armoire could have hidden a stray airman. (Actually, many airmen *were* hidden in armoires during the war.) Michèle wore a bright red skirt, a black sweater, and pearls. She had white curls, intense hazel eyes, and a fluttery, enthusiastic manner. She served me coffee, fruit, chocolate, and *pâtisseries*.

Her English was much better than my wobbly French, but we con-sulted her well-thumbed dictionary. She had always intended to write her memoirs, she said. But she had procrastinated. Sighing, she said, "It is too *difficile*."

Since the nineteen-eighties she has been active with other former politi-cal prisoners in documenting the deportations, and she (a former teacher) takes her scrapbooks about the war years to the schools to show children what life was like then.

As she showed me one of these scrapbooks—full of ration books, let-ters, news clippings, photos, and a secret notebook in which fifty aviators had written their names and addresses—she seemed flustered and clumsy, scattering the photos and papers.

A photo fell to the floor. Picking it up, she said, "This is Jean Carbon-net. I went with him on the train to guide pilots. Sometimes we went to

Noyon or Chauny. Once we went to Lizio, a petite village, where nineteen pilots were hidden. We escorted seven of them to Paris in one journey."

Michèle described how the handsome young man in the snapshot was arrested with her family, how he survived (barely) Buchenwald, how he was forever changed by the war ("his head turn-ed"). Although he had died years before, he struck my imagination and I thought I had found my Frenchman.

In the scrapbook was a stenciled number cut from the clothing Michèle had been forced to wear as a prisoner. She had no tattoo. As she began to tell of the arrest and deportation, her English lapsed and her French sped up. I was having difficulty following.

After several months in prison, she and her parents, as well as Jean Carbonnet, a priest, and two English airmen who were arrested with them, were deported on the last convoy out of Paris before the city's liberation in August, 1944. Michèle and her mother arrived at Ravensbruck, a women's concentration camp where political prisoners were sent. It was a shock beyond imagination. Some weeks later, as punishment for their part in a protest against being forced to work in a munitions factory, they were sent to a labor camp at Koenigsberg (now Chojna, Poland). During the hard months of winter on a windy plateau, five hundred women were forced to construct an airstrip—with their hands. At first Michèle had only a cotton dress to wear. The women dug out large squares of frozen sod and heaved them onto a wagon on rails. They had to shift the rails by hand periodically to extend the track. They had no socks.

In February, 1945, as the Russians closed in, the Germans sent the ambulatory prisoners on a death march back to Ravensbruck, but Michèle hid in the infirmary with her mother, who was too sick to walk.

"The *incendie!*" she cried.

The runway, the heavy wagons, the sod, the cold.

I tried to piece together what she was saying. The Germans set fire to the camp and fled. The Germans left; the Red Army came.

I decided not to probe further that day. Her son, Francis, drove me around Paris and showed me the various locales that figured in his mother's story—the Jardin des Plantes, Gare d'Austerlitz, the Colonnade on the rue de Rivoli where the Photomaton was located, and the site of the infamous Gestapo headquarters on the rue des Saussaies.

The camp at Koenigsberg was not extensively documented because there were so few survivors, but I managed to gather some more details about it and Michèle told me more a few days later.

After being rescued by the Russians—almost a year after their arrest—and spending four months in a hospital in Poland, Michèle and her mother arrived at Hotel Lutetia, the welcome center in Paris for returning deportees. Anxiously they searched the bulletin boards for word of Michèle's father. A cheerful aide said, "Oh, we do have a Monsieur Moët. Wait here." The aide returned with a long face of apology. "It wasn't Monsieur Moët. It was Monsieur Chandon."

I had never heard such a cruel twist of fate, like a mean joke.

I don't know why she trusted me to transform her story into fiction, but it was clear that she wanted it told. What could I possibly write that would do justice to this painful past? It is never easy to write about actual people, but her resilience, her high spirits, inspired my character, Annette.

I visited Michèle several times, each time filling out more of my picture of wartime Paris and her difficult history, and we became friends. I became aware of the fun she had before the arrest—an exuberant girl ready to take risks, willing to use her schoolgirl advantage to fool the Germans, and infatuated with the "big American boys."

In the story I wrote, I couldn't resist inventing a romance between the character Annette and the young man she accompanied on the missions to collect aviators. I thought it gave an added dimension of sorrow—a young couple whose possibility of raising a family was lost. That wasn't Michèle's story, but I was writing a novel, I reasoned. On the other hand, I felt strictly bound to use exact details about the Koenigsberg airstrip. In writing about concentration camps, the imagination cannot trump reality.

Eventually, "The Girl in the Blue Beret" appeared in print, and Michèle read it avidly, quickly. I was concerned that her family might think the teenage romance in the novel was true—an embarrassment to her. "I didn't like that part," she admitted. But she forgave my liberties, granting that fiction goes in a different direction from a documentary.

When I did a reading at Shakespeare and Company, she was there, and the audience loved her—a real live member of the Resistance. Seeing the impish smile on her face, I imagined again the schoolgirl with a book satchel, strolling through the Bois de Vincennes with several awkward, gawky

Americans in ill-fitting French garb following at a distance, trying to keep that blue beret in sight.

In my own walks, I had noticed the many plaques honoring the Resistance on buildings around Paris, and I wondered why there was no plaque on the apartment building where Michèle's family had sheltered aviators. As an American with typically big ideas, I inquired, although I suspected that I'd be stymied by the French bureaucracy. But it turned out to be a reasonable request, especially coming from abroad from a representative of an Allied aviator. The Moët family was long overdue for recognition, and to my amazement, a plaque was ordered. As the Second World War generation recedes, there has been in France, the same as here, a determined effort to document and remember stories from the war.

This year, National Deportation Day, the last Sunday in April, was also the anniversary of the arrest of the Moët family, April 28, 1944. Sixty-nine years had gone by. At midday a ceremony dedicated the plaque on the building in the suburb of Saint Mandé where Michèle and her family had lived during the war. The day was cold. The street was blocked off for about a hundred of her family and friends (all generations) who were gathered to honor Michèle, her brother, and their parents. I was freezing, and I was the only one wearing a hat, except for one grandmother. Michèle had brought a blue beret, but forgot and left it in the car.

The mayor of Saint Mandé, dashing in his official, ceremonial, red-white-and-blue sash, addressed the crowd, which included two women who, like Michèle, had escorted airmen.

Michèle's eight-year-old grand-nephew, from a ladder, pulled the string that dropped the bunting and revealed the plaque. Then he read the words aloud.

*Après avoir accueilli ici de nombreux aviateurs alliés en 1943 et 1944, la famille Moët à été arrêtée par la milice et remise à la Gestapo le 28 avril 1944, puis déportée. Gèrard Moët est mort à Buchenwald le 6 Mars 1945.*

*La ville de Saint Mandé en hommage à leur courage et à leur sacrifice. Le 28 avril 2013*

(After having sheltered here numerous Allied aviators in 1943 and 1944, the Moët family was arrested by the Milice and taken to the Gestapo April 28, 1944, then deported. Gerard Moët died at Buchenwald March 6,

1945. The town of Saint Mandé in homage to their courage and to their sacrifice. April 28, 2013)

Michèle read a lengthy, carefully prepared text, telling her story movingly, insisting on an explicit, factual accounting of what had happened. Many in her family had not known the whole story before. She told it without faltering until she came to the part where she and her mother returned to France after the end of the war. Her voice broke, and then she wept when she told of finding her little brother again. When they were arrested, he had been left behind on the sidewalk with his teddy bear.

The honor of the plaque was not for her, she stressed, but for her father, who loved France enough to die for it.

Michèle had written her own story at last. She ended by quoting Primo Levi,

> *N'oubliez pas que cela fut, non ne l'oubliez pas.*
> (Never forget that this has happened, do not forget it.)

# XIV

# Zanies

*In recent years I collaborated with flash-fiction writer Meg Pokrass on a few strange experimental pieces.*

—BAM

# Whale Love

Featured in the online journal *The Nervous Breakdown,*
August 21, 2013

With Meg Pokrass

### LOUISA

Louisa, who tucked up her skirts and went running every day or she would
go mad, was confounded and smothered by the whales of Concord, like
Mr. E, on whom she had a crush when she was a child and left him flowers
under his window, flowers found and laughed at by Mrs. E, who had to put
up with all his giggly acolytes, who arranged themselves prettily at his feet,
including that lunatic Jonas Very, to whom Mr. E was always so kind even
though Jonas Very was very very unpoetic and it would kill him to think
so, but aside from Mr. E and stately Mr. H, whom she privately liked to
call Nat, because he was so very very formal and distant, always walking
along the Lexington Road with his head bent in thought, there was princely
Henry, and on that spring evening she was running to meet Henry in his
rowboat—Henry in his rowboat, playing his flute!—and overcome by her
freedom from the whales of philosophy she did a sort of handspring in the
path and accidentally felled a small dead tree.

### THE WHALE OF WALDEN

In his sturdy personal cabin within sight of the great pond, Henry wrote
and wrote daily in his journal, of all the comings and goings of warblers
and chipmunks and geese, but he never dared to record his sightings of the
great heavy fabulous creature that surfaced from time to time, white in the

night, with a spout of Walden water so forceful it reached the shore and he felt the spray and heard the thrashing, and he knew there was only one—stranded, grown to giant size over the years, without a mate. . . . or perhaps with one, a little minnow who failed to grow and was fated to trundle the bottom of the pond—wherever that was, as it was so deep the bottom had not been found.

WALDEN BY NIGHT

The moon crept up daintily through the trees, highlighting the white birches and extending a broad pale shimmer across the surface of the pond, as Louisa let Henry row her through the night, while he jabbered about nighthawks and unknown thrumming insects—the insect orchestra being so loud as to drown out some of his words—but she thought he said, "There is a secret out here, and I want you to see it, to thrill to it, but you must never tell it to anyone," and being a truthful and earnest girl, she made the promise and also, in a moral quandary, felt both abashed and quaky, trembling to the sound of his voice, the slosh of his rowing, but then suddenly he let out a stifled cry, the boat rolled and rocked, and the water heaved high, and a great white shape jumped in front of her, moonlit and slick, and a fountain blew to the sky and Henry cried, "Don't tell, don't tell!"

TWICE-TOLD TALES

Louisa never told, not exactly, but she was haunted by troubling visions and on her morning runs she avoided Walden and instead ran through the woods from Hillside to the Old North Bridge and often saw Nat and his bride in their garden, and once she saw them in a shocking embrace on their porch, her bonnet askew and his chest bared and one day she ran into Mr. H, or Nat, as she had heard Mrs. Sophia address him, on the path where he was muttering along, and he invited her for tea with him and his wife, so on the day of the tea she brought them a sketch, which was not so good as her sister May would have done but it came from her heart and it was not telling the secret to portray a fanciful image of a spouting whale and anyway who would know it was secretly established in a local pond? And Nat H seemed so pleased with the sketch, and Mrs. Sophia declared that she would etch a whale onto the window glass with her diamond, and Louisa was delighted, for Nat and Sophia behaved like children, children who were allowed to get into each other's clothes.

## THE TALE TOLD

The book in the Boston bookshop was not prominently displayed, and Louisa would not have noticed it except for the word "whale" on its cover. It was not her cup of tea. She would not read about a mad sea captain obsessed with punishing a whale. That sounded absurd. But Nat knew this author. Nat must have given him the idea of the whale. Her knees buckled. She had betrayed Henry. She felt as though she had opened Pandora's trunk. Now that the whale had been revealed, it would wreak mayhem throughout the world. It would overwhelm prose, curtail sentences. She gasped, staccato breaths. You can't fight a whale.

## WHALE PRINCE, M. DICK

Romancing the big whale prince M. Dick, Nina the Hussy-Seagull feels, is not effortless; she imagines him blowing her a swan-bubble of air as she leans on the current, which is her crutch maybe, so feels like a mute starfish, dumb star of fish, a bit anxious but hey, lighter at least, emerging for her fantasy groom, M. Dick—probably bi-sexual or at least carrying the taste for the adorable Pequod and crunchy Ahab and other bobbing objects of water, especially that sarcastic beast, Ishmael, passively mocking Nina just home from the second water-bounce gull-orgy, gold-green seaweed shapes in her hair, a mammal smell or shell or Ahab's hamburger-leg in M. Dick's cavernous mouth jiggling at her lusty bird-heart again, it is M. Dick, prince of mammals, his cold, rudderless lips.

## HUSSY-SEAGULL IN MODERN TIMES

Nina, the Hussy-Seagull of Russia, fully possessed by the devil-spirit of twelve-step-averse sailor, Ahab, and repelled by the savage cannibalistic disabled Queequeg, an extraordinary harpooner, battled her own afflicted brain, which was pecked with chronic anxiety and soul-sickness, dreamt of many handsome seagulls but of only one misplaced, poetic whale, M. Dick, commuting to Walden Pond from Moscow for freedom—orgies over water—guiltlessly dumping her capricious lover, Jonathan Livingston, a mean-bird who acted out and found relief by dirtying the nearly-bald head of daytime television actor Ahab Trigorin (known for ungainly character roles and public displays in bare trees) while the hussy-seagull could not watch, she squawked sorrowfully and flagrantly flirted with many birds in different flock arrangements, performed deck-duty very well with the Roomba, or at least did some of the dishes by webbed-leg to reduce energy usage, so in a dream or a real day, Nina flapped upward to the top of the Pequod's crow's-nest, ready to plummet and land on the first under-dressed whale who swam by, but she was inevitably seduced and raped by a Russian "soul of the world" with a flight-fixation, thus ruining the fragile seagull's sense of balance and rendering her mute.

NINA OF WALDEN

When frustrated, water-logged M. Dick the whale of Walden discovered Nina the Hussy-Seagull with morning sickness, lying prone upon the Rock of Walden, the great gentle whale burped in his mouth a bit—which scared three nearby fishermen to death—and seeking relief, M. Dick popped his vacuum-sealed cave a crack, uttering forth a cloud which covered Walden with Dick's famous blend of breath reminiscent of organic oak bark and chocolate-nib laced with hints of cat-food breath (alcoholic content both mellow yet dangerously high), producing a sweet, organic after-flow vintage ambergris and immediately curing the sorrowful seagull of everything and injecting the hussy-bird with the creative desire to be not only a whale-wife, but to settle there forever on the shores of Walden with her long-lived lover, the indomitable Dick. They would drink fermented pond-water and plant a garden. She would make the ground speak beans.

WHAT WE SQUAWK ABOUT WHEN WE SQUAWK ABOUT WHALE-LOVE

"Helluva tourist draw," the casino mogul mused. Adventurous nighttime rides, honeymoon special, cozy fiberglass jet-boats.

Legend bubbled that the whale surfaced when a love-sick seagull performed a swooping dance in the moonlight. One of the location scouts had observed through a telephoto lens a seagull hovering above Walden—a lone seagull sporting what appeared to be a necklace with an albatross pendant, and a tattoo that said "Call me Fish Meal."

No one in the forensics lab recognized the line, and with no whale to show for six months of sonar, immersed sub and bubble-bath ultrasound, the developers proceeded briskly with their plans for Sunrise over Walden Waters retirement condos, built on the site of an old ruin where an odd, gloomy man had once scribbled some words not worth beans anymore.

And yet the ghostly ambergris vapors of M. Dick will haunt the shores of Walden Waters (a name chosen because it was more poetic than Walden Pond), and the residents will complain of seagull shit on the balconies and a foul sweet smell rising from the waters at dawn.

# Talking through Hats

Featured in *Five Points: A Journal of Literature and Art,*
Winter 2015

## With Meg Pokrass

*TV Voice*: It's time for "Talking through Hats" with your host, Geoffrey Chase.

*Chase*: Good evening and welcome to this week's edition of "Talking through Hats," in which our guest critics opine and cogitate, jaw and argue while they probe and dissect, worry and flay a Poem. They Pick A Poem Apart, academically scrubbing it, much as if they were in a classroom and forced by an irritable English teacher to Find the Meaning—much as if it were a Christmas pudding with a hidden coin. Here on our show we ask the question: are these coins counterfeit?

Let us meet tonight's guests. The lady in the blue hat is the distinguished editor of the anthology, "Feminists and the Forgotten Others." The lady in the yellow hat is a veterinary receptionist.

Welcome, ladies in hats.

(*Head nods and half-smiles.*)

Tonight's poem was sent in by a viewer in Boise, Idaho, Ms. Lily Larkin. Ms. Larkin is a maintenance engineer for the waste treatment plant of Boise, and in her spare time she adores knitting and kayaking. Allow me to read her poem.

*She Dwelt Among the Untrodden Ways*

She dwelt among the untrodden ways
Beside the springs of Dove

A Maid whom there were none to praise
And very few to love;

A violet by a mossy stone
Half hidden from the eye!
—Fair as a star, when only one
Is shining in the sky.

She lived unknown, and few could know
When Lucy ceased to be
But she is in her grave, and, oh,
The difference to me.

*Chase*: Lady in the yellow hat, let's start with you. Would you say this poem is reflective of our time?

*Yellow Hat*: Yes! Yes, I do. The poem is under one hundred words! Bravo! Indeed, this poem can be read while rollerblading, unicycling, in line for a muffin at Starbucks—on any handheld device. This is clearly a modern poem. In the past, so many poems were just unbearably long. For example, "The Wasteland" was so very wasteful of the land. I believe it was over four hundred lines. Think of all those trees that poem murdered.

*Blue Hat*: Hold on, hold on. How is this poem modern, or even postmodern, or post-postmodern?

*Yellow Hat*: What do you mean? Desi tries to do away with Lucy! No surprise! Imagine that tension. It is a rerun we do not need to watch, and yet we do. It grabs us hard, those menacing muscles of an angry Cuban. This poem grapples bravely with the universal "maid" in trouble. Or the need to hire a maid.

*Blue Hat*: I object. For starters, the word Maid. With a majuscule no less, I see (*gestures to screen*). That won't do, won't do.

*Yellow Hat*: Would you prefer the word "hussy"?

*Blue Hat*: I will ignore that, thank you. This poem demeans women. It is sentimental. "Beside the springs of Dove," "Fair as a star . . ." Further, the poet—no offense to the lily of Boise—is devoid of vision. The narrator wallows in his own private grief—I'm assuming *his,* but that is narrow of me. Lucy's lover could have been—

*Yellow Hat*: Ethel.

*Blue Hat*: A pre-streaming TV Lucy from fifty years ago is past her expiration date. A poet of our time should at least be *au courant* with binge TV and contemporary zombie melody. Our post-911 *angst* needs to find its expression. You wonder where these untrodden ways can possibly be if there is no ATM machine along the paths. And is there electricity? What was Lucy wearing when she disappeared? A hat? We need poetry that makes its music from the uninhibited pixies of our pixilated world so that it can lead us to a stratospheric dance. A poet should be a one-man Hubble telescope, not a vexatious crank turning himself inside out. *Her*self. One-*person* Hubble. I fail to see the necessary gravitas.

*Yellow Hat*: Gravitas? Listen. This poet envisions a black-and-white world, filled with visceral emptiness. We mourn for the fresh-smelling Lucy Ricardo, violet-tinted Lucy, bathed in Dove. "She lived unknown, and few could know . . ." An imaginative reader delights in a lovely vision of Lucy and Ethel headed downstream, but is also aware of the saddened, emasculated yet still narcissistic Desi, standing with raised hands beside pot-bellied Fred and bawling, "Lucy!"

*Blue Hat*: If you're going to infer Fred Mertz from a poem, it is going to need more concrete details, but I will grant the multicultural aspect—Lucy plus Cuban. More specifically, Lucille Esmerelda McGillicuddy Ricardo. An A for trying.

*Yellow Hat*: Details. The success in this poem lives in what is *not* said. There are hints of terror and a bit of relief. One smells a cigar being lit, and then put out too soon. Most American poems having to do with Lucy's legacy fail to address the universal problem of mouse-brown roots and the fact that no comedienne could genuinely fill Lucy's shoes.

*Blue Hat*: I must be going insane.

*Chase*: Ladies, stop this. Allow me to interject. Could you each address the music of this poem? Does it sing? Or does it warble, off-key?

*Blue Hat*: The silly rhyme scheme is a-b-a-b. Oh, please. And the meter is simply old-fashioned iambic tetrameters alternating with trimeters. It's greeting-card meter—the same as the meter of "The Rime of the Ancient Mariner," for fuck's sake. The Anglo-Saxon hemistich b-b-b-c stresses of a rap song would be more modern than this antiquated, petrified heartbeat. I don't hear real music here, for there is nothing at stake.

*Yellow Hat*: But the lines are melodious! The rhyme scheme is like a pulse; it dribbles our heart's pant-o-meter. And I do feel that there is a lot at stake. A red-headed kook named Lucy is dead but still causing trouble. We're looking at a poem bravely skydiving before heading into unwieldy adult diapers. Few poems are willing to tiptoe into that place of stillness. Few would dare to hint at the word *morte,* or Mertz, with anything like conviction.

*Blue Hat*: A poem so obscure and vague can mean anything you want it to mean. Our poets should use the textures of our own time—our techno wars, our steroidal sports team, and our creative obsession with heart-smart fats—to create globs of profundity. Poems are artful literary truffles.

*Chase*: And now we come to the part of the program where we reveal the Trick, the McGuffin, if you will. The poem submitted to us by Ms. Lily Larkin, sewage maven of Boise, is not a poem of her own devising. It is, rather, the timeless poem, one of the Lucy series, written by the venerable William Wordsworth, in the early nineteenth century. Thank you, Ms. Larkin, for playing Trick the Critic, and thank you, guests in hats, for chancing humiliation, and thank you, lovely audience, for tuning in. Next week we will pick on Walt Whitman. Send us your favorite Whitman song of himself, and we will probe his body electric.

## XV

# Dancing

*I'm fascinated by stories that go back and forth in time and place. Characters retell their stories to themselves, reshaping episodes in light of new information. Characters who try to puzzle out where they have been and what their lives have come to are always on the verge of something. Regret and hope ride in tandem, a jaunty couple on the road to transformation.*

—BAM

# Quinceañera

Featured in *Good Housekeeping*, July 2013

The rented hall had a flat, gray, dense carpet and a bandstand that seemed too large for the room. The mariachi band had only six musicians, and the trumpet player drowned out the violinist. Bob had inserted his ear plugs before leaving the car. Margo walked ahead of him, stylish in stilettos and a swirly black skirt.

He and Margo sat at the head table, on a dais, in a row with their friends John and Dee. Miguel was their mutual yard man, and Miguel's daughter was now fifteen. This was her quinceañera. Wearing a giant pink Civil War dress, she floated around the room, greeting guests and smiling through her glowing pink braces.

"She's lovely," Margo murmured to Dee. Or seemed to murmur. Bob's hearing was a wall of fuzz and noise.

A knockout, Bob and John telegraphed to each other with their eyes. The girl standing next to her wore a shimmering tight dress that hiked up her butt with about a millimeter to spare. Several other barely dressed teenage girls strutted about the room, their long dark hair slinking with their sinuous bodies.

Bob took a deep breath and settled in his seat for the evening, content not to make conversation. Margo had insisted that they be here because their presence meant so much to Miguel. Bob agreed, although he disliked noisy social occasions. Margo liked going out, and he usually gave in because he felt guilty for being away so much on flights. He flew for UPS out of Louisville. Long hours of tense, uneventful piloting often made him crabby when he got home, but Margo would say, "Let's do something fun." Although they had met in the anonymous clubbing scene in L.A., when he was working as a flight instructor, Bob never thought clubbing was fun.

Here in her native Kentucky Margo had a large network of friends from her job in retail clothing, and she liked to plan event weekends with them. He didn't see the point of arbitrary social occasions that amounted to little more than shallow, forced pleasantries and a lot of driving. He would rather read a book. But he felt that a quinceañera was different. It was genuine.

Margo and Dee were watching some children playing with balloons in the center of the dance floor, but Bob and John were fixated on the teenage girls.

With a giddy grin of pride, Miguel brought a bottle of bourbon especially for the four guests on the dais. He had offered cans of Bud to the other tables.

"It is special," said Miguel. "Enjoy for me."

"Congratulations, my friend," John said, twisting open the bottle.

Bob had a six-o'clock flight to Stockholm the next morning, and he didn't want to get loopy here, so he opened a bottle of water for himself. Margo sipped a little of the bourbon from a plastic glass. He thought she would have preferred wine. But maybe he was wrong about that. She rarely confided in him anymore. He didn't know what she liked. A rift had opened between them in the last year or two. She said he never listened to her. He felt she was overly critical of him, so why listen?

The mariachi band, having played "La Bamba" and "La Cucuracha" and other obvious old songs, was touring the tables, taking a request at each.

"'Malagueña,' por favor," Margo said, when the band stopped in front of the dais of the four affluent bosses. She clapped her hands gleefully and her clunky gold jewelry glinted in the light.

The violinist reacted with animated delight, as if they had been asked to play something authentically Mexican—obscure and special. The musicians ripped into the song, playing with more energy than they had with "La Cucuracha" and the others. Why would a song about cockroaches be featured at a banquet anyway? Bob wondered. "Malagueña" was inspiring, varied, wild, and energetic, sounding tropical, historic, dangerous—and by turns lonesome and frenetic. The musicians were lost in their fervor, each soloist singing with eyes closed.

Bob was surprised that Margo knew this song. He wanted to talk to her about it later. Margo knew so much more music than he did. At her job the satellite radio played the world-music channel all day. Her iPod was a world of mystery.

He hated himself for thinking her gaudy baubles made her seem older. She would be thirty soon.

The high-priced mariachi band, hired by the hour, left the stage and a tattooed D.J. took over, cranking up the sound—the test of Bob's tolerance. With his earplugs, Bob felt he had a deficiency of sensation-sorting syndrome, or something like that. He couldn't distinguish words of conversation from background noise. All the talking around him flowed together. John, on his third plastic glass of bourbon, and Dee and Margo were having an uproarious discussion. They knew him well enough to leave him out in a noisy situation, which was fine with him. He could drift around like the girl in her billowy dress, paying attention to everyone and no one. "He's on auto-pilot," Margo sometimes explained to people when he tuned out. Once, she had said to him, in front of friends, "You may as well be flying to another planet." "Hauling freight to Mars," he replied.

Margo and Dee were on the edges of their chairs during the quinceañera ceremony. The girl's mother, Maria, and some other women set her down on a throne and pinned a tiara on her head. Then Miguel (in his cowboy shirt and ten-gallon hat) and Maria (tall in her silver heels) joined her. They removed the girl's shoes and set them aside. They took a pair of new shoes from a box—silver shoes with very high heels, stilts—and slipped them on her feet.

"Cinderella," Margo's lips said.

Miguel danced with his daughter around the room, her new shoes invisible beneath the dress. His cowboy boots expertly slipped beneath the hem of her dress without catching it. A skill a gardener would have, Bob thought, imagining a trowel. "Miguel is a treasure," Margo was always reminding him.

On the dance floor a dozen family members made a hand-linked circle around Miguel and his daughter. One by one they took turns dancing with the princess in her tiara and floating dress and new shoes. Three small wiggling children in the circle danced with her. When the dance finished, Maria brought her daughter a pink-frocked doll wrapped in cellophane like a gift basket. The girl accepted the doll, and with a giggly grin, she fumbled with the wrapping. She hugged the doll and held it in her arms like a baby. Then she began to dance with it, tilting and swaying in her new shoes. The lights dimmed and she danced with her doll—slowly, mournfully, lovingly, tearfully, in a farewell dance. Three times she circled the dance floor alone, lost in a reverie of childhood.

"That was so beautiful," Dee and Margo were saying to each other for five minutes afterwards.

John was killing the bottle of bourbon.

Bob said to Margo, in what he hoped was not a shout, "I'm going to get some air."

"The cake is next," Margo said. "Cake!" she screamed. Her lipstick had faded.

"I'll be back."

He left by the side exit and zipped through the parking lot, relieved to be out of the noise for a while. He had been moved by the fresh beauty of the dance, but he didn't know how to explain that to the others above the noise. The girl's mood fascinated him. She seemed to be acting an ancient role that she had been taught to play, but at the end she had flung the doll away and flopped down at a table with her gum-chewing chums.

The mariachi band was in the parking lot, loading their instruments into a van.

"Gracias, amigos!" Bob shouted. They shot back a stream of friendly Spanish.

"Your band is better than that noise," Bob said. He heard the thump of the amps shaking the building.

It wasn't dark yet, but he could see a slim sliver of the moon through the clouds, a soft silvery glow like a pale marble. He had always loved the moon and liked to keep track of its phases. Flying with a full moon rising made him feel like David Bowie's Major Tom, about to drift away.

He walked up an embankment behind the parking lot to the grounds of a pioneer fort built by the first settlers of Kentucky. Perhaps the fort nearby was only a reconstruction. He had never been here before. Probably he should pay more attention to local history. He didn't remember ever learning anything about Kentucky in California public school. Margo had dragged him to Kentucky five years ago because she was homesick in California, but he had never made an effort to fit in here.

He had gotten off on the wrong foot with her father because Bob refused to go hunting with him. And lately John had been urging him to go hunting with him. John wanted to bag some sandhill cranes. It was legal now. In a wildlife refuge once Bob had seen a pair of sandhill cranes perform a mating dance. The majestic male, in his plain gray plumage, hopped around the female in a circle, jumping up and down and flexing his wings as though he didn't want to take off without her.

Bob didn't want to shoot a beautiful bird down from the sky. He didn't want to fit in. He detested Bluegrass music. He didn't care about basketball. He didn't want to play dress-up. So many people went about in costumes. The orange-clad hunters. The Civil War re-enactors. The festival goers. The basketball fans in "true blue." He had to work in his mud-brown UPS outfit, and off-duty he never wanted to put on another costume of any kind.

Bob found himself in the pioneer cemetery. A plaque told him that there were about five hundred graves here, most marked by simple blank stones. "To the Wilderness Dead. Those without graves . . . unknell'd . . . uncoffin'd and unknown."

One stone stopped him abruptly—the grave of the first white child buried in Kentucky. Two years and two months old.

Another stone read "JANE."

He lingered, drawn by these slim clues to former lives. He would like to bring Margo here before they went home tonight, but he knew it wouldn't be her idea of fun. She was expecting him to dance. Still, he wished they could get through to each other, the way they used to when they were younger and silly—but so sincere. They were still young, but soon enough they would lie mute in the shadows of two stones. It was a far-fetched thought and he brushed it away.

He wandered through the cemetery, bounded by a low stone wall, then came to a white memorial stone at the opposite end. There he read in the fading light that the pioneer cemetery was dedicated in 1974 "by Neil Armstrong, astronaut pioneer to the moon. . . ."

Overcome, Bob had to sit down. He sat on the stone wall, his feet in the grass. He didn't believe in signs or omens, but he believed wholeheartedly in the power of coincidence. He felt profound pleasure that he, Bob, a flyer and moon lover, should stumble upon Neil Armstrong's presence here.

It didn't mean anything, but it was pleasing for all these similar things to come together in an unlikely way. He was glad to be sitting on this historic stone wall, at this point on the earth, in the moonlight, alongside the first settlers of Kentucky, with the ghostly footprints of the first man on the moon. And nearby a mariachi band and a gathering of Mexicans—pioneers too, crossing a border—were celebrating a girl who was entering her quinceañera, her flowering. In his enthusiasm, Bob jumped up, to go tell Margo.

# The Horsehair Ball Gown

Featured in the *Virginia Quarterly Review,* Spring 2013

On Thursdays, if the weather was pleasant, Isabella Smith drove her older sister, Maud, to Lexington to have lunch at Harvey's, the best place outside of Louisville to get a Kentucky Hot Brown. They liked the friendly old-time atmosphere, with its Venetian blinds and antique portraits of forgotten families, and although alcohol was on the menu, the restaurant was never rowdy. It was clean, and their usual waitress, Shannon, knew their preferences.

But they had not been to Harvey's for two weeks. An incident that had occurred there during their last visit was so unnerving that Maud was afraid to get in the car, even for the ritual delight of traveling to Lexington, which she said was like "going to heaven in house shoes." What had happened at Harvey's had Maud so nervous and confused that Isabella was increasingly distraught. At church, her mind wandered, replaying the perplexing incident, and Maud, sitting next to her, silently clasped her hand, as if they were riders on a Ferris wheel.

Maud was near ninety, and it was Isabella's duty to care for her, much as they had both cared for their mother in her declining years. When Isabella was a child, Maud had helped to take care of her, babying her and calling her "Little Bit." Isabella called Maud by the familiar term of affection, "Puss." They still used these names with each other. They were the sort of women who remained little girls around their mothers. They spoke childishly to their mother even while Maud was married to Mr. Burnham—for a tragically brief time. A heart attack felled him at the spring stock sales, and the surprise of it made Maud never trust love again.

Isabella herself, being unmarried, had led a life of tabbyhood—one of their mother's quainter terms. At seventy-four and climbing, she still refused age a place at the table and intended that no infirmity should strike her down. Maud was remarkably healthy, too, except for twisting her words around on occasion. She didn't dither over what she couldn't remember, and she still groomed herself impeccably as the gentlewoman she had always been. Isabella worried about her sister, though, for refusing medication. Maud had had twenty-four bladder stones once and didn't give a sign of discomfort. Ever since Maud found out that the "police-bows" the doctor prescribed were just sugar pills, a tricky experiment to see if her heart flutters would abate, she hadn't trusted any medication. She'd had anesthesia for her bladder surgery, but she declined to take the opiates and dopes afterwards. "Pain helper," as she called such medicine.

On the telephone now, one of their nieces, Louise, was fussing at Isabella. "Aunt Isabella, you get yourself back in that car and drive to Lexington."

"I don't know, Lou-Lou. I can't get Maud to go. I told her we could try some other eating place." Isabella steadied herself against the glass-fronted china cabinet, which had a wobbly foot.

"You know how much you love Harvey's, and I know how you love to drive that Lincoln Continental."

Isabella gazed at a line of dust on the wood trim of the cabinet.

Lou-Lou ignored Isabella's silence. She said, "I hate to bring this up, but I got concerned when I didn't get a note from you after Easter. Remember I brought you those two trays of sausage-twirls? Usually I hear from you first thing. Was something wrong with them?"

"Oh, Lou-Lou, I'm so sorry. I should have written you a thank-you note. I've lost my head."

"You don't have to apologize. I was just afraid—well, it wasn't like you."

"I didn't have my manners showing." Isabella paused to grope for an appropriate response. Impulsively, she said, "Those sausage-twirls were the best things. You are so good to us."

"Did you freeze one of the trays?"

"Oh, yes. We're really looking forward to having them for breakfast one of these Sundays."

Isabella had thrown both trays into the garbage. She had always hated Lou-Lou's sausage-twirls. They were made with pasty pop-open canned biscuits.

Lou-Lou said, "What if I pick you two up at six o'clock and we'll go eat at Long John Silver's?"

"I'm afraid it'll be too much for Maud. She's been disturbed since . . . since the incident. And I already had plans—I have some hose I need to wash out."

"I forgot—it's Tiptoe Day!"

On Wednesdays, the sisters had their hair done, and Lou-Lou always laughed at them for the way they tiptoed around, trying not to muss their hair. Maud wore a hairnet, but Isabella liked a modicum of bounce in her hair and refused to wear one. Maud had pointed out that Eleanor Roosevelt was on TV recently wearing a hairnet.

"What was Eleanor Roosevelt doing on television?" Isabella asked. "She's been dead for decades."

"It was an old film reel, without any color."

Now Isabella thought about her sister's hairnets wadded up in her drawer like little bundles of spiderwebs. They were too gossamery to wash. Her niece was saying, "Don't you worry about that man anymore."

Isabella cried, "Don't worry about that man? For heaven's sakes, Lou-Lou, I told you how upset Maud was!"

"You're so old-fashioned, both of you," said Lou-Lou. "But you're sweet to a fault."

Lou-Lou had some kind of job in the tall blue building in Lexington, and Isabella thought she acted as though she lived in an advanced civilization.

"Bring us some of that Better-than-Sex Cake next time," Isabella blurted out. She hadn't meant to say that. "It was so delicious."

After hanging up the telephone, she stooped to retrieve the matchbook that had become dislodged from under the shaky foot of the china cabinet. She squeezed it into place and tested the cabinet.

On that last visit to Harvey's, Isabella and Maud had been sitting at their favorite table, with the sunlight shooting through the slanted blinds. Maud said she was tired of Kentucky Hot Brown, and they had decided to split an order of ribs after Maud said she couldn't hold a whole order. Isabella asked for some extra slaw and beans. Shannon brought more yeast rolls, too, along with several napkins to sop up the grease from the ribs. She spoke cheerfully about her young son, who was in a special magnet school. After

Shannon left the table, Maud and Isabella had a discussion about whether she meant magnet or magnate. They didn't know if the child was deformed somehow or couldn't learn, perhaps, but it would be impolite to ask.

Near the end of the meal, as Shannon was freshening their iced tea, she said, "That gentleman in the corner has paid for y'all's lunch."

For a moment, Isabella couldn't imagine what she meant. "What gentleman?" Isabella looked to the corner to her right and then glanced behind her to the far corner, and all she saw was a black man drinking coffee.

Shannon gestured toward the man. Both sisters stared at him, then turned to each other. Maud murmured, "No, that can't be."

Isabella, embarrassed, said, "Tell him we don't want him to do that."

"But he already did it," said Shannon.

"Tell him he's not obliged," Isabella said. She spoke quietly, not wanting to make a scene.

"It's all right, ladies. He was just being nice," said Shannon, waving and smiling into the corner where the black man sat.

Maud muttered, "This isn't done." She had turned quite pale, Isabella noticed.

"Don't worry, Puss," said Isabella, reaching for her sister's hand.

"Mother would have a fit if she could hear such an idea." Their mother had always let the maid eat in the kitchen.

Shannon had vanished, and they were afraid to glance at the man again. Isabella opened a packet of sugar for Maud's tea, but Maud pushed her glass away. She was twisting her paper napkin nervously.

Isabella tried to finish her slaw and beans, but they had lost their savor.

Then the black man was standing beside their table.

"Ladies!" he said. "I've seen you here many times, and it's my pleasure to extend a little good feeling your way. My name is Herbert Brewster, and my mission is to spread joy and sunshine."

Isabella was afraid Maud was going to faint. She clutched the edge of the table, her knuckles white. She stared at her lap as the man continued to prattle and gab about spreading sunshine. His large dark shape, silhouetted by the sunlight, leaned toward them as if he might pounce. They shrank— ever so slightly—as his goodwill burbled forth. Isabella could not make out his features, but he wore a loden-green wool jacket and a seagreen turtle-neck. His hat, a derby style, was bobbing in his hands.

"I want to invite you to my church," he said. He laid a card on the table next to the salt shaker.

He placed his hat on his head, then quickly doffed it about two inches.

"God bless you, ladies," he said, and he strode away.

Shannon was there again, clearing the dishes. She said, "Oh, he's real nice. He comes in here all the time."

"We'll have to send him a thank-you note," said Isabella, staring at the card.

"I was too stupefied to utter a word," said Maud.

"Don't worry," said Shannon. "He's just a lonesome, sweet guy who wanted to do something nice. I hear he's a dynamite preacher."

As Isabella and her sister drove home, they chattered nervously, their talk running together like a monologue.

"Reckon what he wants with us?" . . . "Wonder *why* he paid for our ribs?" . . . "Did he think we couldn't afford a whole dinner apiece?" . . . "How shameful to give such an impression." . . . "What if he wants us to buy *his* dinner next time?"

Isabella almost slammed into a dog in the road.

"The nerve, inviting us to his church," said Maud, who still had her tattered paper napkin, which she had worried into the shape of a twist of tobacco.

"We don't have to go, do we?"

"Did he think he could buy us a dinner and get us to come to his church?"

"Maybe he feels it's his duty to feed widows and orphans," Isabella said. "You're the widow and I'm the orphan."

"I'm an orphan, too," said Maud, patting a platinum curl that had escaped her hair net.

Maud couldn't sleep that night, hurting from her arthritic hips and knees. Isabella had a bad night, too. When she heard Maud thrashing, Isabella brought her a glass of water and offered her some ibuprofen.

"No. And I don't want any of those police-bows either."

"How would you know which is which?"

"I'm not taking the chance."

The next morning at breakfast, Maud said, "Little Bit, I can't get my mind off of this. It carries me back to when Mother was alive, how she would get so distressed at any little thing. She could work something up in her mind and then it would take over."

"You're not that much like Mother." Isabella realized she sounded snappy.

"All the same, Mother wouldn't have stood for this."

Although Maud argued against sending a note, Isabella wrote to the preacher, a simple, proper thank-you on one of her floral, sachet-scented notes. Too late, it occurred to Isabella that he might interpret the fragrance incorrectly. The church was some sect Isabella had never heard of, the House of Glory on Harrodsburg Road.

Maud began having her little dizzy spells, and her stomach bothered her. She stayed in bed for two days, eating broth and boiled custard until her digestion improved. Although usually patient, Isabella was growing irritated by her sister's behavior. She was tired of not being able to watch the news. Maud had refused to have the news on since Obama had been elected president. Sometimes Isabella stayed up to watch the eleven o'clock news, with the sound barely a whisper, and she got goose bumps at the sight of the President.

Maud, who had slept unusually late, seemed agitated the next morning when Isabella brought her breakfast on a tray. A little sigh and a groan escaped as Maud twisted in the bed to sit upright.

"Did you have bad dreams, Puss?" Isabella asked.

Maud nibbled a triangle of toast and sipped her coffee. Isabella stood by her sister's bed, listening to her tell about her dreams.

"We were all in a wedding, and then it rained and all of a sudden we couldn't get across a creek that was flooded, and Mother said, 'Hold on! Hold on!' Oh, it was dreadful, and Gisela was on the other side, but she got washed away, like a big washtub floating away."

"Gisela!" Isabella hadn't uttered Gisela's name aloud in years. "Puss, why did you dream about Gisela?"

"It was her—holding her head up high and singing to beat the band!" Maud paused to reach for more toast from the tray.

"What happened then?"

"She was hanging around here. She wanted some scraps, and I said we didn't have any scraps. They were reserved for the dogs."

"How did she look?"

"She looked like a Gypsy. Long, tangly hair and a scarf."

Isabella remembered Gisela only vaguely and hardly ever thought about her.

Maud said, "She was a pitiful sight."

She wadded her napkin—the pale-peach linen napkin from their mother's absolute best breakfast set. Isabella had not meant to use that, it was so hard to iron. Now it had coffee stains on it. She lifted the tray and stood there with it, spoons akimbo.

"It was just a dream," she said. "Gisela wasn't here. She can't worm her way back in here. She won't bother us." Isabella tried to comfort her sister, assuring her that Gisela wouldn't be returning. They didn't have to worry.

But Maud began to weep. "I haven't seen Gisela in over sixty years," she said. "We don't know if she's dead or alive."

With the tray shaking, Isabella retreated into the kitchen, her heart pounding. Her sister had dreamed about Gisela, of all people. The family had lost contact with her decades before, when she was only nineteen.

"I always hated that," Maud called out. "I lost Mr. Burnham and I lost my sister."

Isabella was afraid to hear any more. She didn't know why Maud should suddenly be wrought up about Gisela, after all this time.

While washing the breakfast things, Isabella accidentally broke a coffee cup. She had never liked the Blue Willow pattern, but it was Maud's favorite. She fished the pieces out of the sudsy water and gratefully flung them into the garbage pail. In the laundry room, she hunted for something to remove the coffee stains from the peach napkin, but she forgot what she was looking for. She didn't know what to do next. It seemed as though she had a list of important matters to take care of, but she kept losing it.

She sat rigid for a long time, with the memory of Gisela raging through her mind like a fresh blaze.

Maud was sleeping. As quietly as she could, Isabella hauled the step-ladder into the dining room and stepped up to the third step, holding on to some molding, until she could reach a high cupboard, where some boxes of pictures had been stored. Balanced precariously, she lowered several of the dusty boxes onto the table. They were filled with several decades' worth of postcards, greeting cards, and snapshots. She rummaged through the boxes, not allowing herself to become distracted by the bygone messages, until she found a solitary photograph nesting in a glove box beneath a sheaf of postcards.

The girl in the picture was young and fair, with curled bangs and flipped hair—not a beauty, but someone whose rebellious air always attracted attention. Isabella could recall the amusement Gisela had generated. With her careless laugh, she seemed to encourage disapproval. In the picture she was wearing a big hoop skirt with a strapless bodice. Her bare shoulders were bony and shiny. Isabella remembered little about her sister, but she recalled the dress quite well. It was the horsehair ball gown, a gift from overseas, from a cousin who had toured Europe. It was foreign, a style not worn here. The cousin had sent it to her as an amusement, knowing it was outlandish, but Gisela loved it and paid no attention to the sneers it elicited. Gisela's features in the photograph were unclear, but the dress stood out like a haystack, which it resembled. Isabella remembered the gown's stiff texture—the loose, lacy weave shot with gold and the black taffeta undercoat. It was round and bouncy, large enough for a small child like Isabella to hide beneath. Gisela was determined to wear it to the Harvest Ball, but their parents disapproved of the strange garment. Isabella could remember her mother saying, "Horsehair is so dirty. Who could wear such a thing?"

"You have a fur coat yourself," Gisela said. "You can't say muskrats aren't dirty!"

"Young lady, don't you talk back to me!" Mother cried. "And it's not muskrat. It's mink!"

The Harvest Ball was on the last weekend of October, while their mother lay ill with a seasonal complaint at their grandmother's and their father was away in Lexington at a tobacco sales meeting. Isabella, too young to go to the ball, had stayed at home with two garrulous aunts who played gin rummy and whooped and sipped gin. It was her impression that gin was sinful, because her father was in the bourbon business. The aunts, she recalled now, told her to keep quiet and do as she was told and to study her Bible verses. "You're a good little girl, Little Bit," they said, as if they were speaking to the cat.

When Father came home the next day, he demanded to know if Gisela had worn that damnable dress to the dance. Gisela, lying, denied wearing the horsehair gown, and Isabella, who had seen her sister pirouetting in the dress before dashing out to the ball, sided with her. But when Maud came in, she told Father that Gisela had indeed worn the disreputable horsehair ball gown.

A day passed, during which Isabella's lie seared her conscience like a coin burning a hole in her pocket with its desire to be spent. Gisela had slipped away from the house—for a rendezvous with her young man of the moment—without even thanking Isabella for her loyalty. Maud, who had spent the afternoon at the Burnhams, admonished Isabella for her lie. Her enthusiastic report about the Burnhams' Thoroughbred yearlings seemed to diminish the significance of Gisela's behavior. Maud urged Isabella to confess her lie. "Father doesn't know which of us to believe," she said.

Isabella found him in his "counting house," the mahogany-paneled room where he calculated his tobacco and whiskey profits. She felt that she was being a good girl, but she was trembling while he leaned over her, annihilating her with his shadow as she confessed. "Remember, your reputation is your fortune," he said, as he caressed his gold watch absently. "Good girl," he said like an afterthought as he dismissed her with a pat on the head.

It had never occurred to Isabella that after all these years, Maud still anguished over their missing sister. Maud's dream of Gisela washing away in the flooded creek gripped Isabella's own mind, and she could hear Maud still sobbing. Thinking that Maud needed a tonic of sassafras tea, Isabella set the teakettle on its hob. She had dug some fresh root. Even though sassafras had been discovered in recent years to be a poison, she did not believe it was unhealthy. Sassafras, which her grandmother used to call "sass'ras," had always served them well as a spring tonic.

While waiting for the water to boil, she shuffled through some more of the old snapshots. She paused over a few poses of Gisela and Maud together. Her sisters, wearing similar drop-waisted frocks and cloches, appeared relaxed, smiling at each other, sharing some secret—a sisterly love that excluded Isabella, who was still little. And in another set of snapshots, there was Isabella, in her prim pinafore and bonnet—a goody-goody child who was jealous of her big sisters! She hadn't seen herself that way before, but now she observed her priggishly superior countenance—a spitefulness that suddenly evoked her father in a way that made her shudder.

She had lied to her father, and she had confessed, and she had been forgiven. Then later that night she had witnessed her father with Gisela in the foyer when she returned after midnight. Isabella could see them from the dining room. Armed with the truth, he greeted Gisela and held it in her face, swinging it like a lantern to illuminate her sin. She had turned out wild, he said. She had disgraced herself and the whole family by wearing the nasty dress to the Harvest Ball, and she had disgraced them all further by her behavior with a Mr. Pettigrew. The family could not abide her indiscretions. He went on and on, his face puffed and crimson. Isabella remembered Gisela saying, almost calmly—as if she were saying, "Pass the butter, please"—"I'll run off and never come back again." And she left. She departed with Mr. Pettigrew, a ferret-like little man, for Joplin, Missouri, and points beyond. She wrote home, but no one answered her letters, and eventually she stopped writing. Her last letter was from California.

Isabella had always felt justified that her confession had helped push her wayward, disobedient sister out of the family. But now the tears that began flowing down her face were for that lost sister, for whom she had never before shed a tear, and for her sister Maud, who had suffered the loss without complaint. Isabella, eight years old, had believed she was being good. She hadn't let herself care about Gisela. She had confessed to her father, whose mistreatment of Gisela was only one of his crimes. He had been a dirt farmer who forgot his raising. His children should have been brought up in a hillside tobacco patch, hoeing and gleaning like people in French landscapes, Isabella thought; but Silas Smith had had aspirations, marrying a lady from the horse-and-bourbon country and angling his way into the gentry with his artful real-estate ventures. Eventually he owned tobacco land in Cuba, and on that he claimed his fortune. There was really little fortune, and he was dispossessed of it during the revolution, but he denied his loss, still handing out fine cigars to business associates as if his wife had just had another baby. Again and again, those cigars appeared, and, she thought now, they may not have even been Cuban, but only show cigars, devised for the occasion.

But Maud had always upheld his deceptions. Isabella was shocked by the vehemence she suddenly felt rising from her closed heart. She hated her father and resented Maud for complicity in Gisela's exile. It was Maud's own fault that Gisela had run away. She had told on Gisela when she should have lied as Isabella did. Instead, Gisela had been driven away, and Isabella had been bound to Maud in a little teacup-and-doily world ever since Maud's Mr. Burnham died. She and Maud had never been anywhere and they didn't know the world. Isabella felt she should have been like Gisela and run away! Instead, she had been tied down, tiptoeing around Maud all these years.

The teakettle blew, and Isabella angrily splashed boiling water over some splints of sassafras root bark to steep. She selected another Blue Willow cup for Maud. It clattered in its saucer on the tray but did not break. The Reverend Brewster's House of Glory card caught her eye. It lay on the secretary desk like a butterfly that had drifted in. When the black man had appeared at their table, his presence a dark silhouette like something jumping out of the shadows, it was as though a slit had opened into the past, where there was more sorrow than she could grasp.

Maud was calling her, and Isabella rushed in to assure her that she was near and that the tea was brewing.

But she would save the surprise she had for her. She was going to invite Brother Brewster to visit. She would not write another sachet notecard. She would select a different card, one bolder and more colorful. She turned back for the tray, the words forming in her mind already. *Brother Brewster, please come to visit and to pray over my ailing sister, who is troubled in mind and has a lot to answer for. There will be tea.*

# XVI

# Flash Fiction

*After exploring the past in the memoir* Clear Springs *and the novels* Feather Crowns *and* The Girl in the Blue Beret, *I wanted to settle down in the twenty-first century. It was a time shift.*

*In fiction of the eighties the popular use of the present tense offered the immediacy of watching movies. The writer seemed not to know what was going to happen any more than the reader did. I might note that in the present tense, making progress from A to B, or from one room to another, is a challenge. It is tricky for the writer, immersed in the moment, to skip ahead a year, or even an afternoon.*

*Now, in the throes of attention deficit, we may experience a different kind of immediacy—the sudden splash of light or explosion, a flash of dynamite, a flashlight in a dark corner. I've never found poetry to be suitable for my sensibility, but flash fiction, what might have once been called prose poetry, is appealing, and in the last few years I have dabbled with this form.*

*Ideally flash fiction attempts to be a poem that reads like fiction, or a story that has the intensity of a poem. Flash seems quick and easy, but it should be penetrating and difficult to shake loose. There are no precise definitions, and the form lends itself to experimentation and often absurdity.*

—BAM

# Corn-Dog

Featured in the online journal *New World Writing,*
Spring 2014

Here he is—unmarried, fat, with few cravings, stuck in a stucco house waiting for parcels to arrive by UPS, waiting for anything to come out of the blue. Anything would be welcome—bill collectors, laryngitis, UFOs. But a letter from Laura would be nice. He really wants nothing else. On the sidewalk a neighbor walks her mutt, which resembles a carnival corn-dog. He saw a dog like that on *Animal Planet.* The necks of the neighbor and her corn-dog stretch similarly toward their mutual goal, the curb. She wears creased shorts that end just above her less than thrilling knees. Her hair is wispy, frothy, like something from a French bakery.

The disgruntled old guy with asthma struts by with his fuzzy Standard Poodle. He imagines this old guy with a whiny wife who tries to make him eat goat cheese and arugula. The old guy must sing "Hallelujah" when he is out the door with the Standard Poodle. They march down the sidewalk, ready to spank any corn-dog that crosses their path.

A wasp has sneaked into the stucco house. Trying to shoo it away, he is stung between two digits, and a welt arises. He doesn't flinch. He stares at the sting stoically. He is stoic in his stucco house. Since Laura left he feels nothing but her absence. Yet now he searches for some sticky gunk to soothe his finger, for the wasp sting is not fake. It is a true wasp sting, and he feels it. The salve on his finger is like mustard spreading on a light crispy crust.

# The Canyon Where the Coyotes Live

Featured in the online journal *New World Writing,*
Spring 2014

She lives near a canyon with four cats. The Post-it notes on the bulletin board keep track of the cats—their special needs, the diets, the vet appointments, little notes about their charming pranks and romps.

Yesterday she recorded Annie chirping at a snail. Normally Annie chirps at the sparrows who bathe in a bowl outside the large window.

Billy chirped at an invisible fly. He was leaping high into the air, reaching and chattering. Carrie and Davy have other hobbies—spiders and tiny furry fake mice, respectively.

The cats do not go outside because of the canyon where the coyotes live.

There is a husband around the house, too.

"That sounds like a children's book," he says. "*The Canyon Where the Coyotes Live,* something written to scare children."

"But stories like that make them laugh," she says.

If there were children, she thinks.

She would love to see the cats play outside, but the coyotes from the canyon come forth at night. Even in the daytime coyotes have been sighted. It would be delightful to see the cats on the patio stalking the sparrows, where the coyotes come to stalk the cats. It would be even more delightful to see a toddler pulling a cat's tail.

"Everything's gotta eat," he says, closing the refrigerator door. "Including me," he says.

"Have a Pop-Tart," she says.

"Pop-Tarts are for kids. Why do we have Pop-Tarts?"

Exactly.

He works late shifts in the bottling industry. Often when he comes in late in the night he tells of a coyote crossing the road or an animal he can't identify that always must be a bear or a cougar.

In the night while he is gone the sounds are magnified, and the howling coyotes seem to be at the back door but may be across the canyon. She hears the cat at the scratching post, the *click click click* of the door lock when he returns—if it is him and not some mugger who has commandeered his car and made him drive home at gunpoint.

Yesterday he said to her, "Don't you see how nuts you're becoming? Everything is fraught with terror and apocalypse with you!"

"Fraught? I'm fraught with nothing." Empty. Flat-bellied.

"You're afraid to let the cats outside because of the coyotes. If there weren't any coyotes you'd find something else to be afraid of."

"They would get killed on the road."

"Right. See what I mean?"

"It's better for cats to stay indoors. They live longer."

The Pop-Tart is like limp pasteboard. He eyes it ruefully, then her.

"Furthermore," he says. "We are lucky we don't have any kids. I see how you would be with them."

She snatches the Pop-Tart from his hand. "I'll make lunch," she says.

She makes a salad with artichoke hearts and palm hearts. Her own heart could be the centerpiece, ripped out and posed on a platter like the head of John the Baptist. There is nothing to do but dance.

# Car Wash

Featured in the online journal *New World Writing*, Fall 2014

Hi, Betsy,

Got here on Tuesday and had a job by sundown! They say the economy is in the ditch, but I'm just a lucky guy, I guess. I'm not pushy, but I can speak up for myself. I hit just the right balance.

The job is at a service station with a car wash. It's kind of upscale where people leave their cars to be cleaned. And they mean *clean*. There is a fancy waiting room with trays of cookies and cold drinks free. Little cubicles with TVs, La-Z-Boys. These are rich people, who don't need free snacks, and some of them are so rich they don't even bring in their own cars. Their "people" bring them, I never knew this but if you are a movie star out here you don't have to get your own gas or a lube job or anything. Someone does all that for them. I guess if you're famous you don't want to be seen pumping gas or doing anything ordinary. They must think they live in a sort of heaven where they eat things with ginger and seaweed and can take a dump in the shag carpet if they've a mind to and somebody else will clean it up. Their people won't tell who they are working for either, so we do a lot of speculating. Wednesday there was a vintage Corvette that belonged to George Clooney—and it was true because there was a book on the seat with his name written in it.

Yesterday I had to clean out a car that smelled like puke. No real mystery there, the way these people binge, or so I'm told. I had to use four rounds of deodorizer on the carpets in that car. The leather upholstery wasn't ruined, but it was borderline. Of course they can just have that replaced, or buy a new car.

Today I cleaned out a glob of something chewy that had to be cut out of the carpet. I felt like a surgeon, trying to cut the fibers of the carpet so it wouldn't show. I'm sure this is a skill that will be useful in a better job. I got the damned chewy stuff under my fingernails and had to use industrial solvent to get it out.

But I like this job so far. Most of the other employees are Mexican and I wish I had paid attention in Miss Garrity's Spanish class, but I can say *amigo* and that goes a long way.

I'm sorry I left in such a hurry, but I hope you change your mind and come out here. You know I didn't mean to slap you that way. I just get carried away sometimes, I know we could have us a fine time out here. I don't see any way but up.

Love,<br>Mark

P.S. I wrote this yesterday but haven't mailed it yet. I don't know where the post office is. This morning I had to clean up a car that had blood in it. The guy who brought it in said he had to deliver his sister's baby himself on the side of a busy freeway, and he had to cut the umbilical cord with his hunting knife. He talked like he was a big hero. He said she would have died if he hadn't been prepared. Like some pimply Boy Scout, I reckon. That was the guy's story, but it sounded fishy. You never know what really happened when people are telling you things out here. So much out here is just stories.

# Cumberbatch

Featured in the online journal *New World Writing*,
Spring 2014

"The Giant Pacific Octopus starts out as plankton, microscopic at first. Then it is the size of a grain of rice." *The schoolchildren sitting at my feet are disbelieving. Shrugs, but no astonishment.*

"This octopus is named Cumberbatch. He weighs thirty-two pounds and is not full grown. The Giant Octopus often weighs up to a hundred pounds. Right now you see him tucked into a slit in this rock. He can squeeze his body into tiny openings, like this soup can." *The soup can I am holding is open on both ends—a virtual vagina. I feel a little spin down there.*

"Listen carefully, kids. Be quiet. The octopus has three hearts. The extras are for oxygenating blood." *My blood rushes when I think of my ex-lover. If I had three hearts, perhaps I would have a spare, one that is not broken.*

"Cumberbatch can open child-proof medicine bottles and screw-top jars. He is smart as a cat. An octopus has a superior sense of taste, with taste sensors all over the body. Imagine that you could taste everything you touched. The bathroom floor. The driveway." *I tasted his liquid but I sneezed and it went up my nose and that gave me the giggles. What I would give to have that moment again! My worldly possessions? My precious cat?*

"Sometimes we put his food inside a Mr. Potato Head or other toy for stimulation and to keep him from being bored." *I was never bored. We had toys. He brought me lovely, velvety, rubbery toys, wiggly toys. I like this texture. I really do!*

"Children, do octopuses have tentacles or arms?"

"Octopi," says a kid, who is maybe fourteen.

"Smarty," says another kid.

"No, they are octopuses, not octopi. That ending is Latin. Pus is from pod, the Greek, meaning foot, but are they called tentacles or feet or arms?"

The kid who said "smarty" is smirking. "Arms," he says.

"The octopus can change color to blend in with his surroundings." *When I was with him I turned color, blushing all over. He painted me with kisses and licks. Red dribbles of his red-zinger drink.*

"Octopuses don't live long. The octopus is a terminal breeder. When he nears the end of his life he is ready to mate. The female eats a lot while she is preparing to mate. The male inserts one of his arms into the hole on the side of her head. The arm has grown round and hard. It has changed shape, the suckers have stretched out and blended in. It is rigid and purposeful." *He thought I had an abortion. He thought he would never have to see me again. I bought a car with the money.*

"After inserting his spermatophore packet into her oviduct—it can be up to a meter long—the man octopus is spent and he dies."

*Oh.*

*A meter. A metaphor. A broken heart.*

"The mother accepts the spermatophore packet and she hides in her den, overloading on carbs. She waits a week before she punctures the packet and lets the sperm fertilize her eggs. She hangs her eggs on the ceiling of her den and cares for them. She sweeps them and aerates them for seven months. She stops eating during this brooding. After her eggs hatch, she has used so much energy that her body breaks down and she dies. She dies more quickly than the guy." *I am dying like the mama octopus brooding, fussing with her broom, sick with brooding, sick with thinking and wishing. Dying. A terminal breeder.*

A small pigtailed girl is asking, "About the thing going into the hole in the head. Where does it go—into the ear?"

*No. Into the heart.*

# The Girl in Purple

Featured in the online journal *New Flash Fiction Review*,
Spring 2014

Near dawn, Dennis Moore saw the iron gate to the courtyard inch open
and the wisp of a girl squeeze through, clanging the gate behind her. Two
minutes later, on the boardwalk, she halted as if for an invisible dog, then
resumed her dog-walker gait. He followed her down this wooden walkway,
known as the Promenade. The surf, retreating as if pushed by the hurry-
ing sun, murmured and slurped. The girl, he could see now, was dressed
in purple, and she wore a thick long scarf twisted in an elaborate slip-knot
around her throat.

His thoughts wandered. The Auguste Macke poster of "Promenade
1913" above his mantel. Andy Kaufman wrestling women in the videos he
had watched. Lisbeth Salander with the dragon tattoo. The nutrition facts
on the back of the granola bar in his pocket.

The girl in purple was coughing. She paused on the Promenade and
coughed repeatedly. Something had gone down the wrong way. He knew
the feeling.

This was the right moment to grab her, but he felt dizzy and sluggish.
He had to concentrate. She was lighting a cigarette, cupping it from the
beach breeze. He saw that her scarf was a tartan. He thought of Scotch
tape. Quietly, he tiptoed behind her along the bare boards. When Mark
Twain steered the riverboat around the bend where the Mississippi meets
the Ohio, he had to proceed very carefully. But he dumped Huck and Jim
there on a flimsy raft in those dangerous waters where Illinois, Missouri,
and Kentucky come together to shake hands. Now Dennis Moore had to
go very carefully, pitty-pat. He could not stop himself now. This time he
would do it.

A light bulb lit in his head. Fuck hen. Until this moment the spooner-ism of Huck Finn had never occurred to him. That old jokester, Twain, was probably still laughing, wherever he was. The granola bar would taste good right now. Pay attention! She coughed again. The scarf was many shades of purple flashing in the sudden sunrise.

# The State Pen

Featured in *Elm Leaves Journal,* Winter 2016

Sandra went with me to visit my boy at the state penitentiary, an unforgiving castle-like fortress with a splendid view of the lake from the cellblock. We were walking past the pleasant house outside the gates. It had a dog house inside a chain-link fence. The dog, a cute pug, was running around in the yard loose. And then I saw the kitten, who was meowing at the front door. The dog jumped up on the porch and the kitten playfully chased it off. I was thinking how sad it was that they had to live next to the pen. And then I saw the little girl open the door and call her pets inside.

"That could be me," Sandra said. "When I was growing up in that house. We moved away when I was fourteen."

"Weren't you afraid to live next to the pen? Weren't your parents afraid to bring up children so close to the worst mess of hardened criminals in the state?"

"Honey, my parents knew one thing for sure—if one of those guys busted loose, he wasn't going to tarry. He wasn't going to come to our house and ask for a sandwich and a change of clothes. He was gone."

"So you weren't afraid."

"Oh, no. We played in the yard on the grass. We would peek through the wire and watch them do their exercises. There were some mean looking guys. There was one guy with a scar right down the middle of his face, top of his forehead, down the nose, down the middle of the lips and chin. A big slash. It was fascinating."

Sandra has a sweet nature and a sense of fairness, all maybe gained from growing up next to the pit of evil.

But they're not evil. I can't believe they are all evil. Some of them maybe. Not Kevin. Not my sweet boy. That trouble in California? He says it wasn't him. I believe him. It has been nothing but agony and despair from the beginning, from the first news of his arrest to the time they locked him up here. I should be grateful they brought him back here, close to home. I can visit him. I can lay eyes on him.

"They still used the electric chair when I was growing up here," Sandra was saying. "Sometimes if I stayed up late—and I did on the scheduled executions, they couldn't stop me—the lights would flicker around midnight. I knew what was happening, but my parents never said a word."

I was gazing into eternity when suddenly I saw another kitten shoot across the grass and leap onto the porch.

# Falling

Featured in the online journal *New World Writing*, Fall 2014

## 1 Synopsis of My Day

George had a fitful night, the nurse said on the phone. Surgery scheduled for nine a.m. Frantic about getting to hospital in time. First: I zipped Squirrelly Girl over to the groomer—her spring molt. It took a month to get the appointment so I didn't want to cancel. Had to leave her there for the day.

Waited for Shelby to arrive. She can't manage dogs and vacuum cleaner at same time so I had to leave four dogs outside with storms forecast.

Walked Bootsy and shut her in laundry room for the day so Schotze wouldn't bother her.

Tractor Guy called about picking up lawn tractor for repair. No, don't know where key is.

Rain and storms.

Dropped Kookie at the Cat Clinic on the way to hospital. She was very dehydrated. George always gave her IV fluids. I cannot even get the cap off the needle.

Yesterday, when George lay unconscious on the deck the dogs did not jump on him. They circled and kept barking. They howled when they heard the siren. I fastened them indoors and they were afraid.

Downpour and thrashing windshield wipers. Traffic, hellish circling in parking garage, shuttle to hospital.

Reached hospital just as George was arriving in his room from recovery. Asking for crackers.

Could have been far worse, a cheery nurse said. She said there was a rod in the leg. Another nurse said it was a plate with sixteen screws.

A third nurse said, "Third ladder fall I've seen in two weeks."

No sign of a doctor.

Loved the new hospital. Wanted to move in. Charming guest nook with daybed, desk, Internet.

"There were helicopters outside the window all night," said George.

When he fell asleep at four something I left to get Kookie.

Met with vet about Kookie and arranged drop-off for fluids again tomorrow and Sunday. $325 today for blood tests, etc.

Took Kookie home. Driving rain.

Went to get Squirrelly Girl. All pretty and fluffy.

Talked with groomer about the dog's paw—the limp from her last fight with Schotze. Groomer suspects a "joint mouse."

Home with Squirrelly Girl.

Fed everybody. The dogs wouldn't eat. Kept looking for George. I ate a bowl of soup and fell asleep. Woke up several times, hearing that ladder slide and thump once more. I woke up too early.

The moon was a little grin in the dawn.

## 2 AT HOME

I bought George a luxury recliner to coddle his hurt leg. It raises your feet higher than your heart. Your head flips back and your feet aim for the stars. Your torso remains perpendicular to your legs, as if you were sitting. It's the astronaut position. Whoopee, but can he sleep in it, with a broken leg?

I ordered this over the phone and got the store to agree to a two-week trial, since I was buying it sight unseen. It is a floor model, 35 percent off. Bargain.

The store manager brought it himself. He and his burly man unpacked the chair and showed me the chair's tricks. The astronaut position is supposed to take the pressure off of every square inch of your body. I keep wondering how you calculate the surface area of your body in square inches.

The chair uses backup batteries in case of power failure. But it didn't come with batteries. Would anyone ever expect batteries? George was afraid the electricity would go off during the storms last night and he would be stranded in take-off position on the launch pad. I fetched the 9-volt batteries from town.

I fetch everything now.

Here comes the hard part. You send the chair, on its own, into astronaut take-off position. Then you find the little receptacle with a wee plastic door where the leads for the batteries are stored. To connect the batteries, I had to poke my head into a cave under the chair and, at an awkward angle, try to fit the male part of each battery to the female part. But in my strained position I couldn't get them to make love. The sex parts failed to grab, so I couldn't press them together. I recently watched a pair of orangutans on TV grappling with this same problem, up in a tree.

I worry about trees. Last week I saw a dead tree with a jagged crack near the base. It could fall any moment, I thought, so I didn't go past. It fell within the day and brought down a live tree with it, and two or three other dead trees also toppled, encouraged by the crashes and thuds.

While I was studying the devastation I saw another dead tree tilted at an angle of about 50 degrees. I thought it was leaning on another tree for support, but as I inched closer I saw that the two trees were not touching at all. I backed away swiftly.

Storms in the night. The electricity flickered off momentarily, but the chair was untroubled. Dulled by oxycodone, George lolled in his easeful new electric chair, so far away from me, strung up like a man on a rack.

Rain, rain today. Momentary hail. Going out to look for the dead tree, to see if it has surrendered to the earth.

# XVII

# The Hot Seat: Interviews

*In interviews I rarely manage to say what I mean, or I don't realize until later what I meant to say or should have said. Writers, who may spend months and years fussing over words to get them just right, are somehow expected to talk off the top of their heads during interviews. It can be a greater challenge than writing a story or a novel, for it calls on skills the writer doesn't necessarily possess. One may be tongue-tied on the spot but later able to imagine carefree witticisms, brilliant comebacks. Roger Angell calls this condition "retardant Wildeanism."*

*Interviews I have done that manage to be informative or enlightening were conducted by superb, understanding interviewers. Here are a few.*

—BAM

# *BOMB* Magazine Interview

By Craig Gholson, Summer 1989

Craig Gholson: We're both from Western Kentucky, and I always refer to
it as the South. But I have friends, particularly ones that come from
further south, who pooh-pooh the notion of Kentucky as being of the
South. They talk about it like it's a plain stepsister. Is Kentucky of the
South to you?

Bobbie Ann Mason: It's a border state. I think the place we come from, the
Jackson Purchase, has a lot of history. And it seems to be more Southern than other parts of Kentucky.

CG: Your stories are rife with aphorisms and sayings particular to Western
Kentucky.

BAM: I get them from my mother.

CG: They're phrases I heard all throughout my childhood, like: "If 'ifs' and
'buts' was candy and nuts, we'd have Christmas every day." And: "It's
as ugly as homemade sin." I put the book down and laughed for five
minutes on that one. Do you use a notebook to keep these phrases? Do
you remember them? Or do you use them yourself?

BAM: No, I write them down in a notebook. My mother is always coming up with one. And she does it quite unselfconsciously. She'll come
out with some expression that either I've never heard before or remembered, or it's something I had forgotten and I'll whip out my notebook.
Or I'll say, "Now, what did you say? Say that again." And she'll protest
that she didn't know where it came from, and she wasn't even aware
that she said it. It's just so natural to her. And, of course, I then make
something out of it.

CG: So you go on these fact-finding missions.

BAM: (*laughter*) You might say that, but I happen to be there, anyway.

445

CG: I think one of the ironies presented in your work is that these older clichés have the ring of truth about them, and seem profound compared to the latter-day clichés that have replaced them. In "Hunktown," Debbie says, "We're always caught in one cliché or another." It almost seems as if one of the tragedies of modern life is that everything, including clichés, have been devalued, or marked down, or means less.

BAM: The nature of language is that metaphors die, and then they are just used unthinkingly, and they lose their meaning. But my mother's language, for example, seems fresh and new because it's so old that we've forgotten it, and she still uses it. And she usually can't explain to you the source of it. My father uses a lot of it, too. For example, our dog was very happy, so he was running around in figure eights, in circles. Daddy said that Oscar was "cuttin' didoes." Do you remember that one?

CG: No.

BAM: I guess it's D-I-D-O. Cutting didoes. I said, "What in the world does that mean? Where did you get that expression?" "Well, he's cuttin' didoes." "What does it mean?" "Well, it means he's happy." "But what does the expression come from?" And he said, "Well, it just means cuttin' didoes." (*laughter*)

CG: I think some of the most poignant passages in your work come when your characters make up facts. It's a kind of poetry of misinformation. For example, Joe, in "Memphis," tells his kids that marabou feathers come from the marabou bird, which is a cross between a caribou and a marigold. These are pure storytelling moments and they are some of the few moments when your characters really seem connected with one another and are really happy. But those moments are basically lies.

BAM: Lies?

CG: Yes, because they're nontruths. Is that a more cynical reading than you would intend?

BAM: I think so. I thought all people told their children stories and made up things. I don't know.

CG: That particular example just happened to be a father and child. There are other moments when adults do that amongst themselves, too.

BAM: Let me ask you something, since you come from that place. Do my stories seem depressing or bleak to you? Some people—usually people from quite far away from that world—think they are.

CG: I don't think of them as being bleak and depressing. They are, however, lives of middle-class hardship.

BAM: It seems like some people look at a story and think, "Well this is about a factory worker. How depressing." Or, "These people don't read books, they watch television. How depressing."

CG: Well, who only wants to read stories that confirm their own reality?

BAM: It seems to me that the reader, then, is judging in terms of his and her own experience and value judgments. Whereas I feel that in the world of my characters whether they read books or not is beside the point. Of course they don't read books, they're doing other things. And I don't feel that their lives are at all bleak or depressing. The factory worker, for example. If you work all day in a factory and you get a chance to go to Disney World and take your family, that's great. That's a big deal. And the same way with the shopping malls. A lot of sophisticated people find shopping malls and people who shop in shopping malls very depressing. But the thing about my characters that maybe others don't notice is that my characters don't actually have a shopping mall. They have to go all the way to Paducah. And people come to that mall from a hundred miles around because it has a certain strong presence.

CG: For me, those people have an immediacy to their lives that I, basically, don't have anymore. That's the way I read them. They have a different set of problems. However, one of the ways that I think that people may see the stories as depressing, is that a larger theme of your work is that the center doesn't hold anymore. Your characters constantly say, "I don't understand what's happening to people, the way they can't hold together anymore." In "Sorghum," Ed and Liz are getting their pictures taken in Wild West costumes, and the woman who runs the booth says, "Everybody gets a kick out of this, because it takes them back to a simpler time." And Ed says, "If there ever was such a time." Do you think that there ever was a simpler time?

BAM: No. I mean, yes and no. There is a lot of nostalgia abroad for a simpler time. And I think that simpler time was full of hardship. It didn't have the same set of problems as we have now. Basically, what I write about is how people are dealing with their relationships in the face of the phenomenal swirl of change going on in this world. And it's what we're all doing, all of the world. And it's very confusing and scary and hard for the center to hold, and hard to know where you belong and what's going to last. But, on the other hand, these characters are facing change and what they think of as progress, and they're getting a lot of advantages out of it, opportunities that their parents' generation didn't have. There's a lot of optimism and positive value coming out of this. I may find it more exciting than some of the characters do because they're the ones who have to go through it. For example, in the story "Memphis," Beverly is cutting loose from a marriage that no longer works. It's scary and confusing, and she's not sure what she's going to do or how she's going to make it. But in thinking about this, she's thinking about her parents' world, in which people stayed married whether they liked it or not. And nowadays they don't have to. There's a passage toward the end which has her thinking about how many choices we have these days. And she's seeing this in a very positive way; it means that she could do something with her life. And so it takes courage, and I have a lot of hope that she will make it through this chaotic time and make some sense of her life, and get beyond the trap that she was in. So, in that way, I'm very optimistic, and I feel that there's a lot of energy emanating from these characters, because they're not jaded. They're not really disillusioned yet. A lot of them are holding onto the tag end of the American Dream. So I'll go with them and see what they're doing and care about them, and hope that they have the courage to get through it and not turn cynical.

CG: One of the things your characters constantly struggle with is expression. Words seem to fail them. In "Hunktown," there's a line: "Debbie had her tubes tied rather than tell her husband in plain English to treat her better." There's this myth that has grown about the oral tradition in the South, about how storytelling has fed the fiction coming from the South. Your fiction seems to go contrary to that, and I've read something in which you talked about how nonverbal your father was. Or that he wasn't particularly loquacious. Do you think that that particular oral storytelling tradition is a myth of the South, or just wasn't pertinent in your particular case?

BAM: I really don't have any way of knowing. I think there must be a strain of reticence, especially among farm people, who don't see a lot of other people. This may be a cliché, coming out of the South, but the idea is that some people will say what they think, which means that those people are uninhibited and straightforward and not hypocritical. And then other people will put up a pretense, put on a front and be polite. But some people are bold enough to say what they think. And the character you just mentioned, Debbie, apparently didn't have the courage to say what she thought in her marriage.

CG: There's a lot of noise in your stories. Mainly it's from the television, like *M\*A\*S\*H* or MTV, or the radio, where you'll hear Bruce Springsteen or Michael Jackson. It's noise that once, in another age, probably would have just been in the background, or for entertainment. Now, however, it's a noise that has become louder both physically and emotionally. It's insistent and your characters use it to shape their values and to define their thoughts.

BAM: Well, if you take a story by, say, John Cheever, or somebody, if there was a TV set on in any of his stories—and I don't know that there ever was—it probably would be just background, something not very important. But in my characters' world, TV is very important. They spend a lot of time with it, and they care about it. They get a lot of information about the outside world from it.

CG: Yes, but I'm always surprised that the songs and TV episodes don't just collapse under the weight of all the content that your characters put onto them.

BAM: But there seems to be a difference between these stories in *Love Life* and where I'm headed now, and where the stories were in *Shiloh*. I think back then the characters were at home at night watching their favorite network shows, and the TV shows were very important, and they would never miss an episode of *M\*A\*S\*H* or whatever. But by now, they've gotten cable TV or satellite dishes, and there are too many channels to choose from. So TV actually has less importance in their lives in an odd way. And I think it throws them back on their own resources, or it makes them seek out other diversions. So I think people are out and about a lot more in the newer stories.

CG: What is it that you think that these things—TV and music—have replaced in these people's lives? What do you think would have been there before that was there?

BAM: I think you'd have to go back to about 1930, because we've had TV and radio constantly in our lives since then.

CG: And what do you think would be there?

BAM: (*pause*) I think the romantic view is that people would be telling stories and making their own music and having fellowship. The reality might be that people had to put up with each other a lot more. (*laughter*) I had a passage in *Spence + Lila* where Lila is remembering her childhood and how people sat around after supper. The uncle ruled everybody, and he did as he pleased. And the cousins bickered, and they had to do their work, like their ironing. They bickered, and there was no entertainment to do the work by. It was just each other and a very small world. I don't think that's so romantic. I'm sure it isn't all like that, but I don't think TV is the great destroyer that people want to think it is.

CG: In "Sorghum" Ed says to Liz, "It's a tradition, one of those things that's supposed to mean something." What do we end up doing with these lost traditions, these traditions that end up being a civilization's detritus?

BAM: I think that suggests that traditions lose their value. I never trusted holding onto traditions for the sake of tradition. I think I do look for value, and I don't like empty ritual. I don't like rituals for the sake of ritual, and I'm excited about things that are new and challenging, things that shatter the old ways. (*laughter*)

CG: An example of that would be in "Love Life," where Opal sneers at the tradition of the burial quilt that her niece, Jenny, wants to see so badly. A tradition unravels for one character, Opal, while another character, Jenny, reinvents the meaning of that very same tradition.

BAM: Yes, yes. The contest in that story is between Opal, who hadn't been much of anywhere and who hadn't broken out of that small world, but who had wanted to and had been too afraid to. And Jenny, who had broken out much more easily and then came back searching for her roots, as young people are wont to do at a certain age.

CG: And the burial quilt ends up serving a purpose. It unleashes all the feelings Jenny had about an old boyfriend who she lost track of, and found out had died. So the function of the burial quilt or its tradition, still, in a very oblique way, seems real.

BAM: Oh, yes. We can't get away from those basic processes in human life and nature: grieving and celebration, change, growth.

CG: Another way of asking this question would be to ask how many ways do you think the Old South can die? Or has it died, or will it ever?

BAM: Oh, dear, that's a real broad one. I've not been very knowledgeable about the really deep South. I don't know. I think the South is still very defensive. There's a line I have in "Love Life" where the real estate agent, Randy, says, "We're not as countrified down here now as people think." Southerners have always, since the Civil War, had this sense of inferiority and fear that Yankees aren't going to think that they're as up-to-date or as sophisticated. This image of being "country"—Southerners have had a terrible time with this. And you probably know yourself, in going North, how Southerners feel about their accent.

CG: Going back to when we were talking about characters that speak in a blunt language that cuts to the heart of things. A large preoccupation and a major source of tension in the stories is the way in which times have changed. Opal says: "Girls used to say they had the curse or they had a visitor. Nowadays, of course, they just say what they mean." But really saying what they mean still doesn't say it all. Yes, it's a more blunt way of saying it, but it still doesn't express all that it is and means.

BAM: I feel that my style derives from the language of farm life which is very practical and not decorative.

CG: It's a language of service and serviceableness.

BAM: And I hang onto that language, and polish it and care about each word, because I think that that style of language conveys an attitude that I want to get across, an attitude about the world that's not layered over with a veneer of polite society or Southern hospitality. And it's a class distinction. It's not the language of Southern hospitality, the upper classes. It is, for the most part, more direct and closer to what people think than sophisticated, polite ways of dealing with people. And it can be blunt and hard—painful.

CG: I'd like to talk about structure. The way I look at the structure of your stories is that they're centripetal; they spiral in. They seem, to me, to track their prey. They circle and circle, getting tighter and tighter. And they're usually moving in on a specific emotion or a specific image, and when that image or emotion gets stretched, taut, the stories end. Does that make sense to you?

BAM: I never heard of that.

CG: (*laughter*) How do you deal with structure? Do you have a structure that you go by? Is it instinctual?

BAM: It's instinctual. I never map it out. It's what feels right. There's a movement to it, and it comes to a certain point and you leave it.

CG: In "Airwaves" there was a passage that illustrated how I think you structure stories: "It was that everything in her life is converging, narrowing, like a multitude of tiny lines trying to get through one pinhole. She imagines straightening out a rainbow and rolling it up in a tube." When I think about your stories, that's the motion I see in their structure.

Your stories generally do end in one image and it's usually an image of stasis or entropy. It's a moment, a pause, where things are about to change. They're suspended moments; moments of very uneasy equilibrium. One that comes to mind, even in its title, is "Residents and Transients." It ends: "I see a cat's flaming eyes coming up the lane to the house. One eye is green and one is red, like a traffic light. In a moment I realize that I am waiting for the light to change." Do you believe that there are resolutions in life? And, if so, what form do you think they take?

BAM: Students very often want to know why the stories never come to a complete end, why they're never wrapped up clearly. And I try to tell them they do come to an appropriate end, which is that they just place the image. And I point out that in life nothing's ever wrapped up for very long. So resolutions in life are evanescent. Life has that structure of sunrise, sunset; day, night. It goes through cycles and seasons. The times of life. So there is something very natural about movement and balance and change, but resolution—final resolution—I suppose that means death. Or of living happily ever after.

CG: Which is a form of death. Raymond Carver spoke about the "aftereffect image" of your stories. And I think this comes not only from the whole story itself, but from that one image that you end with. Do these images come to you and then you write towards them?

BAM: Usually not. It's usually in the process of writing that they burst out at the appropriate moment. It's so exciting when it happens. It's not that they're all that spontaneous, but sometimes it happens, and then I'll have to work on it to get it to feel just right. No, I don't usually work toward the end. I don't have the ending and write the story to fit it.

CG: One of the biggest sources of grief for your characters is when they somehow get above their raising, so to speak. Like in "Memphis," when Beverly calls Jim and Tammy Bakker the biggest phonies she ever saw, her mother says to her: "Do you think that you're better than everybody else, Beverly? That's what ruined your marriage—you're always judging everybody." This essentially is a writer's dilemma. Not that you judge everybody, but in the process of writing you have to pull away from them. You've spoken of yourself as being an exile. Have you become less connected to where you were born by focusing in on it?

BAM: No, I don't think so. I think I'd be much less connected if I had gone back to live in Kentucky. I think about it; I write about it. Lots of people move away from the South and don't look back, so they are cut adrift. The one thing that is paramount is my relationship to my place, to Kentucky, to my family. Being a writer, moving into the world of being a writer, into the literary world—I can't forget where I came from in the world. It's very important to me to still be who I am, to still be from Kentucky, to still be that person and not to become a Literary person, with a capital L. That makes me very uncomfortable.

CG: I think one of the real strengths of your stories is that you are infinitely compassionate to these people.

BAM: Well, they are my people. I'm part of them, and so I see myself implicated and reflected in their lives. So I can't become this Northern Literary person who looks back on them from some great distance and judges them.

CG: No, you really seem like you're among them.

BAM: But, yet, in order to write about them, I have to have a certain amount of distance. Just enough.

CG: This exchange is from "Sorghum." One character says: "I just feel like something's going to happen." And another character, Ed, says: "I always feel like I'm on the verge of something." A cynic might say that the truth is that these people are on the verge of nothing, or, at best, they're on the verge of just being on the verge.

BAM: Again, that's maybe somebody who's way, way outside and is very sophisticated and has been through it and knows that it might not amount to much. But my characters don't know that.

CG: What is it, do you think, that they think they're on the verge of?

BAM: Something about to change for the better.

CG: How do you think your first stories, the stories in *Shiloh*, differ from the latest ones in *Love Life?*

BAM: That remark I made about television describes one way I think they've gotten more complex. I hope they have. They seem more complicated to me, and I hope they're more mature artistically. I find the whole process of writing gets more and more complicated. The more I know about it, the harder it is to do. Because I think one's vision of things and how the story should be gets more complex. But the first draft of a story is just as clumsy and innocent and awful as it ever was. So the task gets harder, shaping it into something that matches your vision.

CG: For me, the newer stories are more specific and more complex in fewer words. There's more air in them. When I went back and looked at *Shiloh,* it's inundated with details. The atmosphere is much heavier than in *Love Life.* Another way I thought that they were different was that in "Shiloh" for example, Leroy says: "Nobody knows anything. The answers are always changing." In the later stories, it seems as if there are no answers, or the characters don't look for them as much. I don't know whether you think that's true or not.

BAM: I don't know. It's hard for me to really generalize about them as a whole. Things like that, I don't know where that comes from.

CG: You've said that the language of the place is the key. And in your stories, the wants and needs of the characters are very human and very general—what it takes to love and be loved. It's the details of the stories that make your stories specific. I think it was Flaubert who said that "God is in the details."

BAM: And Nabokov said: "The detail is all."

CG: Does this minutiae of life constantly prey on your mind? Do you make lists and keep notebooks to make things specific?

BAM: That's really the starting point for a story, and it's the raw material, and it's your access to the heart. When you stop to think about it, you don't really know many other people very well, very intimately, so if you see something you want to write about, if you see a person, you probably don't really know what's going on. And you have to use your imagination to get at them. So usually I find that physical details or description, observation, what's going on in the outside—those are clues about what's going on in the inside. And you have to use more imagination to get across what's going inside, because you don't have as much access to that.

"Midnight Magic" was prompted by a guy I saw one morning in a supermarket parking lot. He was in this blue car, hiked-up rear end. It had "Midnight Magic" painted on the rear and he was sitting in his car eating chocolate-covered donuts and chocolate milk, and he hadn't shaved, and he really looked like hell. And I wondered, "Who is this guy? What is his story?" So I just took it from there. My first paragraph is that description. And then because those physical details sparked my imagination, I was able to make up his story.

CG: What, to you, is the biggest misconception about your work? What really gets your goat?

BAM: I think it's attitudes that are elitist, or that come from people who may not have known people who watch television. (*laughter*) How should I say this?

CG: So it's people who think that these characters aren't worth writing about?

BAM: Yes. Who judge them in their own terms rather than in the characters' terms. And, you know, it may be my own failing that I don't present them fully enough, but I do think the reader should judge the characters in terms of their own, and in terms of the characters' context, and not in terms of their own context. So, in general, it's disparaging comments about these characters who watch television. The fact is that most people, most Americans, watch a lot of television. It's quite an ordinary thing to do. Some people fail to understand that TV has a role in other people's lives, and that they're not necessarily having their brains turned to mush; they're interrelating with it.

CG: For your characters, a lot of their hard news information comes from *60 Minutes* or *20/20,* shows like that.

BAM: I have a character in one of the *Shiloh* stories who finds a lump in her breast and has a mastectomy. I'm quite sure she wouldn't have found that lump in her breast before television. And she wouldn't have known what to do about it.

CG: What do your parents think about the stories?

BAM: Oh, they love them. They're really proud of them and get a kick out of them and think they're funny. And enjoy seeing the familiar, and they recognize a lot of the language and behavior.

CG: Yes, I think we all recognize those things whether we come from there or not.

# *Missouri Review* Interview

This interview was conducted by correspondence over a period of several months in 1997 by Jo Sapp and Evelyn Somers of the *Missouri Review* editorial staff.

MR: How did your background, growing up on a Kentucky dairy farm in the forties and fifties, contribute to your becoming a writer?

Mason: It was a somewhat isolated social setting, although we lived close enough to town that its pleasures and privileges seemed within easy reach. I suppose the desire to go to town helped make me ambitious, and the allure of the worlds that came in over the radio also helped. But the rewards of growing up on a farm were far greater in many ways than life in town. There is nothing that compares to the familiarity with natural detail: with knowing about grasshoppers, the anatomy of a leaf, the texture of high weeds, the color of a robin's egg.

MR: Is that part of the reason you returned to Kentucky, after living in the Northeast for a while?

Mason: I moved back to Kentucky eventually for family and cultural reasons. I'd returned to nature, so to speak, during graduate school, when I was writing my dissertation about the nature imagery in Nabokov's *Ada*. I moved to the country in Connecticut and planted my own garden then. Most of the time I was in the Northeast I lived in the country, and I think that helped me to discover my material for writing.

MR: So your home, the place you came from, and your interest in nature gave you a lot of material. Were there also ways in which these things gave you the motivation to write?

Mason: My motivation to write was complicated: for some reason, probably because I was the first-born, I was treated as special. I lived on the farm with my parents and grandparents. I had no playmates as a young

457

child, and I was indulged. I helped my grandmother piece quilts, and we made pretty albums, an old-fashioned pastime. We cut poems and pictures out of magazines. I suppose I had the sensibility of a writer— the attentiveness to texture and detail and sound, and the desire to learn. But in order to become a writer, I had to rebel against the limits of my surroundings. We weren't poor, but we were well defined, circumscribed by generations of folkways and the rigid expectations of a farm culture. I wanted to get out. I wanted to go places, see the world. This ambitiousness developed at a time historically when it was first possible to leave—to go to college, to seek a livelihood other than farm wife. So you could say the early ambition to write was part natural sensibility and part idealism.

MR: Was the feeling of being constricted more intense, do you think, because you're female? Gender roles seem to be a concern in your early work especially. Sam Hughes, for example, is disgusted by her friend Dawn's pregnancy and her own mother's new baby, and she's very aware of the limited—and limiting—potential of her relationship with her boyfriend. Norma Jean, in "Shiloh," is discovering her capabilities in a way that Leroy doesn't understand; he's worried that it's "some Women's Lib thing." Would you say that was true of you and your ambition? Was part of your desire to achieve, and get out, a feminist desire?

Mason: I rejected the traditional notion of "women's work," but I never thought of my early ambitions in a feminist way, exactly. Primarily I rebelled against apathy and limited education. I was rejecting a whole way of life that I thought trapped everyone. I didn't see women doing much of anything in my region except having babies and slaving away on the farm. They might work in stores or factories or teach school, but none of that was for me. But I didn't see men doing anything I wanted to do either. When I went to college, all the intellectuals and writers were men, so I aspired to crash into that world. I never had that feminist sense of wanting to prove myself by having a job. I didn't know of any women trapped at home in a fifties paradise with nothing to do. The idea of working outside the home as a matter of principle was a middle-class notion that I had little knowledge of. My mother worked in a factory some of the time, and she didn't do it to make a point. She did it for money. I was trying to get an education so I could escape from the labor force.

MR: You've said elsewhere that your early reading was typical: children's series like the Bobbsey Twins and Nancy Drew. You've even written a book about female detectives in some of those books, *The Girl Sleuth*. How, if at all, did those series influence you?

Mason: The Bobbsey Twins and Nancy Drew fed my aspirations to see the world, to become something else. The Bobbsey Twins always went on vacations, and of course a dairy farmer does not take a vacation, not even a day off, because the cows have to be milked. The Bobbseys frustrated me with their endless travels. The girl detectives' adventures made me long for something exciting to happen. I got the notion that everything exciting happened elsewhere, so I was filled with desire to go places and find out things. I tried to write stories patterned after the girl detectives, and that was the first thrill of writing—finding adventure through it.

MR: How has the traditional farm culture that you came out of changed in the past fifty years or so? If you were growing up on the farm now, how might your trajectory be different from what it's been?

Mason: Growing up on a farm nowadays is not that isolated or autonomous, and the family farm as I knew it hardly exists. You couldn't feed a family on fifty-four acres now. Anyway, the wide world is much closer and more accessible than it was when I was little, so a kid today would have more choices. My ambitions were fed mostly by illusions and lack of information. I had little to go on except the movies and songs on the radio. I often dwell on that impossible question—what would my life have been like if I had had more advantages? Or what if I'd had fewer; what if I had lived in my grandmother's time? That's the personal question underlying *Feather Crowns*. I can't really answer it.

MR: You made a foray into academia before becoming a writer. You went to graduate school at SUNY-Binghamton and the University of Connecticut. Did you plan to teach literature?

Mason: I went to graduate school in literature because I wanted to read and write and didn't want to work at a meaningless job. I had no plans for a teaching career. I was just trying to find a situation where I could read and write for as long as possible. I had wanted to go to a writing program, but there were only a few of them then. In fact, I had applied to the Stanford creative writing program but I wasn't accepted. So I went into literature. I was a graduate assistant, and I taught freshman English, but the class wasn't only composition. It was a survey of Western literature course.

MR: What was teaching like for you?

Mason: Frightening. At Binghamton all the students were smart, sophisticated kids from New York City, and as a quiet Southerner I was terrified. I look back on that time with a shudder because it was so embarrassing, difficult, and scary—that classic situation where you feel everybody else in the room seems suave and articulate. That was what visiting a professor's house was like, too. At one such gathering at the University of Connecticut I found myself seated next to the poet John Berryman, a genuine luminary who had just given a reading there. I was nobody, with nothing in my head, unable to speak. Poets lived on another plane. What would you say to a poet? I found myself catapulted into situations like this, where I felt I didn't belong, and I had neither the confidence nor the social graces to manage.

MR: How did the experience of living in the North affect your notion of regional differences?

Mason: The North was, in our Southern mythology, the land of arrogant Yankees. They were the authorities. We felt inferior; we were losers. When I lived up there, I subscribed to that notion so completely that it was years before I could begin to get out from under it. Jimmy Carter had to be elected before the South in general could get ahold of its shame and start to turn it around. In the North, I was in few situations where I could tell about things like my Granny wringing a chicken's neck or how my chore was washing the milk cans twice a day. If I did tell people a little about my background, they tended to misinterpret it in terms of quaint stereotypes, something out of *Ma and Pa Kettle*. There was a yawning cultural gap between North and South in those days, and bridging it seemed almost impossible for somebody as bashful as I was.

MR: Do you think of yourself as a Southern writer?

Mason: I'm a writer from the South and I write out of a Southern culture, but I'm not immersed in the South. I think my exile in the North gave me a sense of detachment, a way of looking in two directions at once.

It's an advantage. I don't want to celebrate the South more than it deserves—which it does to a great extent, of course, but I'm wary of too much regional pride. It's important to pick a place and be there, but not to be provincial about it. So much country music wallows in that provinciality—like saying "I'm ignorant and proud of it."

MR: Did you "pick your place" early on, or did your subject come to you over time?

Mason: I think, given my background and my earnest endeavor to lose my Southern accent—to find my place in the North—that it was unlikely that I would know early on what my material was. I started writing fiction in college, but it took me a number of years to get the right perspective on my material. I hadn't really recognized what I had to write about. I was looking outside. In the late sixties I wrote a novel about the Beatles, inspired by Donald Barthelme's *Snow White*. Finally, in the early seventies I wrote the obligatory autobiographical, coming-of-age novel. These were great practice and got me started, but I was slow to get into focus.

MR: It's hard to imagine the Bobbie Ann Mason who wrote "Shiloh" and *In Country* being inspired by an experimental, satirical book like *Snow White*.

Mason: *Snow White* was right up my alley. Early on, I was interested in stylists, writers who loved language and played with words. In college, I loved Max Shulman (*Rally Round the Flag, Boys!*); his writing was sophomoric, but then I went straight to James Joyce. Barthelme's story "Robert Kennedy Saved from Drowning" gave me the idea that you could write fiction about somebody famous. *Snow White* was written in short bursts and had a sustained tone of disconnectedness. The technique was very alluring. Nothing had to be explained, no full context and development—just hits. It looked easy and revolutionary. I wrote most of the Beatles book in 1967, the summer of *Sgt. Pepper's Lonely Hearts Club Band*. It was a time to throw the graduate school reading list out the window and just go with the times.

MR: Were you also writing short stories during this period?

Mason: I wrote short stories in college, published one in the college literary magazine, but I didn't write any more stories to speak of for fifteen years.

MR: But then you started writing them again, and you made an immediate impact with the stories in *Shiloh*. How did that come about?

Mason: In the late seventies, as I neared the mid-life identity-crisis time, I decided it was now or never. I think the crisis went back to my childhood conviction that I was special, and I followed the notion, picked up in college, that writing was a calling, that writers were different and could indulge their sense of apartness by writing. All that seems a little silly to me now, but at the time it helped give me the determination I needed. When I realized that I hadn't yet done anything of note, I got busy. I wrote a story that was about five pages long and took it to a writers' workshop. I got some inspiration from seeing that people were actually writing and it looked possible, so I wrote a couple of other stories and immediately sent them to the *New Yorker*. Do you see the ten-year-old child there answering the Famous Writers School ad in the back of a magazine? What was I thinking? To my surprise, I got encouraging responses from Roger Angell, one of the *New Yorker*'s most illustrious editors and writers. He took me under his wing, responded to all my submissions with great care and interest, and gave me the first real encouragement I had ever had.

MR: What was the writers' workshop you attended?

Mason: For three summers in the late seventies I went to a week-long workshop run by Joe David Bellamy from St. Lawrence University. It was at Saranac Lake in the Adirondacks. It was pleasant, a chance to hang out with some writers. I attended workshops run by Gail Godwin, Charles Simmons, and Margaret Atwood. They were all encouraging, but I think what charged me up most was the rediscovery of a notion I had gotten in college that writing was a passionate commitment and an honorable thing to do. I had always believed that, but my writing ambition had gotten so dissipated by lack of confidence and various diversions. The typical story for women writers seems to be that they spend twenty years raising children and then they go back to their original ambition of writing. I didn't raise children, but it took twenty years just to get my head together.

MR: *Love Life* is dedicated to Roger Angell. What was that writer editor relationship like?

Mason: Roger Angell was the first person who said, "You are a writer." His encouragement brought me to life as a writer. Finally, I believed I could do it. As an editor he has always been very professional, yet he deals with a story on the level of emotions; in those early stories he helped me understand that I should go deeper into the characters' lives. His responses were subjective, never prescriptive. I heard how the story made him feel. He was always very careful not to tell me how to do it. He said he didn't know, but he made me think that I did. The story "Offerings" was the first story he accepted—the twentieth one I sent in. He telephoned me and said he liked the story but thought there was something lacking in the portrayal of the absent husband. It needed something a little darker. I studied the story for a long time and worked on some revisions. I was going to New York about three weeks later and I was going to meet Roger for the first time—November, 1979. I took the revisions with me—only about three sentences' worth—and met him in his office. He passed the story along to William Shawn, the editor, who made the ultimate decisions. The next day, a Friday, I met Roger for a drink at the Algonquin Hotel. I still did not have a story accepted—I would know on Monday—but there I was, being entertained at the celebrated Algonquin. It was awkward, but exciting. I kept looking for the Algonquin cat, Hamlet. On Monday I was to call about one o'clock, which was when the messages ordinarily came back from Mr. Shawn. I phoned from some place on Fifth Avenue, and Roger said the word hadn't come yet. He said to call again in fifteen minutes. I called again. Still no word. Then I had another appointment and couldn't call until 3:15. I called from the ladies' room phone at Saks Fifth Avenue and learned that the story was accepted. Roger wanted to know my social security number. I spouted out some numbers, but realized later they were wrong. The rest of the day is quite unclear in my mind. I was probably never so thrilled in my life.

MR: What about the editing of your books? Do you have any insights into the working relationship between a novelist and her editor?

Mason: I have been fortunate to have had some of the great editors—Roger Angell, William Shawn, and Ted Solotaroff. I was spoiled by the *New Yorker*, and so I expect careful, close editing that serves the work. Ted Solotaroff's great quality is his ability to penetrate the heart of a work and to push for something deeper. In the early stages of writing *In

*Country*, he pushed me to confront the subject of Vietnam. I'd worked on the novel for some time before I realized it really was about the effects of the Vietnam War. When I did realize it, I felt somewhat intimidated. How could I write about such a big subject? What authority did I have? But Ted helped give me the confidence to stay with it.

MR: Critics said of your first book something to the effect of your being, already, a full-fledged master of the short story form. *Shiloh and Other Stories* was nominated for the National Book Critics Circle Award and the American Book Award, and received several other honors. With the exception of the Nancy Culpepper stories, the characters are all ordinary, small-town people who work at ordinary jobs—the "Kmart crowd" as they've been stereotyped. You were obviously well on the way to developing your vision by the time that collection was published. How did that happen?

Mason: I don't know how I developed a cohesive "vision," if that's what it is. The subject matter is a given. The vision is something internal, and writing helps me find it and bring it out. For me, the process of writing is a matter of dealing with inhibitions, to find out what I have hidden down inside; if I can get it out, it seems to fall loosely into shape, and then I help it along in a more deliberate way. My stories typically start out very rough. But if I see there's something in a story, I'll work and rework it over and over, making small improvements with each draft until it finally reaches its finished shape. In writing most of the pieces in *Shiloh*, I just fooled around with what randomly came to mind. In that way I made discoveries that I could work with. I wrote about fifty stories, of which sixteen went into the collection.

MR: Most of your early short stories are told in third person, and they're almost all in the present tense. You use present tense and the same center-of-consciousness viewpoint in your first two novels, also. Why is that natural for you, and what do you think are the respective advantages and disadvantages?

Mason: The later stories moved into the past tense—stories like "Memphis" and "Coyotes"—when I got really tired of that convention of present tense. Present tense seems quite natural for characters meandering through a vague situation. It prevents the author from overtly asserting *authority*, the privilege of saying "Once upon a time . . . this happened, and I know how it is going to end and I'm going to tell you how it was."

MR: Critics and readers have commented, too, on the consciousness, in your early work, of popular culture and of the media, especially film and TV.

Mason: I'm a little sensitive about being reduced to the terms of "popular culture," since it's often a pejorative term. I don't think the culture of the people ought to be dismissed like that. Their lives are just as important as the lives of those who read the *New York Times* and go to the opera. I often write about characters who happen to watch TV. Most Americans do watch TV. It's a big deal in their lives, especially if they work hard at some mind-numbing job. I try to write what is appropriate to the characters, the attributes and interests that are meaningful to them. For most of them, the TV is not a malignant force droning in the background, as it might be in a Cheever story. For many of my characters, it's a source of pleasure and escape, although that's changing now, as they get cable and find fifty-seven channels with nothing on. As a writer I can maintain a bit of detachment from the characters, showing them in their world and seeing a little bit more than they do. But I'm not looking down at them.

MR: You've had some magazine writing experience, also. You've written quite a bit of nonfiction for the *New Yorker*.

Mason: Since I began publishing fiction in the *New Yorker* in 1980, I've been contributing occasional nonfiction pieces as well. I've done a couple of dozen "Talk of the Town" pieces, some humor pieces, and some reporting. I had a little background in journalism—writing columns for my college paper, and teaching journalism for a while during the seventies. In certain ways, I was influenced by Tom Wolfe and Lillian Ross and some of those "new journalists" anthologized by Wolfe.

MR: How did those writers influence you?

Mason: I absorbed them because I had to deal with them so much in teaching journalism: Tom Wolfe's use of point of view—"the downstage narrator"—and his accumulation of what he called "status detail." Lillian Ross's wonderful deadpan reporting. Those writers wrote about real events by using techniques of fiction. It was the techniques of fiction I was most interested in, and so I picked up on some of them.

MR: What would you say are your literary "roots"?

Mason: I think my aesthetic principles derive from James Joyce and Vladimir Nabokov. From Joyce I learned about how a work is organic—how sound, for instance, is meaning, how the language is appropriate to the subject. If the story is *about* a journey, then it should *be* a journey. From Nabokov I learned that the surfaces are not symbolic representations, but the thing itself, irreducible. Rather than depending on an underlying idea, an image or set of images should be infinitely complex—just the opposite of what we're sometimes taught about symbols and themes as hidden treasures. You can hack off an image and examine it, but it would be like trying to cut away light and shadow. The work should shimmer.

MR: You mention Joyce as an influence, but you generally eschew the Joycean epiphany as a way of ending a short story. In your stories, because we're so much in the minds of characters who aren't necessarily all that self-aware, the "recognition"—if there is one—is left up to the reader. How deliberate is that?

Mason: The goal is to leave the story at the most appropriate point, with the fullest sense of what it comes to, with a passage that has resonance and brings into focus the whole story. It has to sound right and seem right, even if its meaning isn't obvious.

MR: How, in your mind, is that different from what a novel does?

Mason: It's principally scale, the size of the canvas. I write novels in much the same way as I write stories—that is, the process is the same, but the effect is larger, more developed. In either case, though, I revise and revise. I fuss over every word.

MR: While we're on the subject of what fiction does, perhaps I should ask what you see as the role of the writer in society. How does literary writing matter—other than, obviously, as a sort of catharsis for the person doing it?

Mason: It is tempting to say that writing does serve the writers first; I often think many of us are misfits who can't hold a job and who achieve, at best, some kind of mystique by virtue of our quirks. But I look back to Emerson and Thoreau when I think about why literary writing matters. It's easier to see the writer's role in the smaller world of Concord, Massachusetts, in the mid-nineteenth century. Thoreau was certainly a quirky misfit, but *Walden* comes down to us as an instruction manual for the heart and soul, as well as for getting a crop out. Emerson was famous, a very public figure, but both of them were quite visible in their community. In Concord, a town of two thousand, they could simply go to the Lyceum and give lectures. They engaged their neighbors in their discoveries. As writers, Thoreau and Emerson were lively and curious and demanding. They took on the world and tried to figure it out and then to translate what they found to the public, all in terms of the deepest questions about the nature of reality and morality and aesthetics. They led with their genius, turning their observations of nature into poetry and essays. They were standing on the verge of our time and they could almost see what was going to happen to us. They were leading their readers and listeners into the future. Writers belong on the edge, not in the center of the action. Nowadays we don't have leaders who are worth much when it comes to the heart and soul, but if writers can make us feel and appreciate and explore the world, then I think that's an extremely valuable function; it goes far beyond entertainment and steers well clear of politics.

MR: How do you see your own role as a writer?

Mason: I don't make any claims for myself. I'm sitting on the toe of Thoreau's boot. I'm not a natural storyteller. I see writing as a way of finding words to fashion a design, to discover a vision, not as a way of chronicling or championing or documenting. In other words, it is to applaud the creative imagination as it acts upon whatever materials are at hand. Creative writing is not to me primarily theme, subject, topic, region, class, or any ideas. It has more to do with feeling, imagination, suggestiveness, subtlety, complexity, richness of perception—all of which are found through fooling around with language and observations.

MR: You've written two story collections, two full-length novels, and *Spence + Lila*, which is really more of a novella. Your work has been pretty much equally divided between long and short fiction. Do you consider yourself a novelist first, or a short story writer first?

Mason: I don't know. I've written only eight or nine stories in this decade. In the eighties, I wrote about seventy-five stories. I have been busier with novels and nonfiction in the nineties. But in the future, it could go either way. There's more of an immediate gratification in writing a story, but in the long run, writing a novel is more deeply gratifying. It's not really something I can consciously control. But I try to be wary of jumping into a novel too casually. Some notion has to really grab me hard for me to get into a novel. Stories come and go. If a story doesn't work, it's no great loss to throw it away. But a novel . . . that's years of my life.

MR: And a bigger challenge?

Mason: Yes. The challenges keep getting more and more complicated, as you become more aware as a writer. Committing to a novel is so risky and uncertain, and there is so little to go on when you begin. With *In Country* I couldn't find the story that held those characters together; with *Feather Crowns* I had to sustain a long narrative on a subject that threatened to be grotesque. I had to show how the characters' actions were justifiable in the terms of their world.

MR: That novel was quite a departure for you. Like your other fiction, it's set in Kentucky but it's Kentucky of the turn of the century. What made you turn to historical fiction?

Mason: I don't think *Feather Crowns* was a major departure. It's the same people, the same landscape I have been preoccupied with since the start. The contemporary characters in my stories are the descendants of the rural people who were rooted on the farm for generations. On the farm, they were independent, land-owning yeoman farmers—in rural terms, the middle class. The Depression, the decline of the farm and the lure of cash sent them out of their culture into what they called "public work." In many ways, it was a demotion. In working for a boss, they lost their autonomy. That transition since the Depression has had profound effects on rural and small-town culture. It formed my expectations that I would have to work in a factory or at a clerical job. I dreaded and feared the loss of independence. Writing was my way of keeping my own life.

MR: Can you say something about the genesis and writing of *Feather Crowns*?

Mason: The book was inspired by a true story, the birth of quintuplets in 1896. It happened in my hometown—in fact, across the field from where I grew up. I did not hear the story until 1988, and there wasn't much information about it, but it was enough to inspire me. I had been wanting to go back into the world of my grandparents when they were young, and that true story was just right for the journey. I seized on it for my own, as a chance to get into the language and folkways of the rural culture of the turn of the century. These things have a deep connection to the present, because the old ways are still hanging on; change is much slower than we imagine. So I see continuity between *Feather Crowns* and *Shiloh* more than I see a radical juxtaposition.

MR: The project itself was somewhat different, though. For one thing, it must have required a lot of research. It's also a bigger novel than any that you've written so far—longer, more characters, richer and more complex thematically. Did you feel at all like Christie, at the start of the book, who fears that the baby inside her—which is actually five—is so big and wild that it must be a monster?

Mason: The historical research wasn't as extensive as you might think because I knew that world intimately, through my parents and grandparents. The language, superstitions, landscape, farming methods—all of it came down to me in my lifetime. The rural community didn't change that much from the turn of the century to the nineteen-forties. Much of my research involved asking my mother questions, and much of it I simply knew firsthand. I spent about the same amount of time writing it as I did writing *In Country*. The story was clear to me from the beginning, whereas with *In Country* there was so much I didn't know about what was going on. I actually spent more concentrated time writing *Feather Crowns*, whereas with *In Country* I spent most of the time searching and trying out various directions for the characters.

No, I didn't feel quite like Christie. I knew from the beginning that it was a big book, and I could see what it required in terms of pacing and emotion and goal. I had to invent most of it—the characters and their world—but I had a clear sense of direction.

MR: Among other things, the novel is about the loss of privacy, and Christie and James's inability to defend themselves against the damaging effects of the public's curiosity. The babies are the product of a very intimate kind of desire, but they thrust the Wheelers' personal lives into public view. Christie is referred to by someone as having "dropped a litter," and James is leered at by other women, who assume he's extremely virile. Eventually the Wheelers' grief, too, becomes a public affair. Was that part of the real story you learned, of the 1896 quintuplets? Or is that your imagination, operating on the historical incident?

Mason: Some of it was true, but there was very little information on the 1896 quintuplets. I know they were besieged by the public. I think the litter-dropping and a sense of the public invasion was also part of the reports surrounding the Dionne Quintuplets. Everything else I had to imagine.

MR: One of the very significant events in the book, which actually takes place prior to the main action, is Christie's trip with her friend Amanda to the revival at Reelfoot Lake. It becomes a sort of focal point for Christie—and not just because it's one of the only times she's ever been away from James and her children. What, in your own mind, is the importance of that event in the novel?

Mason: The focal point had to do with guilt—Christie has impure thoughts about that sexy evangelist, Brother Cornett. So she builds on this guilt when she realizes her pregnancy is unusual. She imagines she's carrying a monster, a devil. But the true monster turns out to be the public response. Also, in her attraction to Brother Cornett and the sideshow atmosphere of the camp meeting, we have the seeds of her vulnerability to celebrity that she encounters later. Her innocent desire to experience something new also leads her into danger.

MR: Can you comment on your current writing project?

Mason: I don't quite know what to say about it, as I'm still in the midst of it as we speak. It's called *Clear Springs* and I hope it will come out sometime in 1998. It is a personal story of the fate of the family farm—my family's farm. It includes a lot of memory of childhood and some autobiography, but I don't think of it as a memoir. It's less about me than about my family, especially my mother. By extension, it's about a way of life that's disappearing—the small family farm, the small rural community, that was once seen as the ideal for American civilization.

MR: How does your notion of what Bobbie Ann Mason, the writer, is about differ, do you think, from the public and/or critical perception of your work?

Mason: I don't think of myself as the Kmart realist. I hope that what I'm trying to do is more than document patterns of discount shopping in the late twentieth century! Many teachers and scholars seem primarily concerned with themes and ideas, but that's not the way I think. If that was what I was after, I'd write a term paper. I think more in terms of literal details and images, as well as sound and tone—all the textures that bring a story to life. Sometimes it seems I'm working mostly with sounds and rhythms, the voice in my head. I write a story over and over until it sounds right. If it works, then the themes will be there. I don't plant them.

MR: So you're more concerned with character and place than with any overriding theme in your work.

Mason: I'm not saying I'm uninterested in what a story means, it's just that I find it hard to isolate that, either during the process of writing or in the final analysis. I think theme sometimes gets separated out too much from a work. The themes are important, but the artistry is just as important. Ideally, form and function are inseparable. That's what I read for most: writing that can't be torn apart, a story that can't be told any other way. I read a writer for the way he tells the story. And when the substance and style are perfectly wedded, you can't reduce the story to a set of abstractions.

# *Transatlantica* Interview

By Candela Delgado Marin, February 2015

CDM: *New Yorker* author Hannah Rosefield wrote a piece ("No More Questions," 2014) this January reflecting on the struggle or nuisance interviews may represent for writers. She reported that in 1904, Henry James said in his first interview: "One's craft, one's art, is his expression, not one's person." And Joyce Carol Oates claimed earlier this year that a "writer's life is in his work, and that is the place to find him." How do you approach interviews?

BAM: What is difficult about an interview. . . . A writer spends weeks and months and years working with words, trying to get them into a final shape that works, so that the whole can't be easily broken apart, so that the words chosen are exactly the right ones. Then the writer, who is maybe not a talker, is suddenly on TV and expected to talk off the top of her head and make sense! The transition is startling. Also, the writer may be expected to be articulate, to talk in confident analytical terms, while writing fiction is so different! It is more like singing a song while swimming underwater.

CDM: And yet I find your answers literary, as well as analytical. Your language seems to be unconditionally linked to the musicality of fiction. Don't you feel that interviews for writers are created to receive answers that maintain the tone of the author's fiction? What are the emotions that you relate to the image you just described, "singing a song while swimming underwater"?

BAM: The approach of the literary critic is so different from that of the fiction writer. The critic wants to explicate and comprehend what the writer may not be of a disposition to explain. The writer is not thinking in those terms. The metaphor above draws from the mystery and the fear of creation and the music that is its aim.

CDM: In your latest novel, *The Girl in the Blue Beret,* Marshall Stone, an American WWII veteran who was a B-17 bomber pilot, now a retired widower in his 60s, revisits France in the quest to find the members of the French Resistance that helped him and other Allied aviators escape occupied Europe once his plane was shot down in Belgium. One of the people he is most keen to locate is Annette, the young girl from the Resistance, who wore a blue beret to be recognized and whose family hid him until he could be safely transferred to Spain. Marshall Stone is inspired by your father-in-law's experience of being shot down in World War II, and Michele Moët-Agniel, whose family helped him escape from the Germans, is your real model for the girl in the blue beret. When you met her in Paris in 2008, you learned that she and her parents had been arrested during the war. Her father died at Buchenwald, and she and her mother were sent to labor camps. In the novel, Annette's family is betrayed and they are imprisoned in labor camps. Annette and her mother survive.

You visited Chojna, in Poland, in September 2013 because the WWII labor camp, where five hundred women worked in inhuman conditions to build an airfield runway, was located there. The trip could be seen as a follow-up to the publication of the novel. When you showed her photos of the abandoned airfield, where she was forced to work, Michèle, in her eighties now, stared for a long time at one of the pictures of the runway. In your notes from the encounter you describe how her eyes focused on a point "where flowers were growing through the cracks in the pavement." You add: "Finally she said, 'I built that.'" This report of such a moving anecdote marks for me the clear difference between your novel and history. I would really appreciate hearing your take on the fine line between fiction that deals with history and the study of a historian.

BAM: Although they may want to discover and present the fascinating story within their subject, historians don't normally take the liberties fiction writers do. Fiction writers are generally dedicated to showing a kind of truth that the known facts alone might not reveal. What was it like to be a bicycle courier in World War II? How did it feel to fly a bombing mission? In realistic fiction, within certain boundaries of historical fact, the writer is free to invent characters, descriptions, plots.

On the other hand, my friendship with Michèle Agniel has provoked profound thoughts and feelings about some things that actually happened. And that, in turn, is different from reading fiction.

CDM: Writer Daniel Swift in his review of the novel in *The New York Times* states the book is a work of "remarkable empathy" ("A War World II Veteran Revisits his Saviors," 2011). How does it affect your conception of the story when research intertwines with the establishment of personal relationships, when the sources being investigated are loaded with emotions?

BAM: *The Girl in the Blue Beret* was an unusual venture for me because it was inspired by real people and their stories. Normally, I am not restrained by any desire to stick to someone's story. It is much easier to invent. But in this case, not only did some real stories draw me into the subject, but I began to feel a deeper commitment to doing justice to their stories. Still, that did not mean I followed them literally. Rather, it meant that I felt motivated to go as deeply, imaginatively, as I could into the possibilities of their history.

CDM: Present and past frequently merge in your novels and short stories. At times, recollections seem to assail the characters. This is a constant in *The Girl in the Blue Beret,* as it was for the Vietnam veteran Emmett in your novel *In Country.* You explained that the main character in your latest novel, Marshall, had been avoiding the past, and during his European quest, memories start to come forth, at times, when he least expects it (Bloom, 2012, *The Art of Word Making*). How do you interweave the present and remembrances? Do you approach the representation of traumatic war memories with a specific technique?

BAM: It was the interplay of two narrative lines—the present, 1980, and the past, 1944. Incidents in the present triggered memories of the past. Psychologically, it was fairly simple. Not all the memories would come at once. For instance, the memories of Marshall's B-17 being shot down are doled out from time to time—for narrative suspense—before Marshall can face the full impact of the crash-landing. So the reader experiences it gradually, and likewise Marshall slowly comes to terms with his memories.

CDM: You state the following in the "Introduction" to your short story collection *Midnight Magic*: "Like me, these characters are emerging from a rural way of life that is fast disappearing, and they are plunging into the future at a rapid saunter, wondering where they are going to end up . . . I am excited to meet them at a major intersection" (xii). Much has been written about the concept of the Post-Southern reality, an ever-changing simulacra of what the South used to be. As a writer, how do you work with this "intersection" as the setting, with the Post-Southern everydayness?

BAM: I don't think about it in these broad terms. I'm an observer of detail. I notice what people have in their shopping carts at the grocery, what they are saying when I overhear them, what they're wearing, what kinds of jobs they have. The particulars going on in a character's life reveal this larger concern. You can't address "intersections" and "simulacra" straight on. You have to hear a character saying, "It's amazing that I have strong feet, coming from two parents that never had strong feet at all." I actually overheard that, and it entered my story "Shiloh." That sentence contains so much. It is the sound of it, the attitude.

CDM: Is it then from the language, the chosen words, and the details being described that the current South and its features spring up? How do you think a reader unfamiliar with the American South could read, and pick up on, this subtle contextual information?

BAM: Actually, I think it would be very difficult, without an intimate knowledge of the sounds and nuances of the language. Sometimes I think that what is most important to me about the sound of the prose is just not something that will be noticed! Even in English.

CDM: History, tradition and legacy are essential concepts in your writings. Your characters are not completely disentangled from their roots. In your story "The Heirs," the narrator explains how the main character appreciates a box of her family's letters, pictures, and a stick of dynamite. The objects, somehow, narrate her family's past. There is a respectful approach to the materiality of memories: "Nancy saw herself in this group of people, lives that had passed from the earth as hers would too. She felt comforted by the thought of continuity, even if a stick of dynamite could be called an heirloom" (*Nancy Culpepper,* 202). Do you play with objects as somehow speaking for your characters?

BAM: I don't really know how to answer that. I'm usually dealing with objects like sticks of dynamite on a fairly literal level. This is what makes them work for the reader ultimately as symbols or narrative objects or whatever. If you get the surfaces right, in the right combinations, at the right angle, then they will embody in the larger story those themes, symbols, concepts, etc., that entertain the classroom.

CDM: When observing these details that surround you, do objects ever work as triggers for stories? How?

BAM: Very often it is an image of some sort that sparks the inspiration for a story. That stick of dynamite found in a box of letters may very well have been the trigger for that story. In the opening of "Shiloh," Norma Jean is lifting weights. The novel *In Country* was initially inspired by the sight of a couple of teenagers selling flowers on a street corner, but that scene was eventually dropped.

CDM: In the article "Honoring her Fathers" (Mason, 2011, *Book Reporter*) you narrate your reconciliation with the South by re-establishing a bond with your father. I was intrigued by your choice of the verb "to gravitate" in order to create the metaphor:

> *But in the last years of his life we found common ground as I gravitated back to the land. We shared a love for animals. He liked to have a small dog with him in his car, so they could go motivating down the road listening to Chuck Berry. I got my musical tastes from him.*

For me, your use of the word "gravitate" also suggests *gravitas* in the sense of "dignity." How do you convey this Southern gravitas, which is still often ignored in cultural representations and the media?

BAM: "Gravitate" is from modern Latin "*gravitare*," to move, from Latin *gravitas,* weight. In that quote, I was more concerned with the echo of "gravitating" in the word "motivating," a word Chuck Berry uses in his 1950s song "Maybellene." ("As I was motivatin' over the hill, I saw Maybellene in her Coupe de Ville.") Motivating implies purpose, and Chuck Berry's creative misuse of the word suggests he is motoring purposefully—with a strong motive! Maybelline has been untrue and he is speeding after her. I don't know if you can get gravitas out of that sense of vitality and purpose. And humor. As for my father, I'd think of humor before I'd think of gravitas.

CDM: Female friendships are a constant in your writing. In the story "Bumblebees," three women have decided to move to a farm together and work and live off the land. You portray their intimacy in the following way: "With the three of them cooped up, trying to stay out of each other's way, Barbara feels that the strings holding them together are taut and fragile, like the tiny tendrils on English-pea vines, which grasp at the first thing handy" (*Love Life,* 109). Three women confront their fears within the narrow limits of the house, creating a sense of tension and annoyance, simultaneously with a strong loving bond. How do you recall your own experience of living in a house full of grandmothers, mothers, and sisters?

BAM: I don't remember it exactly that way, and "Bumblebees" is fiction. I grew up with one grandmother, one mother, two younger sisters. My grandmother and mother were always working with food. And they made our clothes. I wanted to read books and escape farm life! That was the tension for me, but I've imagined these women in "Bumblebees" who choose that life.

CDM: But you eventually moved back to Kentucky; would it be fair to say that you also "chose" that life after having left it behind?

BAM: Not entirely. I had escaped the narrow confines of the cultural and economic expectations and I was able to come back on my own terms.

CDM: I am really interested in the volume *Missing Mountains: We Went to the Mountaintop but It Wasn't There* (2005), where you contributed an article denouncing the disastrous environmental effects of mountaintop mining. Here you show your commitment to the preservation of the American landscape. Previously in 2000 you published the article "Fall-Out: Paducah's Secret Nuclear Disaster" in *The New Yorker,* which conveys a disappointment with Kentuckians for their passive attitude towards the poisonous presence of the nuclear plant in their land. You generally praise the resilience of farmers but also mentioned then that the lack of drive to fight for their rights was not surprising "in an agricultural region, where farmers forgive the forces they cannot control." Do you ever reflect this attitude in your characters?

BAM: Yes, I would say so. My novel *An Atomic Romance* features a man who works at a uranium enrichment plant, within a culture of denial.

For the nuclear-fuel workers, it is a matter of livelihood. It is too scary, too uncomfortable, for them to ask too many questions, so they close their eyes to the dangers.

CDM: How do they reconcile their instinct of survival and resilience with their love for the soil and landscape that might be endangered?

BAM: I don't know about those folks, but I think that often people in denial about something can find convenient rationalizations, and often they seize on wrong-headed beliefs that prevent them from having to confront what they fear.

CDM: Talking about your novel *An Atomic Romance,* is it true that Salvador Dalí's *Atómica Melancólica* (1945) served as an inspiration for it? When did you come across the painting and what was your reaction to it? The connection of these two artistic pieces became significant for me in reading the following words about the main character Reed, the engineer with a passion for astronomy: "He tried to imagine what an astronaut would see, peering down on that patch of green earth with its gray scar, the earth still steaming from its little wound" (50–51). Are we peering through those scars in Dalí's painting?

BAM: The painting wasn't an inspiration. It was just a pleasing discovery that seemed to corroborate the impulse of my novel or reflect its concerns. I don't remember when I became aware of it, certainly when I was well into the writing of the novel. I tried to see the painting in 2005 in Madrid but it was not on display.

CDM: In April 2012 you read a poem from Wendell Berry's *Leavings* in the National Endowment for the Humanities program at the Kennedy Center for the Performing Arts. Berry was selected by the NEH to give the Jefferson Lecture, a prestigious honor granted by the federal government for distinguished intellectual achievement in the humanities. I find a strong connection between his lines and your work. Allow me to quote Berry:

> *I will be leaving how many beauties overlooked?*
> *A painful Heaven this would be, for I would know*
> *by it how far I have fallen short. I have not*
> *paid enough attention, I have not been grateful*
> *enough. And yet this pain would be the measure*

*of my love. In eternity's once and now, pain would*
*place me surely in the Heaven of my earthly love.* (2010, 71)

Could you tell us why you chose this poem and what it means to you?

BAM: I did not choose the poem. It was chosen by the program planners, perhaps with the approval of Wendell Berry. I was merely asked to read it aloud at the program. I do like the poem and agree with its joyous embrace of the delights in this world, as opposed to those promised by heaven. Yes, heaven would be this world, with all my favorite pets, and my family still here.

CDM: Later in the year, in your speech "Don't Live a Throwaway Life" at the 2012 Earth Day Awards Ceremony for the Kentucky Environmental Quality Commission, you declared: "Growing up on a farm taught me to be observant, to pay attention to every detail in front of me—a bird feather, a funny bug, a patch of moss. This is a habit of mind I have found indispensable for writing fiction, which after all is like piecing quilts from scraps, something I learned from my grandmother" (Mason, 2012, *Courier Journal*). Could you elaborate on how being observant influences your creative process?

BAM: For me, stories are made out of tiny details stitched together. I consider that growing up on a farm provided me with the richest textures and sensations as well as a solid grounding in the natural world. I didn't have many books when I was growing up, but I did have bugs and chickens and blackberries and cows and an infinitely complex world to explore.

CDM: It might be in the complexity of a simple life, a rural life, where elements of the landscape sometimes articulate intimate emotions for people. Christie, the mother of quintuplets in the turn-of-the-last-century novel *Feather Crowns*, dreads the death of her babies. She observes one of them: "It was the one that made Christie see the dark winter branches of a rained-soaked tree, with the deep blue sky coming through from behind. She heard him cry—a strong, healthy cry" (88).

Is Christie decoding nature, with the sharpest skills, as if it were a book to be read?

BAM: I seem to recall that in that novel Christie associates specific imagery, particular sensations, with each of her five babies. It is a blending of the senses and feelings. She is attuned to the natural world and her babies are part of it.

CDM: I would like to talk to you about a paradox I have myself encountered in reading Southern literature and that is related to this contemplative attitude we have been discussing and the idea of storytelling in the South. Eudora Welty wrote in her essay "Place and Time: The Southern Writer's Inheritance":

> It is nothing new or startling that Southerners do write—probably they must write. It is the way they are: born readers and reciters, great document holders, diary keepers, letter exchangers and savers, history tracers—and, outstaying the rest, great talkers. Emphasis in talk is on the narrative form and the verbatim conversation, for which time is needed. Children who grow up listening through rewarding stretches of unhurried time, reading in big lonely rooms, dwelling in the confidence of slow-changing places, are naturally more prone than other children to be entertained from the first by life and to feel free, encouraged, and then in no time compelled, to pass their pleasure on. They cannot help being impressed by a world around them . . . (163)

This paragraph summarizes the primary contradiction I find in Southern literature: characters are storytellers and yet, at the same time, they are introverts. When you are creating a character, do you find any compatibility between these two traits?

BAM: Well, these two traits can't be true of every character, and I can't say that I have given this idea any thought in my own writing. I don't recognize much of what Eudora Welty says about "great talkers." I'm not a natural storyteller, I didn't grow up with a traditional storytelling Southern background, and my characters are probably mostly introverts. What affected me was the *sound* of talking, perhaps because it was not a constant. The sounds came out of silence, so they were surprises—noticeable, memorable. At any rate, most of my characters are restrained in their speech and often reveal more by saying less. In many situations it is difficult for them to speak, and that is a tension that is more interesting to me than listening to the storyteller who never shuts up.

CDM: Without imposing literary labels on your writing, and as a closing remark, are there any writers, storytellers, that you feel close to?

BAM: An author I feel especially close to is Alice Munro because our backgrounds—growing up on farms—were so similar. Reading her autobiographical works is especially interesting to me. Of course her fiction is so widely adored. I can only regard it in stunned admiration. My favorite writer is Vladimir Nabokov, the word wizard. And his life was worlds away from mine. His writing genius too, but I do feel I share something of his sensibility. And we were both exiles.

CDM: What are you currently reading?

BAM: Right now I'm reading *Anna Karenina* (1877). And before that I read a nice novel by Judy Troy, *The Quiet Streets of Winslow* (2014), and Frederick Barthelme's new novel *There Must Be Some Mistake* (2014). Recently I also read *Sweet Tooth* (2012) by Ian McEwan.

CDM: Would you like to finish up our interview by commenting on your current work? What have you been focusing on and devoting your days to lately?

BAM: I have been writing stories, all of which either take place in California or have some link to California. I am imagining a book called "California Stories." Some of the stories are very short—forays into flash fiction. I have three flash pieces in a special flash-fiction issue of Frederick Barthelme's online journal, *New World Writing*. And I may be doing some more collaboration with Meg Pokrass. She tickles my funny bone.

CDM: Thank you very much, Ms. Mason. Please, keep your pen close to the page for our delight.

BAM: Thank you for bearing with me.

# 2paragraphs.com Interview

By Joseph Mackin

*What do you like least about writing?*

In a way, what I like least is the thing that is best—that state of mind when your Muse kicks you off a cliff and you go flying without any thought given to gravity. You just go. I often have an airplane image in my mind, taking off or landing. Somehow in that state, the energy is directed and you get into the story and you don't have to stop until you run out of gas.

That is the best feeling, when it happens. But the worst thing about it, the worst thing about writing, for me, is how that exalted Muse-lifted state in its defeat of time—its timelessness—robs me of time because I don't remember it that well. I recognize that I did it, but where did the time go? Suddenly it is six o'clock. Where was I? Writing a novel is like that for big chunks of your life, not just an afternoon. Someone asked me how long I spent writing the novel "Feather Crowns." I thought for a moment and said three years. The next day I had to correct my memory; maybe it was four years. For me the first year of writing a novel is the agony of the blank page, the all-too-obvious presence of time—empty time when I am sitting there fooling around, wishing I could get to the jumping-off place. And then come four or five years (who knows?) of disappearing into the novel. Eventually, seeing the finished book, I know I did it somehow, but I don't remember it. I know I was in there, and it was intense, and I recognize the complex workings of it. But the time disappeared—so quickly. I always hesitate before launching into another novel. It had better be worth it or I won't go near it. It has to steal me, kidnap me.

# Copyrights and Permissions

# About the Author

Bobbie Ann Mason is best known for *Shiloh and Other Stories* and the novels *In Country* and *The Girl in the Blue Beret*. Her many awards include the PEN/Hemingway Award; the Arts and Letters Award for Literature from the American Academy of Arts and Letters; the Southern Book Critics Circle Award; and the Kentucky Book Award. Her memoir, *Clear Springs*, was a finalist for the Pulitzer Prize.

Her fiction has appeared in the *New Yorker*, the *Atlantic, Harper's Magazine, Mother Jones, Ploughshares*, the *Virginia Quarterly Review*, the *Paris Review, Story, Five Points*, and other publications, and it has been featured in *Best American Short Stories, The O. Henry Prize Stories*, and other collections. She received a Guggenheim Fellowship and a National Endowment for the Arts Fellowship.

Mason was writer-in-residence at the University of Kentucky (2001–2011), and she is a member of the Authors Guild, PEN America, and the Fellowship of Southern Writers. She lives in Kentucky.

www.bobbieannmason.net

BOOKS

Fiction
*Shiloh and Other Stories*
*In Country*
*Spence + Lila*
*Love Life*
*Feather Crowns*
*Midnight Magic*
*Zigzagging Down a Wild Trail*
*An Atomic Romance*
*Nancy Culpepper*
*The Girl in the Blue Beret*

Nonfiction
*Nabokov's Garden*
*The Girl Sleuth*
*Clear Springs*
*Elvis Presley*